WARRIORS
IN THE MIST

Susan D. Kalior
M.A. in Education in Counseling
Human Relations and Behavior
B.S. in Sociology

Blue Wing Publications, Workshops, and Lectures
Tualatin, Oregon

Warriors in the Mist
Medieval Dark Fantasy
Copyright 2001 by Susan D. Kalior
First Printing August 2007
ISBN978-0-9795663-1-8

Published by Blue Wing Publications, Workshops, and Lectures
Cover Design by Laura C. Keyser, Logo by Sara C. Roethle

Blue Wing Publications, Workshops, and Lectures
P.O. Box 947
Tualatin OR 97062
sdk@bluewingworkshops.com
www.bluewingworkshops.com
Readers' comments welcomed.

Other Books by Susan D. Kalior

The Other Side of God: The Eleven Gem Odyssey of Being (Visionary Fiction)

Return to Innocence: Undoing Social Programming
A Collection of Social Psychological Essays

Growing Wings Self Discovery Workbook:
17 Workshops to a Better Life

johnny, The Mark of Chaos: An Urban Dark Fantasy

Manufactured in the United States of America

Dedication

to me

Author's Note

"Warriors in the Mist" is an epic masterpiece that took form and came to polished life over the course of fifteen years. The story glows, the kind of glow that can only evolve over time. Writing this novel carried me through intense life transformations. The last sparkle embedded, marked my freedom into a new plateau of being.

Acknowledgments

I would like to honor those who played a part in helping this book become all that it could be. Cindy Kalior and Robert Kalior were the first to embrace my work, deepening its foundation. Thank you "Miller Canyon Women" Susan Bortman, Mary Means, and Laura Ellis, whose exuberant response from reading the book, became nutrients in the garden of my creativity. Thank you to Rosalie Sanzone, Anita Savi, Kevin Bowman, and Ron Jarvis were also among the first to read early drafts. Their encouragement and support inspired me to dive further into the story, and make it even more than it was. Ron, who also made some great story suggestions, was so touched that he gifted me with an antique sword from his collection. I want to thank Michelle Mancini for using my book as a college project in which she was required to make a cover. That cover further inspired me in many ways. I want to thank Katie Govier for suggesting some names that I used. Thank you to Sara Roethle for helping decide the title, and for her eagle-eye proofreading skills. Thank you Laura C. Keyser for her amazing talent in designing the cover, and Matthew A. Keyser for lending knowledge on war and fighting. Thank you Zack and Wes Cotner for helping me with the cover photo. Thank you to Linda Post who helped with the logo, and offered great encouragement. Others who have believed in me and my work are Mark Kalior, the late Carole Kalior (always with me), Jennifer Kalior, Stephen Roethle, Anita Mitchell, Helen Levison, Mary Thompson, and Gail Barton. Thank you all!

Prologue

It happened in the Dark Ages,
in a Province called Kantine, ruled by
Sakajians. Sakajian warlords vied for power,
the mightiest of whom controlled even the King.
Brotherhood was vague. Sisterhood was held
only by the Priestesses of the Mist, who
were nearly diminished.

Ж

Chapter One

Kiers Region in South Kantine

The dark woodland was damp with vapors that seeped from the ivory stone of her castle walls. She required no army to secure her lands, knights to guard her dwelling, swords to slay her enemies, nor man to champion her honor.

She was an enchantress, empowered by the Sacred Mists of Cohesion that absorbed the singular into the whole, changed enemies to friends, and the lost to the found. She could bring the sick to health, the meek to their heights, and the imperious to their knees.

She was a luminary, led by wisdom, ruled by compassion. Her actions served to bridge the cracks in time, space, people, and hearts. She accepted strangers into her castle, the ill-fallen needing sanctuary, wayfarers needing a home, sinners needing salvation, and philosophers needing—more.

She was young and she was old, living in a benevolent dream that was to her—reality. While the reality of her war-ridden province was to her—but a dream. Though her days were filled with giving light, guiding, teaching, and healing—her nights grew darker, consuming her with fitful dreams, drawing her ever closer to the edge of uncertainty.

Groaning and writhing, she sleeps this night—trapped in her nightmare. Brilliant moonbeams slash through the small open round window, highlighting her down feather bed. She sweats under white linen covers, soaking her white night shift, as she labors to sustain her white, white world.

Her head thrashes side to side, but her golden brown hair remains splayed like sunrays upon her pillow. Her damp hairline arches like a rainbow over her moist, delicate face, taut with pain. Her spirit wilts in the relentless light of her martyr ways that command denial of her human need. She exists only to navigate herself into the dark and desperate hearts that oh so need the shine of love. She, like the moon, traverses dark.

However, in her nightmare, dark traverses light.

She dreams she is in sunshine, curled against the trunk of a rough barked oak tree. She wears a soiled white night shift, not her own. She trembles, for all around her warriors fight: swords, arrows, blood. There is an open window yonder. Beyond that window, blackness. From that blackness, an incubus emerges, glides to her and lands, taking human form—a barbarian male. Beneath his chubby bare toes, shiny black bugs wiggle out, climbing up his thick hairy legs over a brown fur strip that conceals his loins. His broad, bare chest parades dominance. His coarse, black whiskers sprinkle his wide face. His eyes are vacant, his laugh more empty.

She searches for a sparkle of light within him that she may use the Sacred Mists of Cohesion to bring him into Divine Love. However, she can find no light. Therefore, she cannot enchant him. She cannot heal him. She cannot bridge him to the human race.

Never before had her power failed her. He thrusts her back flat on bristly ground, his massive body crushing her slight frame. Never before had she been helpless. He hoists up the edges of her gown. Never before had her ideology betrayed her. Screams form in her heart, but she is breathless to emit them. She gasps in barely audible tones, "Wait, wait," as if maybe, by some chance, he would. He does not.

He jams his erect organ into her, again and again. Her body rivets pain. Dry heaves rise to her throat. All she stood for, all she was, all she had ever been, was now in question. Oh, horror of horrors—to be emptied of all the rare and beautiful beliefs that gave life meaning! He climaxes, and throws his head back in a roaring laugh. Her tears stream. He slurps them with his fat lips, and whispers, "Kamara Lania, you are mine." He swallows her spirit, and the world fades—into nothing.

Kamara screamed long and loud. Awakening from her nightmare, she bolted upright in her bed. The covers dropped to her lap, chilling her sweat-soaked body. One quivering hand went to her heart, the other against her glistening brow.

Her devoted confidante, Michael, flung open the chamber doors and raced to her side. The moonlit room illuminated him: disheveled brown hair and bearded face fraught with concern, naked chest glowing peacock bold, taut tan pants and bare feet.

He questioned breathlessly, "Kamara, what ails you?"

"I had the dream again," she blurted in a suffocated whisper, "but this time the Cold One took human form and then he . . . he—" Her ragged breathing was too irregular for speech.

Michael knelt softly by her bedside, and engulfed her trembling hand in his. He examined her pale shaken face. "Your nightmares worsen. My concern grows, for always your dreams come to pass." His jaw tightened and ire threaded his voice. "If this savage be human, I shall reclaim my sword and—" He arrested the crude

3

words that nearly gushed from his mouth. Instead, he said, "—protect you."

She yanked her hand from his grasp as if he'd become too hot to touch. She straightened her shoulders. "No, Michael. No sword shall be drawn. That is a man's way. It shall never be mine."

"A man's way might be your only hope."

She shook her head.

"Kamara—"

"No, Michael. No." She cradled her stomach and rocked gently, her body knowing what her mind rejected. She stared into the dark, reciting what had been told her since birth. "My great grandmother journeyed far from Gateland, enduring great hardship to build this domain in Kantine for the Light Priestesses of the Sacred Order of the Mist." She stopped rocking. Her eyes turned to his, almost imploring. Repressing heavy tears, her voice fell like powdery snow. "I'm under vow to uphold the teachings."

"Kamara—" he stopped short, uncertain how to educate her about the amoral side of life without implying disrespect.

She shut her eyes, inhaling confidence. Exhaling determination, she snapped them open. "For three generations no sword has been drawn. And none shall be drawn for the fourth."

His heartbeat quickened. "Times have much changed. In your grandmother's day, the Priestesses were many. Now, there is but you and your guardian. The Sisterhood is weak. The Mists are weak. You *must* let me champion you. I beg you change your mind."

"My mind cannot be changed."

Michael wanted to roar his protest, but she was too gentle-hearted for roaring. "Kamara, I don't wish to offend you, but you do not comprehend the dimension of this malevolence."

"In the dream, I fail because I panic and lose faith. I must strengthen my resolve to pacify the Cold One. He is a lost soul—that's all. I shall bridge him with spiritual love, just as I've bridged all who have come upon me." Her eyes deepened. "If I could but find in him one spark of light, just one, then—" Her eyes turned to Michael. Her hand went to his forehead, brushing back his tousled bangs in a motherly fashion. "Go now Michael, I shall be bright with the morning light."

Her touch melted his frustration, but not his concern. Never his concern. He guided her mothering hand to his lips and kissed her fingers. "As you wish."

He rose. Her hand fell from his. He saw her demise. His somber gaze lingered upon her a moment more. Then he turned and made way for the door.

"Michael!" She cried.

He turned around, waiting for her to speak. Was that not the way of it? She called. He answered. Moonbeams slashed his bare chest and the waist of his pants, leaving his head obscure in the shadows.

Her voice enveloped him. "Your despair weighs heavy upon me. Please, take heart. A solution shall present itself, I am certain."

Michael's face hurt, harboring futility. "There is no certainty here! You are tethered before me Kamara, in my old world, in my old way. And the old me begs righteous resurrection!"

"No reason merits violence, Michael. I know this proves difficult for you who had been so great a warrior, but to think as such shall land you back in the heartless world. Think Michael, what saved you from that brutal existence? 'Twas not the sword, but spiritual love."

Michael's voice softened, "Dear Kamara, spiritual love saved me, yes; but it was the sword that brought me down. You spent two days healing my wounds—remember? I was vulnerable then, near death, easy to bridge."

"I remember," she said quietly, and then blurted, "but I could have bridged you, even in your prime."

Michael shook his head, but she could not see his head buried in the dark.

Her strained words erupted in his ears. "I believe in the Sacred Mists with all that I am, and I'd sooner die than take a sword to another!"

Michael's chest caved. "You well may," he said.

5

He left, closing the heavy wooden door behind him. Cold stone chilled his bare feet, plodding one in front of the other, down the hallway to his bedchamber. He crawled into his down feather bed, wishing more, he could crawl into Kamara's. He longed to consummate his love.

His loins ached to release his seed into that feminine cavity men so love to conquer. He wanted to feel that old familiar warmth again, skin against skin, his manhood enveloped, his lips upon a woman's breast. Even though Kamara seemed absent of sexual desire, he was unwilling to sleep with another, fearing he'd destroy his chance to win her.

He wondered if his mammoth lust would cause him eternal suffering, for even if Kamara developed a procreative urge, she ever believed lovemaking would connect her with male aggression, and poison her constitution. She believed it would kill her.

Oh well.

If he couldn't win her body, he would win her life. She was naive to think she could defeat the Cold One with spiritual love. But then, how could she know of the outside world, when in all her life she had never left her lands?

She had been born and raised to heal the victims of the warring world. What use had she for fighting? None, until now. Maybe she was to learn there was a worthier place for a sword than the secret chamber where his lay rusting. Perhaps *he* was meant to show her. Perhaps *he* was meant to teach her the merit of the sword.

But no, her words rang true. If he gripped the sword, he'd embrace old ways that he no longer desired. He had accepted sanctuary in her castle of light, and for the first time, he experienced a sense of himself beyond his own bloodlust.

He had come to know the joys of cleanliness, the passion of sunset, and the pleasure in humane behavior. He had come to know a sense of connection with the beetle, the flower—her. He had come to know the bounty of the inner world, of higher wisdom, and the soul of self. However, he hadn't forgotten what he'd known before he met her. And what *he* knew . . . *she* did not.

He knew that if the sword hadn't taken him down, she could well have been his victim. He knew that she couldn't bridge the Cold One, for such men were void of love and light, and could never be bridged. He knew that *this* battle required the sword. And he knew, sadly, that he wasn't the one to wield it. Not only for himself, but for her too.

If he fell into his old ways, he feared she'd suffer and die, for they had become empathically bonded, perhaps too much. She'd not only feel the killing act through him, but also the victim's pain. She couldn't survive such brutality—of this, he felt certain.

But, if he couldn't help her, then who? His old liege and best friend came to mind: cold blue dancing eyes, hard-lined face with lightly scarred jaw, jet-black long hair, war-hardened chest, and venerated sword at side. Aye, indeed . . . the Warlord Kayenté Ketola, commonly referred to as Panther, not only because the Panther was in his family's coat of arms, but for his shrewd and beautiful swordsmanship, for his love of play in war, and for his sharp clean kills when the playing was done. Kayenté had always preferred the name Panther. It cast a shadow on his humanity. It instilled a healthy, fearful respect in his subjects. Most importantly, it helped him subdue his conscience. Yet, his conscience was there, buried however deep, but—there. Enough to aid Kamara—probably, hopefully. Michael auditioned Kayenté in his mind with frank scrutiny.

Lord Panther Ketola: capable of ruthlessness, yes, but also a man who governs himself by ethic of the civilized upper class, known to reward fairly those who serve him, capable of manners, shrewd strategist, master swordsman, and the second born son to the Duke and Duchess of Kanz . . . well maybe not the Duke.

Kayenté, in a once drunken state, told Michael he was likely the son of a rapist. That life long suspicion kindled in Kayenté a furious rebellion against the rules of nobility, compelling him to make his own rules and dominate the very aristocracy that might one day strip his title. He had acquired more land and power than even the King, along with one of the most distinctive fortresses ever built.

Michael sighed, recalling those years when he and Kayenté were warrior comrades, overthrowing castles, and pushing back the boundaries of bordering provinces. A different life, Michael thought, forever ago, even though only two years had passed since he dragged himself to Kamara's door, wounded and dying.

"Kamara and Kayenté," Michael whispered, envisioning them together. Kamara curing butterflies, and Kayenté killing men. He laughed quietly. No two humans could be more mismatched. And yet, who could better help the woman he loved? Besides—Kayenté owed him. Yes, Kayenté was the one.

Michael spent the last hours of night devising a strategy to manipulate Kayenté into accepting the challenge, and Kamara into accepting Kayenté. And when the sun finally rose, sleep had not yet touched him.

He donned his short-sleeved russet brown tunic, and strapped on his leather belt. He had an urge to wear his sword, but he fought the temptation to seek it. He pulled on his calf-length, brown leather boots over the calves of his tan pants.

He wrapped what he needed for his journey in a burlap sack, and exited his room in search of Kamara. He walked halfway down the corridor and tapped on her bedchamber door. No answer. He peeked inside. Her rumpled bed was empty. He closed the door lightly, and journeyed down the stone stairway into the great white hall.

A cool rush of air embraced him. His spirits lifted, as always they did he stood in this hall, this glorious Great Hall—more ventilated, brighter, and whiter than any Great Hall he had ever visited. And he'd visited many during his castle ravaging days with Panther.

He scanned the room and spied Kamara's guardian, Teeah, who was also the cook. She and several helpers were placing clay bowls piled with stewed cinnamon apples on the three large round, birch wood dining tables. The sweet pungent aroma made his mouth water and his stomach grumble, but he had no time to eat.

He hungered more to execute his plan. He walked toward Teeah who somehow always knew Kamara's whereabouts.

Teeah was lean and wise, fooled by no one, and respected by everyone. Her gliding steps were concealed under her velvet gray, ankle-length tunic. The sleeves shaped the thinness of her arms moving smoothly as she set the table. The velvet neckline scooped above her small round breasts that had never been suckled.

Apricot freckles sprinkled her light skin, climbing up her neck, but fading before they reached her gaunt face, weathered and wrinkled from the march of time. The crystal ornament that held her silvery hair in a bun glimmered in the natural sunlight that poured through numerous round openings in the stone walls. Her mature age matched her talent in creating meals that earned applause.

However, there was more to Teeah than her culinary skills and sharp wit. Once upon a time, Teeah and Kamara's mother were two of over sixty Priestesses that lived in Lania Castle. They all carried the same last name . . . Lania, not only to unify them, but also to mask any link to their fathers. The Priestesses sought no men, except for spiritual ritual or to conceive children. And even then, the chosen males were peace loving, and the children born were always female. When Kamara was an infant, all the Priestesses save Teeah, vanished or died. No one seems to know the truth (except for Teeah, who won't tell anyone—not even Kamara). Teeah was bequeathed guardianship of the infant priestess, left with the task of educating her as a healer and mentor for light seekers that she may carry the sacred teachings of Divine Love into the future.

Michael stopped before Teeah, and cleared his throat to gain her attention, hoping he wasn't making a mistake. He feared she'd read the truth behind his facade, for she, like Kamara, had that ability.

He'd spent all night creating a mind shield to block such access, but as Teeah tended her table, she said nonchalantly, "Kamara dwells at the front court with the roses." She pointed to a burlap pouch on the end of the table. "There's food and drink in there—" she looked up at him and winked, "—for your journey."

9

Michael blushed. "Thank you."

Teeah had read him. She'd read him easily.

He put the pouch in his sack, wondering how much of his plan she knew. And why, if she knew what he thought she knew, wasn't she stopping him? She was a Priestess, and Priestesses don't condone violence, not even in self-defense.

He slung the bundle over his shoulder, slanting a last hard glance at Teeah. He turned away and sighed, praying Kamara wouldn't read him the same. He moved toward the outside entrance, convincing himself that Kamara would be easier to hoodwink than Teeah. Kamara was gullible. He had a few tricks in mind. Even so, he needed to concentrate harder on placing the illusion in front of the truth, convincing himself that the story he was going to tell her was real.

He opened the arched white wood double doors and stepped onto the half-circle marble deck. He gazed down at the pearly sheen that held his reflection. He saw a traitor. She'd hate him for saving her this way.

He descended seven steps edged with rose bushes. He reached the flat grassy yard below and spied Kamara off to the left in her little rose garden, kneeling in front of a rosebush—picture perfect with her white silk gown fanned around her, stroking a fully blossomed snow-white rose with delicate reverence. She seemed lost in the world of the rose. Her face held that same softness. How did she do that? How did she look like a vision in the concrete world and move like a dream in reality?

Michael shook his head lightly and blew out a slow hot breath of admiration. He wanted to remove the glittering crystal ornaments that held up the sides of her fawn colored hair, so that he could slide his hands through the waist-length downy strands.

"Kamara!" he called, setting his pack down on the bottom step.

She turned her head toward him. Her large amber eyes glowed angelic innocence. "Yes?"

"I too have had nightmares."

She rose and approached him gracefully, question upon her face. "Of what Michael?"

"My sister."

She cocked her head. "I didn't know you had a sister."

"Well, a half sister. We were not raised together, but the same man sired us. I've had so little contact with her that I never considered her my sister. That's probably why you haven't seen her in your visions. Besides, I've been ashamed to claim her as my blood because—" Michael paused, visualizing a whore he once slept with, and then added, "I've heard it told that she sells herself to men."

"Oh." Kamara lowered her head shyly, and blushed. Her childlike view of sexual matters conflicted with her image of what a priestess should be. The priestess won. She peered up at him pretending she hadn't blushed. "What of your nightmare?"

"Each night, I dream she calls me to free her from the men."

Kamara's forefingers flew against her lips. "Oh!" she gasped, as if it were the most terrifying tale she'd ever heard. Her hands clutched her heart. "She must be helped! She must be saved! I can send her Mist. I can—" She paused. Her jaw dropped in a moment of dead silence. Her face crumbled. She finally realized what he was trying to say. "I suppose then . . . that you . . . must go to her?" Her earnest eyes awaited his answer.

He felt bad dusting up her emotions, but such villainy was required if he was to obscure her second sight. He knew his story would discompose her. Sexual issues always did.

But not wanting to appear insensitive to her needs, he said, "I don't have to go to her. If you need me, I'll stay."

"No," she replied with sad softness. "You must go. There is nothing you can do for me anyway."

He clamped his jaw so hard his temples hurt, riled by her stubborn insistence on being a martyr. Swallowing his ire, he said, "I'd like to bring her here to live with us."

Her eyes brightened. "Do you think she'll come?"

"Yes," he lied.

"But—" her brow creased with worry, "are you ready to leave the castle, Michael? I mean truly ready?"

"I believe I am. And I should leave at once."

"Without a sword?" She held her breath.

"Without a sword," he said.

She exhaled relief, "Very well then." Quite suddenly, bewilderment crossed her face. "I have a vision of a warrior with long black hair and bright blue eyes—and a most calculating stare."

Michael nearly choked on his saliva.

Kamara's eyelids slid half-shut. "He has sword in hand, and—"

Michael gripped her shoulders, and spoke firmly to break her focus. "Kamara, don't you have enough to manage without taking on the troubles of every face that pops into your mind?"

She looked up at him. Suspicion glinted in her eye. "Are you to see this man?"

He cleared his throat as he took a step back. "No, of course not. You have my agenda."

She stared into him. He knew he must move before she locked onto the truth. He began pacing with joined hands behind his back, thinking hard, thinking fast, gaze fixed upon the soft dirt ground. "I cannot think why you see such a man, unless . . . maybe, well, no—."

"Unless what, Michael?"

"He does sound like a relative of mine." He froze for a moment and then snapped his head toward her in mock revelation. "Perhaps you are seeing a future that I have not comprehended."

Her eyes deepened. "Perhaps."

Michael nodded. "Probably."

She walked to him.

His heart pounded. Had she bought the story? Had he successfully obscured Kayenté's true identity?

She rose on her toes, planting a light kiss on his bearded cheek. She whispered in his ear, "Return to me," her voice broke, "as you are . . . as the man I know." Landing flat on her feet, her eyes flickered apprehension.

He smiled faintly. "Fear not. The old Michael is too far gone—" He lifted her chin with his fingers, forcing her eyes to greet him, and said with a joking smile "besides, you'd not let *him* live with you."

Strength gathered in her eyes. She pushed words past the knot in her throat, for she very much did not want him to leave. "I'll keep the Mist about you, faintly though, to avoid drawing attention. Darkness will make the vapors more visible, but that cannot be helped. They will keep you safe. That's what's important."

Her amber eyes glossed with tears, but apparently, they had been forbidden to fall. More than ever, he wanted to return her kiss . . . but not on her cheek. Only the touching of lips could honor such tenderness. He lowered his head and ever so barely lighted his mouth on hers. He lingered there with eyes closed, worshipping the intimacy. And to his surprise, she let him. He pressed his mouth a little harder against hers, tasting the residue of honeyed tea mixed with the salt of a tear that had found its way into the corner of her mouth.

He opened his eyes to behold the dreamy look of longing he hoped was upon her face. His heart lurched, speared by her frantic stare. She seemed more shaken by his kiss than his leaving, but clearly traumatized by both.

He stepped back, upset that he'd upset her. "Kamara—" he said, unable to say more, because he'd already done too much. He wanted to tell her not to fear his love, and that it hurt him to leave her, more than it hurt her to be left. And he wanted to spill his heart and reveal that he was only departing so he could save her. But he swallowed the truth. "Give my goodbyes to the others."

Her face softened with a nod.

He retrieved his bundle, and with a pang in his chest and longing in his eye, he said, "Fare-thee-well, Angel."

"Fare-thee-well, Michael."

She watched him turn away and walk to the stables east of the castle. Her hand rose to her heart, confused by the love in his kiss, and her own feelings toward him. Was he merely her very good and most positively perfect best friend, or was he—more?

She watched the equine attendant saddle her swiftest dun steed. She watched Michael mount and lope north across the field of purple heather. She watched him disappear over the green grassy knoll. And then, there was nothing more to watch. He was gone. Her beloved Michael was riding into the chaos of the outer world.

She stared at the vacant hill. Loneliness brewed in the pit of her stomach. She was sad. Not just because Michael had left, but there was something in the way he left that felt—crooked.

Maybe he just wanted to leave so that he could taste his old life again. Or maybe this was a ploy to make her want him more. Both notions upset her, for if either were true, then he'd betrayed her trust with duplicity. The priestess image of who she thought she should be, again conflicted with her child-like view of men. The child won.

Even if Michael's story was true, she felt betrayed, for he'd not given her half the farewell she expected considering he believed the Cold One would kill her, maybe even before his return.

But, what was she saying? The Cold One couldn't harm her. If the powers of heaven and earth could move mountains, then sure-they could hearten the heartless. *Oh please let it be so,* she prayed, *please let it be so.*

Ж
Chapter Two

Kaquenda Region in North Kantine

Michael traveled hard for two days through forests of maple and pine, past the duchy of Kanz where Duke Ketola lived, through the burgh of Kanis, beyond the nunnery, into the massive northern Kaquenda region until he reached Kayenté's castle at dusk.

Five massive black stone cylinders stretched to the sky, the setting sun splashing over the highest conical roof. He stopped in front of the moat and glared into the dark odoriferous waters vaguely reflecting his image perched on horse. Again, he viewed a traitor, not only to Kamara, but also to Kayenté. He had left Kayenté for Kamara, and Kayenté was short on forgiveness.

Several guards recognized him and shouted from the D shaped towers of the thick outer curtain wall that surrounded the castle. "Sir Michael, you've got guts coming back here!" and, "Panther's going to kill you!" and "Hey Michael, we heard you were eaten by the witch, Kamara." Another voice bellowed, "Or seduced." Another hollered, "Is she a witch? Is she as ugly as they say?"

Michael's blood boiled while he waited by the barbican for permission to enter, and for the drawbridge to lower. He had an impetuous urge to pummel the loose-tongued imbeciles, but more disturbing to him was the ease with which his old self begged return.

A voice bellowed from above. "Permission to enter—granted." A cool wind gusted past him as the drawbridge lowered. The chains jangled and the wood creaked. Nervous anticipation knotted his stomach. Would Panther bare ill will that his second in command and best friend had left him to live the life of a pacifist?

Once the drawbridge was completely lowered, Michael trotted his horse over the oak planks of the causeway, through the opened gate of the first curtain wall that surrounded the castle and into the outer courtyard.

His mind reeled with rich recollections as he passed the dozen square pinewood domestic buildings that housed the outdoor servants, the massive stables filled with snorting restless warhorses, the pen with pigs rolling in mud, and the coop of cackling chickens awaiting the chopping of the neck. But his memories almost came to life when he passed the four-acre exercise yard where he'd won many a nefarious tournament.

He rode through the gateway of another curtain wall of more manned towers into the front courtyard, to the entrance of the keep. He stopped and dismounted. A skinny blonde-haired page appeared and tended his horse.

"Sir Michael Randanscene!" A small distant voice sounded from high above him.

Michael took a few steps back and looked up to see an armored man waving from the crenellation at the top of the keep. But he couldn't recognize the foot long soldier from such distance.

The man shouted, "It's me, Sir Robert Durham! Remember the day we single handedly cut the hearts out of thirty-one Rudels?"

Michael waved and shouted, "Aye, I remember!" He shook his head brusquely as if to awaken from a dream. Had he really committed such atrocity? Was it truly he who had enjoyed mutilating men and then bragging about the deed afterward?

Not wanting to remember more, he again waved and walked forward, sighing anxiously. He made haste up the six black marble steps that led to black double doors, ornately carved into life-size panthers leaping toward each other—the Ketola Coat of Arms. The original Ketola Coat of Arms consisted of two panthers leaping away from each other. But Kayenté, well, he was rebellious.

He looked intently upon the panthers, waiting for the doors to open. Warmer memories flooded his mind—like the times he and Kayenté had played at Duke Ketola's castle, hunting, hawking, and whoring together. Even though Michael was not a noble and merely the son of one of the Duke's warriors, he and Kayenté had been the best of friends since childhood, and Kayenté had given him the title, Sir.

The doors opened, manned by two house guards. Michael entered. The guards closed the doors with a dull echo. Michael almost lost his breath when he viewed his former lord at the far end of the Great Hall crossing the shiny black marble floor with a speed and venery that made the knot in Michael's stomach grow harder.

Kayenté looked cruel and wild in his black attire: sleeveless tunic bearing muscled arms, his long loose hair edging his hard lined face. As the distance closed between them, Michael grew more agitated. What if Kayenté had dissolved the ties between them? What if Kayenté viewed him as a mutineer, punishable by death? Even Kamara's mists would fade in Kayenté's wrath.

But when his lord arrived, malice did not taint his face. He was bright with energy, smiling even, handsome even. His deep-set blue eyes sparkled in brilliant contrast with his night black hair.

"Sir Michael Randanscene!" Kayenté seized Michael in a manly hug, and expelled him just the same.

Michael looked Kayenté up and down, reacquainting himself with the man he'd once known so well. Silver studs lined the v-neck of his collar. A black leather belt held his sheathed broadsword. Black hide pants and soft black boots completed his slick appearance. His form held true to a knight who lived and breathed the hotness of war.

"Lord Kayenté," jested Michael, "I feared you were set to slay me."

'Not yet," Kayenté said in a hard teasing voice, countering the flash of coldness in his eyes. "We'll talk first. Then I'll decide."

Michael swallowed nervously. Same old Kayenté: playful, but deadly. Kayenté had not changed, but Michael had. And he feared that once Kayenté discovered this and the true purpose of his visit, he'd be deemed a coward for not championing Kamara himself.

"Come," said Kayenté, "let us retire to the sitting room."

Michael nodded and followed Kayenté through the colossal Great Hall. Footsteps resounded on the ebony floor as they passed black and gold tapestries of panthers, bestial heads and furs hanging on the dark stone walls, busy servants, house guards, and intermittent black marble ribbed pillars towering high to the ceiling.

Finally, they arrived at the small sitting room, darkening with dusk. "The light from the oil lamps cast a ghostly glow. He surveyed the chamber, unchanged since his departure. The walls were covered with worn and frayed maps of Kantine. In front of the huge unlit fireplace, laid a brown bearskin rug with the head attached. But best of all, Michael's old favorites were still intact: two soft black leather armchairs facing each other with accompanying round side tables of ornately designed wood, upon which they'd been served delectable cuisine and goblets of the finest wine. Michael smiled faintly, remembering those great old days.

He had often sat with his friend in these very chairs, devising war strategies and contemplating ways to make his lord, King. But now, standing next to Kayenté, he felt paled, effeminate in his faded bloodlust and weakened musculature. He was no longer willing to do what men do to call themselves men. So, what did that make him?

Kayenté gestured to the chair. "Sit."

Michael lowered his body stiffly onto the cool leather. A hard lump formed in his throat.

Kayenté sat across from him, slouched back with open legs, rubbing his chin in contemplation. "So Michael, are you here to restore your status?"

Michael swallowed the lump and tapped his foot lightly on the floor. "I fear not. I've . . . I've come to ask a favor."

Kayenté narrowed one eye. "A favor?"

"Yes lord, I've—"

"What the—" Kayenté squinted, "—hell is that substance about you?"

Michael blushed. "Protection."

"Protection?"

"The Sacred Mists of Cohesion. It's the paste that bonds life forms together. If the prey feels connected to the predator, then the predator finds it difficult to assault itself."

Kayenté eyed him suspiciously. "And this works?"

"Yes."

"Mist . . . protects you? A vapor that you can put your hand through . . . protects you?"

An attractive woman servant entered the sitting room. Her ankle-length deep blue velvet tunic shaped her curvaceous body. Her shoulder length hair was reddish and wavy, her face timid and pleasing. On a golden tray, she carried two shiny gold goblets and a black bottle of wine. She set the tray down on the wooden table next to Kayenté and poured sparkling crimson liquid into the goblets.

She handed a goblet to Kayenté, then curtsied. "My lord."

When she turned to serve Michael, Kayenté rapped her playfully on her behind. She jumped, peeved, but respectfully afraid. She handed Michael a goblet, then hurried from the room.

"That was Allysa," Kayenté said. "She's enjoyable under the covers. Yours for the evening," Kayenté raised his brows, "if you like."

"No," Michael said hesitantly, wanting to say yes. "That won't be necessary."

Kayenté's eyes widened. "Michael! You've changed." He asked curiously, "What is it like to reside with a witch?"

Michael scowled. "Kamara isn't a witch."

Kayenté's eyes narrowed shrewdly. "The mists that protect you," he swilled down half his wine, "is that not her magic?"

"Yes, but—"

"She took you into her castle, tended your wounds, so they say. Soon after, you sent word to me that you'd retired your sword. You, Michael? She would have to be a witch to keep *you* from your sword."

"She's no witch!" Michael said, fearing ill fate upon her if so labeled. "She is a Priestess, an emissary of compassion."

"Perhaps she has cast a spell on you to make you believe such nonsense. Perhaps soon she will steal your spirit, if indeed she has not already."

"No. She could never harm me. She is as a nun, motivated by spiritual love, not by a lust for power and position. And she's as an angel, healing and caring for all who enter her lands."

Kayenté swilled down the rest of his wine. "She performs no evil ritual?"

"No," Michael sipped his drink, "she turns us inward to find our souls."

Kayenté gave a wily grin. "So my friend, have you found your soul?"

Michael slapped the wine goblet on the table next to him, sloshing red liquid. He rose abruptly. "This is no joke!" He turned to leave. "I doubted you would understand."

"Halt," said Kayenté with his usual deadly calm." I see you've still got the Randanscene temper, which is the only part of you I recognize."

Michael rolled his eyes toward Kayenté, his temper calming. "I've changed."

"Too damn much," said Kayenté. "The Michael I knew was a foul-mouthed, beer guzzling, whore chasing, blood thirsty warrior in search of riches. Now you don't even carry a weapon. Hell Michael, you have manners!"

Michael faced him with a poignant stare, typical of Kamara. "Perhaps, I have found my soul after all."

"Perhaps you have." Kayenté motioned Michael to sit. "Now, what of your . . . favor?"

Michael hesitated. "You'll take me seriously?"

Kayenté scowled playfully. "I'll try to behave."

Michael sat warily. He reached for the goblet, drank down the wine, and set the empty chalice on the table. He inhaled deeply, laboring to form his next words without sounding like Kamara had emasculated him. Not finding any, he sighed. He inhaled again, searching for words and paused with held breath.

Kayenté blurted, "You love this woman—don't you?"

Michael's head jerked back, surprised by Kayenté's keen appraisal of the situation. He bit his lower lip and nodded with timid despair.

Kayenté asked with a twisted smile, "Is she your mistress?"

"No," Michael said, wishing he could say yes. "Her body is void of such passion. She swoons over no man."

"Hell, she sounds dull."

"Dull—she is not. Cautious perhaps, but dull? Never! She believes man's basic nature is destructive, that sexual merging would destroy her."

"She's no witch, but she's got bats in her belfry."

Michael's eyes steamed anger.

"All right, she doesn't have bats in her belfry. She's merely . . . peculiar, simply and without a doubt—peculiar." Kayenté raised his brows, freeing the twinkles in his eyes. "And there's nothing wrong with loving a peculiar woman."

Michael's glare bade Kayenté stifle his grin, but behind his straight face, he was laughing still. He said, "Continue my friend."

Michael cleared his throat. "I love her enough to keep my distance, and yet remain close enough to help her any way I can."

"Mm, so she is the reason for your visit. Trouble has befallen your nun-angel?"

"Yes. There is one who would destroy her. She calls him the Cold One."

Kayenté straightened a little. Violence was his favorite subject, and warranted serious attention. "Why don't you find this rogue, slay him, and be done with it?"

"She forbids me."

"Hell Michael, do it anyway. She wouldn't have to know."

"It's not that simple. She is spiritually bonded with me. If I were to kill, she'd feel the act, and that would destroy her."

Kayenté's face froze in a skeptical expression.

Michael read him clearly. "It's true!"

Kayenté leaned forward, elbow on knee, chin on fist. He smiled derisively. "You're telling me . . . that if you kill another, she will die?"

Michael's eyes sharpened. "It could happen."

"Ah huh." Kayenté leaned back. "After fifteen years of lopping heads, you retired your sword to keep one female from empathically experiencing your deeds? The bats are in your belfry, Michael."

"I retired the sword on my behalf, for my own good. I've vowed never to touch it again."

"Ever?"

"Ever. Upholding that vow has opened me to a whole fresh world that I very much like."

"You've been deluded, Michael. You cannot survive without a sword."

"But I have. And so has Kamara—up to this point anyway. She enchants people out of their corruption. In the twenty years she's lived at Lania Castle, no one has invaded her realm. She's never been struck or seen another stricken."

Kayenté lowered his eyelids. "I question that."

"She has never journeyed beyond Lania lands into the outside world. All within Lania Castle are pacifists. Thus, she has never

22

known violence, only its victims, whom she heals and protects. She's lived peacefully, that is, until the Cold One found her."

"If she can enchant, then why does she fear this man?"

"Enchantment requires light in his soul. But the Cold One has no light. If he did, she'd have pacified him by now. Each day he nears. Each day she weakens, yet insists she'll find that spark and pull him into spiritual love, as she did me."

"You don't believe she can?"

"I don't know. She is naive about such men. Perhaps she's right. Maybe she can bridge him with spiritual love, but what if she's wrong?"

"She's wrong."

Allysa entered the room with another golden tray that carried two gold platters, each displaying a whole chicken, brown roasted, and steaming hot. She placed a platter with a red cloth napkin on each table. Michael noticed her trembling hands. But more, he noticed the soft curves of her body. He'd been two years deprived. He left his chicken on the table, his appetite on Allysa, until her absence left the room colder somehow.

Kayenté reached for his chicken. "You can have her if you want Michael." He tore off a leg and bit into the succulent meat.

Michael wondered if he tore at Allysa the same. "She fears you," he said.

Kayenté almost choked on his food, swallowing a bigger glob than he'd intended. "Me! It's *you* she fears."

"Me? Why?"

"Because she knows you live with a witch."

Michael glared two unsightly beams of protest.

Kayenté's palm shot up. "I know, she's no witch . . ." his hand drifted casually to his knee, "but she lives in a child's dream."

Michael's eyes deepened with mysticism. "Perhaps, it is we . . . who live in her nightmare."

Kayenté slouched back in his chair and contemplated Michael's statement. He bit slowly into the chicken leg, sparing his throat further terror, and ripped a strip of meat, licking it into his mouth, chewing lightly. He swallowed, cocking the chicken toward his ear. "Michael, my friend, I respect you. You have served me well in the past, but your whole way of thinking has become . . . well, moonstruck—a little off, you know?" He took a hefty bite of chicken, and chewed heartily.

"Maybe so, but still, Kamara is in danger. I'm asking you to champion her."

Kayenté swallowed another oversized hunk, terrorizing his throat again. He threw the poultry haphazardly on the platter. "Me! Are you mad? I have a kingdom to conquer. I don't save women." His eyes darkened. "You should know that. Anyone could meet the challenge," Kayenté raised one brow, "even you Michael. You know you could." He grabbed a red cloth napkin and wiped his mouth.

"I'm asking *you*."

Kayenté wiped his hands and squinted, realizing that Michael must have assessed her adversary too strong for an ordinary man to defeat. "Just who is this Cold One?"

"We don't know. He comes in her dreams."

"Her dreams? He's not . . . human?"

"He's human. Her dreams foretell."

Kayenté stared at Michael blankly for a moment, then reached past the chalice for the wine bottle and took a fervid swig. "Assuming he exists then, where is he?"

"We don't know."

Kayenté bobbed his head lightly, forcing patience. "When is he to come?"

"We don't know."

Kayenté huffed, "You want me to protect a woman who doesn't want protection, from a man she saw in a dream, not knowing where he is or when he will arrive?"

"Well—yes," Michael said.

Kayenté paused, stunned by Michael's ludicrous request. His friend had gone decisively, perhaps irrevocably 'over the bend.' A more kindly tact was in order. He stated calmly, "I gather she doesn't know you are here."

"Well—no. She thinks I'm with my sister."

"Michael," he said carefully, wondering if his friend was salvageable, "you don't have a sister."

"I know, but it was the only excuse I could raise to leave the castle."

Kayenté sighed, relieved Michael knew he didn't have a sister, relieved that Michael had signs of sanity in him, relieved that he could refuse Michael's request without compunction. "She does not wish my help, so that's—that. She'll not receive it."

"I'm asking you to help *me*."

"By begging a woman to let me protect her? No." Kayenté shook his head, "No." He reached to his plate, and pulled off a chicken breast.

Michael watched Kayenté eat vigorously as if he no longer had company in the room. After thirty years of friendship, Michael felt he deserved more from Kayenté than this. By God, he would get it. His face sharpened. His tone sharpened. "You owe me, Kayenté. You do."

Kayenté put the bare chicken bone down on the platter, and grabbed his napkin. He crossed his ankle over his knee, and wiped his hands slowly, taking his time. Then he stared contemplatively at Michael, and exhaled a long sigh.

Michael sensed an opening in Kayenté's hard mental shield. "I only ask that you come and stay at Lania Castle for several weeks, and when the time comes, slay the bastard. I'll not have broken my vow. Kamara will be safe. And you can return home."

"What makes you think she'd allow a blood thirsty, power hungry warlord into her sanctuary?"

"She turns no one away who seeks 'the light.'"

Kayenté leaned forward. Michael's plan was taking definition. "You want me to feign *needing* her . . . to save my soul?"

"Well," Michael's brow raised. "Yes."

25

"Why can't we claim that I simply wish to join the group? That way she won't try to *save* me."

"She is going to read you somewhat no matter how well you block her. If our story is to be believed, we must skirt the truth as closely as we can. This will make it difficult for her to read you accurately. So, we will not hide that you are a warrior. We will just say you are battle-weary, and even though you are hesitant to relinquish your sword, you will, if it means finding 'the light.' "

Kayenté stilled, dangerously so. Issues of saving and being saved sometimes did that to him.

The sharp fangs of Kayenté's silence bit Michael, raising the hairs on the back of his neck. Had he pushed Kayenté too far?

Kayenté rose and stepped toward him.

Sweat beaded on Michael's brow. Humility and Kayenté did not mix. Humility equaled shame. And Kayenté would not be shamed. And he was famous for slaying those who shamed him. Michael had always before been exempt from Kayenté's revenge, for their kinship had been strong. However, in the lapse of two years, exemption seemed tenuous.

Kayenté leaned over Michael, clutching the arms of the leather chair.

Michael gulped, wondering if Kamara's mists were still there.

Kayenté's deadly glare struck Michael, clean and cold—his stare, his blade, were one. What next? Would Kayenté draw his loyal companion from the inner sheath of his boot, his old and well-used friend that had sliced many an enemy's throat with lightning speed?

Kayenté spoke through clenched teeth, "You ask . . . too much." Fury widened his eyes, but lethal calm possessed his voice. "I am a warlord—*Michael*. I believe in war—*Michael*. I like war—*Michael*, and I don't ask women for help—," he straightened his body and stepped back, "—*ever*." He walked to the wall to a detailed map of Kantine and brushed his fingers over the rough paper.

Michael sighed with relief. Kayenté still cared for him. Not as much, but some. Kayenté hadn't slit his throat, and that meant a lot.

Kayenté said, "If she wants my help, she must request it." He faced Michael. "I'll not abandon my manhood . . . as you did."

There it came, Kayenté's assault. Michael preferred the knife. Death to dishonor, any day. He ground his teeth—hard, temples exploding pain. He labored to quell his temper, but he could not. He was a pacifist to Kamara, not Kayenté! He lunged from his chair toward Kayenté, red faced with balled hand drawn back. An old-fashioned punch would feel better than hell. "You make it hard for me to stay my fist from your face!"

Kayenté pointed to his jaw, "Come on, let's see some of the old Michael!"

The old Michael? Michael's face softened, realizing what Kayenté was after . . . the old Michael.

"Oh," Michael's hand uncoiled, and his arm floated down. "So that's it. You want me violent. Peace frightens you."

Kayenté's lips tightened. "You're insane."

Michael sauntered back to his chair and plopped against the soft leather. Kayenté desired him alive, or dead he would be. Kayenté had missed him, or talk would not thrive. Kayenté would assist him, for his heart, though bludgeoned, was not slain. Not yet. Michael knew he had the advantage. Bravery set in. "Do you know why people who enter Kamara's lands seldom return to the outside world? It's not that she eats them for supper. They prefer peace, so they stay."

Kayenté squinted one eye that twitched, repressing rage. "You think I fear that the witch woman will change me?"

Michael raised a brow. "Well?"

"I fear no woman!"

"Then come."

Kayenté walked indignantly to his black chair, sitting roughly, slouched, forearms hanging over the sides, rebellious, teen-age style. His hard face glazed insensitivity. "I see no reason to go with you. I've my lands to protect. Her adversary is not even of flesh and blood. I'm neither monk nor magician."

"The Cold One *is* human."

Kayenté tipped his head back. 'Make it worth my effort."

"So," Michael sighed and walked over to him, "our friendship has come to this. Protection comes with a price of land or riches?"

"Yes." Kayenté's cold eyes turned up to Michael. "*You* left *me*—remember?"

Michael knelt, eye level with Kayenté. "Do you recall the day we tried to take the east land of Rudelia and how badly our army was slaughtered? You were severely injured, gouged in the stomach, deep in enemy territory. Your blood spilled. I, though slashed in the leg, searched relentlessly for you. You would have died, had I not found you and brought you home."

Kayenté exhaled sharply. "I remember."

"I beseech you, Lord Kayenté. A few short weeks of your time. I ask only that, for the years I fought by your side to help you acquire and retain your lands. You have powerful knights to defend your castle in your absence, among them—Sir Robert Durham."

Kayenté's somber face birthed a sadistic smile. "I gave Sir Robert your every possession: your bedchamber, your whores, and your position as my champion and second in command."

Jealousy grabbed Michael, but remembering Kamara, he overrode Kayenté's obvious attempt to punish him for becoming a pacifist. "Sir Robert is worthy of your trust, is he not? Let him guard your interests while you are with me. You always pay your debts of honor, and with all due respect, lord—you owe me."

"I will send Sir Robert. And that is a sacrifice."

"She needs the most able man alive to conquer this foe, lord. With your sword in hand, you are infallible. You know this to be true. Only you will do."

Kayenté sighed, almost grieving. "So be it! I will give you ten days, no more."

"But—"

"Ten days. Do you want them—or not."

"Yes," Michael said, hoping ten days would suffice.

"And for what you ask," Kayenté lowered his lids, "you will owe me more than land or gold. You will owe me the favor of my choice, no matter how much you despise it."

Michael nodded reluctantly, wondering what Kayenté would request. Judging by his hard glare, something unsavory. But, for Kamara, yes, he'd do anything.

He was surprised though that Kayenté labored in accepting this minor task, minor anyway, compared to his major accomplishments. True, playing the part of a needy man would prove an embarrassing challenge, but more challenging for Kayenté would be the temporary surrender of his sword, which was ever in his presence.

Michael said, "You will still be able to attain your sword. It just won't be on your person."

"What!" Kayenté thrust his body forward. "You said nothing about me parting with my sword!"

"She won't believe you seek peace if you won't part with your sword!"

Kayenté sprung up from his chair. "And if I do, how the hell do you expect me slay this . . . Cold One! Wasn't it you who said with blade in hand, I am infallible?"

Michael rose and walked across the room with hands joined behind his back, cogitating an explanation of his plan without further aggravating his lord.

He turned abruptly and faced Kayenté. "She will hide your sword with mine. I'll follow her and locate the hiding place. When the time comes, we'll sneak it back."

Kayenté's chest heaved a sigh of defeat. "I'd like to sneak you back and trade you in for the old Michael."

Michael glided back to his chair and sank comfortably into the cushions. "The old Michael wouldn't have convinced you to do as I have asked."

"Precisely my point."

"Precisely mine." Michael smiled faintly. "See the power I've attained?"

Kayenté grumbled, leaning back into his chair, shocked by his acquiescence to Michael's ludicrous request.

Michael swung his ankle over his knee and tilted his head up, pausing in thought. "We'll need to change your identity, of course."

Kayenté glared, jaws clenched because Michael asked *more* of him yet.

Michael felt the weight of Kayenté's disapproval, and looked straight at him. "Well, it's necessary we do it this way. I told her much about you during my recovery. I even referred to you as Panther. With a name like that and the reputation I told her you had, she'd never believe that you would seek pacification."

Kayenté's eyelids lowered slowly until they were almost closed, seething acrid warning.

Michael had stumbled into another sore subject for Kayenté. Though Kayenté was shrewd and self-serving, he didn't view himself evil. However—being the suspected spawn of a sadistic rapist, he sometimes wondered if he was.

Michael added sheepishly, "Of course you're not the devil, my lord." He climbed quickly away from that topic. "How about James for your name? I'll tell her you are my cousin and that we grew up together. That way, if she has visions of us as children playing, there will be a plausible explanation."

"Your cousin?" Kayenté's voice was taut with sarcasm. "You're gaining quite a family Michael, first a sister, now a cousin. Don't you fear your claims will attract suspicion, considering you are the only child of deceased parents who have no surviving siblings?"

"I can make her believe me. I have ways."

"Ways Michael? You mean lies upon lies entangling you in hypocrisy. You are a pacifist, but you want me to kill for you. You respect her way, but you don't believe her capable."

"You are not innocent of such manipulation!"

"I manipulate. I calculate. I persuade and dissuade. I do not lie. I'm bold and clear about who I am and what I want. I take what I please, and I make people obey my wishes. You should do the same with your nun-angel, for this scheme of yours compromises your honor."

"It's her honor, wherein my concern lies!"

"She doesn't seek your help. You waste your time on her. You waste your heart on her. Such action leads to ruin."

"As long as it is not she that is ruined."

"No, Michael, it is you who'll be ruined. You cannot save a woman who doesn't want saving. This I know," he said spitefully, remembering a past he preferred to forget.

"I will save her!"

"You may save her life, but you'll lose her respect in this . . . subterfuge." His eyes deepened, seeing the past once more.

"I know my plan is distasteful to you, but it's the only way I can save the woman I love—the only way."

"She'll hate you when she discovers the truth. And that she's bound to do if she's truly endowed with such mystical powers as you have described."

Michael sighed. "I hope it won't come to that. I hope this whole matter is settled before she suspects. There are ways to block her from reading minds and hearts. And these ways, I intend to teach you."

Kayenté grumbled, feeling Michael's plan take on, new and not bargained for, dimensions with each passing moment.

Michael reached for his plate of food from the table and devoured his chicken ravenously. And with a mouthful, he pointed to the chicken leg on Kayenté's plate. "Eat up, Panther, eat up."

Kayenté sighed. "My appetite has vanished."

"Come on Panth—it's not that bad!" Michael said cheerfully.

Kayenté glared at him. "Oh Panth—is it? . . . now that you've got me where you want me."

"I call you Panth when we are brotherly close. Correction . . . closer. If you, Taran, and Marc are an example of brotherhood, I decline such status."

Kayenté felt scattered and lost, tormented by the agreement he'd made.

Michael tried to comfort him. "I'm merely asking you to slay someone. And you crave bloodshed."

Michael's words didn't alter Kayenté's somber face, so he decided Kayenté would fare better if distracted. "Tell me, will you ever wed?"

Kayenté said impassively, "I plan to wed Lady Winnefred in six weeks time."

"Lady Winnefred? I thought Taran was to wed her over a year ago."

"Winnefred's guardian had a sudden change of heart a week before the wedding. Taran didn't seem disappointed. I doubt he condemns my engagement to her."

"I wouldn't be so sure. Taran condemns all you say and do. But what of Winnefred? Are you sure she's your best choice?"

"Best choice?" Kayenté echoed, as if Michael was insane for asking. "Hell, Michael. Her guardian is Gatish with lands I could acquire through marriage. Her dowry is enormous, and she's a beauty!"

"And," Michael said, "she a glutton for wealth and power."

"As am I, so what's the problem?"

"If that's what you want . . . I mean if that's all you want, then congratulations."

Kayenté leaned forward. His eyes hardened, "My bride-to-be is nothing like your nun-angel, is she?" He fell back into his chair. "Well, at least I'll be able to sink my hands into her, not to mention—"

"Enough," Michael said, "I get the picture."

Kayenté tilted his head curiously. "Don't you ever want to—"

"Yes."

"Then take Allysa, tonight," Kayenté said with a sinister smile.

"I don't—"

Kayenté interjected with sarcasm, "—remember Michael, you don't remember how?"

"No, Kamara, I don't know if—"

"—if she'll feel you feeling it, and then it'll kill her?"

Michael speared Kayenté with hateful eyes.

Kayenté said, "Sorry . . . sorry. I was just wondering if there was any part of your manhood left."

"Bastard," Michael said darkly. Remnants of who he used to be blended with who he had become. He hoped it would not affect Kamara adversely.

"All right, all right." Kayenté's face lightened. "We'll depart in four days. I must make ready my castle if I'm to be gone for this time."

Michael sighed, agitated. "Can we leave no sooner?"

"No, we cannot."

"Very well." A gleam crept into Michael's eyes. "Then tonight I'll take the woman."

Kayenté smiled. "Now, that's the Michael I know."

Ж
Chapter Three

Lania Castle-Kiers Region, South Kantine

Kamara sat in the front courtyard gazing absently at her favorite rose bush. She had watched the creamy full blooms wilt slowly with each passing day that Michael had not returned. The cool dawn breezes lapped at the hem of her white cotton dress, simple yet eloquent: scoop neck, snug over the torso, and puffed sleeves narrowing over the forearms. A white velvet cape rested on her shoulders, the hood under her long silken ponytail.

The sun had risen six mornings now. Each day she'd hoped to see Michael riding over the hill. And with each passing night, her hope shrank like the moon, her faith . . . dimming. The Cold One ever stalked her in the land of sleep, luring her into the outer world, challenging her to bridge him, laughing demonically at her when she could not.

She and the people of her castle had been holding vigil in shifts during Michael's absence. Teeah and Kamara took turns flowing the mists almost constantly while their people chanted "the light" and visualized Michael safe. They had called to Great Spirit Mother for wisdom in dealing with the Cold One. There was no reply. If only the people of her castle could do more. If only they could invoke the Sacred Mists of Cohesion, like she and Teeah, then surely with such united power, the Cold One could be bridged.

Unfortunately, "misting" was a gift utilized only by those born of a Light Priestess. The sacred runes, however, revealed that in rare instances, those not born of the blood could become like her. But as of yet, no one she knew had accomplished that feat, although her protégé Camille was close.

Kamara longed for others to become like her, lonely in her distinction. Teeah had told her that Light Priestesses were part angel, but to Kamara, everyone was part angel—even the Cold One. He just had to be. And the mere thought that he wasn't made sickness churn in her stomach and crawl into her limbs.

She needed Michael to comfort her. She detested admitting that. Priestesses weren't supposed to require men that way, but for some reason, she did. Oh, why had he been called away now, when she needed him most? She felt the rippling in his vast spirit, temptations melting into him like warm butter, bumping up against her heart. Would he change while he was gone? Would he cease to care for her?

She could wait no longer for the promise of his comfort that had soothed her far more than she'd realized. Without Michael, she was unable to stand one moment more of the Cold One's torment. She would seek her antagonist today and confront him once and for all. She would journey west, for that is where he lurked in her dreams.

Did she believe in the Sacred Mists of Cohesion, or not? Was she her mother's daughter, Teeah's protégé, and a true healer? If so, then fear had no place. Yes, she would meet the Cold One's challenge.

Teeah's strong voice sounded near the marble steps. "You're leaving?"

Kamara rose and sprinted into Teeah's arms, pressing herself against the soft gray velvet of her guardian's tunic. "What is happening to me?"

Teeah held her with motherly kindness. "Perhaps you are becoming more than a healer."

"What?" Kamara stepped back and wiped tears from her face.

"When you were a little girl," Teeah stroked Kamara's cheek, "you were fascinated by dark, wild summer storms. You'd press your hands against your bedchamber window and implore, 'Let me run into the storm Teeah, please!' I always told you, 'No, not until you are ready.' "

She cupped her hands over Kamara's cheeks. "You are ready!"

Kamara absorbed the impact of her guardian's words and again fell into her arms. "I'm frightened!"

Teeah's warm hand cradled the back of Kamara's head. "Even so child, your time has come. Summon courage. Remember, you are a Priestess of the Mist. You and I are the last. You *must* survive." She kissed Kamara on the cheek and eased her away.

Kamara stepped back, plagued with a sudden urgency to solve all the mysteries in her life in the span of a single breath. If she was going to confront the Cold One and expose herself to an uncertain fate, she wanted to know all that Teeah had held back from her for the twenty years of her life.

"What happened to the Priestesses? Are they dead, or did they just leave Lania Castle? Why did they leave our homeland of Gateland and come to Kantine? Why did they build a castle instead of a temple? What happened to my mother? Did she leave me, or did she die? Why won't you ever give me these answers?"

Teeah said, "If knowledge is given at the improper time, it cannot be heard, even though it has been spoken."

Kamara's face sank. Would she never know the truth?

Teeah pulled Kamara's waist length ponytail around to the front of her chest and held the tip. "This is the hair of your childhood." She traced her fingers up the mane to the top of her head. "Look how you've grown!" She released the hair, teary eyed. "Your mother would be pleased. She's ever with you, though not here."

Kamara said sadly, "I know she's with me—in my heart. I feel her in my heart." She paused, and began to speak, but paused again. Finally, she blurted, "Remember the drawing you gave me of my mother?"

Teeah nodded.

Kamara eyed her guardian hopefully. "She resembles you."

"Child," Teeah said, "when the Priestesses were many living together, we mothered each other's children. It was of no importance from whose womb the child sprang. We did not advocate possessiveness between mother and child, and I urge you to release your need to possess your mother. You are a Priestess of the Mist. All Priestesses are as One Being."

"But I must know if she abandoned me. If you are she then—"

"Hush," said Teeah, "it matters not what your mother did or did not do to you. What matters is what you do to yourself. What actions will you choose? And it matters not who I am or who I'm not. All that matters is who you are. Who will you become?"

Kamara sighed, expelling the last traces of her resistance. "Very well, I shall leave at once. Instruct the others to continue the vigil for Michael. Do not search for me, under any circumstance, no matter how long I might be absent."

"I'll tell them, but first let me prepare food for your journey."

"I feel too ill to consume food." She held out her unsteady hands. "Witness how I tremble."

Teeah landed her palm warmly on Kamara's shoulder. "Then go, child. Go and be done with it."

Kamara's hand flew over her heart. "You do believe in me?"

Teeah's eyes hardened. "Believe in yourself."

"I shall," Kamara said, with only half her usual confidence. She stepped backwards, away from her beloved guardian as if she would never rest eyes upon her again. "I shall try," she said, with the same lack of conviction. She turned suddenly, and ran in an uncontrolled, almost hysterical manner toward the stables, her white cape billowing behind her.

Teeah watched Kamara reach the stable. Then she gazed at the trail of Kamara's boot prints in the soft dirt. "Such a trusting child. A trusting child indeed. Forgive me Kamara. But spring is over and summer is here. The storms are coming, and the devil can no longer be detained."

The stable attendant saddled Kamara's favorite white mare, aptly named Twilight for the symbolic hope of a new and better dawn. Her favorite, for the animal had a gentleness akin to hers. She mounted quickly and rode out the corral gate, held open by the attendant. She cantered west under a pinkish blue sky, her long ponytail bouncing against her long drop hood.

She appeared angel-like with the half-risen sun splashing golden light about her form. The hem of her cape circled the horse's alabaster rump. Her soft ivory boots rested lightly in the stirrups.

The bobbing of the horse eased her jittery stomach. She inhaled the cool morning air, filling her lungs to the brink, exhaling slowly, expelling her fear. This settled her nerves, so she repeated the process frequently, even though it made her light-headed.

On she went. On and on and on. She loped through a wind swept wheat field, walked her mare through a fragrant apple orchard, and cantered over a meadow dotted with dainty white and red flowers. She hastened and slowed the gait of her mare often, flowing as a wayward river compelled to find the sea. When she entered the thick forest of green maple trees, she slowed almost to a stop, plagued with an eerie sensation. Stillness. Silence. The forest seemed empty.

Her mare jolted, trying to turn toward home.

She yanked back the reins, forcing abeyance. "Sorry Twilight, but we must both be brave." She called for the love of Great Spirit Mother. The Sacred Mists of Cohesion steamed from her breath and fingertips, engulfing her and her beloved horse in a vaporous cloud, calming them both.

She tapped her heals, and her mare moved forward, step by slow step. She came to a grassy clearing, edged by a shallow trickling creek that marked the western boundary of Lania land. Her stomach lurched when a surge of wind blasted past her like a cold ocean wave, washing away the mist.

She halted her mare, darting her eyes frightfully about the countryside, searching for signs of the Cold One. Her throat tightened. She choked until she coughed. She pressed her hand over her heart, trying to calm its fluttering from lack of breath.

She summoned the will to face her tormentor, but she felt absurdly vulnerable and already defeated. Panic rolled painfully up her torso, turning her face pale and her skin cold. She must return home—now!

She pulled the reins hard to the left, twisting Twilight's head. The mare began turning around just as Kamara caught sight of a brilliant white apparition in the distance, across the creek.

The ghostly angelic figure hung in the air with arms outstretched as if reaching for her. The face took definition as seconds passed. Kamara was entranced. Could it be? Could this be her mother's spirit? The face resembled the drawing she had of her mother. Of course, she had also thought Teeah had resembled that same sketch. But what if—?

Her heart pounded. "Mother? Have you come to help me?"

The spirit remained silent, reaching to her.

Kamara moved forward, hope renewed. The earth vibrated beneath Twilight's hooves. Kamara's chest tightened, straining her breath. Cold fear. She misted heavily. Twilight jerked her alabaster head right, then left, then backward. The mist calmed neither of them.

Twilight reared her front legs into the air with a screaming whinny, expressing Kamara's terror. She tightened her knees on the saddle as hooves clunked the ground. Frenzied, her once gentle mare bounced on all fours.

The mists seemed ineffective now. Twilight grew wilder. Kamara tried calming the frightened beast by stroking her thrashing sweaty neck. But still, they both wanted to run.

The spirit woman signaled her forward.

Kamara exhaled sharply, summoning courage. She managed to move her bouncing mare sideways across the creek. "Faith," she said aloud. "Faith," she said again.

The ground rumbled violently. Longer. Louder. Unending. Her snorting mare bucked with increasing violence. Kamara slipped in the saddle. Right. Left. Her every muscle tightened to resist falling.

She shrieked to her mare over the rumbling, "Calm down Twilight, calm down!"

She pulled the leather reins hard to the left, trying to give the horse a direction to flee. However, the frightened beast bucked harder, not going anywhere. Kamara held on for a seeming eternity, trying to outlast the earth's rumble and the mare's tantrum. But neither stopped. Siphoned of strength and will, her arms began to spasm with pain. They gave out when she gave in.

She didn't remember falling, though she must have, for she was laying flat on her back on stilled and quiet earth, looking up at maple trees. Her right hand was wet. The creek water flowed over her open palm. Pain throbbed in her left shoulder and the back of her head. Leaves rustled beside her, and one blew against her neck. It tickled. She let her chin drop toward the leaf, and beheld the rump of her mare disappearing in the thick forest, away from her lands, away.

"No," she whimpered. A pang of shock fluttered her heartbeat. Doom. The feeling swallowed her.

A sooty twisting wind blasted from the trees, ripping leaves from their safe branches. The twister engulfed her, sucking her upward to her feet, spinning her in ever-dizzying circles, faster . . . faster. Worlds seem to spin around her from stories she'd heard others tell, horrible stories of death and destruction.

She heaved herself down on hands and knees, visualizing the earth's core—grasping for it, for her sanity, for *her* world. She mustn't be as the leaves, ripped from their knowing! Her ponytail and cape whipped tightly around her, swaddling, and suffocating. Maple leaves blew in a flurry around her head, some slamming against her as if clinging for salvation. But, they were sucked into the wildness instead. Dirt granules stung her face. She labored to crawl out of the twister, but budge, she could not.

With eyes closed, she held her position with thoughts of the Lania Priestesses, vague memories of her infancy, and the glorious choral of feminine voices that once sang blessings for her.

A sharp rock hit her cheek. She felt blood. Memories of childhood, memories . . . she must concentrate! Around the pictures in her mind, the whirling continued, closing in, trying to snuff the bright reverent faces of her past.

"Oh wisdom, do not desert me!" she cried. She peered through the black fury, her eyes searching to behold the spirit woman. The apparition seemed gone. Had she been tricked? Had the Cold One captured her?

The top of her head buzzed, stimulated by an energy vortex stationed above her. The buzzing turned to a sucking sound. The spirit within her shot up to the top of her head toward the vortex. "No!" she cried, "No!" With all herself, she held her spirit inside her. Mist floated from her breath and fingertips. "I summon 'the light.' I *am* 'the light!' "

The sucking intensified. Resistance was harder. She screamed loud and long, "I . . . am . . . 'the light!' " The sucking gained momentum and she doubted she could fight it. Something whispered, 'Give up, give in.' Her spirit was almost pulled out of her. She shouted, "Great Mother, help me!"

A motherly voice echoed in her brain, "See a cap of light on your head, sealing you within yourself."

She followed the instructions with such sharp focus that her scalp split with pain. "I am capped, capped, capped." The cruel wind sucked away her streaming tears. "I am capped, capped, capped." Weak, she felt weak. No, she must fight. "I am capped, capped, CAPPED! I am sealed within myself. I am sealed, sealed, SEALED!" The sucking sensation began to dissipate. "Capped. Sealed. Capped. Sealed."

The twisting wind transformed into a black wall, yards long and high—blowing cold and forcefully against her, roaring its shrill defiance that tormented her ears. The heavy air crashed into her lungs. Breathing was hard. Her face felt pressed against a solid mass.

She must crawl toward home. She must! She raised a hand to crawl, but the wind force blew her palm to her ear, and almost sent her reeling backwards. It took all her strength to push her hand through the wind back onto the ground. The more she tried to move toward home, the mightier the wind became. She felt paralyzed in her position. The wind blew colder, and harder, ripping her cape and gown, numbing her skin.

'Give up, give in,' she again heard the whisper.

"No!" she shouted, siphoning her resolve to return to Lania Castle. And with that, she began to inch forward. Her arms trembled from the strain of lifting a hand and jamming it through an almost impenetrable pressure to greet the ground, a smidgen ahead of where it last touched. This required total might, an iron-will, but most of all—courage. She summoned the sacred vapors to pour from her breath and fingertips. Even so, the dark wall grew higher, longer, wider, blacker, stronger. Her mind screamed, *Oh love of my people save me! Oh power of heaven, I implore your rescue! Oh, sacred forces, embrace me*! Each and every budding tear was ripped from her eyes and sucked behind her, swallowed by the ever-howling wall of storm. Insanity beckoned, and the whisper settled in her head, 'Give up, give in.'

"No!" Her tone was more desperate than the last time she shouted that answer.

She crept meagerly forward, her exhausted muscles begging rest. Each step managed, likened the climbing of a ladder. Each rung attained, forced her to experience the cold slap of cruelty in its most potent performance. And each succeeding rung was worse than the last. Yet, she had to grip each rung and survive its horrors before she could pass over it. The only way 'out' seemed to be—

'through.' The rung of deceit came first, undoing trust. Then came rape, crushing sanctity. Then torture, maiming integrity. Then murder, destroying will. However, the worst rung to pass over was innocence marred.

Had she fallen into the chaos that lurked beyond her lands? Or was this solely the Cold One's doing? Then she somehow knew the answer. The Cold One was trying to pull her to him with the world's chaos that she was clearly, and to her immense surprise, ill-equipped to handle. The mist and light she flowed simply dwindled in the world's heavy pain of being.

Minutes stretched into hours, and hours into the night, the wall ever expanding, the wind more deafening, the brutalities of life romping inside her. On and on she crawled, with arms and legs cramping, straining against the cold blast. Hands, knees . . . stinging, bloodied, grating against rough ground. Lungs aching. Ears aching. Incessant howling. Insanity beckoning. And the familiar whisper, 'Give up, give in.'

Her head throbbed from concentrating on chants and visualizations that had been reduced to: *I can do this, and I'm breathing through a tube.*

Her dry grit-filled mouth craved liquid. She drew her parched tongue over cracked lips. Even a single precious drop would do. Fatigue weighed her down. Her skin burned cold. Depleted of energy, sheer will, and sheer will alone, gained her slow inches.

The freezing gale had long since unbound her hair into tangled strings whipping straight behind her, blown away her cape, and changed her dress into a rag.

She fantasized death often and the lovely quiet it could bring, but ever shook loose the fantasy when she heard the dastardly whisper, 'Give up, give in.' Determination pushed her through the night and into the light of the next day, on and on, toward her castle into eternity.

Ж
Chapter Four

Near Lania Castle

Michael and Kayenté had ridden their horses hard, closing the distance between the two castles with a speed that had wearied them all. Kayenté's black warhorse, black, except for white shins, had fared better than Michael's dun steed that was untrained for such rigor. The Dun panted, snorting intermittently with a show of yellow teeth, too tired to whinny. Michael had insisted they travel almost constantly, but as they neared their destination in the hot afternoon, they slowed to a walk.

This region of Kantine was much warmer than the Kaquenda region where Kayenté lived, and his northerly attire induced sweat. His long black shirt hung loose over his chain mail shirt and the waist of his black hide pants, sword ever at his side. He'd shed his black cape some time ago, stowing it in the saddlebags. The unpleasant heat generated by his semi-armored attire was countered by the comforting weight of chain, durability of hide, and power source at his hip—a sensation that promised protection in battle should one arise.

Michael's tan cotton tunic and leggings left him comfortable and free. He no longer felt naked without his armor. His promise, his protection, were the mists enveloping his body.

Kayenté was glad when he finally saw Kamara's misty castle stretching long and tall over a grassy knoll of wildflowers under the canopy of hot blue sky. A bead of sweat stung his eye when he squinted to study the distant dwelling in the moving mist. Through the vapors, he viewed the dream like structure, seemingly void of moat or curtain wall, and the many defenses common to most fortresses—save four watchtowers cornering the castle.

He wiped the sweat from his brow and said to Michael, "I searched for this dwelling once, that year you tended your sickly parents. I was curious about the rumors of the witches at Lania Castle causing an uncharacteristic bout of disease. I decided to—"

"Yes, I remember those silly lies," interrupted Michael, as he waved a fly from his face.

"—investigate." Kayenté said pointedly, batting away the fly that had left Michael for him. "I searched for it many fruitless days, with maps made by those who had seen it. Yet, here it is, where it wasn't then. How can that be?"

"It was here. For a hundred years it has been here, seen only if the Priestesses wish it to be seen. However, knowing you, I am surprised you gave up."

Kayenté didn't reveal the truth of the antiquated lure he'd *always* felt toward the rumors of Lania Castle, nor the accompanying apprehension. He puffed his chest, voice assured. "The castle was said to inhabit helpless women and villagers. Those who had professed visiting the place, never spoke of riches or weapons, so I was not motivated to solve the mystery. I simply returned to Kaquenda and announced that no one need worry about the harmless inhabitants of Lania Castle. They put their faith to me, and that was that. However, once we complete this task, I *will* command loyalty from the people of this domain."

Michael smiled faintly. "They are no threat to you."

"That's irrelevant."

"They are loyal to Kamara."

"That can change, especially if I succeed in slaying her tormenter."

"Once you return to your fortress, you will not find your way back here if she does not wish it so."

"I now know her exact location, and I'll not forget."

"That won't matter. The Priestesses generate the Sacred Mists to camouflage their domain from those with ill intent. They can play tricks on your mind. You won't find them."

Kayenté slipped his eyes darkly toward Michael. "My intent is not ill. Their loyalty to me would earn them a place under my wing. That is all."

"I beg your pardon, lord. I didn't mean to insinuate that you possess a malefic predisposition, only that Kamara would judge your goal unsavory, for she abhors any hierarchical system of power."

Kayenté stated, with a cynical laugh, "For an anarchist, she sounds quite opinionated about how the world should be run."

Michael gave a colluding smile. "And of the real world—she knows little."

Kayenté stared at Michael, pleasantly shocked. His statement suited the old Michael more than the new. "You do think then that she's a little—off?"

Michael felt quickly shamed. "No. I don't believe she's 'off.' *You* are doing this to me. You incite my former self. Kamara's great wisdom is to be respected, not mocked!"

"So, is your wise woman going to seize my sword the moment we arrive and thwart my ability to defend her? Perhaps I should hide it now, so that her wisdom doesn't cause her demise."

"That would prove pointless. She would not only eventually see it with her second sight, given you'd be thinking about it all the time—but if you are hesitant to surrender it, which is actually the truth, it will throw her off the mark of suspecting our ruse. And that is why I don't protest your chain mail shirt."

"Had I known you would have protested, I would have worn full armor."

"All right, all right," Michael said, "I know I'm asking a lot, but I must. She *is* wise."

"I prefer to think of her as ignorant."

Michael gave him a hard, cold eye.

Kayenté didn't care. Michael must be punished, however minor, for hauling him into this escapade. He'd rather fight a dragon than feign submission to a woman. And he'd rather be naked than stripped of weapons. But at least, in his boot, he had hidden his preferred knife. He didn't intend to relinquish it. In fact, he'd almost drawn it several times on Michael to make him cease his unending drill on how to block the truth from Kamara. Well, he would block *this* truth from Kamara.

However, his greater concern was the trouble his men might have finding Lania Castle should they need to reach him. If they could not, and his castle fell, his dreams would die, and for that, Michael would have to die. He didn't particularly wish Michael dead, or his dreams for that matter.

A woman raced toward them, her light blue dress and long blonde hair whipping in the wind of her run.

"Kamara?" asked Kayenté.

"No." Michael kicked his horse and cantered in her direction.

Kayenté kept in step with Michael. "Too bad."

"Why? Because she appears innocuous?"

Kayenté flashed Michael a wily look.

Michael laughed. "Looks can be deceiving."

"What are you saying," scoffed Kayenté, "that the woman in blue is a tyrant in disguise?"

"No," Michael said, "I am referring to Kamara. She appears more innocuous than this woman, and yet she maintains harmony between two hundred and four people. This woman," he said pointing toward her, "is Camille, a peasant girl, once raped and beaten by warriors. She sought sanctuary with Kamara." He glanced at Kayenté with glittering eyes. "Her life has much improved."

"Yes, yes," said Kayenté derisively.

They halted their horses before Camille.

She was panting hard. The distress upon her reddened face alarmed Michael. He had thought her speed was motivated by joy for his return. Apparently not.

Kayenté said, "Her life's improved, eh?"

Michael ignored Kayenté, preoccupied with Camille, who had finally gathered the breath to cry out, "Michael, oh Michael! Kamara left yesterday morning to confront the Cold One. She has not returned!"

Michael froze. His heart pounded in his ears, drowning all sounds but imagined ones, like Kamara whimpering and the Cold One grunting atop her.

Camille tugged at Michael's leg. "She forbade us to seek her, but you must Michael, you must!"

Michael could barely feel Camille tugging his leg. And he could not hear her at all.

But Kayenté heard. His blood surged, eager to draw his sword, and preferring to do so before he was required to surrender it.

The wind began to bluster. A screaming howl came toward them from the west, intensifying with each moment. Looking to the sound, they saw a colossal black wall of wind rising over the hill.

Camille shrieked. Her once flushed face had paled. "Mother of Mercy! What is that?"

Kayenté was stunned, and not much could stun Kayenté.

Michael saw the faint silhouette of a woman crawling amidst the dark blasting gale. "Camille! Return to the castle and keep the others inside until I say otherwise!"

Camille nodded and raced back toward the fortress.

Kayenté masked his astonishment, saying casually, "Don't tell me," he pointed to the silhouette, "Kamara?"

"Kamara," affirmed Michael, kicking his heals firmly into his mount. "Come on!"

Kayenté hesitated a moment, trying to break his stupor. This Kamara was beyond peculiar. She was an aberration personified. What was this wall of storm? Where did it come from? How could it be defeated? How—

"Kayenté!" Michael's distant voice carried back on the breeze.

Kayenté preferred to evaluate an enemy before he attacked it, but Michael wasn't going to allow that, so he spurred his weary horse forward and raced to Michael's side. "Damn, Michael! *That* isn't human!"

Michael said, "I need your help!"

Kayenté thrust the back of his hand toward Michael with each sentence he shouted, "Hell Michael! Give me a criminal to fight! Or a knight to slay! Give me a whole damn Rudelian army!" Then he jerked his hand forward to the black wall. "But this? This Michael?"

"I didn't ask for *this*!" Michael shouted.

"Why did you have to fall in love with *that* woman!" Kayenté said, "Why *that* one!"

Coming close to the dark wind wall, the horses would go no further. Bucking hooves flew in the air, and neighing snouts yanked side to side. Kayenté and Michael vaulted to the ground while they could. The horses shot back toward the castle, terror overriding exhaustion.

Michael shouted to Kayenté, "Let's step into it, grab her arms, and pull her out!"

Kayenté furrowed his brows with a sigh. "This isn't the rescue I had in mind."

Kamara was so deeply submerged in her efforts, and so overcome with biting coldness and torturous fatigue, that she hadn't even noticed the men in front of her, or the castle so near. She was startled when her arms were suddenly snatched upward. Her legs flew off the ground behind her. Her chest was drawn against solid warmth. A heart pounded against her chest. Another body pushed against her back. More solid warmth. Another pounding heart. She was interlocked between two people, her own feet not touching the ground. Who was helping her?

Her limbs felt weightless, as if they were rising, though they were limp. Her head rumbled like an earthquake echoing over the edges of her fatigue. She was too weak to hold on to anything anymore, so she hoped that whoever was helping her would not give up, and that they were powerful enough to free her from what she'd come to call, The Black Wind.

She heard male voices, moaning, grunting, and cursing, intermingled with the dissonance of the howling gale. She felt the men's muscles straining against her for a long time. It seemed they were eternally affixed in their position. Suddenly, they all shot through the air, out of the wind's grip, onto still earth.

A weight tumbled from her back. The wailing wind rolled away over the hill from whence it had come. Kamara's ears throbbed with the shrillest pain, and the phantom shriek of the black horror continued to howl in her head. Her mind felt stretched backward from wind speed, and her violently trembling body felt like it was moving up and down. Her numb frozen skin burned from heat beneath her, and she realized she was laying on someone who was breathing hard, hence the moving up and down.

It was over! The nightmare was over! She wanted to cry and release the trauma, but gaining her breath took precedence. Several minutes passed in a choir of panting bodies, until the choir of panting became solo—hers.

And with that, her voice emerged ragged—but audible. "Thank you . . . thank you . . . thank you." She couldn't hear herself even though she knew she was speaking.

Large warm hands stroked her back with a gentleness that brought great comfort. Her cheek lay upon someone's chest. A heart beat in her ear. The strong musky smell of sweat filled her head. She wondered whom she laid upon, but she was too weary to lift her face and see.

"Kamara, are you all right? Your skin is almost blue." She heard Michael's voice.

She gasped for air, shivering uncontrollably, her chattering teeth affecting her words. "M-m-Michael! . . . I'm overj-j-joyed . . . to hear your voice."

"And I yours," Michael replied.

"You s-s-sound . . . miles away." She listened for his answer, assuming she lay atop him, for her ears did not work right anymore. "Did you s-s-say some some something?" "The w-w-winds have affected m-m-my hear hear hearing."

"I am here Kamara. I am here."

She spoke in a suffocated whisper between continuing gasps for air, "Michael, oh Michael . . . I have n-n-ever fought . . . anything . . . so, so d-d-dark . . . and so r-r-ruthless . . . for so l-l-long . . . in all . . . my my life."

Michael lay on his back next to Kayenté, waiting for the feeling to come back to his arms. He laughed softly and said, "Kamara, angel . . . it is the *only* thing you have *ever* fought."

"Well . . . I d-d-disdain it. I disdain it . . . imme . . . me . . . mensly!" Her tone held the ache of her experience, and at that she began to weep gently, too weak to release the sobbing aftermath of horror that she truly felt.

Kayenté rather enjoyed their weary congregation. He smiled faintly, amused by Kamara's sheltered life, favoring her weakened frame upon him, the girlish tone of her voice, and her tears of surrender. He liked her this way—vulnerable. No better way to have a woman.

"You're safe now Kamara," Michael said, "Safe." He wanted to pull her in his arms then and there, but they still would not move. Two years of passivity had shifted his strength from muscle to heart, so for a moment more, his words would do the embracing. "What was that *thing* you were trapped in?"

Kamara's breath began to ease, and her teeth chattered less. "It was the . . . Cold One's attempt . . . to draw me to him." She gasped suddenly, expelling pain. Her next breath rose, and a giant wave of emotion crashed down upon them all. "It was the hell of your Old World, Michael—of *the* world, I guess. I hope not. It was grim and bitter . . . infected with greed . . . plagued with sorrow—brazen hatred coursing through blood. It was innocence twisted and tortured . . . turned evil by the quiet whispers that beckon madness, wilting the flower and crushing the seed! It was the crawling seeping sickness of hysteria . . . permeating the helpless. It was the shadows of deception laughing . . . at the shock on purity's face. It was hideous and horrible and too much to bear! However did you survive it, Michael? How does anyone? How!"

A deep voice resounded in her ear. "Sometimes you have to use a sword."

The strange voice and forbidden words fell into her ears like stones, and her tongue threw them out. "What did you say?"

"I said—"

Michael blurted, "Kamara, may I present Lor," Michael caught his mistake. "Ka." That was a mistake too. Rescuing Kamara had distracted him from the ruse, and for a moment he couldn't remember the fictitious name. But it came to him in a burst. "James!"

"Lorkajames?" asked Kamara, realizing it was Lorkajames, not Michael, whom she laid upon. And she was most embarrassed.

"Yes," Michael said, almost sheepishly, "This is Lorkajames."

Kayenté winced, cursing silently at the idea of being stuck with such a foolish name.

Kamara said, "Michael, where are you?"

She felt her body lifted and pulled to a sitting position, her back against someone's chest. She was far too weary to hold herself up, or open her eyes. Even speaking had proved strenuous.

Michael answered, "In my arms, Angel."

"Who is Lorka—"

"Hush. Rest." Her skin felt arctic, and he intended to warm her, but first he did his best to arrange the remnants of her tattered clothing over the most feminine parts of her exposed skin. He didn't want Kayenté getting any *ideas*, as he often did.

"I'm," she shivered hard, "so cold."

Michael rubbed her arms vigorously.

Kayenté was startled by her appearance, even though Michael had earlier given him a clue. She looked childlike, but she was no child. What he'd glimpsed between the shreds of her white garment proved that.

How could that before him not be warmed for lovemaking? How could this passive creature sustain harmony between two hundred plus people, or possess the supernatural powers Michael described? She seemed powerless, not powerful. Michael was right. Her looks were definitely deceiving.

Through heavy lids, Kamara tried to peer at the stranger who sat across from her, but her eyes wouldn't stay open long enough to view him clearly.

She asked wearily, "Who is this Lorkajames who believes in the sword?"

Kayenté cursed inwardly again at the sound of the insipid name he had to bear.

"Clearly, Michael," she said, her voice weary, "this man is not your sister."

Michael said, "I freed my sister, however, she chose to remain in Kaquenda. But Lorkajames, my cousin, asked to come here. I believe he might be the man you saw in your vision?" Michael thought that was a nice touch to authenticate his ruse. "He is weary of the warrior's life, and he seeks 'the light.' "

Michael glanced at Kayenté, who had sat up bearing a protesting glint in his eye.

Kamara forced her eyes open, focusing on the man in chain mail and black clothes, sitting casually, draped elbow over one raised knee. She drank in his hard-lined features, bright blue eyes, long black hair, and sword that hung like an appendage at his side. This *was* the man in her vision. "He does not appear the weary warrior to me."

"He wouldn't. Fatigue is not a thing warriors openly wear."

Her eyes slid shut. She felt too weak for etiquette and for anything but sleep, yet her mind was jarred by the warrior's essence triggering visions of him in raucous fighting. She cried, "Oh, such callous abandon. Oh, the sword dancing with such deadly precision." Her voice rasped, "The blood cry is his song!"

Michael assured her, "Kamara, you are seeing what he was, not what he *wants* to be. He knows no other way. He needs you to teach him that he can survive without the sword, and that a better life awaits him."

Kayenté glared at Michael, wondering if he believed what he was saying, and if maybe the ruse was on him.

Kamara pushed her eyes open to mere slits, beholding the warrior with distorted view. "But he *just* said, 'sometimes you have to use a sword.' He sounds at ease with his way, the way of the sword. His sword *is* his life. I feel it burning in his bones."

Kayenté smiled inwardly, feeling the truth of what she said.

Michael retorted, "Then why is he willing to surrender it to you?"

She shook her head slightly. "No. He needs war, leads war, is war." She couldn't make her eyes stay open any more, so they fell shut, overtaken by exhaustion. Her body jerked. "Oh—the things I see . . . ." A tear rolled down her cheek.

Michael said gently, "You fail to understand warriors, Kamara. Survival depends upon throwing one's self completely into battle. You are seeing those past moments, not this moment and the man before you."

"No, this man would not seek pacification. Why is he here, Michael? Why?"

Michael eyed Kayenté with a look that said, 'She is reading you.'

Kayenté was amazed by her 'knowing,' and began to under-stand why Michael had drilled him so hard on the fine art of 'block-ing.' The time had come to implement that art. Oh, not so much because it was Michael's plan to fool her. He just wanted to see if he *could* fool her. He recalled one day when he actually was thor-oughly war-weary, and he brought it to life in his mind, vividly, maybe even to sting her a bit. "Fear not, lady," Kayenté said. "While war has possessed me, I detest being its slave, craving blood over water, slaughter over creation, death over life."

Kamara moaned, feeling queasy, still unable to open her eyes.

Michael glared firmly at Kayenté, knowing full well he was toying with her in his creation of imagery, extracting, as always, a price for his sacrifice.

Kayenté continued, "However, I am just a warrior, as any war-rior is, as all warriors are." He concentrated hard on days before he fought in wars, on days he felt helpless, on days when he watched his mother raped by the man he believed to be his blood father, and how helpless he felt to save her. "I use the sword only to survive."

"You are a leader. I feel it."

"If I were, I'd use that power to stop injustice." Not savoring his memories, he hid them with a dalliance of words. "However, I am not. As it has been my station to be a warrior who follows or-ders, yes, I'd rather lead, if only to make humane changes. But if I need not be a warrior, then neither would the need to lead—be." Kayenté delighted in mind games. Given he was being forced to play an unsavory role in Michael's ruse, he would exact his own style.

"I'm exhausted," Kamara said, "and my mind is muddled."

"You must rest now." Michael stroked her cheek, relieved that her shivering had subsided. "You are overwrought with all that has happened."

Kamara's voice weakened with fatigue. "I suppose I must trust your judgment, Michael." She paused nearly drifting off. "Forgive my doubt Lorkajames. Michael was once filled with fight. And yet, here he is, devoted to peace, the fight in him—gone."

Kayenté would have laughed had his ire not been so near. Instead, he touched his sword. He could not help it.

Kamara's voice trailed as sleep began to capture her. "If your sword has been surrendered when I awaken . . . I shall believe the intentions you have stated."

Anger swam in Kayenté's eyes. He wasn't sure he *could* surrender his sword.

The world blackened around Kamara. "Michael, give his sword to Teeah, right away."

"Rest Kamara," Michael said. "I'll see to it that the sword is put where it belongs." He then eyed Kayenté, nodding his head slightly, for they both knew where it belonged.

"I need the Hot Springs, Michael and the Cape of Deep Return—or I may not awaken." Sleep took her. Had not her breath given faint rise and fall to her chest, her stillness would have appeared fatal.

Michael spoke urgently, pointing north. "Panther! The Hot Springs are just over there, beyond those cedar trees. Carry her into the water, quickly!"

Kayenté narrowed his eyes, having been long unpracticed at taking orders.

Michael, noticing Kayenté's steely glare, cleared his throat and restated, "Lord Kayenté, would you mind assisting me?"

Kayenté rose, and walked in front of Michael and the sleeping Kamara. Towering over them, he said, "Don't confuse the game for the truth."

Michael nodded. "My apologies, lord."

Kayenté knelt. He scooped Kamara in his arms and rose.

Michael leapt up. "I must retrieve her cape!"

Kayenté watched Michael dash toward the castle entrance, dotted with a large crowd. He sighed, unnerved by the whole situation, and distressed that some woman named Teeah would soon confiscate his sword.

He walked toward the cedar trees, viewing Kamara's cold, almost lifeless body in his arms. A surreal sensation overcame him. He tried to shake off the dreamy feeling, the soothing sensation of something raw and beautiful, something forgotten but real. He *had* to shake it off, something about being in control.

Her torn dress had fallen back from her legs, exposing her bloodied knees, and the creamy smoothness of her undamaged thighs. The top of her dress covered haphazard parts of her, revealing portions of her breasts and abdomen. Her neck, her shoulders— he could kiss them if he wanted. And the little blood wound on her cheek—he could kiss that too. No one need ever know that he had a tender moment. But he would not kiss her. Her sleeping face seemed sinless in her slumber, but that didn't mean it was.

He reached the Hot Springs and waded into the warm water, sensing no time to undress. Deeper and deeper he went. When the water reached his waist, he lowered her into the steamy liquid, leaving only her face above the surface. Her lengthy honey hair swirled around her body.

She stirred faintly in the twilight of sleep. "Michael," she murmured, "You feel so—beautiful. I love you . . . as never before."

Kayenté didn't respond, not wanting to alarm her.

Her voice was whispery, "I know how to locate the Cold One. Don't tell the warrior . . . shhhh."

She went limp and unconscious so fast, he feared she'd died, and was shocked that he cared. He put his ear to her mouth briefly to confirm breath. It was there—her breath, the breath of this unusual creature. So naive, he thought, so refreshingly unworldly, a pleasant change from all the people he knew, hardened by a hard life. And he pitied her for a moment that she would come to know him, for he was sure to offend her sensitivities with the bloodlust that was his very nature.

Kayenté thought perhaps Michael would one day realize his dream of having her after all, but he was curious to know if her feelings were for the man holding her, or for the man she thought was holding her. Would she swoon over Michael the way she did him? Michael had told him that she swooned over no one, and would be taken by no man—ever. Michael was wrong. This woman could be taken. All women could be taken with the right lure.

He heard the pounding hooves. Michael drove two galloping horses hitched to a cart, coming toward him. When he arrived, Kayenté noticed Camille and another woman in the back of the transport.

Michael called, "Bring her . . . please. Place her in the cart."

Kayenté waded out of the water with Kamara in his arms. Streams of liquid dripped from their bodies and the point of his scabbard. He nearly lost his breath when he glanced upon her soaked form, skin sparkling. Water was pretty on her. He reached the cart and laid her upon an ivory blanket stretched over the wood floor. Camille covered her with a deep plum velvet cape. The older woman smiled at Kayenté. "I'm Teeah, and you are?"

"Lorkajames." Kayenté scowled at Michael.

Teeah's eyes twinkled. "Pleased to know you . . . Lorkajames." She turned her attention back to Kamara.

Teeah, Kayenté thought begrudgingly, *the weapon confiscator.*

"Lorkajames!" said Michael. He jerked his head to the side, meaning 'let's go.'

They walked to the front of the cart and climbed onto the driver's board. Michael took the reins and hastened the horses on a bumpy ride to the castle entrance. The hot sun beat down on the cart and Kayenté's hide pants began drying. He glanced at his sheathed sword by his leg. Maybe with Kamara "out," confiscation would be forgotten.

As they arrived, multitudes of men, women, and children surrounded the cart, asking in varying keys of chorus, "Will, she live? Is she all right?"

Michael ordered, "Stand back everyone. She needs rest."

Kayenté watched the people step back from the area, wanting to do the same. Instead, he climbed off the cart and went to Michael, now standing, and carrying Kamara in his arms. The plum velvet cape was yet draped over her. Her long wet mane hung in the air, water beads dripping.

Kayenté helped Camille off the transport. Her shy glance empowered him. But the empowered feeling faded when he helped Teeah down. She gazed into his eyes, into his soul. He released her quickly and scanned the grounds for his warhorse. Not that he was planning to leave, but he might at any moment decide not to stay.

Michael was at the foot of the steps that led to the entrance. "Come Lorkajames, don't worry, our horses will be collected and tended. Your belongings will be brought to you."

Kayenté raised a brow. "That's not where my worry lies."

Michael carried Kamara up the steps into the castle. Kayenté followed. His brief spell of being dazzled by Kamara had faded. Cold stark reality set in. He had grand plans and Kamara was not a part of them. Maybe not touching her, not seeing her, broke the illusion of loveliness. No matter. It was broken, and he was glad.

Teeah and Camille followed Kayenté silently.

Kayenté felt like he'd entered a great snow cave. The vacant white walls glittered with mineral chips. There were many small round fist-sized windows, the sills each holding a large clear crystal. The sunlight shining on the crystals sprayed rainbow colors all over the room. Though the effect was unorthodox, he rather liked it, and continued gazing upon the colored lights even as they climbed up the ivory marble staircase on the east side of the Great Hall. When they reached the fourth story, Michael carried Kamara down the corridor.

Teeah called out, "Lorkajames, I'll store your sword for you. Once your belongings are retrieved, I'll need the mail shirt as well."

Kayenté growled lightly and stopped in his tracks, still hearing the echo of her words in the long tunnel of his mind.

Michael reached Kamara's bedchamber, and stopped. Panting softly, he looked to Kayenté and watched him relinquish his sword to Teeah.

Teeah glanced at Camille. "Show him to his room."

Michael nearly said, *Place him near Kamara*. But then Teeah, as though anticipating his very words, said, "Place him in the guest room near Kamara." Then she flashed a smile at Michael and walked away down the corridor toward the staircase. If she knew his plan, she was clearly endorsing it.

He glanced at Kayenté whose face showed visible grief as he watched Teeah disappear with his sword up the stairway. Michael sympathized—until Kayenté stabbed him with a hawk-eyed and beak ripping-into-flesh, glare.

Michael nodded at Kayenté slightly, assuring the return of his weapon.

Kayenté's face did not soften.

Camille opened the door to Kamara's room. Michael carried his beloved inside.

Camille said, "This way, Lorkajames," walking one door beyond Kamara's room.

Kayenté followed her, ire brimming beneath his stoical facade.

He passed Kamara's room, glancing in at Michael doting on his beloved, instead of trailing his sword. Liar.

Camille stopped and opened a door. "This room is usually reserved for overnight guests. You are privileged to use it."

Kayenté resented the statement to say the least. A lord is never privileged. He is *lord*.

"Perhaps it's because you're a friend of Michael's?" Camille's face took on a dreamy expression.

"And you fancy him, don't you?" Kayenté said with a vindictive glint in his eye.

Her face flushed.

Vengeance is sweet. Now to get rid of her.

She said, "You may rest here until Teeah or Michael return for you."

He nodded, but didn't go inside. Instead, he lowered his eyelids and gave Camille his cold-blooded warrior stare. She shrunk back, excused herself, and dashed into Kamara's room, just as he'd hoped. He must trail Teeah with his sword before it was too late.

He sprinted down the corridor. Above him, he heard the sound of stone grating stone. He raced up the stairway to the fifth floor and crept along the hallway. He scanned the long walls. No doors. No openings. Could he have been mistaken about where Teeah had gone, or was there a secret passageway?

He decided to wait and see if Teeah reemerged. Once he could ascertain the location of the moving stone, he'd leave and later return to discover the way inside. He knew many secrets about hidden passageways. His own fortress had many. Surely, one of them would apply to this corridor. He cursed Michael. He needn't be in this position, if Michael had kept his promise instead of spending wasted moments with his little witch. Fool.

His attention was directed to the sound of footsteps by the staircase. Michael rushed toward him, and when he arrived, Kayenté slammed him against the stone wall, clutching his tunic with fists, and his attention with threats. "How the hell did you know to come up here if you don't know where she hides the weapons!"

Michael's face paled, startled by Kayenté's attack. "I have . . . have . . ."

Kayenté dug his knuckles into Michael's throat, making him cough. "You'd best not have lied to me!"

Michael spoke in a raspy whisper, "I have always known it was the fifth floor. I've just never known exactly where."

Through grated teeth, Kayenté hissed, "You had best not lose track of my sword. You know my affection toward that particular weapon." He withdrew the pressure of his knuckles on Michael's throat, but not his grip, which still pinned him against the wall.

"I know. I know, lord, six months in the making—"

"Fourteen. Eight months studying and testing the shapes and weights of the most supreme killing blades in the world. Six months more to fashion a sword to surpass all others. Four years hence, with that perfect clean-cutting, impact resistant, quick-moving blade in hand, not even a flesh wound has found me. It's my . . . lucky sword."

"Lord," implored Michael, "I'll find it, I swear, but let us leave this area before our motives are suspected."

"I'm not leaving—" Kayenté glanced down the corridor, "—until that woman emerges. She's on this floor, somewhere."

"I'll obtain your sword when the time arrives! I swear, my liege."

"Former liege."

"My allegiance remains. Only violence is prohibited."

"What good is allegiance if you're not willing to kill for me?"

"I'll listen to your troubles and hold them in confidence."

"My only trouble is you."

"I'll defend your honor with my tongue, even if it means I lose it."

"You may yet, for talking me into this."

"I can't kill for you, but I will die for you."

Kayenté groaned, his face softening.

Michael said, "If an arrow came your way, I'd take it for you."

Kayenté loosened his grip, but glared at Michael skeptically.

Michael continued, "You may appear ruthless. You may speak a callous game. Even so, I know goodness dwells within you. Would I have trusted you with Kamara if I didn't believe that was so?"

He released Michael and stepped back. "If we are to save her, you must attain access to my sword."

"I will," Michael said, "but likewise, if we are to save her, you must start thinking and feeling the need for help."

Kayenté's jaw flinched. "This had better not be some grand scheme to pacify me."

"I respect you too much to deceive you."

"Why not? You respect your little nun-angel, yet you deceive her."

"No offense Kayenté, but I stand to gain more by Kamara accepting the sword than I do by you accepting 'the light.' And I fear your retribution exceedingly more than any revenge Kamara could muster."

Kayenté sighed, shaking his head lightly. "All right, Michael, but this situation had better not worsen. You've convinced me to pretend I want pacification, and to relinquish my sword without knowing its whereabouts, and to be called—" he scowled, "Lorka-james, for God sake." He flicked his hands in front of Michael's face. "That's it! I'll give no more than this!" He stomped down the corridor, indifferent to the possibility of eavesdroppers.

Michael followed, torn between relief and the fear of being discovered.

Moments later, they reached Kayenté's room and entered. Kayenté felt strange. The chamber was as white as the Great Hall, with dozens of sparkling crystals protruding from the stone walls. The white velvet comforter on the bed looked clean and fresh. A large white pillow, puffed like a cloud, seemed to beckon his head to rest upon it.

His hide pants were only damp now, and his belongings had not yet been retrieved from his horse, so he rested on the bed, propping his head up with the pillow. "I feel like I'm on a cloud."

Michael sighed. "Kamara has a way of comforting people."

"How is your nun-angel?"

"Sleeping. She'll probably be out for some time."

"Damn," Kayenté huffed, wanting to sit up, but just too tired.

"I thought you'd be glad. If she sleeps, then you needn't worry about her trying to bridge you with spiritual love."

"Yes, but if I kill her foe soon, that wouldn't be a concern. She spoke at the Hot Springs, believing I was you. She said she knew how to find the Cold One, but that you were not to tell me. The sooner you can get her to tell you where he is, the sooner I can get my sword back, slay the bastard, and get the hell out of here."

Michael eyed Kayenté curiously. "Did she reveal anything more?"

Kayenté hesitated, not sure if he should tell Michael the rest. He decided not to, feeling in some strange way that her words of love had not been meant for Michael, but him. Of course, had she opened her eyes to see who truly held her, she would have died then and there.

"Nothing else," Kayenté answered, "But don't tell her that it was I she spoke to. I think that knowledge would alarm her."

"All right," Michael sighed, "so be it. Rest, Lord Kayenté. Later, I'll show you about and introduce you to the residents."

Kayenté nodded, having grown heavy with fatigue. His eyelids closed. He heard Michael exit. Sleep took him fathoms down into himself.

He dreamed he was trapped in a land so bright that his eyes hurt and his skin burned and he began to shrivel. He searched frantically for his sword in the land of boundless light. His sword had always protected him before. Suddenly, he stopped searching, realizing that a blade could not help him escape 'light.'

Then Kamara appeared in a sheer white nightgown and approached him seductively with his sword in her hand, as if to return it. She looked at him with liquid eyes and said, "I love you Kayenté. I am 'the light.' " Then she plunged the blade into his heart.

He awakened from the dream, bolting upright in his bed, cold sweat beading on his face. He reached his hand down to his inner boot and sighed with relief. The knife was still there.

He labored to calm himself, resting once more on the billowy bed. In his life, he'd conquered ferocious men, sometimes against overwhelming odds. He could fight the cold hearted. This he'd proven. But how does one battle goodness, light, and love? The answer eluded him, but he was determined to find it, for he'd not be seduced by "the light," and pierced in the heart, betrayed by his own sword—in the name of . . . love.

He clasped his hands behind his head, elbows out, summoning his own power. Kamara Lania would not bridge him! Bridge? She doesn't bridge people. She breaks them with love. Love, a different kind of power, but power nonetheless. She probably attained supplies and goods for her whole castle, and had her crops reaped from the fields without paying a single coin! People likely did her bidding—in the name of . . . love.

Michael had her pegged wrong. She's no sweet angel, or even an anarchist! Anarchist. Hah! She's a ruler, just like any warlord, duke or king, lethal as hell, because she lures her victims into voluntary surrender. Then she controls their hearts to get what she wants—in the name of . . . love.

Like Michael. Michael. She has held him prisoner, tricking him into being consumed with protecting her, despite her claims that she didn't need or want his protection. And she's made him obsessed with having her, when she'll never be had by him. Poor Michael, she even had him conned into suppressing his primal desires—in the name of . . . love.

Kayenté smiled, thinking of Michael's affair with Allysa. *Well, we took care of that.* And then he laughed, wondering if Kamara had felt the act. But his laughter was stopped by an unsavory thought. Had she manipulated Michael into retrieving him in particular to slay the Cold One? Maybe she did know about the charade. Maybe she was playing them in *her* game.

Kayenté's mind spun a web of defense. *I'll not be her puppet. Kamara Lania and her love will not know me! If her pursuer is human, I'll slay him—for Michael. And then I'll show her my true power and beat her at her own game. I'll make her desire me. I'll seduce her. Then I'll force her to bow at my feet! And she will do so—in the name . . . of . . . love!*

He relaxed, comforted by his shrewd plan. He fell back upon the white velvet covers, desensitized by his survival instinct. He rested serenely, protected by his cold mental armor. He was safe—for now.

Ж
Chapter Five

Lania Castle—Four Days Later

Kamara had slept four days. Kayenté was beginning to wonder if she'd ever awaken. He and Michael sat with a dozen other men and women on birch wood chairs at the far end of the Great Hall. Kayenté wore black cotton, cooler for the south: black sleeveless tunic, plain styled pants, and soft ankle boots. He'd even combed his hair back some, with two small braids trailing down each side, over the loose mane.

The people were engaging in a pleasant late afternoon conversation. Colorful clay cups of blue melding into white, rose to and fro lips that discussed life's relevance, to and fro the little round wood tables by each chair, to and fro—the conversation sparkled. They drank Teeah's famous gardenia elixir, as Kamara permitted no wine, claiming it could alter the senses unfavorably. With that, Kayenté disagreed fervently, missing the two bottles a day he usually consumed.

His thoughts drifted from the topic of conversation, thinking instead about the residents of Lania Castle. He'd become familiar with this gentle group of over two hundred people, who seemed so vulnerable without an army to protect them, and yet here they were in a castle that had never been under siege.

He partook in their strange meditations, even though he spent the entire time dreaming of his sword. And he came to enjoy their chants of light and love, even though he didn't believe what he heard. And he liked their strange dances and stories, even though they always gave the same irritating message of love, not war. And he rather enjoyed bathing each day in the Hot Springs, even though he felt weird being so clean. And he liked the delicious food Teeah made of fruits, vegetables, nuts, and flour, even though he craved meat.

The people had no schedule. Yet, they harmoniously flowed in and out of group events at will: spinning threads, sewing, cooking, singing, dancing, and producing works of art. Everyone voluntarily pitched in to keep the castle and surrounding grounds clean and well maintained—farming lands of cotton, wheat, vegetables, fruit, and nuts—growing grow silk from worms, and digging wells from the earth. Each held the duties with which he or she felt most able, and most comfortable. And each had a personal agenda for self-improvement, while also aiding others in their endeavor to do the same. And the people talked not of war, and riches, and copulation, but of feelings and thoughts beyond mundane concerns.

If Kamara truly had lived this way her whole life, then yes he would agree that she had been completely sheltered from the realities of the outside world. If she were to pay it a true visit, not merely in some conjured reality as in the Black Wind, it may well destroy her.

He took comfort in this thought, for if he wanted to drive her away from him, all he need do is describe to her with ruthless ill-manner, the rough realities of everyday life. Yet, to the contrary, he had an urge to shelter her. Maybe she was an innocent, and not at all capable of contriving any master plan such as the one he had imagined. Such manipulation was more *his* style.

He had slipped into her room periodically when hearing her whimper in her sleep and he surmised she had been dreaming of the Cold One. He had gazed upon her angelic face, less and less able to believe that she was a conniving strategist. Still, he'd not thrown the notion out completely, for he'd never known a woman who wasn't. Nonetheless, he'd found himself viewing her as sincere, and he was charged by the thought of killing the culprit in her nightmares.

Though he was anxious to escape "the light," he didn't want to depart a coward, nor with a commitment unfulfilled. How much longer must he wait? He needed to fight. He'd pestered Michael daily to locate his sword and the mail shirt Teeah had collected. And he went for long rides on his warhorse, seeking signs of danger, ever dismayed when he found none.

"Good evening, dear people," announced Kamara from the stairway behind the group.

Kayenté and the others looked her way. She neared them, appearing freshly bathed, clothed in a dress of golden velvet: snug at the waist, long tight sleeves, and a scoop neck. Her silky hair was tied back into a ponytail, trailing over her shoulder down the front of her gown to her waist.

Kayenté watched her curiously with a kind of delicious apprehension.

She walked over to the group who began to rise, respecting her presence.

"Please, remain seated," she said warmly.

She knelt to each person, touching their hands, greeting each with a delicate smile and liquid eyes. When she came to Kayenté, she did the same, but added, "I thank you for your heroic deed four days ago."

Kayenté nodded in affirmation, unwilling to reveal anything more of himself. But she did not move on. She studied him intensely. He moved restlessly in his chair, ill at ease with her probing gaze. Daring of her, a direct challenge to reach in him what he chose to hide. Should he crush her now?

She said, "There's much light in your soul, even though you wear a thick armor of darkness and deception." She tilted her head as if trying to detect something.

He was surprised that she found his soul good, and wondered how much she knew about him. Had she used the word deception to mean that he was specifically deceiving her, or the way he ran his overall life?

He remembered Michael's tutelage about thinking the illusion, so he forced himself to recall times when he was weak. He thought about when he was a child and no one would hold him, when he so desperately needed to be held.

She nodded her head in light approval, rose and walked over to Michael.

Kayenté cursed silently, haunted with the sorrow of his childhood. This place and this woman were no good for him.

Kamara snapped her head back toward Kayenté, her face in wide surprise as if she had heard his true thought.

Damn her! Shutting out bad feelings was not permitted. He swallowed his pride and resumed his former uncomfortable mode of thought, promising himself that he'd later discompose her, and twice as much.

She looked to Michael, and sat at his feet, resting her head on his knees. The people darted their eyes at each other, clearly stunned by her submissive behavior toward a man.

Kayenté found her openness odd, not caring who heard what. She seemed incapable of harboring a secret, hiding a thought, or feigning an emotion.

He studied her closely when she looked up at Michael with adoring eyes. "Thank you for watching over me, dear Michael, with such diligence, and for fulfilling my uncommon requests. I remember a moment in the Hot Springs, I—" She furrowed her brows.

Kayenté watched. Kamara turned her perplexed face toward him, cocking her head sideways as if questioning. Kayenté's eyes locked with hers, interested to see if she'd relinquish her idolatrous attitude toward Michael once she found her answer. She cast her eyes back and forth between Michael and Kayenté several times. Suddenly, while focused on Kayenté, her amber eyes widened with realization.

And Kayenté knew, that she knew, it was he who had held her at the Hot Springs. Her face held the very expression of confused horror that he'd imagined on her, if she had known that day to whom she had professed her love. Ah, sweet revenge!

Michael whispered, "What is it?"

Kayenté watched amused, as Kamara leaned her forehead on Michael's leg, hiding her face. Michael slid off his chair onto his knees. He drew her into his arms, pressing her cheek against his chest, which made her view Kayenté.

She cast Kayenté a shy look, and then turned her head the other way, visibly fighting tears. "I cannot work with your cousin. I don't want him here."

Kayenté barely heard her, but if she had said what he thought she'd said, he was relieved. At least about the part that she couldn't work with him—that is, until Michael rebutted, "You cannot turn him away. He seeks 'the light.' "

She pushed Michael back from her, and faced Kayenté. "You sir, are far too violent to be bridged. I must ask you to leave."

Kayenté endorsed her appraisal of him by casting his cold warrior stare.

Kamara gasped lightly.

Kayenté knew he frightened her. And he should. He *was* too violent to be bridged, and he couldn't bear to convince her otherwise. He had given her mock control once, and she had nearly taken it for real. If she lost that control, that was her problem. And if Michael wanted her to have it again, then he'd have to give it to her.

Michael spoke as if reading his mind, "He's no more violent than was I. What ails you Kamara? You never turn people away. And you've always believed that the whole world could be bridged."

She assessed Kayenté's steely gaze. Her eyes reflected compassion and fear conflicting.

Kayenté, feeling a little sorry for her, softened his face. "If I am too much for you . . . how do you expect to bridge the Cold One?"

Her eyes became introspective. She bowed her head, gazing at the floor.

Silence pervaded the room, everyone seemingly uncomfortable that their Priestess was behaving like a human instead of a sage.

She raised her eyes softly to Kayenté. "Very well then, I shall work with you—now."

Kayenté squinted one hard eye, resenting himself for getting deeper into what he wanted to escape, and would have, if only he'd kept his mouth shut.

She turned her head shyly to her shoulder. She knew she must work with him now, because later might devour her courage.

Michael's face fell. "Now? Tonight?"

She gazed upon him with apologetic eyes. "If I am to work with him, it must be at once."

Michael frowned. "Very well." He eyed her longingly as she rose and walked over to Kayenté's side.

Kayenté turned his hooded eyes up at her.

"I've been dreaming of you," she said.

"Bad dreams then?" said Kayenté in jest.

She put her hand on his shoulder. "Are you ready to work?"

He slanted his eyes to her hand indignantly, and almost shoved it off his shoulder. He sighed and stared forward with stubborn resistance.

She moved in front of him and knelt, resting her palms on his hands. "You don't trust me. You hide the ache of your heart, but I see the wound anyway. Let me heal you."

She curled her fingers around the sides of his hands, wanting him to respond, but he remained limp.

Her lucid eyes burrowed into him.

He realized that prolonging it was worse that getting it over with—fast. He stood up with a deadpan face. She rose. He wanted to knock her down, peeved not only by her unwelcome invasion of his inner world, but by her public display of such personal issues.

Her manner was contrary to his upbringing, where problems were handled with such secrecy, other family members were clueless.

Detecting his irritation, her face hardened. "You resist me. Do you desire peace or not?"

He glared into her for long seconds, wanting to say no, unable to say yes. Finally, he grunted.

"Was that a yes?"

"Mm hum," was the best he could offer.

"Then come with me."

She led the way out of the room. He followed the gentle sway of her hips, fighting the urge to exert dominance over her in the most primitive fashion and put her in her place—beneath him.

Halfway up the stairs, Kamara said, "You were the one who held me in the Hot Springs, weren't you?"

"Yes," he answered, still following her.

She stopped one stair above him, turned around, and stared directly in his face. "You know, I believed you were Michael."

"I know."

"Whatever I might have said then, you must disregard it."

He smiled faintly. "Done."

She stared hard at him, not moving.

"It's disregarded," he said with glimmering eyes.

She sighed briskly, still not moving.

He said, "That's not good enough, is it?"

"What do you mean?" she said defensively.

"What you said that day was meant for the man holding you, wasn't it? It was meant for me."

She shook her head lightly. "It couldn't have been."

"And yet, it was." He smiled knowingly. "That is why you did not want to bridge me, isn't it? You feared that I'd bridge you instead, in the ways you most fear."

"Of course not," she huffed, her voice audibly nervous, "I can *never* be bridged with a man in *that* way."

"And yet, tonight, in *that* way, you were forming a bridge with Michael."

"Lorkajames," she said, "we are here to work on you, not me, so let us rest this talk."

She turned away and walked up the stairs with the most willowy gait he'd ever enjoyed. He followed, smiling, thinking how easily he could whisk her off her feet, take her outside, and make love to her in the wild heather. He knew that he could control this woman in any manner he wished, and that decision—he'd make later.

They arrived at the second floor and entered a small wooden chamber, lit by thirty blue candles placed in rows on a mantle at the front of the room. The scent of cedar pervaded the air. Central to the room was one large square, blue velvet pillow. She led him across the wood floor to the pillow and bade him sit. He did, curious to see how she'd try to heal him.

She neared his body, sank to her knees, and placed her hands on his temples. Leaning in, her forehead pressed against his. "Relax, breathe deep, and inhale the candlelight."

He smelled the sweet honey on her breath, every exhalation emitting a moist vaporous cloud that eased the strain in his muscles and gave his head the sensation of opening, smoothing out creases of irritation. He inhaled the fragrance of clove on her skin, enjoying the closeness of her body and the kindness in her touch. He followed her instructions, interested to discover her next move that he may analyze her procedure and outwit her, but instead he found himself nearly falling asleep.

She spoke deeply and strangely, as if it was not she who spoke at all. "I see a little boy watching knights in tournament, in particular his older brother. This boy is sad, for he feels different from the rest of his family, as if he doesn't belong."

Kayenté realized she was reading his childhood. So, he followed Michael's mind shield instructions by envisioning a white light curtain around him.

But he literally saw her burst through the curtain, and then she said, "An invader named . . . Ajento, comes to the boy's mother when his father is away. His father is . . . powerful and of nobility. Nobility?"

Kayenté tried to confuse her by thinking of other things, like the moments he'd slain people or made love to a woman. But she continued, "The invader is—" her breath constricted. Her voice quivered, "—violent. The boy has seen him—" her voice grew raspy, "—rape . . . his mother on many occasions. But his mother swears him to secrecy. The boy wonders why. He concludes that he is the son of Ajento, and that his mother fears her son's banishment if all were told. Banishment?" Kamara paused and then said astonished. "The boy lived in a castle. Hmm, a castle."

Kayenté fought hard to block and obscure the images of his childhood, not only because she was on the edge of uncovering his true identity, but mostly because she was dredging up memories that he'd rather forget.

She stumbled on her words, "The boy is plagued with shame, for he has done nothing to save his mother. There is no way out, no way to reconcile his frustration or relieve his rage, no way to know power or feel honor, but to fight and fight and fight. And so at age fifteen, the boy becomes a knight."

She placed her hands on the top of his head and rose, moving around behind him. She knelt, sliding her palms down the back of his head slightly, and placing her lips above her fingers. She inhaled deeply, several times, and then said, "Bring out the boy. Bring out the boy."

Kayenté felt waves of great magnitude crash upon his head, and no matter how hard he fought against her invasion, he could not block the truth.

Her hands slipped down to his shoulders. She spoke in his left ear. "Your father says, 'Protect your mother when I am away fighting with your brother.' However, Ajento pays you handsomely for your silence, and your mother begs you not interfere."

Kamara then shifted her lips to his right ear. "The boy knight thinks, *I will take the money and build my own kingdom—my own nobility. Father won't banish mother, mother won't be angry at me, and Ajento is paying for something.* But guilt tugs at the boy knight. His mother has been shamed and he had not defended her honor. He grows rich off of his mother's suffering. The boy silently screams, *I'm the son of a rapist. I am worthless*! He believes the way to feel like something is to attain more power and wealth than his brother and his father, for he hates them with a secret jealous rage, because they are so noble, when he himself feels ignoble." Her tone intensified, dramatically flooding in his ear. "Fight, Kayenté, fight."

He heard her use his true name, but so deep was his anguish that he didn't care. She had so easily found entry into him, and as in his dream, she so quickly buried the blade deep in his heart to the very hilt. No one, not since his mother, had accomplished that feat.

She continued, "In every enemy's face you see your noble father and brother, your mother who swore you to silence, the cruel man who seduced you into shame, over and over again. Fight Kayenté fight. Fight against yourself by killing others, more and more, forever and ever, but never the shame will die. Never, Kayenté, never!"

Kayenté snapped open his eyes, strong and cold. "Leave me alone, witch."

"Like always," she said, in a cloud-like voice, "you are alone in your pain. Never was there a kind shoulder to cry upon, a friendly ear to listen to your dilemma."

His body stiffened with rage. "Leave . . . me . . . alone."

She trailed her fingers down his temples to his cheeks, over his lengthy hair. Impulsively, she buried her face in the thick strands, inhaling his musky body scent, her heart bursting with adoration.

She whispered passionately in his ear. "Oh strong one, so kingly in nature, cannot you feel how so very pure of heart you are deep within?"

From behind him, she moved her cheek upon his, wrapping her arms around his chest, torn between wanting him and healing him. She chose healing because there was no future in the wanting.

She deepened her trance and pulled his truth out of her mouth, "I feel your honor and capacity to love, buried fathoms away from the outside world that has hurt you so dearly. Release your shame. Forgive yourself. You were but a child. Now you are a man, and day by day you shall be given opportunities to champion heart to the forfeit of conquering. You can heal completely if you do so. That is your work and your pathway to peace. May the high ones bless you." She kissed him on the cheek. "I have taken you into my heart."

He was still as she held him, not pushing her away, nor keeping her close. She had flooded him with her compassion and in one fatal blow he'd been undone. His hand cupped hers. He spoke with quiet resignation, "Damn you."

She began to withdraw her arms, but he held them fast.

"You have enchanted me, witch woman," he said, wanting to push her away but unable to let her go.

She said lightly, almost hesitantly, "And you—me."

"I know you are drawn to me. But why? I am all you detest."

She spoke warmly, her cheek yet against his, "When I was a child, I longed to run in the summer storms. Teeah forbade me, until six days ago when the Cold One called me into his. But his storm did not impassion me—yours does."

"What's the difference?"

"The Cold One is like a tornado, sucking his victims into oblivion. You are like the lightning storm in a dark sky: flashing bolts of warning to all invaders, thundering loudly, defending your space, blowing passionately your right to wild freedom. Yes," she said softly, "that is it. Your natural aggression feels like liberation to me." Her voice changed to a dramatic whisper, "Oh, how I long to be discharged from the great responsibility of healing the world. Oh, how I yearn to run free in your storm!"

"Then do," said Kayenté, realizing that she had indeed bridged him, and at the moment he did not care. He only wanted to bridge her.

She brushed her cheek against his as if saying goodbye. "If I let go my restraint, I might touch the energy of male aggression, and that I could not bear."

"You could learn to bear it."

"After experiencing the Black Wind, I think not. Teeah was wrong to tell me that I was ready for the torrents of life, and I tremble before you because I must resist this temptation. If we are to be close, then it is you who must come into my world."

He scoffed, "You think I can bear your world?"

"My world is love."

"Love is death to me."

"Resist not love," she said, "I'll protect you."

He pulled her around from his back into his lap, holding her in his arms like an infant. "Resist not storm. I'll protect you."

She gazed into his candlelit face, looking down upon her. She reveled in the strength of his hard-lined features and the stallion-like mane that hung over his sturdy chest. The pockets of red heat in his spirit mesmerized her—exceedingly. She desired the red so intensely, her breath quivered.

She distrusted herself to abstain, but more, she distrusted him. Most men in her opinion were hell-bent on conquering. And a man, especially one who conveyed his life story in shades of pale gray when his spirit exuded the most brilliant crimson she'd ever seen—must never, never conquer her. Who was he—really?

She asked pointedly, "Has your tongue deceived me? Are you truly a common soldier? I saw you as a knight, and with the power I feel in you, you would more likely be a king."

Kayenté had to push his next words out, for indeed they were false and he didn't much feel like lying. But then, he never did. "Any man who fights well for the nobles can be named, knight. It is common. I follow orders. I do not lead."

"But the power I felt in—"

"You feel power in me, the willingness to trample all upon my path. Though I am weary and wonder if there is another way, I do have a lust that could make me worse than the knave who sired me. I choose not to do that. Your world feels like death to me, but maybe I need to die."

"Why did I call you Kayenté?"

"Kayenté is the name my parents called me," he said, relieved that Michael had previously referred to him as Panther rather than Kayenté.

"You lived in a castle. You were a noble."

"My family lived in the castle of a noble, my father's friend. He invited us to live with him because my family comes from a long line of skilled warriors. But as I am not of my father's blood, I do not possess that integrity."

She held back her response, pausing in silence. Then she said softly, "Please, if this is not the truth, I must know."

"It is the truth."

She reached her fingers to his lips. "I want to believe you." Her hand fell to her heart. "But you seem much like a man Michael once described to me—his old liege Panther Ketola, nephew of the King. His looks are not known to me, but Michael said that he alone harbored the fierceness of an army, and that he would one day rule Kantine, and that he seduced nearly every woman he met. Michael even said that Panther might kill him for staying here with me, viewing his absence as betrayal. Oh tell me true, are you he? I must know!"

"Why must you know? Would you suddenly pitch me out, or loathe me if I were he?"

79

"No, it's more that—if you were he, I would find it difficult to believe that you were here to find 'the light.' I'd believe you were here to take me from it."

"Well, rest easy lady. I'm not he, although I could be like him if you fail to save me."

"Very well," she sighed, "I believe you. Shall I call you Lorkajames or Kayenté?"

He answered, "It doesn't matter," hoping she'd choose the latter.

She declared, "I shall call you Kayenté then. I think that name suits you better."

He brushed his fingers across the arch of her forehead. "You so fear to take what you have the right to claim."

Her heart pounded. She gazed into his bright blue orbs, shining through the shadows of his face. He was the dark and beautiful storm she had longed for. He was. Tears dripped to her ears.

"Is this feeling so terrible?" he asked.

"Yes," she answered, "because I shan't fulfill it."

He ignored her answer. Instead, he drank in the expression of longing on her lovely face. Her wet cheeks glistened in the candlelight. He wanted to taste her tears, for he himself could not cry.

Her long soft ponytail trailed between her breasts, draped like silk over her belly. He lifted his hand to the top of her head, and slid his palm over the downy strands to the end of the ponytail, resting his hand on her stomach. Her stomach quaked against his fingers.

If she had been any other woman he would have taken her then and there, but he was beginning to realize that she was not just any woman.

"This emotion is new for me," she said softly. "Is it passion? Is passion tied to—" she put her hands over her face in shame. He pulled them down gently.

"Is passion tied to what?" he asked, "sexual engagement?"

She nodded, trying to put her hands over her face again, but he wouldn't let her.

She said, "Is—"

"Sexual engagement?" he asked.

"—related to love?" she said.

He answered, "It can be." In an effort to console her, he said, "This is new to me too."

"Sexual engagement?" she asked.

"No," he smiled, "love."

"But this was never to happen for me."

"Nor me."

"But you are sanctioned to live a normal life. I am not. There's nothing in my teachings of this, no permission from the high ones to relate with men in a personal way."

"Nor is there a teaching to help you deal with the Cold One. Maybe there's a power other than love that you are to draw upon to solve both your dilemmas."

"What?" she asked nervously. "What are you suggesting?"

He said, "Knights fight for holy kings. Do they not? Courts punish criminals to protect the innocent. Do they not? Maybe you need to draw not only upon peace and 'the light,' but also upon storm and the sword."

"No!" She leapt from his lap across the dimly lit room, pressing her side to the wall by the door. "Never!"

He continued, "You crave the wild storm because you need to unleash the storm in you. You need the storm, the sword, the dark!"

She shrieked, "No! I'll never draw from the dark, I shall never appease that passion, and I'll never never touch a sword!"

He flung his cold warrior stare like a dagger into her soul. He pointed his finger at her. "That is your work Kamara Lania, and your pathway to peace!"

Kayenté watched as her knees buckled against the wall. She slouched, holding her stomach as though she'd been gouged. She was gasping for air. Her glistening eyes were as wide as those he had seen on the brink of accepting their death.

"You," she said, glaring at him, "don't need your sword to make a kill, do you?" Tension filled her voice. Her heavy tears fell straight to the floor. "Your words, I should think, are as lethal." She edged her way to the door, thrust it open, and raced from the room.

Kayenté sat in silence for long minutes, baffled by his behavior. Why had he done that? He knew of her sensitivity, her vulnerability. He had waged war with her. She was winning, so when she had shown a moment of vulnerability, he had taken her down.

Was that it? Or was he mad because the only way he could ever have her was to force her into his world.

He didn't know his motive. He didn't even know why the hell he cared. He had never cared before. *Let her go*, he told himself, and then suddenly he remembered why he had come and that when he completed his mission, he had a life of his own waiting for him and a bride arriving in a few weeks.

Michael stormed into the room. "What the hell did you do to her!"

Kayenté leapt to his feet.

Michael lunged, pushing Kayenté across the darkened room, slamming him against the wall, just missing the mantle of lit candles. "Kamara flew past me and closed herself in her room. She won't speak to me. She *always* speaks to me!"

Kayenté slugged his fist into Michael's guts, doubling him over. Then he bowled Michael to the ground, dropped his knee on his chest, and clutched his shirt with both hands. "You remember why I came here *friend*—to do you a favor!"

Michael punched Kayenté in the ribs, forcing him back on his knees.

Kayenté gasped, wrapping his arms around his middle.

Michael said, "Some favor, you ruin her before the Cold One can!"

Kayenté made a fist and hurled a sharp blow to Michael's face. Blood seeped from Michael's mouth, pocketing in a corner of his lips. "Well Michael, now that you're a fighting man again, you can off the Cold One yourself."

Michael held his aching jaw for a moment, then sprung to his feet, almost tripping over the large blue pillow. "Bastard!"

Kayenté rose, and said cynically, "That I am."

They glared at each other, huffing, ragged, and ready for more, looking a bit wicked in the tall light flames of the sputtering candles.

Michael said, "If I'm a fighting man again, then maybe I should off you!" His fist flew at Kayenté.

Kayenté caught Michael's arm, throwing him to the ground on his stomach by the force of his own charge. "So much about you dying for me." Michael rolled over, on his way up when Kayenté kicked him in the ribs. "Come on, Michael, I could use a good fight!"

Michael boosted himself to his feet, seething with anger. He slammed Kayenté in the gut with hard knuckles.

Kayenté fell to his knees.

Michael towered over him, huffing, "At least I fight for my woman's honor!"

Kayenté's eyes smoldered rage as he turned them upward to view Michael. He slipped the knife out of his boot, and rose slowly. With his other hand, he took the blade and pointed the black bone handle toward Michael. "Then kill me," he said cruelly.

Michael stared at the blade, but did not move to take it.

Kayenté said, "What? Are you afraid she might"—he emphasized dramatically—"feel it?"

Kamara barged in the room. "Stop!" She was horrified to see both men silhouetted in the shadows, breathing heavily, their hair tousled, and a knife in Kayenté's hand!

Kayenté addressed her, "Too bad Kamara," he said satirically, "you missed a good fight."

Michael looked at Kayenté with cold eyes of death.

"I did not miss it!" she said. "I have felt your assault upon each other. You may as well have both pounced upon me, for I felt the physical pain of each blow. I couldn't even move to get here until you stopped hitting each other for a moment. Our bonding cannot be treated lightly."

Kayenté wondered how she would take it when he made his next kill.

She looked at each one and then said, "But the physical pain hurts less than my heart to see friendship turn to this!"

She moved closer to them, staring at the blade apprehensively. She scowled at Michael. "You mustn't fight for me. Please don't fight for me, especially against one with whom I've bonded. I can fight my own battles."

"No Kamara, you can't!" Michael said.

She started to speak and then caught her breath. "Granted," she admitted humbly and a bit embarrassed, "I can't. But I'm not bothered by that, and I don't mind the blow if it's to spare another, even if it's the attacker who is spared."

Michael sighed, shaking his head in frustration.

Kayenté blurted, "Damn, woman, it is a wonder you're still alive."

She spouted defensively, "Survival is not an issue with me. Maintaining love is all that matters."

She addressed Michael, "If you hold any respect at all for our hours of work, or for the people here, or for me, or yourself, then you'll believe in love and the way of 'the light' which has made you happy, thus far. Your cousin is new here, and he has much further to go than you."

"But he upset you, Kamara."

"Michael, you've upset me more by reverting back to your old way."

Kayenté and Michael both surveyed her, chivalrous remorse visible on their faces.

Kamara said, "Michael, what occurred was between Kayenté and I."

Michael's face froze. "Kayenté?" he questioned suspiciously.

"That's his childhood name," she said.

Michael and Kayenté glanced at each other with almost a glint of humor.

She continued speaking, "Anyway, what happened between Kayenté and I has nothing to do with you. You and I must separately face our demons." She and Michael cast a brief look at Kayenté.

"That's right," Kayenté said, waving the knife in front of his face with wild eyes, "I am a demon."

"No," she said, moving in front of him as if the knife were not there. She touched his shoulders lightly, and then stroked her hands over his cheeks, staring lovingly into his wild eyes. "Truly, you are not." Her hands glided down his chest and back to her skirt.

His face softened. She was melting him again.

She said, "It was the faltering of my own faith that sent me flying from the room."

Kayenté looked deeply into her eyes, rethinking all his motives.

Reading his mind she said, "Was your action noble? In a cruel sort of way, yes. There is some truth in what you said, although I'm not sure in what way it should apply to me. I forgive you and I hope you can forgive me if I have caused you any pain."

Kayenté was speechless. Even with her sappy way of speaking, she had completely quelled his ire, and he wasn't used to solving disputes in this manner.

"May I have your weapon?"

He looked at her, then down at his blade.

She said, "I ask this purely, for here, there is no need for any weapon."

He squinted and sighed, disbelieving that he was about to forfeit yet another blade to her.

85

She pulled out a kerchief from a fold in her tunic. "Please place it on the cloth."

He did. She wrapped the corners of the material around the blade and slipped it in her pocket.

"Thank you," she said.

She turned to Michael. "Your cousin made great strides this night before your attack upon him. For him to fight you now is comprehensible. For you to fight him after two years of pacification—is not. Search your soul Michael, before it slides away from you. Let me tend mine."

She walked to the door, turned, and faced them. "I hope that you shall again be friends and partake in this kingdom of love. Love, I am learning seems to exist little where else."

She walked away down the corridor.

Michael wiped the blood off his lip. "My apologies, Lord Kayenté. You are still my liege and I shouldn't have attacked you."

Kayenté brushed his hair back with his hand. "Love can blind allegiance." He glared at Michael. "But mind you, you brought me here to solve *your* problem. If you again side with her against me, you will pay—" he paused and then added, "most enormously."

Michael nodded, a bit ashamed.

Kayenté went to the door and looked down the corridor in the direction Kamara had left. "But all that happened was well. I was aching for a bit of a fight."

Michael joined his side, looking down the corridor. "Sorry she took your knife. Sorry it will join your—"

They simultaneously snapped their heads toward each other and said in unison, "The sword!"

Ж
Chapter Six

Michael said, "She's sure to place your knife with your sword. I'll trail her. I can better shield myself from her empathic sensitivities. If you come, she may sense our presence."

"Very well," Kayenté sighed with a vague hint of disapproval, "but do not let her elude you as Teeah did me."

Michael nodded, and hurried down the corridor after Kamara.

Kayenté was uneasy trusting his fate to Michael in view of recent events, and decided to follow him. He crept swiftly down the corridor, and had just started up the winding staircase when he heard faint voices below in the Great Hall. He looked to the castle entrance. Teeah was conversing with someone in the doorway, someone in a black hooded cloak.

Evening had darkened the castle. He couldn't make out a face in the dim light cast by the oil lamps, but he caught the glimmer of a sword before it was swept into the folds of a bright red cape, and handed to Teeah. The mysterious person left. The door closed.

Kayenté was intrigued. He wanted a better look at that sword.

Teeah traveled toward the staircase. Kayenté dashed to the next level and stepped back into the flat unlit nook that led to the third floor. He hid in the shadows, heeding what Michael had taught him about shielding his thoughts. He gathered the concentration he'd always used in battle and imagined himself invisible.

As Teeah ascended the steps toward him, Kamara descended the steps past him. Had Michael found Kamara in time to locate his sword? The two women stopped on the landing in front of his hiding place. The oil lamp on the wall lit the edges of their shadowed forms.

"Child," said Teeah, "the Wise One has brought you gifts."

"Oh Teeah," Kamara said relieved, "what has she brought me? She must know of my troubles."

"Yes child," Teeah said, "she knows. Now close your eyes and open your hands."

Kayenté watched Teeah carefully remove a thirty-two inch broadsword from the folds of the cape. He sucked in a silent deep breath of admiration. The shiny blade reflected the flame from the oil lamp. The steel was bright. A Gatish design of gold inlay spanned the length of the blade, perfectly honed and void of the rough edges born from swordplay. The weapon had been freshly made, or never used. He was dazzled by the sculpture of flames or perhaps wings, on the gold hand guard. There was an etching in the middle of the guard that he could not see. And he thought he caught the glimmer of a large red jewel embedded in the top in the swirling ornamented pommel. He shook his head, awed by the beauteous weapon.

Then he noticed Teeah looking about suspiciously. Realizing he'd broken his concentration on invisibility, he quickly resumed it.

After a long pause that worried Kayenté, Teeah placed the sword in Kamara's hands and draped the red cape over her wrists.

Kamara opened her eyes and shrieked, dropping cape and sword on the stone floor. She slammed her heart with fisted hands. "Teeah!" she said in a tear strained voice, "How could you place a— a sword in my hands? A sword! You *made* me take it. Oh Teeah, why do you do this to me? The Wise One would never give me a destructive device! This is not happening!"

"It is, child," Teeah said.

"Oh," she gasped with horror, moving her head slowly side to side. "My heart rips with grief. This sword I could accept only to take my life."

Teeah said, "There are words that come with the gifts."

Kamara shook her head. "I won't hear them!"

The words are, "You can't bridge the Cold One with love. Wear the Red Cape and you'll not forget that you have blood. Use the sword to keep your blood from spilling."

"You speak sacriledge! Am I to become violent to disarm the Cold One?"

Teeah nodded. "Yes."

Kamara's mouth hung open in shock. "I shan't trust your words! This request defies all the teachings, denigrating the Sacred Mists of Cohesion. 'Tis an offense to my very soul! I dream a world of love and you know I would *die* for that dream."

Teeah gazed upon her with ancient wisdom. "The Sword and Red Cape are your passage into a new life. Nay, a new age. Everything changes—and you must too."

Kamara stepped back from her, shaking her head with eyes of shock. "You . . . and the Wise One are bedeviled. Priestesses *do not* advocate violence. Teeah, I need you so. How could you betray me?"

She continued backing away from Teeah.

"The Wise One isn't a Priestess," said Teeah, "she's a messenger. And as for me . . . it is true, Priestesses have never advocated violence in the past, but . . . times have changed."

Kayenté held his breath and doubled his concentration on invisibility as Kamara nearly backed into him. She stopped and shouted at Teeah, "You're under a spell and you're trying to trick me. I want to see the Wise One!"

"You can't. She forbids it."

"Why! Why am I never to look upon her face or hear the melody of her voice? Now I begin to doubt her existence. Perhaps you have been she all along! Perhaps you have used her phantom existence to manipulate me."

"No child, that's not so. I know your pain is great, and your doubts strong, but you must trust our guidance. When the world changes, so must we. Your mother resisted as you do, and now she's gone. If you resist, gone you shall also be."

"I *must* resist." Kamara cried, "Never have I defied you or the Wise One, but I shan't allow myself to take part in what is obviously a demonic ploy to bring our sacred sanctuary to ruin!"

She moved forward to the fallen gifts, maneuvering the Sword into the Red Cape without touching the metal to her skin. She walked over to the window, inches from Kayenté, pushed it open and said, "The sword of destruction."

Teeah said, "Or the sword of protection."

Kamara ignored her and threw the blade out the window, and then she said, "This cape is red, the color of spilled blood."

Teeah said, "Or red, the color of new blood."

"No," said Kamara, "no." She threw the cape out the window, flapping down after the sword. "The Wise One would enchant me to violence. In the morning, I shall have the sword retrieved and all other weapons we have confiscated over the years. I'll take them to the smithy, and have him meld the metals into a shrine of peace. If I must fight, then my fight shall be against my nightmares and those who would have me sanction violence."

Teeah said, "Until you make peace with what you resist—the battle will never end."

"Make peace with the sword? Accept violence? Never. You betray me Teeah. The Wise One betrays me. I fear Michael and his cousin Kayenté, too, shall soon betray me." She bowed her head. "I'm alone in 'the light.' Truly I am." She ran past Teeah, down the stairway.

Kayenté remained in place until Teeah moved upstairs. Then he crawled out the small window to the outside, almost getting wedged in its scant width. He scaled the castle wall to the ground below, spying the cape. He tossed the cape behind him, and plunged his hands into the tall yarrow bushes. He felt cold metal, grabbed the handle, and lifted the blade upward to the half moon. He kissed the flat steel. "If she doesn't want you—I do."

From his peripheral vision, he saw a shadowy figure in the distance heading in the direction of the Hot Springs. Certain it was Kamara, he followed secretly, comforted by the feel of her sword in his hand, the long walk over.

When she reached the Hot Springs, he watched her silhouette in the gray dark. She shed her clothes amongst sprays of tall grass, and stepped down into the water that reached her waist. Her upper body slumped over the bank, exposing her bare back. Her hair caped her limp arm, sprawled over the grassy earth. The dark water glistened about her defeated repose. And there she lay for a very . . . long . . . time.

He wished he could ease her into the reality of the world he knew. If only he could make love to her, and help her accept the protection of the sword. Then she would learn that the blade was no demon, that men had their merit, and that war had its place.

But no, it seemed there was no hope for her. She appeared to sense this. He stood in the shadows—seasoned warrior, seasoned rebel—pondering Kamara's extreme resistance and strong conviction, not unlike his own. However, those traits, while benefiting him, would cause her demise.

Even so, he understood her dilemma. If she abandoned her belief in "the light," then her faith and confidence to manage her castle, or even herself, would be no more. Yet, by blindly living her belief in "the light" as she always had, the opposition was growing stronger, and in this way also, she would soon, be no more. Either way—she was doomed.

She seemed more willing to die with her beliefs intact than change them. She was brave and significant, standing tall against everyone, refusing to compromise her principles for anyone. She was another noble one, and he sighed sadly at his own lust for power, knowing that if he were in her place, he'd not die with such honor. No, he'd survive at any cost, and if he couldn't, he'd take his enemy down with him, somehow, some way. But that was him.

He stayed with her for awhile, forlorn at the thought of her plight. Never had he felt so tenderly toward a woman, having deemed most of them leeches who fed off men. Getting her to take anything from a man was a feat in itself.

He suddenly thought of his "taken" sword. Why was he obsessing on her? He had his sword to think about. Coming to his senses, he detached himself from her pain. He turned to leave, when he heard her rise from the water. Looking back to her, he gazed upon her dark shimmeing body, fighting a great instinct to move her way. Behind him, someone approached. He stepped back into the tall brush.

Kamara had donned her gown. She was shivering when she walked past him. Then she stopped to greet Camille.

Kayenté had felt like a ghost of late, witnessing transactions not meant for his awareness. He deemed it luck, for fate had not been kind to him.

Camille handed her a white cloak. "Here. Teeah said you'd need this. She said you would wear white. Why did she say that Kamara?"

Kamara slipped the cloak over her head adjusting it to fit her body. She gazed at Camille for a moment, and then took her hands.

"Dear Camille. Do you care for me?"

"Yes."

"Do you believe in the power of spiritual love?"

"Oh, yes!"

"Then I have a great deal to ask of you."

Camille clasped her hands over her heart. "How can I serve you?"

"Great change has come upon me. I fear I shan't survive it."

"Kamara!" Camille's hands flew over her mouth.

Kamara drew Camille's hands down. Then, she touched one finger to Camille's parted lips. "Hush. Grieve not for me." She took

Camille's hands in hers. "I shall rest easy knowing that you'll carry forth the teachings of 'the light' when I am gone."

Camille bowed her head. "Please do not speak this way."

"I do not fear for myself Camille. I fear only that the teachings might die. If you ensure they will endure, then I am fearless."

"What of Teeah?"

"She talks of accepting swords and such. This cannot happen. I trust only you."

"You do me great honor."

Kamara shook Camille's hands softly. "No, Camille, you do *me* great honor." She tightened her grip. "More than any other you've practiced the wisdom of the Priestesses. You are the purest of heart. And in your great effort, you have crossed over the bounds of normal human experience into the sisterhood. Few women can."

Camille's eyes lit. "Do you believe I have?"

Kamara nodded. "Soon, I believe you will chant the Mists. You are near full initiation into the Sacred Order of the Mist. There is no other in this entire castle who has made this transition without being born into it."

"Oh Kamara, do you truly believe I can do your work justice?"

"I do. And you, like all Priestesses of the Mist, shall bear only daughters. So you needn't worry about birthing an aggressive male into this already too violent world."

Camille blushed. "Speaking of men, and I know this question might prove highly inappropriate, but I've something to ask."

Kamara stepped back, releasing Camille's hands. The subject of men always unnerved her. "What is it Camille?"

"Are you and Michael, ah . . . ?"

"What Camille?"

"I mean—" she bowed her head and spoke timidly, "if you're not planning, you know, to one day be with him . . . I should like to—"

"I'll not be with Michael the way you should like to be with him. That possibility has now vanished. Yes." She sighed. "You may pursue him. However, remember that male relations are for breeding, not husbandry. Your daughter must not know Michael as her father, for all the men here will be her father. You must not live for Michael, but for 'the light.' "

Camille nodded lightly. "I will labor to uphold that priority."

Kamara said, "I love you as my sister, Camille"

The women embraced, and their faint weeping serenaded the air.

Kayenté soaked in the sight, Kamara's loose hair strewn over the bright white cloak, angel of the night, soft-spoken, heart of hearts. And Camille receiving the invisible torch of love and light, doomed of course to go out. Love always lied, and light always faded. The sisterhood would die.

Kayenté had heard enough. He had seen enough. But maybe he had not done enough. He made a wide circle around the women, backtracking to the place where he'd found the sword. He slid the blade in his belt and climbed the castle wall, which wasn't easy and only possible because of the many small openings that had been incorporated into its design to let in light.

He climbed back through the window and snuck to his room. Once inside, he wanted to better examine the sword, but hearing Michael call to him through the door, he slid it under the bed.

"Enter," he said.

Michael rushed in and locked the door.

Kayenté lit an oil lamp with cool demeanor.

Michael said, "Where have you been?"

"Spying on Kamara." Kayenté walked to Michael. "She's going to melt all weapons in the morning." His eye twitched. "What are you going to do about that?"

"Relax. I found the secret chamber. I went inside and saw both our swords and your mail shirt as well."

"And . . . my knife?"

Michael pulled it out of his boot, and bowed lightly, presenting it to Kayenté. "My lord."

Kayenté took the knife with a smile and slipped it back in its rightful place. "We'll retrieve my sword tonight."

"But Kamara will be suspicious when she finds it missing in the morning. She would not look for the knife as she would the sword. Is that not enough for now?"

"That doesn't matter anymore," he said, "I've devised a plan based on what has just transpired."

Michael furrowed his brows. "Of what do you speak?"

"Kamara has asked Camille to succeed her. I fear your beloved won't survive, despite our effort. Her spirits are so low."

"What are you saying?"

"She was gifted a sword by a woman called the Wise One. She rejected it and fell into despair."

Michael's eyes widened. "The Wise One gifted her a sword?"

Kayenté nodded.

"If this is so, then she *must* accept it. This confirms our actions. We are right in what we are doing. The Wise One and Teeah wish her to integrate the sword into her way of life."

"Yes, but she thinks that all who carry or advocate the sword are bedeviled."

"We must convince her otherwise."

"She can't be convinced, unless maybe a taste of the outside world would help her see the value of battle."

"No," Michael said, "she'd absorb everything too quickly. It would be too much for her."

"I would have agreed with you before this last hour, but . . . my mind's been changed."

"You work quickly. One day with Kamara, and now you are ready to make away with her?"

"One day is all I needed to understand how to save her. You asked for my help. You asked me to save her. Let me."

"Where would you take her?"

"I will take her to my fortress."

Michael shook his head. "I tell you, she *won't* survive there."

"Does it matter, Michael? If you could only see her as I just did, you'd know—she's already gone. She has given up. She is preparing for defeat."

"That *can't* be."

"It is."

Michael shook his head, not wanting to accept Kamara's reality, nor Kayenté's solution.

Kayenté said, "Ask yourself, just who is this Cold One? She responds to him in her nightmares, the way she responds to the outside world, the sword, and the maleness of men. She resists the passions of anger, sexual union, and survival—all that would make her human. Isn't there a Cold One in us all? Maybe she need not fight the Cold One, but welcome him into her soul? She's trapped herself in her temple of healing, in her light, in her good and noble self. And some other part of her, the human part, is dying, because she refuses to let it breathe. When you and I feel the taste of defeat we'll do anything to survive. She won't. I think we must break her out of her own trap."

"Damn Kayenté, I didn't know you were so deep."

"It's simple strategy, Michael, learning to outfox the enemy by knowing him better than he knows himself. You're just not used to me utilizing my skill to selflessly benefit another."

"Then save her. Do what you must. But be gentle, and shield her from the rough of life." He cast his eyes downward briefly, and sadly looked up. "When will you leave?"

"In the morning."

"But how will you exact this without traumatizing her?"

"I'll find a way, Michael. I always do."

"Very well." He rubbed his brow with his forefinger. "Take her sword with you. In time, she may accept it."

Kayenté walked over to the bed and slid out the sword. "Here it is."

Michael eyed the sword with a similar awe that Kayenté had. "It's exquisite." He looked closer at the design on the hand guard.

"Look Kayenté, the panthers back to back, your family's coat of arms."

Kayenté's intrigue deepened. He brushed his fingers over the design. "Could the Wise One belong to my father's House?"

"I don't know," Michael said. "Her identity seems illusive."

"If she's of my father's house, I'll find out."

"Maybe the panthers on the sword represent you. Maybe this sword bears the message that you are the one to save her."

"Well, if that's so, then we must now retrieve *my* sword."

Michael nodded. Kayenté went to the armoire that contained his few clothes, and slid the sword behind it. They left the room, closing the door securely, and ascended to the fifth floor. Michael led Kayenté down the corridor between ivory stone block walls. He stopped and pushed against a three by three square block that yielded and gave entrance to a hidden chamber. However, the small opening barely lent passage, and once inside, the tiny room cramped them against its white crystal walls.

The air was damp and cave-like, and Kayenté worried about his sword rusting. He waited in nervous anticipation as Michael removed the lid of a long wooden box. Empty!

Kayenté grabbed Michael's collar, pushing him backward toward the wall.

Michael's foot was blocked from stepping back by something on the floor. His knees buckled and he was half sitting when his back hit the wall. His ankle was pressed against the obstacle, a flail apparently, because the spikes against his boot were not pleasant. "Both our swords were here but moments ago! I swear!"

Kayenté clenched his teeth and yanked Michael up to his feet. "Damn Michael, where the hell is the smithy?"

"Outside, at the back of the castle."

Kayenté looked around. "I don't see my mail shirt either."

"It *was* here."

"To the smithy then," said Kayenté.

Michael nodded. "Yes, my lord."

Teeah hid in the shadows of a nook by a window in the corridor. She smiled as the men moved passed her. In her arms lay the red cape. In the cape were Michael and Kayenté's swords and Kayenté's mail shirt. "Relax boys," she murmured to herself, "I'll not let Kamara melt your weapons, nor will I let you retrieve them . . . yet."

Michael and Kayenté searched for the weapons from the smithy to the goat yard, from the highest floor to the lowest, until they began to draw suspicion. They gave up and returned to Kayenté's bedchamber.

"In the morning," Kayenté said, "keep your eye on the smithy. When you find my sword, and you'd better, bring it to the top of the watchtower, the one closest to the front court. I'll be waiting."

Michael sighed. "Very well." Then he began to fidget.

"What, Michael?"

"I've—. I've—"

"Yes?"

"I've one thing left to ask of you."

"Yes?"

"Do not bed her."

Kayenté paused and then declared with finality, "You ask too much."

Michael's face reddened. His lips curled back over clamped teeth. "Even as I have sworn allegiance to you Kayenté, I couldn't forgive you for seducing her. You, of all men, could do her great harm."

Kayenté raised his brows. "And if she wills it?"

Michael pushed his face up to Kayenté. "She would not will it without your manipulation."

Kayenté stiffened. Warning flashed in his eyes.

Michael stepped backed. "You're not right for her."

"And you are, Michael? If that's true, then why is it I who can tend her needs? Is your love for her so weak, you would not want her alive and happy?"

"She'll never be happy with you."

"Perhaps not, but she'll be alive."

Michael glared at Kayenté, torn between love and hate, unable to convey either. "So be it," he finally said, and exited the room.

Kayenté slept lightly, dozing on and off, dreaming and scheming a gentle abduction, when he heard a knock upon his door that opened slowly, awakening him fully. A candle flame lit Kamara's face and the top of her velvet gold tunic.

She tiptoed toward his bed. "Kayenté?"

He said nothing, wanting her to come closer.

She came to his bedside, placing the candle with its crystal holder, on the small table near his bed. She leaned over the soft velvet comforter.

"Kayenté," she whispered softly, touching his shoulder. Then she realized his eyes were open. She jumped back. "Oh my, you're awake!"

"I'm trained to awaken to even the slightest brushing of feet upon the floor. My response awaits the moment when the intruder is at a disadvantage—like you are now."

She stared at him a moment and then straightened her shoulders. "You're trying to frighten me away because you fear I'll cause you to change so much that you'll no longer recognize yourself."

"That is partially true," he said, "but also true is the knowledge that one can never trust anyone, for betrayal is ever imminent."

"Well, if you live here long enough you shall learn to trust, and relax, and sleep deep in the womb of this domain."

"I hope so," Kayenté lied.

Kamara continued, "That is why I needed to speak to you, despite this late hour. I apologize for interrupting your sleep."

He flung back the covers, exposing his sinewy body in tight black pants and no shirt at all. "Come lie beside me then," he said, "and be comfortable."

Her eyes widened. She stepped back. "No, I hardly think that would be appropriate."

"Oh, and coming into my room well into night—is?"

"I must speak with you now, for my fate is uncertain tomorrow."

He grabbed her arm and pulled her closer.

Her voice squeaked, "What are you doing?"

He snared her rib cage and lifted her over him to his other side, landing her on her back. Then, he whipped the covers over their bodies.

She gasped. "I cannot lie next to you!"

"And yet—you are."

She bolted upright. He eased her down with his hand. "Relax. I'm not going to harm you. Rest easy."

"I . . . I . . . I have never been in bed with a man before, and under covers no less!"

"According to Michael, Light Priestesses are allowed to 'be' with men."

"Not me."

"Why not you?"

"I don't know why not me! I didn't come here to talk about that."

"That?" teased Kayenté.

She huffed in frustration.

"I feel sorry for you," he said.

"Sorry for me? Why?"

"While I will learn what you know, you will never allow yourself to learn what I know."

"You mean I'll never know how to punch a man, or slay a human in the name of greed?"

"You have many gifts Kamara, but truly you are naive. If the Cold One was upon you now, and you held a dagger, would you use it?"

"I'd bridge him."

"If you couldn't, would you use the dagger?"

"No. I would die."

"Yes, I believe you *would* die," Kayenté said, "and I believe you *will* die, for the Cold One is upon you, even though you can't see him."

She started to rise abruptly.

He eased her down. "You came to speak with me?"

"Yes." She gathered the covers tightly over her chest. "You upset me so that I almost forgot. My words for you don't regard my fate, but yours. If something happens to me, I've instructed Camille to help you. I implore you not be as forceful with her as you have been with me, for she is somewhat frightened of men."

"And you are not?" he taunted.

"Once again, I am not here to talk about me."

He raised a brow. "Why not?"

"You trouble me, Kayenté. Always you deflect my work with you so that instead we work on me. You are far too aggressive to have an honest yearning for peace." She sat up, turning toward him, still holding the covers tightly against her. "When I moved into your soul, I felt you as a kingly man with vast ambitions that did not include love. Why are you here Kayenté, why?"

"I'm here," he said, lying, "in a way, for a kind of love. And I am learning that good will exists, and that there is a time to take my guard down. But you must remember, I've been conditioned to look over my shoulder, for at every moment there was an enemy at my back. I am a warrior. You cannot expect me to relinquish myself completely to one I barely know. Nor can you expect me not to take an interest in a battle, even though your battle seems to be with a phantom."

"You truly want to learn then? You and Michael are not working against me?"

"Not against you, Kamara, for you," he sighed wearily closing his eyes, "very, very much for you."

"Kayenté?" she asked, but he didn't answer. He'd fallen asleep.

She looked at his candlelit face. Her heart beat hard, for so very much she was attracted to him—to what was *in* him. She secretly wished that she didn't have such exceedingly high standards that seemed nearly impossible to maintain, especially now, when she wanted nothing more than to have Kayenté kiss her.

Hurriedly, she crept off the bed, took the candle, and left the room before her yearnings intensified.

She ran into her bedchamber and screeched, almost dropping the candle. Michael sat on a wooden chair near the foot of her bed.

He tapped his fingers on the chair's arms. "Where have you been?"

"You speak like you own me, Michael."

"Forgive me," he rose and walked to her. "I'm just so worried about you."

He took the candle from her and placed it in the wall holder. Then he held her shoulders lightly.

He stepped forward and pulled her body tight against his. "Earlier tonight, before you rested your head on my knee in the Great Hall, you looked at me in such a way I'd not seen before. I've waited a long time to be with you, Kamara—I mean really be with you."

He felt her body stiffen.

"Don't be frightened. I'd give my life and all my love to protect you. I'd sacrifice anything for your safety. And I have, more than you know. But if it's right for you, I want to show you my love with the closeness of our bodies."

"Michael," her voice trembled, "I'm so confused with all that is happening to me."

She pulled back from him with a satiny movement. "You know I've always cared for you, but what you request I can't even consider, for I'm fast slipping away. I understand now that the Cold One can't steal my light if I don't relinquish. Yet if I don't, I will die. I am almost certain of this. But it's all right. I'll die and live in 'the light' for eternity. It's the only way I can escape the Cold One. You'd fare better to release me and love another."

"No, Kamara. No." He then realized that Kayenté was correct. She'd die if she stayed here. He wanted to tell her that he wasn't going to let her die. He wanted to prepare her for her abduction, to ease the trauma somehow, but he knew that if the plan were revealed, it may not come to pass.

He said, "If you believe you'll soon perish, then let us complete our union? I would treasure that time for always."

"I can't, Michael. I just can't."

She didn't want to tell him that regarding sexual union, Kayenté was foremost on her mind. She also was unable to tell him that she wanted to die clean of male energy, but did not know how to convey that without insult.

He whisked her in his arms and carried her to the bed, easing her down upon the velvet white comforter. He leaned in close and planted kisses along her neck.

"Michael," she said, her voice quivering.

"Hush, Angel," he whispered, "Let me show you my love. Let me pleasure you."

She pushed her fingertips against his chest, but he crawled onto the bed and lightly straddled her. He took her wrists and drew her hands over the top of the pillow.

"Michael, no, please—no."

He touched his moist tongue lightly in her ear.

Her voice broke in a tearful plea. "No! Don't do this—no!"

"I must Kamara, if not now, then it may be never."

A deep voice sounded from the doorway. "She said no."

Michael froze. Then, he turned his head toward the voice where he knew Kayenté stood. Though angered greatly at Kayenté's interference, and even more at himself for his own behavior, he knew he must release her. Kayenté was her best hope for survival. He didn't want to fight the man who could save her.

He left the bed with agitated despair. "Forgive me, Kamara." He ignored Kayenté as he went out the door.

Kamara rolled over on her side and cried, feeling sad for Michael.

She sensed Kayenté standing over her. She stopped crying and twisted her head to see him. He was there in the dim light, long dark hair, rough eyes, bold stance.

He reached down and touched a tear on her cheek.

She sighed. "He's my best friend, you know."

"Mine too," he said.

He turned and left the room, closing the door securely behind him. She threw her hands over her face and prayed for swift death, crying hard . . . as only the pure of heart can.

Ж
Chapter Seven

Kayenté stood high atop the watchtower in the cold dark morning, waiting eagerly for Michael to unite him with his sword. His hand slid beneath the folds of his black cape, touching the gold pommel of Kamara's weapon—thirsty to wield the blade, hard to wait any longer. Soon, his limbs would surge with a thousand balls of sun, slamming steel on steel, sparks flying, gouging flesh, smelling blood, watching his victims lose pomp and mask in whimpers of death.

Oh, to again feel the weight of chain mail, and the shining pieces of armor that bade the dance of war. He felt captive in mortal clothes of mere tunic and pant. These were not the clothes of a fighting man! A gust of wind blew back his cape, exposing his bare shoulder, a reminder that he was here—now. He withdrew his hand from the sword.

Impatience was getting the better of him these long last moments at the castle of 'peace until you die.' The moment his sword was concealed with Kamara's beneath his cape, he would commence his ploy to trick her away with a tale of need at his fictitious lord's castle. She had never asked where he had served or whom had he served, and she didn't seem to care. She'd be most shocked, however, to learn that the castle he served was his own, and the lord he had served was himself.

His heart fluttered when he thought of the future he'd planned for them. She'd become his mistress. He fancied them bathing in streams, playing sex games in gardens, and making love under a full moon. Winnefred's face popped into his mind. Accepting Winnefred would be a large undertaking for Kamara, but in time, she'd adapt.

Rays of light stretched across the land in front of him. The colossal blood red sun rose behind him, silhouetting his body. He sighed anxiously. Morning had broken at last, and still Michael hadn't arrived with his sword. Had he not saved it from a hot death at the smithy?

The castle doors burst open. Kamara ran out in a purple cloak, racing toward the yarrow bushes where she'd thrown her sword the night before. Her velvet hood blew back, plumping against her shoulders. She poked her hands frantically through the foliage. Then she glanced up to the third story window, then back down to the bushes again.

Kayenté whispered, "I've got it little Kamara."

She sprung up and sprinted toward the stables.

Kayenté's curiosity was peaked.

He raced down the watchtower, wondering if he could integrate her course of action with his. However, he preferred not to leave without his sword, and wasn't sure he could. He began to run quietly after her, to appraise her motive for panic.

"Lord Kayenté!" Michael's voice sounded behind him.

Kayenté spun around, torn between chasing after Kamara and attaining news of his blade, which Michael didn't appear to possess, "My sword! Where is it?"

Michael rubbed his thigh hard, a pillar of strength in the soil of shame. "No weapons have yet come to the smithy."

Kayenté squinted an eye. "Are you sure you're not punishing me for last night?"

"No, my lord." Michael's chest caved. "About last night . . . I was wrong."

Kayenté seemed momentarily stunned by a collision of emotions that held him captive. His expression marbled pity, disgust, frustration, disappointment, and bloodlust.

He needed direction. Michael could give him that. He pointed firmly to the stables. "Follow Kamara. She raced past me, mumbling something about a fight on Lania land."

"A fight?" Kayenté came to focus.

Michael knew he would. After all, he'd said the magic word—fight. "Yes, a fight." Michael said. "I'll deliver your sword to you later—" he almost couldn't finish his sentence, "... if it is you must take her now."

"Yes, yes, deliver my sword later," he said, half turned toward the stables, feet already in motion. "Protect it for me, and I will protect her for you."

"Remember, she is sensitive!" Michael said, but he wasn't sure Kayenté heard, for he'd charged over Kamara's footprints with single focused vigor. Michael feared Kayenté would trample Kamara, the same. Michael knew Kayenté's fast feet were spurred by the prospect of battle, not Kamara's need for protection. Kayenté's priorities were backwards. Michael sank his forehead despairingly into fisted palms. Had he erred entrusting Kamara to Kayenté? His liege was more cold-hearted than he'd remembered, or perhaps he only noticed it now because he himself had grown so warm. Perhaps he should abort the plan.

"Let them go." Teeah appeared beside him.

Michael stopped and glanced into Teeah's wise eyes. "You know everything, don't you?"

Teeah nodded. "Yes, I do, including the whereabouts of your friend's sword."

"Where!"

"Safe."

"But Kamara—"

"—asked Camille to oversee the deed, and well . . . Kamara is not here to oversee her. I am. No weapons shall be destroyed."

"Kayenté must have his sword now."

"Oh no," admonished Teeah, "he must not."

"Why?"

"It's not time."

"Then, I've done right?"

"Yes." Teeah's eyes glowed. "You've been of great help. And for all your efforts, one day your heart shall know the satisfaction of love returned."

Michael sighed with relief. "Thank you, Teeah."

Kayenté reached Kamara as she emerged from the tack room, breathless from her run. She scuffled her feet some, weighted by the heavy saddle in her hands, an ivory horse blanket over her arm, and bridle over her shoulder.

"What is our destination Lady Kamara?" he asked cheerfully, sweeping the saddle from her hands, disappearing into the tack room.

She trailed him, anxiously. "What are you doing? There's trouble on Lania land. I must leave at once!"

He placed her saddle on a shelf, fetched his own riding regalia, and hastened out to the corral where his warhorse lived, too antsy to be penned in a stable.

She reclaimed her saddle hurriedly, and lugged it out to the gentle buckskin mare she had led from the stable into the corral moments ago. She missed her lost mare, Twilight, and held hope to one day recover her.

She set down her load, and stole a peek at Kayenté. He'd already saddled his jumpy snorting war-horse, and he in his hide pants, seemed an animal himself.

She slipped the bridle quickly over her equine's muzzle, securing the bit between its big yellow teeth, hoping to finish before Kayenté interfered. She reached down to the saddle blanket, stealing another glance at Kayenté. She saw his black leather boots coming toward her. She flung the blanket over her mare's back hastily, and reached down to grab the saddle, when she felt her upper arm gripped. She tried to lift the saddle anyway, but Kayenté dragged her away before she could get a proper hold.

"What are you doing?" she snapped, glancing back at her un-saddled horse.

Kayenté pulled her across the corral. "I'm taking you to my warhorse."

"I'm not going near that wild thing! And you *must* return to the castle . . . at once. I tell you this for your own well being!"

"And what of your well being?"

She dug her heals in to stop walking, but forward they flew. "Your eagerness to fight clearly overrides your concern for me."

He didn't respond.

"Have you nothing to say?

Still, he did not reply.

"I said—"

"I heard you."

"Then release me at once." She tried in vain to pry his long bronze fingers from her arm. "Kayenté, look at me!"

"I'm not stupid, Kamara. I've seen what your eyes can do."

"This event is for me to deal with—not you. You mustn't fight! And this situation would tempt you—" Kamara's attention was drawn to Kayenté's whinnying warhorse lurching its head up and down. Her voice weakened, "—to do . . ." she glanced up at him, "just that. You are like your horse, craving mayhem, though you need peace."

"And you are like yours, praying for the quiet life, though you need mayhem."

"I don't need mayhem!"

"Then why does mayhem knock on your door?"

"We'll talk of that, when you can answer why love is knocking on yours!"

"You first," Kayenté stated, nonchalantly. They reached the beast. Kayenté glanced at his spirited warhorse, then smiled at Kamara, "mayhem . . . knocking."

She pulled back, but Kayenté's grip was firm.

He said, "You are going to answer mayhem, one way or another, so it may as well be with me." He grabbed the reins.

"Kayenté, leave me to my work. This is wrong for you."

He led them out the corral gate. "A fight then—you've seen it in a vision. Where? Who?"

"I *must* proceed alone."

He closed the gate.

"Kayenté!"

He hoisted her up sidesaddle on his fidgeting warhorse, side stepping, and shaking its head.

"Remove me from this creature, Kayenté! He's much too wild for me!"

Kayenté mounted behind her.

"No Kayenté!" she said, "Stop! You must listen to me." She tried to slide to the ground, but he drew her back against his chest, forcing her legs to straddle the horse, and her skirt to hike up her thighs.

"I'm merely escorting you Kamara. Such action cannot detour me from peace."

She pulled the white chiffon layers of skirt down the best she could over her exposed legs. "Release me this instant!"

"No."

She quite suddenly became calm. "Kayenté." Mist floated from her breath. "I can't heal you if you fight me. Let me help you while I'm able."

"Not today," he said, suddenly feeling warm inside.

"Though hope has eluded me, you can yet be saved. I feel it in your soul."

Kayenté sank into a cloud of comfort. His heart stirred. His voice turned silky. "I'll watch over you while you work your 'light.' I'll not interfere unless you need me."

"I'll not need you." She dislodged his arm from her rib cage, emitting vapor from her fingertips.

Kayenté stroked her hair, mesmerized by her purity. His voice soared on the wings of care. "You're going to arrest a fight single-handedly, are you?"

"Yes. If the fight is on Lania Lands, indeed I shall."

"Where to then?" he asked, resisting the dreamy feeling.

She turned up her nose. "I shan't tell you."

He yawned. "Then here, we stay."

"I must leave immediately—alone." She fidgeted, glancing to the west.

"West hah?" He kicked his calmed warhorse into a lope, moving west, struggling to rekindle the zeal that he'd lost.

She misted him while they galloped across the meadow, but he never slowed.

Her voice crashed through the wind, "You are uncommonly resistant to the Sacred Mists!"

His voice crashed back at her. "You are uncommonly resistant to reality!"

Nothing incensed her more than being told she lived in a dream world. Rage obstructed her misting. Only with love could the mists flow. "You are far too bold!"

"What warrior is not?" He felt his bloodlust returning.

"Surely they're not all so imperious as you!"

He let loose a short stifled laugh, and again slid his arm around her waist. "Truly lady, you live in fantasy."

"I have survived thus far!" She removed his arm.

"Safely on your lands," he whispered low in her ear. Approaching an apple orchard, he slowed the horse to a swift walk. "In the real world, men hack each other to pieces. People are flogged, robbed, raped, beheaded, diseased, dirty, and dying, fighting for food and land."

"Stop speaking that way!" She closed her eyes, and covered her ears, gathering strength until she was calm. Her hands fell to her sides. "I've heard these stories before."

"And that is what they are to you—stories," the sunlight glimmered through the trees speckling his face, "your nightmare, Michael once said."

Her chest caved. "And I shall never be a part of that nightmare, so what is the point in discussing it. Are you trying to frighten me?"

"Yes." He arced his head forward toward her face to observe her reaction. "Michael told me that you'd never witnessed a fight. I'm trying to prepare you. I'm trying to protect you."

She turned her head to face him, their lips so close they could have kissed. And she wanted that kiss, even though he incensed her. The musk of his breath, the heat of it, oh . . . Kayenté was trouble. "Is . . . is . . ." she looked down at her hands to regain control, "is that why you forced me to ride with you, to better protect me?"

"Yes," Kayenté lied, mind shielding the truth, for the true answer was *to better control her.*

She straightened her back and held her head up with conviction. "Well, I don't need your protection. Why do men always want to protect me? You underestimate the power of 'the light.' "

"You, lady, underestimate the power of 'the dark.' "

"I'll prove to you that I can calm warring men without resorting to violence. But you must stay concealed and grant me time to make that happen, even if you assume I'm failing. You must give me your word."

Kayenté was silent.

"Give me your word!"

"I don't have to give you my word."

She grew quiet, moving past her anger, evoking the mists once more. She moved into Kayenté's spirit and lit him with love and kinship.

"Don't do that."

"I don't have to not do that."

His heart felt warm.

She said gently, "Your word—Kayenté."

He couldn't resist the liquid softness of her plea. "I'll give you my word," he said, "if you give me your word that you'll call for me, should you find yourself failing."

"Very well," she halted her mist. "I make this pact with you." She pointed forward. "They are on the other side of that large hill, at its base, near a tall rock wall."

He slowed the horse to a fast walk. "What is the scale of this fight?"

She closed her eyes. "I sense that there was a great battle near Lania lands yesterday."

Kayenté's heart raced.

"The battle carried on through the night. Two warriors have brought their personal fight onto Lania land. I feel a disturbing ripple in the boundaries. Not in a hundred years has this happened."

"Tell me more," said Kayenté.

She paused, opening her eyes, blinking back worry. Then she slanted her face back slightly toward Kayenté. "Something is so very wrong, and I hope I can give you 'the light' before I'm gone. Oh please Kayenté, don't take for granted what I can teach you now."

She looked ahead, hiding the sadness in her eyes.

He slipped his arm around her again, but this time with a depth of commitment, like an anchor against a tidal wave. His low voice sank smoothly in her ear, "I'll not let you die Kamara Lania. This I vow."

"You cannot save me." A tear dripped from her eye. "The Cold One is powerful. All around me, I feel his presence, working through even the ones I love. I cannot defeat him. This I know. But neither shall I join him, and this I vow, a vow I shall take to my grave."

Kayenté's heart whirled in a love storm. Preferring war, he concentrated on the fight. "Are Sakajians involved?"

"I don't know."

They reached the base of the hill. Kayenté stopped, dismounted, and tied his horse to a small oak tree. Kamara was on her way down from the horse when he clasped her waist from behind and guided her to the ground. When she turned around to face him, he perused her slight figure with a protective eye.

"I'll be fine," she said, reading his mind. "I need not be burly and tough to quell this confrontation." She stepped past him.

He pulled her back against his chest, feeling her head under his chin. Her hair smelled of lilac, and he wanted to taste her before another man did. He put his lips to her ear and whispered, "Change your mind Kamara. You don't understand the way of these men."

She rotated in his arms, tilting her head up with trust-filled eyes. "We have a pact."

Her trust melted him. He almost kissed her. To avert the act, he quickly took her hand and pulled her up the gradually sloping hill. He glanced back. Her naive expression was so lamb-like. How could he lead her to the lion's den? He feared she'd come to know men in a bad way, before she could know the man in him in a good way. Oh, why did he promise to not interfere?

He wanted to be the first to kiss her, to really kiss her, slowly, deeply—a kiss she would like, a kiss she would love. His mark on her must precede any other. He turned so suddenly, she almost bumped into him. He engulfed her hands in his and pressed them to his heart.

He had taken her by surprise and he glimpsed the woman in her, like he had at the Hot Springs, that fated day of the Black Wind rescue. Her attraction to him was apparent, the way she peered up with flushed face and troubled breathing. Yet, one second more, and he knew she'd yank the woman of her back into hiding and deny its existence. Before she could, he glided his mouth to hers, sealing their lips, sliding soft, slipping his tongue into her mouth, finding hers, warm, alive, joining at last, dancing fire, succulent, moist, smooth teeth, soft palette, fragrant breath mixing with his.

The air was charged between them. Her body moved into his. Then he felt her freeze, and tremble, and pull away. He released her. When it came to women and lovemaking, he never condoned force.

Her expression seemed enjoyably stunned, but too stunned to be enjoyed, uncomfortably pleased, but too pleased to admit it. Her stance, however, steamed condemnation. And soon her face matched, eyes glaring. "What is this you do to me? What dark magic do you cast to create these feelings in me? 'Tis a dark thing— a seduction? I have heard of this." She breathed hard with tear-filled eyes. You are sinful . . . sinful for doing this to me."

"You like it, don't you?"

"I—I am sinful. Never do that again! I—I . . . think it not good for my soul."

He brushed back a tendril of hair that had fallen over her eye. "You know not at all what is good for your soul, Kamara Lania. It's time you stopped giving to the welfare of others, and began tending yourself."

"There's no place for me in this world. I know this. I am for others. Without that purpose, I am nothing. It has been decreed."

"You are wrong."

"You've detained me long enough. I have trouble to quell." She walked past him and proceeded up the hill.

He quickened his stride, passing her. "Your only trouble is that you won't quell the fires within you."

She blurted, "You stopped Michael last night from behavior most similar to yours just now. How can you excuse your behavior and not his?"

"Me, you want to 'be' with. Him, you did not. I only wanted a kiss, Kamara. Michael wanted more."

"I can't do what I must if you insist on riling me so. I will talk no more of this!" She tried to take the lead as they ascended the hill, but she was pushing hard to keep up as it was.

They neared the peak. Swords clamored. Kayenté stopped. Kamara moved forth, passing him at last. He snatched her hips and yanked, forcing her stomach to the ground. He fell partially on top of her, leg draped over the back of her thighs, taking care the sword was behind him, concealed beneath the cape.

She pushed her elbow back trying to get him off her. "What are you doing?"

"You keep asking me that." He grabbed her rebellious arm and guided it back to the ground.

"Well?"

"Strolling up to combating men, will likely land a knife in your heart."

"Kayenté. I am an innocent woman. What threat am I?"

"You don't understand warriors, nor war. A warrior's instincts are primed, and often what moves, dies. At the very least, move slowly, so they have time to comprehend you are not their enemy. Do you understand?"

"Oh . . ." She loosened her muscles. "Very well, then."

He released her slowly and crawled a little higher up the hill to view the fighting men, a sight worth gold. He caught a glimpse of a shield: panthers and the color red. His man! The other warrior was a Rudel. Why were they fighting? Was his fortress in jeopardy?

Sakajians and Rudels often skirmished, for they shared a common border. But battles, like the one in Kamara's vision, had never taken place on Sakajian soil. Maybe Kamara was mistaken about the scale of the fight. He hoped so, for if she was right, he feared the Rudels were planning to overthrow Sakajian rule in Kantine.

Kamara crawled up toward Kayenté, emulating how he had done it. Her gown and cape kept getting caught under her knees, tangling around her, but she persisted until she reached him. Below, she saw the armored men. Their rivaling swords flashed in the sunlight.

Her face fell to the grass in horror. "They mean to kill each other!"

Kayenté gave her an incredulous stare that required pause, then he said sarcastically, "That is the general point of combat, Kamara."

She rattled hysterically, "How can they strike with no thought for the other? I cannot believe it, and yet such coldness is before me. This is real. This is true!"

He gave her that incredulous stare again. How could she not accept what she already knew? "Did you think the stories you had heard, false?"

"No . . . I," she clutched her heart and exhaled heavily several times as if trying to expel the bad revelation, "the reality of it . . . is much harsher than the vision." She swallowed and couldn't seem to breathe, then finally gasped, "This hurts me."

"Welcome to the real world, little Kamara." He began to move at an angle down the hill.

She grabbed his arm. "Where are you going?"

"To stop a fight." Kayenté could almost feel the sword dancing off his hip. "Return to the horse and wait for me."

"No, I can stop them. I just needed a moment to adjust."

"Kamara, how can you manage these men, if even my warhorse is to wild for you?"

"In spite of their callous behavior, I see light in their souls. They can be pacified."

"I think not." Kayenté tugged his arm free. "I'll descend the hill the way we came, and then proceed toward them from the trees below."

"Kayenté!"

"You can't stop me."

"Do you believe in the power of 'the light'—or not?"

He glanced at the battling men. "Not in this instance."

"However did you expect to surrender your sword if you believed there would be situations that required its use?"

Kayenté stumbled for an explanation, unpracticed in dealing with a female who harbored her caliber of wit. He hated to give her the impression he was less intelligent than she, but he'd trapped himself.

"I don't know," he said. "That scenario never occurred to me."

"Well, I shall prove to you that you don't need your sword."

She began to rise.

He held her down. "I will not let you go into that."

"Nor I . . . you," she said, especially without a sword. You don't possess the skills to do what I must." Her fingertips and mouth secreted mist, enveloping him in a sheer moist cloud. She spoke in a low deep voice, "The mist binds you to the ground and quells your lust for violence."

"Stop your misting," he ordered, fighting against the wave of peace that washed over him. "Return to my horse and await me. I'll not employ violence. I simply care to unravel the reason for their squabble."

"Why?" She glared at him suspiciously.

"I—because—" Again—trapped. He couldn't reveal the truth. Not yet. Her eyes beseeched his innocence. Her sweet face was posed in dread awaiting his answer. How could he tell her that there wasn't a peaceful bone in his body. He couldn't. He almost choked on his words, trying to get them out through the balmy sensations her misting rendered. "If I know the reason, then I can talk them out of their violence. You've never pacified men in the throes of a fight Kamara. You are not ready."

"Kayenté, it is you who are not ready. You're still far too war-like to settle them *without* violence."

The mist made him feel disconnected from his aggression, and he found it hard to counter her anymore.

She looked down upon the fighting men, and chanted with a continuous flow of misty breath. "The joy of friendship supersedes the brutality of war. Innocent child come forth, you are warrior no more. I am 'the light' I am 'the light' and all daughters of 'the light' are with me. I cannot fall. The Mists of Cohesion unite—all."

She rose in a trance, repeating the chant with full toned drama. She moved at a snail's pace down the hill in her vaporous cloud, like a ghost skimming the earth in pursuit of victims.

Kayenté fought the sleepy pleasant feeling that she had cast upon him with the rile that her obstinate naiveté evoked. Out of sheer concern for her, he willed himself to backtrack down the hill, circle around its base, and head through the forest toward the fight. He came upon the rock wall only yards from the confrontation, and squatted by its edge, peeking at the scene.

Kamara circled around the fighting men. Her hands moved in a dance to the chant on her lips.

Kayenté hoped his man would slay the Rudel before Kamara jeopardized herself any further. Yet, he was curious to know if she could truly prove her claim.

The knights glanced at her sporadically until the mists enveloped them, presenting all three in a ghostly likeness. She bowed before them, chanting louder, "I draw you into 'the light.' "

The men seemed confused and intrigued by her behavior. They stopped battling.

The Rudel said, "I think she's a witch."

The Sakajian jerked his head slightly her way. "Let's kill her and finish our fight."

"Let's first behold what's beneath that cape!" said the Rudel.

The Sakajian nodded. "A truce then, to lay down our weapons until we are done with her?"

"Yes," said the Rudel.

Kayenté pressed his hand against the grip of Kamara's sword. He gazed upon the obscure scene, the mists hazing his view. He labored to identify his man. His voice was familiar but altered by the helm. Sir Robert Durham?

Could it be that his second in command was about to rape the woman he'd vowed to protect? He'd made clear to his men that he considered rape a crime, and any man so doing would be punished by death. Yet, to save her, his true identity would be revealed. Then he'd have to take her by force, which may horrify her more than her dilemma with the Cold One. Does a heart betrayed suffer more than a body assaulted? He believed the answer was yes.

He fixed his eyes astutely upon the scene, assessing words, movements and breathing patterns, to ascertain motive and fore-tell action. Kamara remained bowed. The men dropped their swords and removed their helms, exposing their grimy faces through the thickening veils of mist.

"Aye," whispered Kayenté, "Sir Robert—indeed."

Kayenté watched Sir Robert slip his hands under Kamara's cape and hoist her upward like a cotton doll, landing her on her feet.

Sir Robert asked, "Why do you appear before us, woman?"

Kamara replied, "I've come to quell your violence."

"Who are you?"

"A living creature."

Sir Robert laughed. "A living creature!"

The Rudel moved up behind her and squeezed her backside heartily. "And what a creature you are!"

She remained still, void of reaction.

Sir Robert continued his interrogation, "You seem not a peas-ant, nor a noble."

"Who I am, matters not," she retorted stiffly.

"Ah," said Sir Robert, "a witch."

"You—" she looked directly into his eyes, "have much light in your spirit, but your light is imprisoned. You've lost . . . compas-sion."

"I serve the House of Panther Ketola, need I say more?" He removed her cape.

She remained passive. "Panther Ketola? I have heard that he is a brutal man. You have become an expression of his violence, but I shall help you find love."

Kayenté cringed, and cursed hotly beneath his breath. She was practically inviting them to ravage her! In addition, why was Sir Robert describing him as merciless? He had mercy. He had mercy right now for Kamara, for her situation, and for what might happen if she revealed her identity. Sir Robert would ask about his Lord Panther's stay with her, and then she would know who he was. He didn't want her to find out like this.

Why did he care? Why? The answer came. He did not view Kamara as an object. And he'd not ever viewed women as anything but. Excluding rape, women were to be used. And now, he wanted to slay his own man for viewing Kamara thusly.

Sir Robert unfastened her cloak and let it fall to her feet, feasting his eyes on what he now saw of her. He brushed his open palm over the plum velvet bodice covering her chest, downward to the sheer white layers of material over her womb.

Kamara did not react or change the expression on her face. He was impressed that she'd maintained a calm facade thus far, for he knew—inside, she was dying. He had tried to warn her, had he not? Maybe she would learn a lesson.

Sir Robert's fingers journeyed the curve of her hip, up her arm, over the sheer white material of her long sleeves, over her shoulder, and along the velvet scooped neckline of her dress, and then back over her breast.

Kayenté grit his teeth, and whispered almost too loudly, "You will die."

Sir Robert bobbed his head back, scrutinizing. "You dress not as a poor woman. If you are a noble, you'd best tell us now. Or have you stolen these clothes?"

"Why must you know who I am?" she said. "Is it acceptable to degrade a peasant woman, but not a noble? There's no difference in the quality of our spirits. One day we shall all return to the same home from which our souls were born."

The Rudel said, "She speaks like a nun, but I've never seen a nun make vapor."

Sir Robert ogled her. "I don't care who she is." He stroked her face. "She seems a fresh one."

The Rudel, yet behind her, grabbed her breasts. "We will have us a time, now."

Kayenté could not stand by and watch any longer. He slid Kamara's sword quietly from his scabbard. Kayenté readied to make his move, when that whisper came into his head, her voice, 'We have a pact. Are you not noble? Does your word mean nothing?" Everything in him wanted to move, but his feet remained still, and his hand froze on the sword.

The Rudel said, "When I'm finished with you, I'll bequeath you to my lord."

"No," Sir Robert laughed, "*my* lord would enjoy her more! She'd quickly become his number one concubine!"

Kayenté sighed hard and slow with hooded eyes, straining to keep himself in place. Sir Robert must die, not only for dishonoring Kamara, but for slurring his reputation with such an ill reputed lie. Well, not a lie—exactly, but need his man portray him so—distastefully? He again felt consumed with that dismal feeling and age-old enemy—ignobility. Yes, he ruled with an iron hand, but he also rewarded generously those loyal to him. And yes, he seduced women all the time, but he *never* raped them. And he would not witness the raping of Kamara either.

He began to lunge forward from his hiding place, when Kamara's phantom voice scolded, *Remember our pact! Wait for me to call.* Kayenté grumbled, cursing himself for ever agreeing to such a foolish proposal. Then he wondered if what he'd heard in his head was her, or the voice of insanity. Nonetheless, he forced patience once more. If he was so damned ignoble, then why couldn't he break the pact and do what the hell he pleased? Why! He again squatted, sword in hand—watching, waiting, fighting flashbacks, and the trauma of his mother's rapes . . . all over—again.

Kamara closed her eyes, focusing hard on "the light" and not her mortification. She pushed herself into the spirit of the man behind her. "I love you," she whispered emphatically, over and over, "I am one with you."

Sir Robert said, "Yes and we want to be one with you too dear heart."

She moved into the spirit of the man in front of her. "I love you. I am you. We are one."

Mist thickened over the men who inhaled the vapor.

Feeling herself pushed to the ground, she envisioned the two knights hugging. "There is peace between you."

The Rudel said, "In a minute there will be a piece between you."

She visualized them all inside the great Mother Lord's heart that she pictured as the moon. She concentrated intensely. "I believe," she said, living the words, ignoring the edges of fear that threatened to suck her into the violent world.

She heard armor clinking. Her arms were pinned down so hard she couldn't feel her hands. She called loudly, "What you do to me, you do to your Queen."

"No such luck," a voice said.

"What you do to me, you do to the Virgin Mother."

"I never believed she was a virgin anyway," said another voice.

Someone said, "Here, you hold her for a minute."

Kamara's acute concentration obscured the men's voices. She spoke over their jousting comments. "What you do to me, you do to your mother. What you do to me, you do to your baby daughter. What you do to me, you do to your beloved. What you do to me, you do to *yourself.*" Her voice intensified, commanding attention. Her chin pointed to the air. Her eyes rolled to the top of her head, with slit eyelids. "You are too good to incest your mother, dishonor your queen, rape the virgin, or destroy your daughter! You are too good to humiliate your woman, or degrade yourself!"

Her tone grew louder . . . lower, more emphatic. "You are innocent! Your innocence is locked in the stranglehold of your strict and foreboding fathers who care not if your heart is broken, so long as you can bloody the sword of vengeance and call yourself a man! But what of the *real* you, behind the man? What of the grieving child who knows not love? Innocent ones—break free from the cruel jailer! Mother looks at you with a compassionate eye. She's the only one who cares. The only one! The only one!"

Kamara's voice deepened. She drew her tone from the womb of the earth. "Life cracks whips of insane cruelty all around you. You are expendable. Run innocent boys! Run to the only one who sees you, knows you, loves you. Run into 'the light' of mother's heart! Run into her faith, hope, and charity! Run into her heart! Run into her heart—now!"

Kayenté couldn't believe the scene at hand. The knights had fallen into a heap, the Rudel with his head on her shoulder, Sir Robert with his head at her feet. Good God! Were they crying? What greater humiliation could one bear upon a knight? She had succeeded! She had pacified warring men—with love! He'd not have believed such a feat possible had his own eyes not bore witness.

He slid the sword back into the scabbard, watching Kamara awaken from her trance.

The men, minus most of their armor, lifted their heads, with faces drooped in shame.

Kamara sat up and kissed each man on the cheek, then rose. "Embrace your innocence. 'Tis the most worthy part of you. Return to your loved ones. Be with them now, before it's too late."

Sir Robert muttered sheepishly, "I hope we didn't harm you. I am Sir Robert from the House of Panther Ketola."

"You did harm me, Sir Robert," she said, "but I forgive you."

The Rudel said, "I too, am sorry for dishonoring you. I am Sir Bradley from the House of Wincott."

"Sir Bradley, Sir Robert, do remember heart. If you must fight, then fight for the preservation of humane behavior. Fight from the heart, for the heart."

Sir Robert retrieved her cloak and handed it to her softly. He asked, "Just who and what are you—anyway?"

She held her cloak to her stomach. "I am Kamara Lania of Lania Castle."

Kayenté cringed in the shadows. Was all now to be unraveled?

Sir Robert's face turned white. "Ah, please understand, my behavior in no way reflects the reputation of Panther Ketola. Please, I ask you, do not inform him of what transpired here today. None of it. Please, lady."

Kamara's face crumbled in a puzzled expression. "Why would I tell him? Do you think I would have you punished? Fear not. I do not believe in punishment."

Sir Robert sighed with relief. "You are gentle and noble, Lady Kamara, and much to be admired."

Kayenté sighed with relief too.

Sir Bradley said, "Kamara . . . I've heard that name . . . Kamara the—"

"She's not a witch," snapped Sir Robert. He looked at Kamara. "Are you?"

"Am I?"

"I think not," he scrunched his brow, "but what are you?"

"I'm an advocate of spiritual love."

"Then you're an angel," Sir Bradley said.

"If only I was," she smiled faintly, "then I'd fly away from this violent world."

Sir Robert said, "Let us escort you back to your castle."

"I need no escort, as I've just well proven."

Kayenté was glad, not only that she'd denied their offer, but also that Sir Robert hadn't revealed any more than what was already too much. Getting her to his fortress would prove task enough without the Rudel and Sir Robert bucking his strategy, as sure they would, now that the three were comrades of the soul.

Envy washed through him, irritation more. Must she chat so much? Couldn't she seal her melodramatic mouth and move onward to his warhorse so that he could interrogate Sir Robert for details of the battle?

"How can we serve you?" Sir Robert asked.

"Never fight each other again," she said, "and so vow."

They looked at each other and nodded.

She declared, "Forgive each other, and yourselves. Perpetuate good will."

"Yes, lady," they both affirmed.

She nodded and glided away from them, toward Kayenté, as smoothly as she had come.

Kayenté was astonished that she'd actually drawn both men into such sappy female emotion.

Kamara came his way, rounding the rock wall, quickening her pace as she passed him. She said in a low bland voice, "I hate you," then circled round the base of the hill back where the warhorse was tied.

Kayenté stared at her, confounded. She loved the ones who tried to harm her? And she hated him for trying to help her? Now did that make sense? He never did understand woman's illogical notions.

Then he questioned his own logic. What made him think he could help her more than she could help herself? She could defeat warring men! She carried a spirituality that transcended orthodox religion. And she had a goddess like power to bond with people.

Flashes of her more vulnerable moments came to mind. He realized then, that she did need him—not the goddess part of her, but

126

what of the human side, flailing in the righteousness of her holy criteria. Yes, it was the human woman that he sought to free, the one who had just flung her coldness upon him.

He turned his attentions to Sir Robert, hungry for information about his fortress. The well-being of his fortress should come well before a woman, should it not? Kamara had waylaid him long enough, in addition to pacifying one of his fiercest warriors whom he no longer needed to punish, because pacification was punishment enough for any man. After what she'd just done, why should he go to her first?

He tried to move forward to Sir Robert, but his feet went the other way. He was unable to destroy her pacifistic victory, especially after what she had endured to make it happen. He was en route to his fortress anyway. He'd simply feed her some story that required them to make haste.

He sprinted to her, catching up as she neared his warhorse.

She had donned the hooded purple cloak, drawing it around her like a shield. Staring at her walking feet, she hurled venomous words, "Are you disappointed that I did not need defending? Would you prefer me weak, so that I'll be no threat to you?" She reached the horse and began to mount. "Did you enjoy watching what those men did to me?"

Kayenté's teeth clenched so hard his head hurt. He caught her wrist and yanked her around to face him. "I almost killed them for what they did to you."

With teary eyes and trembling lips, she said, "Are you pleased to know that for the first time in my life, I know hate, and that darkness has entered my soul?"

He drew her firmly into his arms. She pushed the palms of her hands against his chest. "Do you treat women that way, Kayenté? Would you have treated me that way had we met under different circumstances?"

"Never," Kayenté said. "You, who know of my past, should also know what I would and would not do to women."

Her expression turned from anger to pain—then shame. He recognized that very look in his mother's eyes oh so long ago. "You bridged those men Kamara," he said, "but at what cost? You gave. They took. They are left with peace. You are left with the bitterness of the invisible wound they slashed upon your womanhood."

"I am at that." She struggled against his firm hold. "I now not only shun the way of men, but I despise man's way with all my heart. I despise the man in you and even Michael. I despise that part of you all, and I feel shame for my hatred." Her head fell. "I have become less than nothing."

"No." He lifted her chin. "You have become more. You have become the storm."

She fell limp in his arms, feeling defeated, even though she'd won.

He kissed her temple. "And I, I have softened. I cannot relinquish my storm, but it has been long since I've felt the warm flame that you've rekindled."

She suddenly clutched his shirt, and gasped, "Kayenté . . . I need you."

"I know," he said.

He slid his arm under her knees and lifted her like a child onto the warhorse, straddling his back.

He untied the reigns and mounted behind her.

She reveled in the touch of her back against his body, so warm and full of life. And if he could love . . . if he could, then hope was his, and her suffering would be less when the Cold One forced her to die.

He secured her waist with his arm. "You need me Kamara, so accept my help. Move under my wing and let me champion you."

"What do you mean?" she asked, "it is *my* help you have enlisted to pacify your aggressions. I intend to see you through the best I can, while I can. Let us hurry home now. I am not comfortable this far from the castle."

Kayenté was about to pitch his lie to her about his lord needing help, when distant voices sounded. They looked across the valley to the next hill and saw mounted knights.

Kamara recoiled. "Oh no!"

A knight shouted, "Lord Panther Ketola! Your grounds were invaded!"

Kamara froze, not even breathing, her thoughts echoing but one word. *Panther. Panther. Panther.*

Kayenté cursed Michael for having dragged him away. His castle . . . his domain . . . all that he stood for, wanted and dreamed of, was in peril! His limbs felt hot. His breath hissed rage, and like a thousand racing stallions, his heart hammered the war song.

Kayenté signaled his man that he was coming, when he felt Kamara slip away from him, off the horse. He snapped his head her direction. She had fallen to her knees, hood dropped from head, golden hair glimmering in the sun. Her skin was red, and she wheezed, clutching her lungs, gripped by deadly shock.

He did not have time for this.

She rose, and broke through her wheezing with a cry. "You are Panther! You are *he!*" She exhaled three quick high-pitched sobs, touching her throat as if to calm the muscles so words could emerge. And when they did, a tearful tone prevailed. "I trusted you!" She cocked her head with an unveiled chastity, and words as pure. "I took you into my heart."

He could barely stand the pain he'd caused her, but there was no relieving it. He glanced at his men. Her trauma was costing him precious time, and yet he was unexpectedly paralyzed.

Suddenly, her tearful tone grew teeth, and he was glad.

"You are the King's nephew, the most brutal power lusting man in all of Kantine. Have you plans to seize my castle and force me to be your mistress?"

"It's not like that," he said softly, feeling himself kicked him out of her heart.

"Of course it is," she cried, stepping back from him.

He gazed upon her face, wrought with belief of betrayal. She turned away with lifted skirt and tread heavily toward her lands. He followed, his horse prancing, matching her step for step.

She flashed her golden eyes at him. Her voice cracked with pain, "You have *mocked* me with your plea for light. I am but a joke, an amusement, a cruel little experiment of yours. You don't *need* me. You have your castle, and your riches, and your fighting men, and most of all your lust to conquer the world! Did you deceive Michael too . . . or is he in on this plot!"

"Kamara, you *must* come with me."

She glared at him, tears streaming. "I will *not* come with you! You broke my trust! You broke my heart!"

Kayenté whispered, "And you mine," but she did not hear.

She turned her head toward home, hoisted her skirt to her knees, and ran. She ran faster and she ran harder, her shiny hair flying all over the place.

Kayenté knew that force had become necessary. He must harden his heart to her words, lest he ride away from her lashing and abandon her to her sad fate. He cantered to her, leaned sideways, hooked his arm around her stomach, and whisked her up in front of him sidesaddle.

She twisted and thrashed, wrenching words from a battered heart. "Traitor! Let me go—or kill me now!"

Kayenté kicked his horse into a gallop away from Lania lands.

She screamed, "If I leave my lands, I shall suffer a tortuous death!"

He replied, "Oh no, dear lady, you shall suffer a torturous death . . . if you do not!"

Off they rode, toward the blood-splattered knights on the hill.

Ж
Chapter Eight

Kayenté slowed his horse. He stopped in front of his men: seven warriors in chain mail armor, round, iron helms removed. Their red tunics, embroidered with black panther heads, were ripped and soiled with blood and dirt. Kayenté was relieved to see among them, his third in command. He was quick to order, "Status report!"

The men spoke, but Kamara could not hear. She was involuntarily soaking in the realities of the warriors before her, their gruesome acts of violence, their kick in killing, their weary bones. Suddenly dizzy, her head fell into her hands. Uncivilized feelings enveloped her and she hated it. It made her sick. It made her want to scream. And she almost did. But she didn't. So she cried silently, *No! No! No!* She was lost in the warriors' cravings, their coldness, their cunning. Who was she? Where was she? Was she them? Was she the animal, the survivor, the male? Her soft love meant nothing. The foot stomps the flower. She was stomped.

As much as she despised Kayenté, she needed him to shield her from the essence of these men. When she had bridged him, she had touched a strong place inside his heart, marked by great innocence. There she would hide. There, he could not hurt her.

She maneuvered her body awkwardly to face him, one knee up on the saddle, one leg dangling down. He didn't seem to care for he continued conversing with his men. She clutched his shirt, pressing her forehead against his chest, moving deep inside his being to that innocent time and place.

Kayenté knew Kamara's fear of his men was great if she had turned to *him* for comfort.

"Your prisoner, lord?" asked his third in command.

"No," answered Kayenté, "just an ailing woman. So, you said King Harold of Rudela hired some mercenary named Merculus?"

"Yes. Merculus was commissioned to lead King Harold's army to invade your realm three mornings ago. Surprisingly, Merculus is Sakajian! He seeks vengeance on the Ketolas', but we don't know why. We heard that he's using the Rudels to his own purpose. We sent your squire to inform you, but he must not have made it. We had to push the Rudels all the way back to Wincott Castle, for they resisted retreat. But from their talk, they mean to next attack your father the Duke."

Kayenté commanded, "Fortify our armies at the castle. Layer them outward as far as you can. I will warn my father and negotiate a joining of forces to counter attack. I'll return in two days.

"Yes, my lord," said his third in command. Then he hesitated and asked with humble curiosity, "Lord, pardon my inquiry, but what is that vapor about you?"

Kayenté looked around. He hadn't even noticed Kamara misting. Was he becoming immune?

He jolted her waist with his hand. "Stop that!"

"Is she a witch lord?"

"She's no witch."

"Shall we take her for you?"

Kamara grabbed his waist tightly.

"No, "Kayenté said, "make haste!"

"Yes, my lord."

The men turned their weary horses and cantered away.

Kamara continued flooding Kayenté with the mists, hoping he'd have mercy and release her.

He said, "Your sacred mists of cohesion seem to no longer affect me, perhaps, because I'm acting on your behalf. I promised

Michael that I'd protect you, and so I will. That is cohesion, is it not?"

"Protect me?" she lifted her head. "Is that what this is about, the two of you plotting to slay the Cold One against my wishes?"

"Yes, Kamara, for your own good."

She pulled back. "For *my* good? You and Michael are not *saving* me. You are *torturing* me!"

"Kamara, without us, you are dead. I think you know this."

"I am resigned to it. I want to die purely, untouched by the dark things of life." Her eyes softened, "Please Panther, do not involve me in your war. Release me."

"No," he said, "it's time you faced the dark things of life, and clearly you are unable to do so alone."

She clutched his arms. "Please, Panther . . . please . . . please let me go. Please!"

"I can't little Kamara. You, seer—are now too blind to see."

She shook her head, hands falling from his arms. "I can *see* this is wrong for me."

"It could not be more right for you."

"I *must* go home."

"Home is your doom."

"I've never left Lania lands."

"Then it is time."

"I am ill with terror."

"It will pass."

"It will worsen, Panther!"

He brushed his fingers down the sides of her cheeks. "You needn't call me Panther—not you. Kayenté is my given name."

Feeling his sympathy, she placed her palms on his chest. "Kayenté, if you have but one shred of mercy, I beg you let me die in peace."

His hands dropped to her shoulders. "Trust me Kamara, once you accept the sword, you will feel renewed."

She shrunk back, turned in the saddle, facing forward, her shin drawn up against the saddle rim. He would not listen to her. He would not listen. With fallen shoulders and drooping head, she clutched her heart. "I have been so betrayed. You . . . Michael, even Teeah betrays me." She began sobbing, deeply and loudly.

Kayenté knew all too well the sharp shocking pain incurred by the dastardly blow of betrayal. And for her to feel betrayed by so many all at once . . . He could not endure her anguish, so he drew her back against him forcing her legs to straddle the horse, and turned his thoughts to war.

She cried and cried.

He galloped onward, along the edge of a pine forest, shutting out the sound of her sobs. He assumed her eyes were shut, for if she were witnessing the aftermath of the battle, she'd be gasping and shrieking. They had passed two dismembered bodies a while ago and a puddle of blood that his warhorse had heedlessly trampled. If her eyes hadn't alerted her, then her nose probably hadn't either, for the newly dead yielded but the slightest fragrance of blood. In addition, fresh blood, well, fresh blood smelled good to Kayenté, but they had passed too swiftly for him to get a decent whiff. He knew that the real carnage would be closer to his castle. He wished he could view it before the bodies were collected and burned. He wanted to revel in the slaughtering of those who had *dared* invade his realm.

They rode along the edge of the forest, while Kamara cried and cried . . . and cried. Hours crawled by with a serenade of Kamara's eternally forthcoming sobs, surpassing all records that he'd ever known for crying without pause, too long for Kayenté, too short for Kamara. She did not want the future as Kayenté did.

At last, Kamara moved into deep silence. Her dream of dying untouched by the darkness of the world outside her castle walls, would not come to pass.

Kayenté felt the weight of her sad surrender as the next hour rolled by. Just when his ears began to adapt once more to sounds of the forest, his nose detected a rank odor emerging from the woods. He halted the warhorse.

Kamara felt his heartbeat quicken against her back. For a moment, he was statue-still.

The forest was filled with the incessant whine of flies. Kayenté dismounted, drawing Kamara down next to him.

"What is that odor?" she asked, her voice raspy from crying.

"A rotting corpse," he answered.

"Hah . . . no. Let's leave. I dare not see it."

"Stay behind me. Out here, there are many surprises, wild animals and thieves, sudden attacks, and merciless kills. If you tarry from me, you are making yourself an easy target." He glanced over his shoulder, checking to see how she was assimilating this information.

She looked up at him child-like with her red puffy eyes. "Let's just ride on. What is the point of walking into trouble?"

"I want to see if the body is my squire."

He drew her sword from his cape, flashing the sun's reflection. "My—my—"

He turned toward her. "Yours?" He turned the blade downward and offered her the hilt. "Take it."

She shook her head. "I don't want it, but I forbid you to use it."

"Forbid all you please," he said, "but if the need arises, your sword will dance."

"No, it mustn't!"

Ignoring her disapproval, he walked skillfully forward into the thick foliage.

She followed reluctantly, but closely. "Why do you continually make me feel so . . . human?"

"You are human."

"Well, I don't wish to be."

"This I know," he retorted with a smile.

She scowled. "You evoke the sleeping demons in me—demons I didn't even know I possessed."

"Good. They've been sleeping far too long," he said as a fern limb flapped in her face.

She batted it away. "You seem anxious for me to turn bad, Panther Ketola."

"Hush," he said. "We'll discuss my plans for you later."

The stench worsened. She pulled back his arm. "Wait—I don't want to do this."

"Stay close," he commanded, moving forward.

"Kayenté, please. I feel dizzy."

He spread open the dense bushes before him. His deceased mutilated squire was naked, caked with dried blood and dirt, and smothered with flies. He felt Kamara's arm drop away, followed by a thump on the ground. He glanced over his shoulder, and saw her flat on her back in a dead faint. He squatted to shake her awake, while darting his eyes about, sensing company.

He slapped her cheeks lightly. "Kamara. Kamara."

Her eyes opened slowly. "I don't feel well."

"You're going to feel a lot worse if you stay here."

Before they could move, seven ragged dirty people with missing teeth and greasy unkempt hair, surrounded them. They held clubs, knives, daggers, and swords—positioned to kill. Kayenté, with one hand, helped Kamara to stand, while his other hand tightened around the hilt of Kamara's sword, plotting their escape. "It will be all right, Kamara. Stay close."

Kamara said, "These people need help."

Kayenté couldn't believe his ears. "You are the only person I know, who would say *that*, in a circumstance like *this*."

"Well, they *do* need help."

"You've got the picture backward Kamara. *We* are the ones who need help."

"I want her clothes," shouted an old woman with a big nose, licking her lips as if Kamara was supper.

"His clothes are mine," declared a tall gaunt man with lifeless eyes.

"His sword is—"

Kayenté nudged her behind him, whispering through the edge of his mouth. "Stay on me like a shadow."

Kamara was torn between compassion and fear, leaving her utterly paralyzed. However, when Kayenté went into motion, she fell into his spirit and copied his stride instinctively, moving unwittingly just as he did, emulating his sword dance behind him. He slashed, thrust, and parried his blade with impressive vigor, maiming the attackers and flinging weapons from their hands. Kamara was in shock, persuading herself that what was happening, was not happening, even as it happened. She was Kayenté's shadow. That's all she knew.

Then the fighting stopped and all the bloody people lay still. She felt pale and sick, and icy. Surely, this was but another nightmare. She put her quaking hands over her gurgling nauseous stomach. She tried to maintain a standing position, but her bones felt brittle and her head felt bubbly. Blackness closed in on the edges of the once fresh and flowery field of her mind, bringing with it, pictures of murderous eyes, and the frigid faces of death. Her knees gave way and her body smacked the ground. Then nothing.

Kayenté turned with ragged breath to see her fallen—again. He had a feeling that she'd be fainting often on her journey into the real world. He wiped Kamara's blood drenched blade on a dead man's shirt. Her sword, much lighter than his, wielded well. However, it required twice the force to execute half the damage that his own beloved sword could render. He slid it in the scabbard, reveling in the sensations he'd so missed while in Kamara's domain. Every shape, every color, shone clearer, brighter, now that he'd parried a sword and slain the ignoble once more. His charged body permeated exhilaration in every particle of his being, wild as ocean waves, clean as the sea.

He knelt down and stroked Kamara's pale face. He shook her gently, attempting to revive her. She bat him away unconsciously. Clearly, revival was not what she wanted.

Finally, her eyes opened. Her voice trembled with soft hope, "I had another nightmare, didn't I? Nothing bad truly happened. There were no mean people, and no one died."

Kayenté sympathized with her need to deny, but he knew that she must embrace the truth to accept the sword.

"Life is harsh," he said, the words deep in his throat.

"No it's not." She blinked. "Life is love, and you are just a long dream I am having."

He slid his arm beneath her shoulders and helped her sit. "You aren't dreaming. Look around."

She glimpsed the dead sprawled about them, and quickly turned her eyes to Kayenté, appealing for comfort. "This *is* a dream. I *am* dreaming now."

"This is no dream. Those scoundrels would have mutilated you with a brutality beyond your imagination."

"Stop!" she said firmly. And then more calmly, she said, "These people could never be that cruel—not *that* cruel."

"Do you want another look at my squire? Would you be convinced if I had let them have at you?"

She sat there for a minute trying to fight the truth, trying to stay calm, trying to pretend. But the truth crashed in, destroying her composure, cracking her beliefs. Was the world truly inhabited with multitudes of bestial behaving people? Was it really as she had experienced in the Black Wind? "Oh Kayenté!" She lunged toward him, throwing her arms around his neck, nearly knocking him over, clinging hard.

He didn't mind, as long as she kept turning to him instead of fleeing.

She started sobbing.

That, he did mind. Her crying of the day had wearied him.

She graduated to low toned screams, and finally words. "I don't understand—the meanness! I don't understand the cruelty! How can this be?" She gasped in a whisper, "I don't understand!"

Kayenté rocked her a little, and cupped one hand to the back of her head. She was an emotional little thing. Although he could not at all relate to what it was she felt, he pitied her for feeling the world's pain. "You'll understand one day," he said kindly.

She lifted her wet face. "You were courageous to fight as you knew how. But not I. I didn't even try to bridge them. I could have saved them! Those poor people. Those poor, poor people. They were lost and in desperate need of kindness."

Kayenté pushed her back slightly. "Why are you so intent on defending swine? They would have taken your kindness and then the men would have raped you over and over as the women cheered them on, entertained by your pain. Then they would have tortured you to death, stripped you of all possessions, and walked away gloating about their catch for the day—smiling and laughing as they remember how you moaned and screamed."

She released Kayenté and sat back on her calves. She rubbed her knuckles against her cheek, as if comforting herself, yet there was an insanity to it. "Love can change people."

Kayenté rose. "Love can change people in search of love. The rest, no. They seek only what material comforts they can get, nothing more, and they will commit any atrocity on anyone to attain what they desire."

Her eyes filled with pleading. "Stop! I'll hear no more of that. If I could have shown them love, I don't believe they would have harmed us."

"I don't think you believe that at all Kamara."

"I do!"

"Then why did you throw yourself into my arms, even though I had shown no love and no mercy for that pack of animals?"

Her lips hung open on suspended breath, preparing to retort, but no words emerged. And though she stared at him intensely, her look seemed more inward as if searching for the answer.

He answered for her, "Because you know you'd be suffering or slain right now if I hadn't been there to defend you."

She sighed, casting her eyes shamefully to the ground. "Maybe so." She shook her head lightly. "I don't know anymore."

He took her hands and helped her to her feet. "You'll learn more of the real world when we get to my father's fortress."

She withdrew her hands and stepped back in a pose of resentment. "My world *is* real and you had no right to remove me from my reality into yours. I'd rather die on Lania Land right now, then experience one more particle of what *you* call reality!"

He shook his head, tired of arguing with her. He walked toward his warhorse, leaving her there, assuming she would follow. Halfway to his horse, he felt the empty space behind him. He turned around. She hadn't budged. She looked a little stunned, though he knew rebellion was what kept her there.

"Shall I leave you here with all your beloved?"

She glared at him, mostly to avoid seeing the scene around her.

He went back to her and took her hand, guiding her forward. She lagged behind, her defiance still intact.

He looked over his shoulder. "When we arrive, little Kamara, you will see how most castles function."

"Stop calling me little," she snapped. "You treat me like a naive child."

He stopped and turned fully toward her. "Well?"

She thrust out her chest. "Well what?"

His condescending eyes darkened. "Children are *less* naive than you."

"—About cruelty," she jutted her chin, "but not love."

"There is more to life than love."

She splayed her hand over her heart. "Not for me."

"Especially for you."

"And what of you mighty warlord?" Barbed words rolled off her once pristine tongue. "Is there no more to your life than killing, conquering, and lust? Do you know love—at all? Or are you a seductive vampire, sucking blood from the weak and ignorant masses, leaving your victims pale and dead. Are you servant to the Cold One, taker of dreams, dasher of hopes, and nightmare of even the bravest warriors? Does the devil's dragon exhale you in his lust to destroy? Do you answer the prayers of his demons who must collect souls to appease his unending appetite?"

Her poisonous words bit into him like a venomous snake, and penetrated deep . . . deep. His eyes narrowed dangerously, burning with hatred. His jaw tightened and flinched. He spoke slowly, and strained, his controlled voice caging anger. "You tempt me . . . woman . . . to leave you to your fate."

Her eyes softened, not with fear—but regret. "Oh Kayenté," she sighed into a well of guilt. "Leave me to my fate then, but please forgive me for what I have said. I didn't speak the truth."

He nodded. "Yes—you did. I know I am a demon."

She stepped up to him, cautiously reaching her hand to his face.

He snapped his fingers around her wrist, stopping her movement. "Should I prove it to you?"

She ignored his threat. "I have felt light in you, and purity of heart—and I do believe you care for me."

He stared fathoms deep into her gold eyes, searching . . . and he found remorse, and he found—love.

She implored, "Please forgive me. I'm terribly regretful. I've never spoken with such an ill-mannered tongue. In less than one day of leaving Lania Castle, I've become so—mean." She lowered her head in shame. "I no longer know who I am."

His grip on her wrist transformed from hate to compassion. He yanked her to him and embraced her, holding her head against his chest so that she could hear his pounding heart.

She wept lightly and vowed aloud, "I swear Kayenté, I swear that I'll never do that again. I knew what would hurt you, and I used it. I did the very thing of which I was accusing you."

His voice reverberated in her ear, "Perhaps you understand now . . . about the meanness—about the cruelty."

She nodded lightly. "It was as if I was deflecting the pain because I could endure no more. Instead of feeling the horror, I hurled it upon you."

"Yes," he affirmed, "just as these people would have done to you. Even if you have compassion for them, you don't deserve to be the victim of their hate. You have a right to defend yourself, even if you must kill."

She pulled back from him. "Do I? Do I have the right to take a life?"

"You have a right," he drew her close again, "to preserve your own."

"But I'm not an individual. I'm linked with all."

He coddled her head between his chest and the palm of his hand. His deep, rich voice fell into her like the fatherly warmth that she'd never known. "I don't pretend to understand your thunderous compassion for the swine of this earth or your need to bridge the human race, but I do know that you also exist as a human being in your own right. Fight for that self, Kamara. Worship your individual existence. Protect your body with a furious love to preserve your life, be it by the tongue of deception, the might of muscle, or the swiftness of the blade." He pulled her head back gently and gazed into her eyes. "You are not good at these things Kamara. Let me help."

"I'm overwhelmed, Kayenté. I *must* return home."

"Home I cannot take you. As it is, we must hurry to reach my father's domain by sunset."

He released her, took her hand gently, and led her toward his stallion.

"Please let me go home, Kayenté."

He did not answer any of the numerous times she asked him that question enroute to his horse. When they arrived, he helped her mount and then swung himself up behind her. He replaced the hood of her cloak on her head and wrapped one arm around her waist. The horse carried them out of the dense woods, under thickening gray skies.

Meadow breezes teased their faces. Brown and green grasshoppers blasted from the horse's hooves, spraying in all directions, before disappearing in tall grass blades. Kamara wished she could dodge danger with such ease. She placed her hand lightly on Kayenté's arm. "I can endure no more. Already I have endured too much. I'm crumbling inside, falling into madness."

"This way is best, Kamara."

"Oh Kayenté! Why won't you understand that if you care for me, you *must* take me home."

His voice melted over her in an almost magical way. "Oh lady, why won't you understand that it is *because* I care for you, that I *must* take you away."

He kicked his horse into a gallop and they made haste until the edge of sunset.

Ж
Chapter Nine

Franz Ketola's Castle-Kanz Region

Kayenté and Kamara had ridden far and long. Fatigue had claimed them both, but when their destination was in view, Kamara's heart hammered away her exhaustion. The castle of Duke Franz Ketola loomed in the distance like a sword thrust up from the belly of the earth, bleeding a salmon pink sunset. Eight square brownstone towers surrounded a taller square stronghold that kissed the sky.

"No!" she cried. "This *cannot* happen. It cannot!"

"You'll survive," Kayenté said callously, distracted by his congesting thinking about war strategy.

Her muscles squeezed around her bones. "This. I shan't survive. You *must* release me, here, now . . . before we enter the grounds!"

"No." Irritation edged his voice. He'd been devising an elaborate counter attack on the Rudels, when her whining crashed into his scheme.

"Kayenté!"

He focused harder, fearing he'd forget the ingenious battle stratagem, unfolding in his mind. How dare she disturb him in his world and his way, when he was doing what he best did, and had most deservingly won that right!

She tried to slide off the horse, but Kayenté firmed his arm around her waist.

Her amplified gasping deteriorated her composure, commanding his attention. It would not do to present her to his father this way.

"Resisting won't help you Kamara. Accept what is to come. There is much of it you'll like."

To his surprise, she quieted. War strategies. Yes, he would—

"Kayenté," she said cunningly. "What might your father do if I informed him that you hold me against my will?"

Kayenté was amused. "Are you doing battle with me Kamara?"

"Well, what would he do?"

"Because if you are, you stated your threat incorrectly."

"What other way is there to state such a thing?"

"Like this, 'I'll inform your father that you kidnapped me.' "

Her jaw dropped. "Very well. I'll inform your father that you kidnapped me!"

He laughed, a snide, slightly stifled laugh.

"Well? What shall he do?"

"Nothing. My father dare not intercede with my choices. He'd not take the chance."

"But he's the Duke. Is his authority not greater than yours?"

"Only by title."

Her face reddened. "Oh! What Michael and Sir Robert said of you *is* true. You can be utterly ruthless. You would stop at *nothing* to rule Kantine. Or perhaps the world. You—"

He clamped his hand over her mouth until he felt her muscles loosen in defeat. "Calm down, little Kamara. Even if my father could control me, he'd do nothing because you're under my protection and there's nothing unlawful about that."

His hand glided from her lips to her throat, resting there like a warden to deal with her mouth should unsavory words dare try to escape.

"I don't want your protection."

There they were. The unsavory words, from his mother's mouth to hers.

"Nonetheless," he said, "you have it."

"Why, because your mother wouldn't let you protect her, so now you are taking an iron hand with me?"

His body tightened, but his words flowed smoothly. "Are you becoming *mean* again?"

Her brave attempt crumbled to dust. "Yes, I am. I just promised you I wouldn't be, and I am. I am falling from grace, can't you see! I *must* return home if there is anything decent in me to remain!"

"See," he declared, "you need something so desperately that you resort to self-serving trickery, and inflict pain on others. Sometimes we become mean to attain what we want. And sometimes we become cold to survive the cold-hearted. That is the way of the world."

"But such behavior is beneath me."

"Apparently not."

"I had no other recourse. Misting no longer alters your itinerary. Pleading is futile. I had to think like you . . . try to fight you on your level."

"I think no less of you for your attempt to imitate me, however far from the truth it was."

"Kayenté, I could hardly imitate you, even if that was my desire."

"No," he said, "You could hardly do anything I can do, so don't try."

Kamara could no longer converse for they had drawn too near the dreaded denizen of combat: warrior-engorged towers, bestial power, the scent of sweat. She had never witnessed such scores of fighting men in all her life. She drew the hood more closely around her face, and pulled the cape snugly around her body, concealing her female features the best she could. This was a war castle, filled with war-like people and war-like ways and she was going to be forced to intermingle as a drop of rain that helplessly falls on a sticker weed.

They rode past a bounty of strategically placed warriors guarding the outer grounds. Acknowledgments showered Kayenté from whomever they passed. "Lord Panther Ketola," they'd say, and bow lightly.

Kamara's stomach knotted. *Lord Panther*, she thought, *Kayenté's malevolent side, not the child of him she'd glimpsed, nor the one who had potential to love.*

They stopped at the drawbridge, waiting for it to lower. The air was potent with war energy. Hurricanes thrashed in her body and earthquakes rumbled in her mind. Oh, was the world falling apart? Was she the world? Would her body shatter? "Oh, Kayenté! I *beg* you take me from here!"

He said nothing, for there was nothing left to say. His course was set; she must remain with him, and that was that.

He softened though when she started gasping again, more silently, deeper, slower. She fell forward, flattening her chest over the horse's neck, its sweaty black fur against her forehead. Mist curled around her fingers and wisped around her head, like some poor desperate thing whose logic had flown, and whose action had fallen to habit. She was doing the only thing she knew. Behaving the only way she could. Trying to survive.

He touched her back. "Kamara. You mustn't 'mist' around these people. They'll deem you a witch, and besides," he chuckled lightly, trying to humor her, "my father would be most displeased if you pacified his armies."

She was not humored. The vapors emerged from her thicker, and faster.

His heart stirred. Porcupines fling quills. Skunks squirt odor. Kamara—mists. He drew her back against his chest and enveloped her with his arms protectively. "I'll let no one harm you."

The vapors grew thicker still, expanding beyond them both. He was genuinely concerned about explaining this occurrence to his father's people. "Enough!" he jerked her slightly. "I command you to stop."

The vapors swallowed the horse and moved outward.

"Very well," he dropped his arms from her. "Mist your heart out, but know you'll never mist this whole domain before they deem you a witch. You'll have great trouble convincing them that you are not. The death of a witch would be more torturous than any you could imagine."

She stopped misting. Her back began bobbing to her voiceless crying.

"That's better," he said, not sure if it really was, for what good was his promise of safety if she died a frightful bird, afraid and shocked, caged in a world she didn't understand? Then again, what alternative would serve her better? None. He had to be hard-hearted with her for her own good.

He kicked the horse onward over the lowered drawbridge, through the gate of the curtain wall, through the portcullis, and into the front courtyard. She'd stopped crying, and had become frozen, so still in fact, it seemed she did not even breathe. His first order of business would be to settle her into a bedchamber and let her feel safe for a time, while he and his father talked of war.

He halted his horse by the stable boy who'd come to greet him. Kayenté dismounted, reaching up to help Kamara down. She grabbed the saddle and shook her head at him with large desperate eyes.

"If you do not dismount," he said, "you will forfeit my presence."

She hugged the saddle tighter with her knees and looked forward stubbornly.

Kayenté shrugged and turned away. She would soon learn the merit of his presence. He sauntered across the grounds toward the double doors of the castle.

Kamara tried to pretend like she didn't care, but as distance shrank his body, her panic rose. The stable boy was crowded out by three warriors who had gathered around her, garbed in chain mail under yellow tunics with black panther heads sewn on the fronts. The men's eyes steamed an almost malicious curiosity. Snaky energy slithered 'round inside her body where it very much didn't belong. She stared at the passive stable boy. He was no help, subservient to his masters. "Kayenté!" she shrieked. "Return at once!"

He barely heard her, but was pleased that he did, although he'd not expected her to respond with such dander and downright disrespect. He turned around and went back to her, knowing he'd have to put her in her place to preserve his reputation and negate her behavior as a precedent to observers. She had much to learn about courtly behavior and the abdication expected by lords. As he approached, he heard the warriors mumble, "She calls him Kayenté, not Panther, nor lord."

"That will be remedied," Kayenté retorted to the warriors, who stepped out of his way.

He arrived at her feet, lifting his head with an imperious stare. "These men fail to understand why you omit calling me, lord. I myself am in mystery of the answer. Perhaps you could provide us with one."

Her chin fell meekly to her chest, preferring humility to harassment. "I changed my mind about remaining on your mount— lord."

He sighed, dismayed that she would not even give him the satisfaction of a good sparring. Instead, his heart tugged once more for the passive young form concealed beneath the soft purple cloak. He secured her ribcage and eased her feet to the ground. She slid under his cape in the crook of his arm, forcing his biceps around her shoulder. Little bird in the nest.

"Your concubine?" asked a warrior.

"No." Kayenté said, "She's—" He was distracted by her behavior. While under the cape, she slipped behind him, and hugged his waist, making him appear hunchbacked. He was startled and half-embarrassed by her movements. He tried to pretend she wasn't behaving as such. "She's—" he tried to continue, but had an urge to show her face when he was talking of her, and to present her with a little dignity. He twisted his head and turned his body in an effort to unearth her and bring her to his side, but she was so stuck on his back that such a feat was too awkward an undertaking. He concluded his comment with ill ease, "—under my protection."

The warrior who had questioned him, smiled and moved around to the back of Kayenté to better view the concealed bump that was denied him. He chortled. "That is apparent."

Kamara sensed the strange man's presence close to her. Maintaining her hold on Kayenté's waist, she moved to his other side, still concealed, until her shoulder was secure beneath his arm. She bore in so close and gripped so tenaciously, he nearly lost his balance. Apparently, she had indeed learned the merit of his presence, maybe a little too well. He peaked under his cape to see her face, tight with fear, pressed against his side.

"Under your protection indeed," snickered the warrior.

"I'm dizzy," Kamara said in a low muffled voice. "I fear I shall faint soon if you keep me in the presence of violent males."

"Who is she lord?" asked another warrior.

Kayenté answered, "Lady Kamara Lania of Lania Castle."

The third warrior inquired, "Kamara, the witch?"

Kamara shrieked as Kayenté thrust her to the side of him. His cape brushed over her head, leaving her exposed. She saw Kayenté's fist fly into a man's jaw.

She fell to her knees covering her face.

She heard Kayenté say, "You will respect this woman as you do the Duchess. She's proven herself worthy to hold her own castle in a kindhearted manner that exceeds your comprehension. You'll *not* dishonor her."

The other two men backed away in silence.

Kamara remained frozen, torn between the shock of Kayenté's violent nature, and the pleasant fact that he truly did seem to respect her.

She felt his warm hands touch her back and then slide to her waist, lifting her to a standing position. "Head tall," he whispered, while wiping off a smudge of dirt from her face, "Hold yourself as you would in your own castle, as the true lady you are."

She nodded her head tearfully, realizing why children need fathers, and women, husbands. Perhaps there was a time for storm— perhaps. Her mind flashed upon a devil smiling. She shuddered. Maybe not.

Kayenté hooked his arm in hers and walked her toward the castle entrance.

She said, "If you are going to force me in there, I must hide behind your shield to avoid feeling the extreme roughness of this place."

He grinned. "I don't use a shield—slows me down from making the kill."

She glared at him. "I don't mean that kind of a shield."

"Oh," he said, still grinning, "you want to meet the Duke and Duchess while hiding under my cape?"

She glared. "I'm referring to your invisible shield. It's thick and impenetrable, deflecting everything but love."

He teased. "If that's true then my shield is not strong."

"But it is. For no shield exists that can deflect love."

"Save the shield of the Cold One."

"I'm not yet convinced of that," she said. "Perhaps there is a way, unlike the usual."

Kayenté smiled. "The word usual must hiss at you . . . for so often you reject it."

She scowled. "And it must lick you all over like a puppy dog in gratitude for constant feedings."

"If you are not careful you're going to poke holes in this shield of mine that you hide behind with those horns that you are sprouting."

"Ah—and what of your horns?"

"I have never denied my horns, little Kamara. In fact of my horns, I'm quite proud."

She roamed his face with serious eyes. "I don't think you are."

His chest constricted faintly, concealed in his arrogant demeanor.

They ascended three steps. The doors opened. House guards stood on either side. They entered. A servant woman whisked off Kamara's cape. Then she tried to take Kayenté's cape but he signaled her away. Then she wished she hadn't let her cape go either. She wasn't ready to part with the cover it had provided. Her dress was torn at the skirt, musty with sweat and grime. And her long loose hair was matted, in dire need of combing.

Kayenté led her into the Great Hall. The tan marble floor shined, reflecting a vague image of her body as they walked. Richly decorated walls held thick rugs, intricately patterned with orange-gold knot designs trimmed with black borders. Servants and knights bustled. Long ornately carved cherry wood trestle tables were being set with silver goblets.

Three finely dressed men approached. The eldest wore a maroon velvet tunic, gray pants, and black boots. His dark hair was peppered gray, matching the mustache on his face. Next to him was a taller, younger man with chest length black hair, wearing gray velvet. He bore a remarkable resemblance to Kayenté. The man next to him wore brown velvet. He was less tall and stockier than the other two, his sandy colored hair cropped short like the eldest man. He had a roughness that startled her.

When they arrived, Kayenté said, "May I present my father, Duke Franz Ketola. My older brother, the Earl, Taran, and my younger brother, the third Earl, Marc. Father, Taran, Marc, may I present Lady Kamara of Lania Castle."

Kamara labored to hold herself proud as Kayenté had suggested. She viewed the three men, stately like Kayenté, and she thought briefly of the night before when she had uncovered Kayenté's childhood, a night that seemed already so long ago.

The Duke lifted her hand gently to his mouth and kissed it. His eyes lingered upon her face with such depth that he seemed to fall into her. When he released her hand, Taran caught her fingers eagerly and lifted them to his lips, planting little kisses, while gazing into her face with a hint of lust in his blue blue eyes.

Kayenté watched him with a critical squint.

Kamara swallowed nervously and ever so slightly stepped back, hoping he'd release her hand, but he didn't. Instead, he speared his charm straight through her. A shiver shot up her arm and down her spine.

Marc rescued her hand from Taran's, into his own, with alarming ruggedness. She stiffened, hardly able to breathe. She gazed into his dark eyes, his oh so very dark eyes, and found . . . his spirit. And within the span of a moment, she saw him as a plow tilling the field, then as an anchor holding the ship. He was the practical one—stable and concrete like a mountain, unmoved by passionate dreams, content with what was before him. And even though the solidness of his energy field disturbed her, she rather liked him—for in all of this, she knew he could inexplicably be trusted. This man did not scheme—ever.

Marc kissed her hand quickly and simply, and then released her.

She bowed her head lightly to each man, beginning with Marc, acknowledging the respect they'd paid her. Then she stepped closer to Kayenté.

Taran smiled. "Excuse us, Lady Kamara, my brother Marc and I have business to tend, but I'd enjoy your company at dinner and perhaps a walk afterward? I doubt Kayenté would mind as he is soon to wed another."

Kamara's face went cold. Wed another? She turned her head to Kayenté, staring at this man so full of secrets. He was looking at her, acting like nothing was wrong. Now that he had dragged her into his world, would he abandon her in this hell, distracted by his bride? Would the affection he seemed to hold for her disappear on his wedding night? She suddenly didn't feel safe with him anymore. But who else would protect her?"

Taran said, "Oh you didn't know. I should say it is a good thing I have informed you."

Kayenté tossed his head back lightly. "Perhaps I should warn the last two or three women left in this castle that you've not yet wined and dined about your ulterior motives."

Marc intervened. "You can tell my brothers are not on the best of terms. Seems they are always drawn to the same lovely women. Even Kayenté's bride-to-be was once courted by Taran. I, on the other hand, favor the sword over the ladies."

"That's right," Taran gibed, "Marc prefers slaying to loving."

Marc said, "Yes because all that I have seen my brothers do is break hearts, a worse kind of killing I should think than stabbing a body clean through." He cleared his throat and addressed Kamara, "Excuse me for the course imagery."

Kayenté glared at Marc, his eyes dark with warning.

The Duke said nervously, "Marc! Taran! Don't provoke Kayenté. Save your fighting for the field. I doubt Lady Kamara wishes to witness you sparring in this Hall."

"Excuse us, Lady Kamara," said Taran, with suave dignity. He bowed to Kamara and then walked away. Marc bowed lightly and followed Taran.

The Duke snapped his fingers, and a middle-aged woman servant appeared in an ankle-length, brown tunic. Her dark visage yielded no facial expression. "Yes, my lord."

"Escort Lady Kamara to the gold room. Draw her a bath before dinner and provide her with a suitable dining gown from the guest closet."

Kamara grabbed Kayenté's arm.

He peeked down at her.

She shook her head at him with wide panicked eyes.

He said, "You will be safe."

The servant said, "This way, my lady."

She stared hard at Kayenté, continuing her silent protest.

The servant lady pried her gently away from Kayenté. Her eyes remained fixed on him, even as her arm fell from his, and she was led away up the winding staircase.

The Duke and Kayenté watched her, somewhat pleasured by her intensity. She didn't see the triad of armed guards descending the steps, and bumped into one. The servant snatched her toward the wall and let the guards pass. When they had, Kayenté saw only the back of her disappearing around the wind of the stairs, with her head twisted his way.

Kayenté smiled. She was his now.

The Duke said, "That woman is strongly attached to you."

"And you father—" he squared his face to the Duke, "—seem most intrigued with her."

"It's just, just—that she's quite lovely. Is she the reason for your visit? Have you changed your mind about Winnefred?"

"No." Kayenté's face hardened. "The King of the Rudels hired a mercenary to conquer my fortress. How Harold can maintain power without ever proving his skill as a warrior befalls my understanding. My men forced his retreat, but I believe he'll attack you next, probably within a fortnight, once his armies recover. Reports are, they lost many. However, no telling how many more they have in reserve. I've come to warn you."

"A mercenary? Who?"

"Merculus," Kayenté clenched his fists, "—a Sakajian traitor. It's been said that he wants vengeance on the Ketola's. We don't know why. Do you know him?"

"No." He touched Kayenté's shoulder, "but we'd best unite our armies and plan an offense. We'll lay out the plan tonight after dinner."

"Good." Kayenté glanced toward the stairs. "Excuse me father, but I'd best check in on Kamara. She's rather—delicate, in some ways."

"Why does she journey with you?"

"Michael asked me to champion her against one who seeks her destruction. I was with her on her lands when I heard word my realm had been invaded, so with me she comes."

"She appears already plundered."

"We had trouble with a band of thieves, but no harm came to her."

The Duke spoke with a far away look in his eyes. "Her kind, I think—attract trouble."

"What do you mean, her kind?"

"What cutthroat is not attracted to innocence?"

"You have a point," Kayenté said, relieved his father didn't know the truth. Kamara was his concern, and he didn't want the Duke's opinions on the subject.

The Duke stared at Kayenté uneasily, scrutinizing.

Kayenté asked, "Why do you study me so?"

The Duke took his arm lightly and led him over to a private corner in the Great Hall.

Kayenté asked impatiently, "What father?"

The Duke fidgeted. "I have to know something." Sweat beaded his brow.

"What?" Suspicion clouded Kayenté's eyes.

"Have you—" the Duke cleared his throat, "—bedded her?"

"Why do you care?" Kayenté wondered if after all, the Duke did know more than he cared to say.

"Have you?" the Duke's voice coiled with tension.

"No," Kayenté said.

The Duke sighed with relief, turning his gaze to the floor.

Kayenté raised a brow maliciously. "But I may yet."

The Duke snapped his head up and stared urgently at Kayenté, "I think it best, you do not."

"Why?"

"Light Priestesses are sensitive creatures."

Kayenté's face tightened. "What do you know of Light Priestesses?"

"I've . . . heard—stories."

"What leads you to believe she is a Light Priestess?"

"It's easy to tell. She's too unearthly for this world. I suggest you leave her here under my protection."

"No. She remains with me."

The Duke paused, sighed, and cleared his throat. "Light Priestesses cannot endure normal lifestyles. If you don't completely understand this sort of woman, your folly could endanger her more than the fate from which you protect her."

Kayenté's jaw flinched. "I understand her better than you think. I have vowed to protect her, and she feels safe with no other."

"But—"

"How is it *really*, that you possess knowledge of these women? Surely, not from mere stories that deem them mostly witches."

"I've lived long," replied the Duke, "I know much."

"Enough secrets father!"

"How I know, doesn't matter. I forbid you to bed her."

"I respect you father, but I'm beyond you forbidding me anything. You were once a powerful man, but never as powerful as I am now. I'll do as I please."

The Duke shot Kayenté a razor sharp glare.

Kayenté returned the glare, sharper yet, until fear hazed the Duke's eyes. Then he softened. "I wouldn't turn on you father, but neither will I submit to your paternal authority."

The Duke cast his eyes downward in resignation and spoke in a low broken tone. "My rebellious son, sometimes—"

Kayenté stiffened. "Sometimes, what?"

"Sometimes I think you are not my son."

Kayenté's heart pounded. "Why?"

"Because you seem to despise me so. Perhaps your mother had a lover. Perhaps you are *his* son."

Kayenté's face reddened, his fury on the edge of eruption. He wanted to grab his father's collar and shake out the emotional contents of his heart. But truth be known, he honored his father too much for such a display, and even if he didn't, the house guards would charge wildly to the Duke's defense.

Then he fought an urge to bellow that he was the son of a rapist. And he fought the desire to at long last defend his mother's honor. It was too late for all of that—too late. The rapist had ceased coming around years ago. What good could be done now by drudging up this ugly truth? And what real good could come from exposing that secret only, when so many other secrets still lay buried in the crowded invisible graveyard of Ketola history. And there were secrets that even he didn't know, but he could feel them there, like nameless faceless ghosts terrorizing his heart.

He was so immersed in his feelings that he barely heard his father speak.

"Why, it's not unlikely that your mother or I could have produced a child without the other?"

Kayenté shook his head in confusion, dazed from the cavalcade of emotion that he was not used to experiencing. "What are you implying?"

"Before your mother, I knew a Light Priestess of the Mist." The Duke sighed, "I sired her child."

Kayenté furrowed his brows. Time stopped. So did his heart. He finally realized why his father had been hedging. He asked, on a breath that hung in the air. "Kamara?"

The Duke nodded.

Kayenté swallowed hard. "You sired, Kamara?" Stupefied, he brushed his hands over his head, stretching his hair against his scalp. He sighed, dropping his hands. "Are you saying, Kamara . . . is my sister?"

The Duke nodded. "I must swear you to secrecy."

Kayenté huffed. The Duke's request was nothing new. "If you only knew, father, how many secrets I've been sworn to keep. Always we keep secrets in this family and that is why I could not remain."

The Duke sighed. "I'm sorry, but some secrets are best kept."

"And so they are," Kayenté said, thinking of his own dark ugly secret that he and his mother withheld from the Duke.

"What of Kamara's mother?" Kayenté asked. "Where is she?"

"Gone now," he said with an ache in his voice. "I've not seen her since Kamara was conceived. I've heard it said that she gave her life to protect her daughter."

"How did you know Kamara was your daughter?"

"Her mother told me that the child's name would be Kamara, which in Gatish, means Storm Tamer—and Lania, the shared last name of all Priestesses, which in Gatish means, In the Mist. You introduced her to me as Kamara Lania of Lania Castle."

"I was under the impression that the Priestesses chose passive men to father their children."

"I don't know why they chose me, and they would not tell."

"Has your curiosity to view her not peaked in all these years?"

"I've heard stories of her existence, but I was forbidden long ago to have any contact with her. I was told my identity as her father would be concealed, as all Priestess's fathers are. We are a seed, nothing more. The Priestesses magic insures their wishes."

The Duke smiled, his eyes teary. "But all these years, I've wondered . . . . She is like her mother in appearance and manner, face shining sweetness, disposition passive."

Kayenté sighed, plagued with a sudden sense that there was more going on between he and Kamara than he had dared realize—but he must. He sighed again, fearing that an adventure into truth would unravel his soul. But he was a warrior—the best, and a coward he would not be.

He drew the sword from his cape and held the hand guard in front of his father. "View the design."

The Duke said, "Our coat of arms. How did you come by this sword?"

"An old woman in a black cape, a messenger for the Priestesses, known as the Wise One, gave it to Kamara, but not personally. Apparently, Kamara is restricted from meeting her. Do you know this woman?"

"No. Years ago, the Priestesses and their messengers became more secretive and took to roaming, but I don't know why."

"Kamara does not roam. In fact she does quite the opposite."

"Yes. I know. She was to remain in her castle in the pureness of 'the light' until twenty years of age." The Duke paused, then raised his brows. "Perhaps that's it. Maybe she was given the sword now, because she has come of age. And because I am her father, her sword bears my coat of arms. And now you, her brother—and I, her father, touch upon her life. If you are to protect her—protect her well, my son."

"Son?" Kayenté asked sardonically, "are you sure?"

"I didn't mean what I said earlier. I spoke then from anger."

"Does mother know about this?"

"No."

"Of course not," Kayenté scowled, "another secret."

The Duke rubbed his hands nervously against his pant legs. "You best look in on Kamara, and I'll see you at the banquet."

"Very well." Kayenté returned the sword to its sheath. He made haste across the Great Hall, up the winding stairway. He was rounding the stairwell toward the fifth floor when he saw his mother descending. She was beautiful as always, but old. She had always seemed old to him for as long as he could remember.

Her gray hair was eloquently pinned up with golden combs. Her dark complexion was stunning against the black and gold of her royal dress, which puffed hugely at the sleeves and hips making her appear mightier than he knew she was.

"Greetings mother," Kayenté said. He stopped hesitantly on the stairs.

"Greetings son." She placed a false kiss on his cheek. Coldness brewed in her eyes, alluding to some strange hate she laid faintly upon him. "Have you returned to assume your rightful place with us, or do secrets of the past still keep you away?"

"I'm here for the night, mother. Are you displeased?"

"You should be here, defending *this* castle."

"Defend mother, since when do you allow me to defend?"

She slapped his face. "Will you never forget the past!"

"No," he said flatly, as if she had not slapped him. "How can you?"

He walked onward, leaving her behind, never looking back.

When he reached Kamara's room she was gone, so he hurried down the corridor to the bathhouse and knocked on the door. "Kamara?"

"Kayenté!" She sounded desperate.

He touched his hand against the soft grain of the wooden door and pushed it open. She was there, damp and dewy, in a velvet burgundy gown that shaped her figure, tight long sleeves, and neckline edging her shoulders. He pleasured to see her as such, but worried about her too much to enjoy it. Her lengthy wet hair dangled over the wine colored slippers in her hand. Her angelic eyes beseeched him.

He surveyed the small bathhouse and spied Taran leaning against the back wall by the wooden tub.

"Greetings brother," Taran said casually, waving his hand in jest.

Blackness masked Kayenté's blue eyes. "Kamara! Where is your woman servant?"

Taran smiled and answered for her. "I dismissed her."

Kamara slid her slippers on her feet. "Oh where is my bedchamber Kayenté? Show me to my chamber!"

Kayenté eased her behind him, eyes deadly on Taran. "Kamara is not a kitchen wench. If you have a problem remembering that, I'll make certain you don't forget!"

Taran strutted over to Kayenté. "I do believe you are in love with this woman. It's a shame," he stared into Kayenté face, "because she won't last long with Winnefred."

Kayenté clenched his fist, and his tongue began to form words that would unleash his secrets. Oh, what shock would come upon Taran's face upon discovering he was Kamara's brother! And oh, what a bristled stupor he'd fall into, when he further learned, that Kayenté himself, was not! Not her blood brother anyway. Ironic, he thought, that for once he was glad he was the son of a rapist. He smiled, knowing the Duke would not sanction Taran pursuing Kamara, while he on the other hand, once in his own castle, intended to do . . . just that.

Taran said, "You smile at the thought of Winnefred tearing Kamara to pieces?"

"Not that thought, "Kayenté said coolly, "but another."

Taran moved outside the door, scrutinizing Kayenté's expression. Then he addressed Kamara, "When he hurts you lady, and he will, remember that while my manner may seem offensive—it is I, not he, who would defend your heart." He then bowed, and said with seductive charm, "I'm at your service."

Kayenté drew back his fist. Kamara, wishing no more violence on top of all she'd already experienced in her exceedingly long and terrible day, cried out, "Oh please take me to my chamber, Kayenté, *now.*" She tugged his arm pulling him away from Taran, who turned and sauntered down the corridor the opposite way.

Kayenté let Kamara move him towards her bedchamber.

She said, "This is the way, isn't it?"

He nodded. "Did he harm you, Kamara, like the others did?"

"No, no." I was pretty much dressed when he entered, however, his manner discomforts me.

"Me, as well," Kayenté said, his fist finally uncurling.

She gazed inquisitively at him as they walked.

"What?" he asked curiously.

"How could you have always believed that Taran was more noble than you?"

"Taran was the first born son of the Duke. In the eyes of the nobles, next to my father, he is given the most authority and respect. He will one day rule this castle. Because of a rapist, my blood is tainted, and my nobility stolen."

She touched his shoulder tenderly. "Is that what nobility is to you, a thing measured by blood and birth?"

His eyes rolled sideways. "What is it to you?"

"Nobility," she said, "is to behave boldly from the heart, at the risk of losing everything."

"I've not done that."

"But you have Kayenté. You have done nothing but that since the moment I met you. Even when I hated you or opposed your actions, you held to your heart. You could have abandoned me many times, and you haven't," she lowered her head demurely, thinking of his bride-to- be, then looked his way, "yet."

Kayenté scowled. He would never abandon her.

Kamara continued, "The point is that you are more genuine and heartfelt than Taran."

"You give me too much credit," he said. "You do not know all my motives."

"No, I don't, but I can feel them. And as long as your heart wins, the other motives don't matter."

"My heart won't win. Ketola's are short on heart," and then remembering that she was a Ketola, he looked down at her, "well not all of them."

"Not you," she said.

"That isn't the Ketola I was referring to, however, I grasp what you imply. Nonetheless, I tell you now, do not invest your hopes in this heart you imagine I have. I'll only disappoint you. I'll give you protection—nothing more."

"What of the evening when you said you were falling in love with me?"

"I was bewitched then."

"And your embraces, your kisses, your confessions of care— what motive lurked behind them?"

"I am drawn to you—your body, your character. I want you safe. But that is not love."

She cocked her head slightly. "I think that is a kind of love."

"I don't love. However, I'm pleased you view me as noble by your standard, but I'm just a self-serving warlord who has taken you behind my shield as a promise to Michael. And you would fare better to view me as such."

"By those rules, you'd best view me as a hopeless dreamer forever resigned to die by the hand of swine."

"Better to die by swine, than a shattered heart."

"Shattered hearts can be resurrected."

He looked at her coldly. "What's the point in doing that? Leave the heart dead, I say."

She was cheated of retort by arriving at her room where the woman servant was waiting. "My lady," she curtsied with a deadpan face.

Kamara stared at her with cocked head, commencing her dive into the servant's soul.

"Kamara?" Kayenté said.

She looked at him with such liquid warmth, his heart hurt.

His eyes glimmered affection. "Lock your door. I'll return for you later. If Taran comes, don't be polite. Tell him to go away."

She nodded and offered him a smile, faint and sweet.

He started to leave, needing to lessen the ache in his heart, but stopped when she blurted, "Tell me I'm right about you, Kayenté."

"I can't," he said, "your words and ways are foreign to mine. All I can tell you is that whatever you think I am—I'm not." He swept his finger briskly from her throat to her chin in a gesture of fondness. Then he turned and left.

She went inside the bedchamber with the servant woman, closed, and locked the door. The servant woman guided her to sit at the ornately carved oak wood vanity, and took a brush to her hair.

Kamara wanted to rejuvenate the woman's spirit, but felt suddenly too darkened by her own feelings. She was grateful for Kayenté's protective wing, yet afraid he would remove it once he wed, and the idea of him marrying pained her. Was Taran right? Would Kayenté seduce her into a world she didn't understand, and then forget she existed? Would Taran then devour her?

Her lamenting sighs matched the woman servant's strokes of the brush through her long damp tresses. Her eyelids slid shut, and she uttered a silent prayer, *Oh, the despairing breed of human best gather 'round me now and partake of my sanctity, for the flame of my once bright epic optimism to bring the world to light, dims. Each moment of each day, it grows darker. And soon . . . it will be out.*

Ж
Chapter Ten

Kayenté bathed and donned fresh clothes, courtesy of his father. His black hair hung loose over the wine colored velvet tunic. Kamara's sword hung on his hip, over the black leather pants that fit him like a second skin. He slipped a knife into each black boot.

He left his bedchamber in search of Kamara, eager to present her to his mother as another token of his rebellion. He wanted his mother to view herself against Kamara's innocent reflection. Kamara wouldn't sell out for riches or position as his mother did, as most women would, as all the women he knew, had.

He wanted his mother to suffer by watching him protect another woman, instead of her. She'd had her chance, long ago, but she had let it pass. He had even offered to slay her tormentor, so that the secret could be kept, but still, she forbade it. And to this day, he didn't understand why.

Anyway, he would never offer her his protection again. And even though he was to marry a woman as selfish as his mother, he would nonetheless enjoy flaunting Kamara for this one evening.

When he arrived at her room, she was absent—again. Only the servant woman remained. She said, "Your mother came for her, lord Panther."

Kayenté cursed beneath his breath and hurried down the stairwell, adamant about shielding Kamara from his mother, perhaps even more so than from Taran.

He stepped into the Great Hall, searching for her, but instead caught a glimpse of an old woman in a black cape darting down the corridor that led to the kitchen.

The Wise One, thought Kayenté, *could it be?*

He changed his course, following the woman. She scurried with clever dodges through crowds of people and commotion, through the kitchen and outside into the night. She scampered cunningly through the secret openings of the outer castle walls so elusively that Kayenté nearly lost sight of her several times.

He followed her relentlessly until at last he caught up and grabbed her arm. "What is your name?"

The woman faced him.

Kayenté yanked the hood off her head, but could barely see her face in the dark. He gripped her wrist and pulled her out of the tree shadows into the dim moonlight. Her old face glowed in the dark. Her white hair caught the iridescent beams of celestial light.

"Who are you?"

"I am all faces and I am as old as time."

"Are you the Wise One?"

"Yes." She squinted, "And you are . . . the Dark One." She paused, then spoke in a low hypnotic tone, "The givers shall take, and the takers shall give. Dark comes to light, and light comes to dark. The risen shall fall, and the fallen shall rise. So has it been, and so shall it always be."

Kayenté loosened his grip, feeling an eerie sense of vastness, as if his spirit had lifted from his body. In his mind, he saw his wedding day, a day to secure more lands and more armies. Then he saw Kamara screaming in his torture chamber. He shook his head, to halt what must be his wild imagination.

The Wise One said, "If only the children of light and dark could integrate each others way willingly, there would be no need for such extremes. But they never willingly integrate. No, they never do."

Kayenté absorbed the wisdom of her words, wanting to discount them, but he could not.

She continued speaking, "Your heart was raided and robbed long ago, Kay—en—té. You filled the emptiness with dark power, and adapted. Kamara is as the light you lost, activating painful recollections of your victimization. You want to turn away from her and yet you feel satisfaction in saving her from *your* fate."

"I care nothing of 'the light,' " he snapped.

"Yes—" she peered at him knowingly, "—you do. You've begun a perilous journey to reclaim the contents of your heart. This journey shall prove more frightening than any battle you've ever undertaken. Will you have the same fierce courage to nurture your love, as you have had in slaying your enemies? If this be done," she smiled, "then you shall at last become—noble." Her voice turned motherly, flailing out to an odd prophetic cheer. She touched his cheek. "Kay—en—té. Kay—en—té. Let your actions be to attain *this* goal and no other!"

He disdained her for attempting to change his way by filling his head with notions of love. She was just another Priestess of the Mist, doing what they do best—emasculate men.

Hence, he needed to get her focus off him. "What of Kamara?"

"You have prolonged her life, sensing her need, defying her defiance. Thus far, you have done well. But the future—" the woman sighed and shook her head, "your personal aspirations may yet kill her."

Kayenté's eyes blazed fury. He grabbed the woman's shoulders and jerked her. "Now, you speak like a witch!"

"I tell you this," she said, "because if you draw her out and then forget her, the Cold One shall impregnate her with a child as once he did her mother."

"*Her* mother?" Kayenté asked, thoroughly confused. "Are you saying Kamara was sired by the Cold One?"

"I did not say that."

"But the Duke, isn't he—"

"I have said enough."

"Is the Duke—"

"I have said enough!"

He feared she'd leave before he'd finished interrogating her, so he didn't probe her for that answer. Instead, he asked, "What of the sword you gave Kamara?"

"What of it?" she returned. "You possess her sword. She possesses yours. All is well. She replaced her hood on her head, bowed, and walked away into the dark.

Kayenté let her go, even though he had more questions. Somehow, he'd already been provided with more answers than he cared to accept. He wanted to cast her off as a charlatan, but her words gave an eerie definition to the nameless faceless ghosts that kept him from peace.

He exhaled briskly, wanting to blow away the mysticism. He yearned to wield his sword wildly, just so that he could again remember who he knew himself to be. These women would not make him forget. He needed no changing, and change—he would not.

He made haste back to the Great Hall. The house guards and nobles were being seated. He spied his mother at the far north of the room, perched on her wood-jeweled throne. Kamara was on her knees at his mother's feet. He admired the way her long golden mane, pinned up at the sides, flowed smoothly down her back.

He strode towards them with the dictates of courtly manner, though his legs wanted to race. He craved to witness her gentle manner, her shy eyes—her innocence. And he thought for a moment how her world would shatter if she were to hear that the Cold One might well be her sire. And yet, she'd also be appalled to regard the Duke her sire, for then her true blue blood would deem her an aristocrat whether she behaved like one or not. Actually, no man, save a monk, would likely fit her dream of a father. Even so, a father she did have. She'd gone from no known father to two possible fathers in one evening.

He saw her try to rise, but his mother's hand landed on her small shoulder and pushed her back down. Kamara moved backward on her knees and rose with a quick turn toward the dining area. His mother flew up and seized her arm with regal command.

Kamara's golden orbs searched the room frantically—for him he presumed. When she saw him coming her way, her face lit with surprise and relief.

When his mother saw him, she scowled and released Kamara. He could well imagine how the Duchess had heckled her, inflicting the same soft vicious bite that she had earlier given him. Finally, he arrived before them.

His mother preened her skirt. "You have retrieved a delicate woman Kayenté. Your father takes a liking to such women." She glared at him directly. "I was that way—once."

She brushed past him and strolled majestically across the room to the dining table, now smothered with meats, breads, vegetables, wines, imported fruits, and chocolates. She sat to the left of the Duke at the center of the largest trestle.

"She's a bitter woman," Kayenté said, "I hope she wasn't too harsh."

Kamara looked at him with a discomforting expression. "She sees through the darkest eyes. Now, I do too."

He knew of his mother's powers to depress even the gayest of souls. He feared Kamara was reaching her limit of real world experience for the day. He hooked his arm in hers and began walking.

"After dinner," he said, "you can sleep."

She hung her head and spoke faintly, "I want to die, Kayenté."

He looked down upon her forlorn repose, distressed that she'd fallen so low.

She returned his gaze. A single tear spilled from her eye and streaked her cheek. "Put your sword through me, Kayenté. Spare me this pain."

"Hold fast, Kamara," he said softly, "I won't let you fall."

"Yes you will, Kayenté, the minute your bride comes, you'll let me fall."

He stared at her earnestly, wondering exactly what he meant to her? If she could have her way with him, just what way would that be? No matter. He would not let her fall. Why did everyone keep saying he would?

He stopped walking and lifted her chin with his fingers, so she would see his face. "Trust me."

She shook her head in doubt, tears glossing her eyes.

He moved her onward to the table. "You must dine and gain strength."

"I have no appetite."

"Eat anyway."

He seated her at the table reserved for nobility and guests. His place was between his mother and Kamara. On the other side of Kamara, Taran appeared and sat, eyeing her boldly.

Kamara instinctively touched her hand to Kayenté's knee.

Kayenté stared at his plate, not needing to view Taran to see what was happening. "Mind yourself brother if you choose to savor another meal."

Taran smirked. "Your threats have proved idle thus far."

"I can remedy that." Kayenté cast Taran a death stare, and began to rise from his seat. But he stopped when the Duke said, "Taran, listen to your brother."

"As he listens to me?" snapped Taran. "I am first Earl!"

His mother said, "He has a point, Franz."

Two servants came up behind Kamara and placed a large platter on the table. She could hear the family continuing their argument, but she could no longer hear their words, for she was consumed and paled by the vulgar display before her: a glazed brwon pig with bulging eyes. If the poor animal had not been dead, she would have sworn it pleaded for help. Benumbed by the utter coldheartedness involved in preparing such an exhibit, dizziness sizzled in her head, turning everything black.

Kayenté jumped when her head bumped his shoulder. He barely caught her before she fell to the hard marble floor. Holding her in his arms, he glanced around the table. Everyone was staring.

"She faints often," he fumbled to explain. He then noticed the pig and presumed its presence had caused her collapse. "The pig," he paused, hoping everyone would get the gist of the problem, but they didn't, so he continued, "it upset her."

His mother snickered. "My Kayenté, that girl needs more care than a child. Why, my every word left her quivering. You'd best send her back from whence she came."

Kayenté cast his mother a frosty glance, when his father declared, "She's an innocent! Dear wife, hold your tongue."

The Duchess tensed her jaw. Her silence was loud.

The Duke addressed Kayenté, "Carry Lady Kamara to her bed chamber. She'll be served supper there when she feels better, nothing of the meat variety."

"Let me do the honors." Taran's eyes gleamed.

"Yes," said his mother, "let Taran do the honors."

Kayenté warned, "Silence Taran. I won't tolerate you now."

"Now? When have you ever?" Taran smiled cruelly.

Kayenté lifted Kamara, her hair pinned under his arm, and her long gown draping over the other arm. He carried her up the stairs to her room. He laid her carefully on the gold silken bed cover and gazed upon her pale face.

In a low voice, he said, "You must cease fainting, and causing scenes by virtue of your far too merciful nature. How I would have wished for your tears . . . oh, so many years ago, when I remembered how to cry—when I still cared about love. But now . . ." He shook his head and walked away, leaving her to rest.

He journeyed downstairs back to the feast. When he sat down at the table, he missed the shine of her kindness. He ate heartily and talked more of the Rudel's attack upon the Sakajians. The officers of war took interest and the topic of conversation had set itself for the evening. Kayenté was nearly finished with his meal when he saw Kamara dart across the hall, her arms outstretched in front of her, chasing a manservant who carried a child toward the castle'.

"Oh no," Kayenté muttered, jumping up from the table. He sped towards her, embarrassed by her less than courtly behavior.

He heard her call out, "Sir, I can help that child!"

Kayenté reached her, just as she approached the servant.

The servant stopped, turning to Kamara with a hopeful gaze. His gaunt face held small eyes and a long thin nose. His long lean body was clothed in gray velvet, most fancy for a servant. The wheezing twig thin boy in his arms, burned with fever.

Kamara's red troubled face empathically matched the boy's.

Kayenté noticed, and said, "Haven't you had enough for one day?"

Kamara answered, "If this boy cries for help, I am obligated to save him."

"This boy is too ill to have cried for your help."

"His spirit asked me."

"Curses woman, do you never see the greater picture? You've just experienced the worst day of your life. You must rest and gain strength for tomorrow, which may be more turbulent than today. Your life is in peril—remember? You're under my protection. And since I've responsibilities to protect thousands more, you must adhere to my way, and not be sidetracked with the needs of a single child."

The manservant looked to Kayenté pleadingly and bowed. "I beg you, Lord Panther."

Kamara touched Kayenté's arm. "Please?"

Kayenté groaned, rolling his eyes derisively. Then he looked to his father, for the servant and boy were the Duke's concern—not his. The Duke nodded.

The manservant asked, "Where should I take him, lord?"

Kayenté grumbled and turned left into a corridor. "This way, and be fast."

They followed him down the stark hall. Kamara had to run to keep up with the stride of the men—a difficult task, for she felt the boy's symptoms in her body. She arrived at the servant's side, laboring to match his steps.

She asked panting, "What is your name?"

"Munson," answered the servant. "I am personal servant to the Duchess."

"Where were you headed with your boy before I stopped you?"

"Outside, to the stable. I have a friend who lives there. He has his own remedies. I have nowhere else to turn. The house doctor said nothing can be done for him. Even leeches didn't work. I fear my son will perish if I do not try everything."

Kamara took the man into her heart, feeling the depth of his anguish, unfairly subdued to suit the nobility of the court. They entered a small cold room that harbored a three-foot high russet cobblestone slab—nothing more.

Munson laid his son on the hard slab. The boy's fine-featured face turned brighter red, and his white nightshirt stunk a sickly odor.

Kamara looked from right to left at the yellowed stark walls that had absorbed the terror of many a previous event. A pang of horror shot through her limbs. "What is this place?"

Kayenté answered, "A punishing room for servants."

Her expression was horror-stricken. "Punish? You . . . you punish your servants?"

"Get on with it!" he snapped, sensitive to her punitive glare, all too much like his mother's.

She went to the cobblestone table and scanned her hands over the boy's body without touching him, honing in over his neck and head. She closed her eyes. Mists floated from her fingertips and mouth.

Munson jumped back. "She's a witch!"

"No," said Kayenté. "Watch!"

Kamara placed her hands above the boy's throat and wailed dramatically, "You need air, dear child, air." She took her mouth to the boy's neck.

Munson cried, "She's a vampire! She's going to bite him!"

"Silence," Kayenté said, "or I'll dismiss you from the room!"

In truth, Kayenté wanted to observe her performing this dubious act of healing, and the manservant was irritating him.

Kamara began sucking the base of the boy's throat.

The boy coughed. She rubbed her hands over his chest, and then laid her head over his heart.

"Oh child," she said, "why do you resist? Let your spirit speak to me. I'll listen."

She was quiet for at time. Then, she looked up at Munson. "He tells me that you have stolen him from his mother who lives in the country. He longs to be with her, and if death is the only way he can accomplish that, then he shall die."

Munson's eyes grew wide. "She *is* a witch!"

Kamara stared boldly at the servant and raised a pointed finger at him, emitting a beam of faint white light that shot into Munson's heart. She spoke in an eerie tone that even gave Kayenté the chills, "Do you ... wish—" she squinted, "—your only son," her eyes flared, "to live—or die?"

"Live, live, live." Munson said nervously.

"I can cure his illness if you promise that he'll be returned to his mother. You disdained her family, so you took the child as an act of vengeance, and this is the result."

The man said sheepishly, "I'll ... return him, I promise."

"If you do not, he shall become ill again, and not even the most adept healer shall succeed in saving him."

"She's put a curse on him!" Munson said.

Kayenté grabbed his collar, yanking him close with glaring eyes. "Do you want her help—or not?"

Munson gulped, then nodded.

Kayenté released him with a jerk, sharpening his eyes with a look that forbade further complaint.

Kamara frowned at Kayenté's rough treatment of Munson, then returned her attentions to the boy. She placed her mouth on his neck, intermittently sucking the skin and turning her head to exhale a dark yellow haze. Sweat formed on her strained brow. Then she stopped, and looked to be in deep concentration. Her trance like voice wailed, "I call you back from the clouds, child. I call you back with motherly love . . . in the name of 'the light.' The sisterhood shall watch over you, and always a sister shall come, in spirit or body, whenever you call with all your heart. Come back into your body—now!"

The boy's body jolted. He broke out in a profuse sweat.

She sank to her knees, and leaned her forehead on the stone edge that had grown hot with healing energy.

Minutes later, the boy's eyes opened. His fever had broken. He sat up and looked to his father. "Return me to mother, please."

Munson's face twisted with surprise, suspicion, and shame, but most of all—relief, and least of all—gratitude.

"Will you?" asked the boy.

Munson nodded.

The boy's face lit. "When?"

"Within the week," Munson said, "when you've fully recovered."

Kamara rose. The boy looked to her, jumped off the slab and lunged into her arms, almost bowling her over. He clung tightly to her waist. "Thank you, Angel—thank you. I called for an Angel—I called so hard—and you found me."

Kamara returned the embrace.

Kayenté perused her. Was she a living angel? She healed the boy's body, and she worked with his spirit to accomplish that feat. What else could she be?

Munson eyed her, almost abusively, while prying his son from her body. But the boy's appreciative gaze didn't leave her until his father had towed him out of the room.

Kayenté was speechless and a bit dazed by what he'd just witnessed. He studied her matter-of-fact demeanor, which told him that indeed she often healed the sick.

"Kayenté," she said, "when I scanned the boy, I felt the pain of a man in chains, in a dark and terrible place that has many strange devices. The man's heavily bearded face is caked in blood. He suffers horribly. He begs for mercy. Is there such a room in this castle?"

Kayenté jaw dropped. "No!"

"No, there is no such room?" she asked innocently.

"No, you are *not* going to the torture chamber! You are naive to the realities of such a place. You've fainted thrice today already over sights menial compared to what's down there."

"Menial!" She threw up her hands. "How can it be that you label your dead squire, and the death of seven mutilated bodies, menial?"

"Because they died swiftly, little Kamara. The ones in the dungeon are—well, let's just say that it's worse."

"But I've fainted at those other sights because in those instances I was not called upon to heal, therefore I was less able to override the gruesome details of the situation."

His voice grew stern, "You need food and sleep." He grabbed her arm and guided her down the corridor.

"Kayenté, please, I must aid him. He calls and I *must* answer!"

"No," he squeezed her arm tighter, "you will forget about that man!"

"But—"

"No!" He lowered his voice when they entered the Great Hall. "You'll never find an end to the suffering in this world, and you can't save everyone."

"Let me aid this one last person. Then I'll stop."

"You can't help a prisoner!"

"He is a human being. Surely you do not relish that he's in pain."

"I do. Prisoners are prisoners because they have performed criminal acts. They must suffer."

"Kayenté, please stop speaking like that!"

"Why? Because you can't accept that I'm a cold-hearted bastard?"

"You're not!"

"I am."

"You're not!"

Her resistance wearied him. "You'll save no one else today."

Kamara scowled, frustrated that she could not make him understand how she was compelled beyond her own desires to answer every call. She scanned the Great Hall, trying to sense the location of the torture chamber. Minstrels bustled about preparing for the evening's entertainment, but the people seemed more excited by the miracle Kamara had performed. They were gathered around Munson and the healed boy.

The Duchess emerged from the crowd, and headed toward Kamara and Kayenté, her black and gold dress trailing the floor. Kayenté stayed on course toward the staircase, wishing to evade her before she actually reached them. But she headed them off just before they arrived at the steps.

She addressed Kayenté. "I should like to speak to this child in private." She glanced at Kamara.

"No," Kayenté said with a devilish smile, "she's under my— protection."

"No?" hissed the Duchess. "Very well, than I shall speak to her in your presence."

Her eyes flicked hatred at Kamara. "Do you know my name?"

Kamara shook her head.

"And my husband, did you know of his name before you arrived here today?"

Kamara nodded. "My friend, Michael Randanscene spoke of him a time or two."

"Of course, that is the way, is it not, that the man is remembered and the woman fades away as if she never was. I am the Duke's wife . . . and the mother of three sons . . . and I'm nothing more. Even Michael, who I treated well, did not utter my name to you—not even once."

"What is your name?" Kamara asked.

"Jela. Does that name mean anything to you?"

"It is your name, "Kamara said softly, "and that means a great lot."

"You've never heard that name before, not even as a small child?"

"No," answered Kamara, perplexed by her line of questioning, "but I shall remember it."

"But in what way? Jela—the bitch?"

Kamara felt the pleading in Jela's heart, and reached her hand slowly toward the Duchess's face.

The Duchess grabbed her wrist forcefully as Kayenté had done earlier that day. "I do not wish your pity child, nor do I care if you remember my name. You are my nemesis. Remember that!" she shouted, casting Kamara's wrist away.

"But why?" Kamara asked.

Kayenté felt the Duchess close to physically attacking Kamara. He instinctively stepped between them, protecting Kamara, facing his mother. "Enough!"

The Duchess huffed, "Get rid of her Kayenté. She's trouble." Her voice thinned and cracked, "Son, oh son. Come back to this castle—come home."

Kayenté peered at her in silence, analyzing his mother's un-characteristically desperate behavior.

The Duchess grew teary and fled up the stairs.

"Oh, how she suffers!" Kamara said.

"Damn, Kamara!" he lashed, "who doesn't?"

Her face fell. "Oh, you suffer too, don't you?"

His eyes flared. "Silence, woman! You annoy me with your unceasing appetite to devour the sorrow of every man, woman, child, beast, bug, and blade of grass that you come upon!"

She stepped back from him, intimidated by his manner. He suddenly seemed so tall—and large. He stepped closer, enveloping her passivity.

His voice turned steely and low, edged with threat, and he spoke as if acting in a play, lines that came from somewhere very real within him. "Cast no more upon me those soft hearted eyes, nor open again your velvet rose mouth spiked with thorns, not even to so much as whimper. I care not for the heart of anyone, not even my own. The destruction of heart altogether would pleasure me greatly! Treat me justly, and I shall—you. Ignore my efforts, and you will be punished!"

Her gold angel eyes cried out, but her lips did not move.

He groaned, hurling her up the first stair step. "Climb!"

"No!" she said hotly, turning toward him. She stood on the first step, still shorter than he. Her tone sharpened, "I'm not your child. And I'm not little Kamara. I've kept harmony between over two hundred people at Lania Castle, and I've not only held order, but I've led each one to peace and I've saved the hearts of a hundred more. I have power—but my power is love. And I shan't let you reduce that and all of who I am to the size of a fly that annoys you." She shouted in his face. "Love matters! It just does, and you can't kill it, no matter how many hearts you bludgeon, because love . . . is mightier . . . than you!"

Kayenté's face steamed rage. What she said was bad enough, but did she have to cause a scene, airing her opinions in public as if she stood in her own castle?

He sighed heavily, regaining his wits that could be shaken by no one more than her. Even his mother and Taran could not distract him from his goals as quickly as she. He reminded himself that protecting her was only a debt of honor that he was paying Michael—nothing more, nothing more at all. So he enjoyed doing it— so what? He had battles to plan and political strategies to exact. He thought about the Rudels, about his goal to eventually rule Kantine. And that was everything, and the only thing that mattered.

He climbed the stairs past her, aware that she was searching the crowd who watched the minstrels sing, searching for one whom she could successfully manipulate to help her bring relief to the prisoner.

He reached back and grabbed her arm, hauling her up the stairs. He said lowly, "If you ask anyone to help you with the prisoner, they will accuse you of sedition and maybe witchcraft, especially after the miracle cure you just performed on the servant boy."

She felt truth in his words, and abandoned the idea. She stared at his back, following forlornly. "You are right, of course, so I beg you. Please let me tend this man in secret."

"You will return to your room and rest and respect the law of this castle. I have spoken."

"Please Kayenté." She stepped up to his side.

"You've become quite bold for a pacifist," he said. "However, are you prepared to challenge the one whose shield you hide behind? Should I turn you over to my mother, or Taran? Would you be happier in the arms of my father's men?"

She looked up at him with soft eyes. "You wouldn't do those things to me Kayenté. I know you wouldn't."

"I could."

"You wouldn't."

"I might."

She quieted, remembering all that he had done for her, and that he had indeed done nothing but protect her since the moment of her abduction. In spite of his badness, he was good too. He was. Not wishing to upset what little favorable connection they actually had, she decided to fulfill her mission in secret. She began mind searching for the distressed man's location. She felt his pain grow stronger when her mind reached east of the castle. She smiled faintly. She could find him now.

When they reached her bedchamber, Kayenté opened the door and pushed her in. "Stay. I'll have food brought to you. You will eat and then sleep."

"Perhaps you are right. I overreact when I am weary."

He scrutinized her. She did appear exhausted. Perhaps reason had found her at last. Perhaps. He nodded lightly. "Goodnight. Lock the door." He left, closing the door behind him.

He walked down the corridor and descended the stairs, when suddenly he had a feeling that she wasn't at all going to stay where he'd put her. She had too easily acquiesced, and healing others was the one area where she'd proven herself fearlessly assertive. He sprinted back up the stairway, flung open the door, and glanced into her empty bedchamber, for the third time now in this one evening.

Knowing she could locate places with her visionary power, he dashed down the corridor over the transition that led to the east tower. He reached the tower, and descended the stone slant through the tubular passageway that gave way to the torture chamber. He reached the passageway's end and looked down the short hall nearing his destination. Kamara was misting the guard at the door of the torture chamber. The guard turned toward the door, key in hand.

"Kamara!" he shouted with cold command, rushing toward her, "return at once!"

"Hurry," she told the guard, yet under her spell.

The guard slipped back the bolt, put the key in the keyhole, turned the key . . .

"Hurry, hurry!" said Kamara.

The guard pushed the door open.

Kamara's lifted her foot to step in. Before it touched the floor, Kayenté snatched her arm and swung her in a wide arc away from the door with such force, her face nearly slammed into the stone wall on the other side of the corridor. Her hands had risen to the wall instinctively. Her fingers were plumped with pain from repressing the healing power meant for the ailing man. Her own body riveted the shrill agony that the prisoner suffered. The cold stone seemed less cold than Kayenté's heart.

With a sturdy grip on her shoulders, he turned her body with his to face the guard. "Undo your spell."

Kamara beheld the guard, who was still ready to do her bidding. The door was right there, and the man who "called" but steps away. She tried to walk, pretending Kayenté wasn't there, but he was, and she went nowhere. "I'll undo the spell after the man is healed."

"Undo the spell now, Kamara, or you'll wind up a prisoner too, in there—with them." Then realizing that though such a threat would horrify anyone else, she'd jump at the chance to heal the imprisoned lot, even at her own expense. "Better yet," he said, "I'll torture the guard for disobedience, and make you watch."

"Oh!" she gasped, and then cocked her head innocently, "you don't really torture people do you?"

He almost laughed, but the predicament soured his humor. He looked her straight in the eye, and nodded.

"You do not!"

"I do."

"You wouldn't torture that poor man!"

"Oh, yes," he said cruelly, "I would."

Though she didn't believe that he really tortured people, she feared he would perform the deed just to make good his threat. She sighed long and hard, accepting that her attempt had failed. She said to the guard, "Sir, we are no longer bonded."

"That's it?" huffed Kayenté in disbelief.

"That's it!" she huffed back. "The power is in the focus, not the words."

The guard shook his head. "What am I doing? Lord Panther, forgive me . . . I—"

Kayenté interrupted, "Lock the door! And study this woman well. Do not trust her!"

The guard's face flushed. Then he turned to lock the door.

Kayenté wrapped his hand around Kamara's elbow, and towed her down the short hall. "My mother was right. You're nothing but trouble."

"Then send me home."

"Soon," he said, "and gladly."

"If you permit me to heal the man, I'll do as you bid until you send me home. But if you deny me, I'll fight you every way I can."

"You have changed since I've taken you away. The spring shower has become a thunderstorm. But you can't overpower me, little Kamara. I am a hurricane." He whisked her feet off the ground and slung her stomach over his shoulder.

"Put me down! Do you wish me to feel that man's pain all night?"

He turned up the sloping tunnel with his burden. "You are forbidden to engage with the prisoners, Kamara. Your refusal to obey commands will be met with punishment."

"I care only to ease the suffering of one man!" She tried to straighten up and slide off his shoulder but his grip on her legs did not yield. "Please, I beg you, if there is one shred of nobility in your forgotten heart, then grant me, you brute, this one last token of mercy!"

Kayenté answered flatly, "There isn't, and I won't."

He was right. Even as thunderstorm, she could not overpower him, for his thunderstorm could eclipse hers. Kindness was her weapon. She exhaled the Sacred Mists of Cohesion over him like a net.

He said, "I've told you, your mists no longer work on me, for I have set my task in motion to protect what is left of the ignorant poison tongued human part of you."

Guilt grabbed her. She had spoken ill of him again, breaking her promise over and over . . . and over once more. In her effort to save another, she had hurt him, and that hurt her. "I apologize for my tongue."

"I would not disarm your rotten tongue," he said.

"You wouldn't?" she asked, surprised.

"No. Your foul words enable me to dispassionately put you in your place."

"Oh! My place! My place! My place is to heal people. You *must* care that they suffer."

"Oh, back to that again. I don't care Kamara. I . . . don't . . . care."

"How can you *not* care!"

"I don't! We all suffer. We all die. We all have our turn."

His view saddened her. She went limp. "Release me, and I shall go peacefully to my room."

"Angel's honor?" he asked, with a light smile.

"Angel's honor." She would go to her room. But she would leave it again. She must, for Kayenté would never understand.

He lowered her feet to the ground, eyeing her suspiciously. Then he nudged her gently ahead of him up the walkway. "I am grateful I do not suffer your affliction."

"What affliction?"

"—the compulsive need to dally your heart in the cruel and bitter open."

She stopped and turned to him with a mystical gaze. "Your appraisal of my heart is most inaccurate."

"How is it then, soft lady, that you wilt and whimper upon the mildest sting of everyday life?"

"Because I find it abysmal that in everyday life, people's hearts are so hidden."

"An exposed heart only hurts and then dies. Look at you, suffering because you can't save a prisoner, or bring the Cold One into love. Are you not a victim of your own heart?"

"No, I am a victim of the coldness, of the lost conscience, of humankind disconnecting from its source. I am a victim of the people's failing memory. They have forgotten that we once all belonged to each other. They have forgotten that they were once a part of me." She gulped down the pain rising to her throat. "Oh no, heart is not my enemy. 'Tis only the lack of it, that pains me so. And I believe it pains you too."

He closed his eyes with grinding teeth. Would she never cease her eternal effort to convince him that heart, his in particular, had merit? He forced down his ire with a tense controlled exhale, and opened his eyes. "Exclude me from your fantasies." He grabbed her arm and led her toward her bedchamber.

She scowled at him all the way there.

When they reached her bedchamber, a woman servant was standing by the door with a plate of food, a goblet, and an open bottle of red wine.

"No wine," she said miserably, "'tis the devil's drink."

Kayenté said, "Drink the wine, Kamara."

"I can't," she said, "wine shall make me feel odd."

"Kamara, you are already as odd as you can be." Kayenté's expression glimmered with a hint of levity. "Drink it and maybe you'll feel normal."

Her peeved eyes slanted up to him in silence.

He told the servant to place the tray in her room and leave.

After she left, Kayenté said, "I'll see you in the morning."

He closed the door. She heard a click on the outside. She tried to open the door. She could not. He had *locked* her in. Locked. Her. In. "Kayenté!" she called, but he had already gone. She cursed him, for he had left her to endure the agony of the bearded man. She cried, "help!" by the door for so long, her plea became a scream. Either no one could hear through the heavy walls, or they'd been instructed to ignore her, for no one came.

She paced the floor in a frenzy, blood racing, body hurting, her rapid breath impeding air. The pain intensified, harder, sharper, throbbing, cutting, biting, stabbing—stabbing her eyes, her face, her limbs, her stomach! What was happening to her? Never before had she been restrained from healing another, and always the victims' ailments became hers until she could cure them.

She tried to cure the ailing man with her spirit, but that was not enough. She needed to flow the mists first hand, absorbing into his skin and muscle and bone. He needed food in his belly, and drink on his tongue. He needed to lie down and let the blood even out in his body. And sleep . . . he needed to sleep, safely. She *must* go to him. Her mind was unhinging, crazed, birthing a wild-eyed monster of hysteria—thrashing, and crashing inside her to get out.

Hold on. Hold on. Stay sane. Oh, dark of dark! Oh, hell of hells. Her skin felt afire. Her struggle in the "Black Wind" had been more bearable! Her nightmares of the Cold One had been less frightful! Hold on. Stay sane.

The pain mounted, roaring over her, unceasingly. Endurance was not possible. Let go. Become insane. The wild-eyed monster took her. After that, she knew not what she did, nor what happened, but the bedchamber walls contained primal screams retched free of reason, utterly ripping off the heads of hope and rolling them into the grave.

Kayenté sat through the last of the evening's entertainment, enduring jealous comments from his mother regarding his father's preoccupation with Kamara's 'goodness.' He empathized with her though. He'd felt that very way all the years she worshipped Taran.

After dinner, the Duke called a meeting with his sons and war leaders to discuss retaliation against the Rudels. They all agreed that while it was common for Rudels and Sakajians to engage in petty skirmishes over land boundaries and the like, something more was brewing. The skirmishes were escalating. The consensus was that the Rudels were planning to seize Kantine. Wincott Castle bordered Rudelia and Kantine, and further seemed the source of many recent uprisings. And King Harold Wincott of Rudelia had interestingly enough placed his own son in that castle.

The Duke planned to seek audience with his brother, King Aldos Ketola, to discuss strategies that would insure the stability of Sakajian rule in Kantine. If the King agreed, in three weeks time, Sakajian armies would unite. Kayenté would lead them into full-scale war on Rudelia, beginning with the seizure of Wincott Castle, and ending with seizure of all Rudelia. Kantine territory would increase substantially and a century of Rudelian threat would end. This would secure the ill King Aldos' decision to appoint Kayenté his successor. Eager to actualize that dream, Kayenté planned to return to his fortress in the morning and prepare his armies for the greatest battle of his life.

After the meeting was adjourned, Kamara came to mind. Had he been too hard on her? For all her strength of heart, she was a frail little thing. He decided to confide in his father about the incident. Maybe he wouldn't mind easing that one prisoner's discomfort—a little. The Duke may wish to please Kamara. After all, he believed her to be his daughter.

He called his father aside and explained the situation.

The Duke said, "Let us see how she fairs. If she sleeps, we will leave things as they are. If she is yet distressed, we can see to the prisoner."

They journeyed to her room. Kayenté unlatched the sealed door, while the Duke knocked lightly. There was no response. The Duke knocked harder. Kayenté did not possess such patience. He pushed it open, the door creaking on its heavy hinges. He did not see Kamara. The room was intact. The faintest whimpers sounded behind the bed's upper corner.

"Kamara!" Kayenté raced to her.

The Duke followed.

She was huddled on the floor in the tiniest compression, face pushed against her knees. Her disheveled lengthy hair was split on either side of her shoulders, exposing the back of her neck, making visible a large red welt. Her barely audible whimpering was constant.

They knelt to her. Kayenté lifted her face gently. Her skin was pasty white. She stared blankly through puffed black and blue lids, whimpers forthcoming. Faint red marks streaked her cheeks and chest.

"Good God," said the Duke, "the prisoner's wounds have appeared on her!"

Kayenté was choked with remorse. His little Kamara, his little bird. His fondness for her burned warm, causing pain in the once comfortable coldness of his heart. He said, "I never dreamed such an occurrence possible. Had I known this to be the result of my action, I'd have chosen an alternate course."

"Stay with her, Kayenté. I'll see to the prisoner." The Duke raced away, closing the door behind him.

Kayenté rolled her gently into his arms, and lifted her ice-cold body. She felt broken to him, perhaps irrevocably. He lowered her carefully to the bed. Though her faint whimpers were unceasing, she seemed unaware of his presence.

He took the soft wool burgundy blanket from the foot of the bed and tucked her in with artistic care, while she stared blankly. He crawled onto the bed and settled next to her on his side, curling his limbs around her to make a human nest for his little bird. He visualized his arm bleeding energy into her body, into her broken spirit. Had he done to her, what had been done to him? Had he destroyed the best of her?

His eyes were wet. Tears? Could this be? He was on the brink of attaining everything he wanted, so why should his eyes do this? Early boyhood was the last time the liquid rose. What was this woman, this mere . . . woman, doing to him? He laid with her for a long while, feeling the tension in her body ease. She had fallen asleep.

The door sounded with a light knock. Kayenté crept off the bed lightly, just as the Duke entered.

The Duke took an oil lamp off the wall and approached. "I had the prisoner removed from the straps, and relocated to a solitary room with a stone bed, bread, fruit, and water, and ordered salve upon his wounds."

"Then, that is why she sleeps at last," Kayenté said.

The Duke lifted the oil lamp to her face. "The marks are fading,"

Kayenté sighed hard. "They should have been prevented."

"You see, you must realize the extent of her sensitivity. I ask you to reconsider letting her stay with me."

"No. She stays with me."

The Duke walked to the door, signaling Kayenté to follow. Kayenté went to him, though reluctant to move farther from Kamara. The Duke replaced the oil lamp on the wall and spoke in a low tone. "Remember then, all I have told you. Light Priestesses are supernatural creatures, the true carriers of unconditional love, and many times more sensitive than we. And remember . . . no matter how tempted you may become, you are her brother."

"I've many women to please me. I don't need her."

"Yes, but Light Priestesses are alluring, especially to warriors whose lives are diametric from theirs. Get some sleep son, not in here though, that I wouldn't advise. I will see you both off in the morning, unless of course you decide to leave her here?"

"No, father."

The Duke nodded. "Very well then." He walked out the door.

Kayenté felt queer inside, almost dizzy. The man who had raised him was her blood father. Or according to the Wise One, maybe not, yet—she didn't actually say the Cold One was her father. Perhaps Kamara's mother had more than one child. And what if the Duke was his father and hers? What strange coincidence had befallen him? Could it be that she *was* his sister? Could he lust for his own sister?

He walked over to her, guilt-ridden, cursing silently for the substantial crack she'd made in his steel facade. He murmured lightly, "If the Cold One exists . . . I must slay him soon and send you back to Michael, before it's too late—for me. I should think you of the Duke's blood, for you, like him, are so noble. And I, I am more like the man I believe to be my true father. No, fair lady, you are not my sister."

He left the room, and called for several woman servants to change her into a soft bed gown that she may rest more comfortably. Then he went to his own room and laid upon the bed, the very one he had slept in as a boy. He drew his hands behind his head and stared into the black night. The old tentacles of his childhood plight with his mother, crawled up inside him once more, twisting, tormenting, torturing his heart, resurrected by Kamara—his little bird, refusing protection the same.

"Damn," he cursed lightly. He drifted to sleep muttering, "These women are going to kill me."

Ж
Chapter Eleven

Kamara awoke the next morning in dim light. The pain had ceased and the softest white nightgown clothed her body, low on the shoulders, nearly weightless on her skin. She searched her vague memory trying to make sense of what had happened, when she was overcome by a terrible thirst. She went reluctantly to the wine.

She'd never tasted wine before and though she'd heard stories about its powers, Michael and others had told her a few glasses were nothing to fret over. She lifted the wine bottle and filled the silver goblet with the dark red liquid. She drank the repugnant bitter drink straight down, much preferring fruit juice. To ease the bad after taste and her hunger, she began consuming the wilting vegetables, browning fruit, and stale bread from last night's supper.

As she ate, she recalled her last memory of the night before, when she had fallen insanely to a heap on the floor. How she got in bed or why the pain went away, she did not know. She did remember some one touching her kindly, but the details were fog.

However, of one thing she was quite clear: she *must* return to her own lands, her own world, her own way. Never again would she be denied the right to aid another. Kayenté's world seemed as awful as the Cold One's. Granted, the Cold One hadn't haunted her in her dreams last night, but why would he, she was already in hell.

She heard a terrible din outside and dashed to the casement window, pushing it open. Dust hung in a cloud around neighing horses and scurrying knights, who were yelling words she couldn't make out. Beyond them, she viewed pointy silver helmets rising up above the stone wall of the inner bailey. The helmets became heads, and the heads became bodies that flooded the courtyard. A horde

of Sakajians on foot swarmed the invading men and swords clam
ored. The castle was under attack! She could hardly believe her
eyes. War here! War now!

She slid her feet into the wine colored slippers, and flew out
the door, hoping to use the incident as a chance to escape Kayenté
and return home. She couldn't save this castle or the cold-hearted
people in it, but she could preserve her own domain. The wine suddenly hit her head and the world seemed to spin around her. She
wavered dizzily, unable to run straight, bumping the corridor walls,
and searching for passageways that might lead her to a remote
exit. Oh, the drink was cursed! Far worse than she'd imagined.

An armored knight in black and silver, raced toward her, fading in and out of sight. The metal on his smooth helmet, caught the
flames on the oil lamps and bounced a shine that hurt her eyes.
And when she could glimpse him once more, she noted a black brigandine that was a vest over his chain mail shirt, and metal pieces
covering various parts of him, wrists, knees, throat and the like. His
hips were laden with weapons she preferred to blur into non-
identity. She swallowed down the bile rising to her throat.

As the warrior came at her, she did her best to dodge him, hoping he was Sakajian, and under order not to harm her. But when
she sailed past him, he grabbed her waist. Their opposing momentum's collided and her feet left the floor, spinning her in a half circle. "I'm happy to see you, Kamara." He landed her feet on the floor.
"You look better! I am pleased."

Her speech was slurred, "Kayenté, is that you?" Her head fell
against his chainmail arm.

"Come along now, Kamara. We're going to my castle."

She drawled, "You are wearing armor. Remove it this
very instant!" She shook her finger. "I forbid you to fight."

"You're drunk," he said, with a half-cocked smile. He moved
her down the hall, her head heavy on his arm.

"I was thirsty," she replied. "Remind me not to get
thirsty again."

"It is well that you were thirsty," he mumbled, almost to himself. "Perhaps you'll fare better with what is to come."

He led her through secret passage ways until they emerged outside at the back of the castle. She shivered in the cold, gray air. He pulled her across the back courtyard, his eyes darting to spy the enemy. Then he fairly threw her to the top of a brown stone wall.

She sat precariously on the edge, her world whirling. He scaled the wall, jumped down on the other side, and instructed her to fall into his arms. Without thinking of the danger, she fell. He caught her tightly, and eased her to the ground.

He felt the enemy at his back like Black Death crawling on his skin. "Be my shadow Kamara, like before." He spun around with sword swinging, met by the swords of two Rudelian knights.

Kamara simply stood there, disconnected from reality, watching Kayenté parry the blade so prettily with a speed and precision that seemed alien to humankind. Or maybe, the wine made it seem so. Anyway, she found it beautiful. The sword dance, she thought.

Then she realized that the men weren't dancing, but fighting before her very eyes and she had not the where with all to stop it. She wanted to avert her gaze, scared of seeing something bloody, but the dance was so stunning, she couldn't.

Kayenté thrust his blade into the stomach of one attacker. With bulging eyes, the victim moaned and uttered something in another language. Kayenté yanked out the blade. The man dropped to his knees. Blood streamed over his hands that sought in vain to plug the wound.

Kamara muttered, "A dream, right Kayenté?"

"Yes Kamara, a dream," he said, as he blocked a strike above his head, from the other Rudel's sword.

Two Sakajian warriors appeared behind his opponent with shouts of death, and the Rudel began swinging at them. Though Kayenté craved to kill another, he tore himself away and let his fellow Sakajians take the fight. He towed Kamara in her daze, over to his nervously flinching warhorse. He mounted with sword in hand,

and hauled Kamara up behind him. She landed roughly, her legs straddled and gown hiked up in a most unlady-like fashion. But as she was only dreaming, what did she care? And when the stallion started to go, she leaned her cheek against Kayenté's back and circled her arms lightly around his middle.

They rode through a passage in the outer curtain wall, crossing the deep moat by way of a hidden bridge inches below the water's surface. They emerged in the outer courtyard. In seconds, Rudels and Sakajians surrounded them, on foot and horseback, locking them in the middle of vicious combat.

"This is a very bad dream," she mumbled, though aware on some level that it was nothing of the sort.

Somebody yanked her to the ground, holding her tight. Then she realized Kayenté wasn't on his horse either. The battle was so thick that all she could see were pieces of swords, and axes, parts of armor, patches of horse, and flashes of ground, spinning round and round.

The person holding her groaned and fell limp, releasing her from his grip. Had he been killed? Who was he? Friend. Foe. Kayenté? She could see no one and nothing clearly in the kaleidoscope of battle. How could they?"

She crawled carefully through dancing feet, under clanking swords, and a rain of blood. She heard whisking and whipping, thumps and thuds, grunts and groans, curses, prayers, and the blasting beat of a thousand hearts, the world yet spinning round and round.

She prayed the warriors would be too engaged in battle to bother with her. Her gown kept catching under her knees, pulling the neck down around her shoulders. Metal feet slammed down around her. Something wet poured over her neck and dripped down her skin curving around her throat. It smelled like blood. However, everything reeked of blood. She kept moving, forbidding tears, wishing she'd drank a second glass of wine, for the elixir seemed to distance her somewhat from the horrors she normally felt.

Ahead, on the outskirts of the battle, she glimpsed a lone oak tree ahead of her, looming there, a live thing, like a mother bidding her to come and fall upon her breast.

Thinking only of the tree, the tree, the beautiful tree, she found herself more quickly there. She dropped her shoulder against the fragrant bark, and curled into a tight ball, very still, afraid to move, lest a knife come flying at her, the way Kayenté had once told her it could.

Her eyes were closed, but the image of swords and bludgeoned bodies flashed erratically in her mind. This battle was like the one in her nightmare: warriors, swords, blood, and she curled against a tree in a dirty white gown, trembling. Would the Cold One appear next?

Her arm was snatched. Someone pulled her forward so swiftly, she felt like a shooting star. Her vision blurred, so fast they did run. When they stopped, she fell to her hands and knees in the thick foliage, panting hard with burning lungs. Some one stood next to her. Would she now behold the Cold One? What was, was. And what was to be, was to be. She could not change it, so she sat back on her knees and looked up to see dust covered leather pants, and a sword dripping blood. Raising her eyes further, she saw Kayenté's face. It was Kayenté who towered over her!

Her hand flew to her heart. "You aren't the Cold One."

He squatted, resting the sword over his knees. "I don't know about that."

"Nor I!" she said, seeing a blood spray on his sweaty brow. She thrust her palm against his chest. "You abandoned me in that chaos Kayenté."

He glimpsed his chest where she had pushed him, and watched her hand withdraw, surprised by her uncharacteristic attempt at aggression, so subdued that it amused him. "I did not abandon you. I guarded you constantly. When that Rudel grabbed you off my mount, I sunk your sword into his neck. As you crawled along, I maimed and slew every Rudel around you." He glanced at her sword. "It performs well, better than I'd hoped, lighter than I like, but perfect for a slapping parry."

She held her turbulent stomach. "Are you trying to make me feel better, Kayenté?"

He pointed toward a field of tall green grass. "You'll feel better if you crawl out there and hide in the grasses. Stay low, move slow, and you won't be noticed. I want to fight more. Then I'll find my warhorse and we'll be off."

"You *want* to fight? You wish to revisit that butchery?"

He landed a primeval kiss on her lips, a kiss that boasted merriment. And then, he was gone. He seemed a chipper fellow, happy even—no, he was virtually ecstatic, or maybe the wine was yet hazing the truth. Now, she wished she'd not drank the first glass. Oh, when would this dazed and whirling sensation end? How could one tell what was what under this influence!

She looked to the meadow, hiked her gown to her thighs, and crawled away from the action. She moved slowly but steadily, willing herself to pass unseen in the brush. Yet, the further away she got, the faster she moved, needing sanctuary too badly for patience to matter. Her hands and knees burned, but she focused on the flowers as she mowed them down in her heedless flight, praying silently for them to forgive her.

The sun was dissolving the gray air, lending vibrant color to the meadow foliage that looked greener by the moment. She thought of how she so very much loved the sweet things of the earth, and more than ever, she longed to be home.

She crawled and crawled—and crawled, until she felt that she had crawled enough. She rolled on her back, breathless and closed her eyes, too shocked to think or feel, numbed by all that had happened to her in only the short while she'd been gone from her castle. She lay for some time, drifting in and out of sleep from the whirring in her head.

"Kamara!"

Her eyes flew open to see Kayenté looming over her. His skin glistened with moisture. His wild black hair was capped with a shining helmet, against the backdrop of a brilliant blue sky, under a bright yellow sun. Blood streaked Kayenté's bruised cheekbone. Sweat dripped around his azure eyes.

She was happy to see him, grateful he'd returned alive, relieved that the fight must be over.

He squatted beside her, elbow on knee, the grasses taller than his head. "Are you all right?"

"No," she sat up, much less dizzy than before, the wine wearing off at last. "I don't like this sort of thing. I don't like it at all."

"This sort of thing?" he asked with a half smile.

"You know what I mean," she said, her eyes watery, "I've experienced more violence with you in one day than I have in my entire life."

"Kamara, what you have experienced *is* everyday life."

"Everyday life! Maybe for you. How can you live this way?"

"It's exciting."

Her mouth dropped open. "Exciting!" Her throat tightened. "I. . . you . . . I . . . exciting? You . . ." She looked at her lap silently, too exasperated for speech. Her long hair fell over her face and blood-smeared throat. The suffering of others—excited him. Had hers? She snapped her face toward him and blurted, "You put me through hell last night."

"It wasn't my intention," he said, "and I ensured your escape."

"Oh," her eyes softened, "so that was you." She paused, and then said, "I wonder, were you *excited*?"

"Not even a little," he said. He realized she needed some small token of victory over him, and thus added, "My father and I saw to your prisoner."

"You did?" Her eyes lit. "Truly?"

Kayenté nodded.

"Well," she crumpled her forehead in determination. "I shall never let you put me through that again."

"We'll handle it differently, if there's a next time," he said.

She cocked her head and studied his sincerity.

However, he rose and changed the subject before she could arrive at a conclusion. "Now that I see you are well, I will locate my mount, and then we'll make haste to my castle."

She jumped to her feet and stepped backwards, blasting her open palms in front of her as if to block him. "Oh no, I *refuse* to go there. I'm not going to experience one moment more of *your* reality!" Hearing an uprising in the distant din of war, she turned her head to the fighting.

He could see the shadow of her body through the sunlit bloodied gown, drooping low on her shoulders. His animal instincts were peeked, and he barely arrested the eruption of a wanton moan.

She snapped her anxiety-ridden face to him. "They—they are still fighting! I thought it was over, that you came to me because it was over!"

"Kamara, an attack rarely ceases in sight of an hour."

"Kayenté, you cannot . . ." she began to see him differently, "go back there."

"I can. I will. And soon I'll return."

"Kayenté, this isn't you! This apathy about killing, I mean this joy you have for it, this adoration, this is *not* you!"

"Now you see me, little Kamara. Look hard. Look well. Study every detail. And remember this the next time you want to convince me that my heart is noble."

She saw him then, full fare, as he was—a killer. Her horror-filled eyes stretched wide in shock of her newfound sight: *blood* blotched black leather boots; *blood* splashed metal on his knees, elbows, shoulders, mail shirt; *blood*-wetted black brigandine with a hunk of sinew smashed above the waist; blood stained belted, weapons of axe and some spiky thing. His sword's sheath was not bloody, but she knew the sword was. His metal-gloved hands were bloody. His naked fingers poking through were bloody. His helmet was bloody. *Blood* smeared face. *Blood* matted hair. Blood, blood, blood! Butcher! Cruel, bloodthirsty warrior fed by the carnage he'd made! Carnality ruled his eyes. The devil ruled his soul!

Her chest heaved with weighted breath. "Haaa," she gasped, barely able to suck in enough air to speak further, "Look at you . . . you—" she pointed at him, "Lord of Destruction! Lord of Darkness!" She whispered in a gasp, "*Such* darkness. I did not see it before. Your lust to kill exceeds defending life and land. You kill for . . ." she clutched her heart, and shook her head with the deepest sorrow, "pleasure."

"I do at that. I've not ever told you different."

She gasped with teary breath, "I don't know this side of you!" She turned to run, but he caught her arms and made her face him.

"Side?" he said. "This *is* me. And I'm too far gone to be saved, little Kamara—even by you."

She snapped her head to her shoulder, appalled, ashamed, and sick to her stomach, "It can't be. How can I be drawn to—"

"—a man who lives to kill?"

She nodded her head profusely, her eyes averted to the grass.

He replied, "You are drawn because, as once you said . . . you need me. You need storm. You need freedom from your self built cage."

She blurted defensively, her eyes yet averted, "I was wrong!" Each word rang with a cry. "I . . . need . . . to go . . . home!"

"Then you don't know what you need," he retorted. "Wait here while I retrieve my warhorse."

She flung her head up to face him. "How can you remain calm about this? Your brothers, your father, could be lying in a pool of blood right now. If you go back there, the pool of blood might be yours!"

"That is a chance warriors take."

"Have you no fear!"

He stepped back, "I have hate, Kamara. And that is enough." He began to turn away.

Surprising herself, her hands flew up and grabbed his arm. "Kayenté, please don't go back into that violence! Come with me to my castle. You can rest there and let me take care of you."

He stared at her bright face, so alive with hope. His eyes softened, genuinely touched by her out of the question proposal. He soaked in her radiance before his answer would make it fade. He smiled faintly. "That's a sweet offer, little Kamara, but I have other plans."

Her body stiffened. She drew in a shaky breath, and exhaled, "Not I." She withdrew her radiance, a faded flower that could only be vibrant under certain conditions. "I'm going home." She turned, and walked away.

"Kamara! Wait here for me. I will come for you, if you do not."

She whisked her body around to face him, crossed her arms over her chest, and sat down in a huff. "I detest you."

He declared, "Even so, you will return with me to my castle."

"Why?" she wailed, flinging her arm upward in a gesture of exasperation, "Go back to your castle and greet your bride, your lover, your comrade in conquering. Protect her, flaunt her, and make her your Queen. I am not anything to you anyway. Killing is your passion, violence your treasure, and blood your reward! Consider your promise to Michael fulfilled. Your part is done, over." She trembled hard.

Kayenté removed his gloves and then his helm, dropping them in the grass. A little spray of gnats flew up around the metal.

Her bewildered expression grew fear. Why had he done that? What consequence had her words initiated?

He strolled over to her with seductive eyes, wild blue oceans promising adventure.

She rolled her golden orbs warily upward. His war-worn face glowed fire, baking something wonderful.

He knelt, gazing into her with what exceeded manly want. There was something more, something lost—but hiding still, just peeking out, barely. He placed his palms on her shoulders. With pressure firm, he rubbed his hands slowly up and down her arms, calling forth what she suppressed.

She thrilled with each snaky tendril of sensation that slithered from her womb, out of hiding. She loved the warmth, the comfort of that movement, what came through his fingers, that thing peeking out. And she was ashamed for feeling it.

He slid his fingers under her arms, touching the sides of her breasts, drawing her up until they both stood. Molten lava desire filled her womb; lightning charges followed. She fantasized his touch would fill her more. Her mind flashed shameful scenes of bodies entwined. She craved, wanted, needed his touch. Her body wanted, needed, begged exploration. Oh how sinful of her body to be needing, begging, and demanding more! Oh how sinful was she!

Proper action dictated that she should slap his face or some such thing. He'd no right to elicit uncontrolled passions from her. But the heat he kindled proved so pleasant, she could not bring it upon herself to object. She could only look at him naively. What next?

His lips came slowly to her. Slowly. Slowly. Forever. Oh, when would they land! When would they touch her! Then she felt it. His tongue on her mouth, licking softly, like tasting honey, mixed with blood. And she almost licked him back, but no, resistance was imperative, for there was no future here, not now, not ever!

He drew her against his armored body. Remnants of death soaked into her gown. He clutched the back of her hair and pulled her head back slightly; his light kisses turned deep and probing. Then he withdrew his mouth from hers. "You were saying?"

She tried to halt her heavy quivering breath. He mustn't know her desire! She cleared her throat and spoke in a high broken pitch, "I said, ah," she cleared her throat again, "that your part . . . is ah—done, over."

He smiled richly and retorted with confidence, "Oh no, little Kamara, it has without a doubt—just begun."

He backed up a few steps, locking his gaze into hers, in an arrogantly provocative stance. He turned and walked away, scooping up his gloves and helm, replacing them on his body as he sauntered in a smooth long stride back toward the fight.

Even with all his arrogance and . . . wrongness, she wanted to race after him, but no. She would not submit. Though her body was yet charged with sensations almost too strong to deny, submission was not an option. She watched him grow smaller and smaller as the distance between them lengthened. When she could barely see him anymore, she muttered, "No, it must be over." To darkness, she would *never* submit.

When he was out of sight, she walked south toward her castle, trying not to smell the scent of death that stained her gown and caked thick on her neck. She 'misted' herself and journeyed all the day until the air turned chilly and dark.

Kayenté hadn't come for her. Was he dead? Or had he given up on her after all? She sought a place to sleep, scanning the moss covered pines and thick shrubbery that yielded the most pungent scent. Insects emerged with the darkness and a little black winged bug lit on her face, embedding its stinger in her skin.

"Ouch." She brushed the pest from her cheek and accidentally squashed it in her palm. She looked upon the mashed creature. "Oh," she said, "I'm your murderer, yet my heart holds no malice towards you. Violence it seems cannot be avoided. And I know that even as I run toward love, in any given moment, I may meet my doom as did this poor creature on my hand. Oh the prey and the predator, how I dread that contact!"

She brushed the insect off her hand and rested her body in a circle of scratchy bushes. The cold hard ground chilled her bones. She curled on her side. In the palm of one hand, she rested her cheek; the other, she pressed against her rumbling stomach.

She yearned to sink her teeth into the white pulp of a juicy green apple. Even a single drop of water would greatly please her parched tongue. Her soiled gown lay heavy like grease upon her body. If not for the cold air, she would have shed the garment in haste.

Night breezes numbed her face and hands. She rolled on her back to gaze upon the starry sky, vast and brilliant above her. Suddenly, the ground seemed less harsh. And for a glorious moment she felt swept into the star clusters, her troubles gone, her faith renewed.

Tears dribbled over her temples, wetting her hair. She cried aloud, "Oh, Great Mother of Heaven, I want to come home to your divine white light before the Lord of Darkness makes me one of his own. Already I've seen and felt the forbidden. I've hidden behind the sword, not trusting love to save me. I've run from love, hating the beast that seems to lurk in every human being. Even me!—even me.

"I cannot stand that I am as they, dripping in scorn and tainted desire. My body craves to merge with a man whose spirit wreaks of spilled blood, a man who would cast love away and marry for material consumption. I shame my body for having such longing. If I were to live the life of a woman, at least I should choose a man who wouldn't have me discard my cape of honor, though it be frayed and unkempt around the edges."

And then she thought silently, that even Michael would not suit her honor, for he'd sold her to the sword. And though he did so in exchange for her life, she couldn't forgive him for such a sale, when he knew more than most the sanctity of her way.

Then she said aloud, "If a knight is sanctioned to die with honor, then why can't I? Am I to live that I may know the shame in forsaking my people, and—myself? Am I to live only to experience falling from 'the light?' Oh Sacred Mother, have mercy! Sweep me into your heaven, I beg you, before temptation locks me in hell!"

She jumped when she heard the neighing of a horse. She bolted upright. Was Great Mother somehow answering her prayers? Or had Kayenté at last come for her? She peeked through the tall shrubs, and saw a white glow in the darkness. She rose and stepped lightly through the blinding blackness nearing the glowing object. Twilight! She'd found her mare!

She sprinted to her glorious horse that she had thought forever gone, lost to the Black Wind. But alas, the dear animal stood before her! She stroked the soft fur and pressed her cold cheek against its warm muzzle, feeling the bridle in place. Then she walked to the mare's side and felt the saddle. Even though it was dark, she wanted to mount, deeming the occurrence a sign from Great Mother.

The frigid wind blew, rustling leaves, teasing hair tendrils over the shadow of her face, in the oh so very dark and moonless night. Then a tingle shot up her spine. Her heartbeat sputtered. Danger?

She sensed the presence of a foreboding mass to the right of her. She held her breath, turned her head slowly, and saw a large figure, a shadow dark against the even blacker night.

"Whose there?" she asked.

"Your doom," returned the dark mass. His voice rumbled low like thunder rolling toward her. "Your . . . nightmare." He blew a frosty breath at her, blowing her hair upward behind her back.

She shivered and stepped away. "You are the Cold One."

He stepped forward, the bulk of him eclipsing her.

Her skin prickled.

"You left your shield behind. How fortunate for me."

Her voice trembled with her body, "My shield?"

"The Warlord!" he roared.

She jumped.

He laughed. Then his voice softened, "You are so easy. Light Priestesses always are."

Slightly incensed by his assumption, she asked bravely, "Who are you? I mean, who are you really?"

He answered, "I'm whoever you don't want me to be. And I can be what ever I choose. With your mother, I was the vampire, seducing her into a world far beyond her dreams, shaming her for all time."

Kamara's face paled. "My mother?"

"With your warlord's mother, I was the barbarian. Ah! Noble women are most delicious."

"What—what did you say?" she stuttered, not sure she heard him right. Had the Cold One been Kayenté's tormentor as well?

"And you—ah yes . . . you are most frightened by brute force, so, I gift you with the barbarian."

She shuddered. "You . . . are . . . so . . . very . . . wicked."

"I—?" he said, "—am not wicked. The exceedingly lustful who stop at nothing to satiate their desire, for blood, copulation, wealth, and power, like your Warlord—they are wicked. I crave none of those things."

She swallowed hard. Trepidation scourged her soul. "Then—if you are not wicked, what—what are you?"

In a breathy whisper, he answered, "Why—I am The Nothing. I am the destiny of those who inhale life, taking until there is no more to take. And I am the destiny of those who exhale life, giving themselves away, until there is no more to give. Without each other, the charitable giver, and the self-serving taker—fall prey to me."

"So," she said, her voice still trembling, "if I were to take and fulfill my human needs, then you would not come for me?"

"I've not come for you. You have come to me by your own act of self-deprivation, refusing shield and sword to guard your life force. I am your inevitable desolation. You had a chance with the Warlord, and he had a chance with you."

"But now," he said, "you are both mine."

He slashed her gown with a knife, cutting the cloth until the shredded pieces fell to the ground, leaving her naked. She couldn't move or speak, or calm her choppy panting breath. She was even too frightened to mist, and if her dreams held true, 'misting' was useless anyway.

His large hands engulfed her shoulders. "Kamara Lania, angel who would not fall—so now she is taken."

He forced her to the ground, flat on her back. She felt the top of her head suctioned, the same as when she was in the Black Wind. But this time—all hope had fled. She could not survive this situation. She was defeated.

His naked body came down, crushing her beneath him, pressing pinecones and rocks into her back. Her nightmare had come to pass. Air. She needed air.

"You have submitted to me." His hard shaft bumped against her womanhood, trying to break the seal to enter.

She thought of Kayenté, wishing he was present, wishing he could save her. A sudden wave of rebellion consumed her body. Her hands pushed against his muscled arms. "No!" she screamed with full lungs at a pitch so high and loud, she felt it not her own. "N o . . . !   I . . . d o . . . n o t . . . s u b m i t!" Her hands pushed increasingly harder against him. Then she was pushing against the air. He was gone.

She rolled to her side and sobbed hysterically, squeezing her eyes shut, denying what had happened. After a few minutes, she feared the Cold One may have returned, so she peeked through her eyelids to see if he was there. A red thin light hung before her. She was so baffled by its appearance that her sobbing transformed to whimpers.

She rolled onto her hands and knees to better view the thin red line that hovered before her. A sword it was—a sword of light.

A male voice echoed in her head, "Accept the sword—or die."

"Oh, but what shall I lose," she wailed, "if I accept the sword?"

"Oh, what shall you lose," said the male voice, "if you do not?"

She snatched the grip of the red light sword. Power charged her hand, numbing her arm. The sword grew larger and larger, as large as she, and flew inside her body.

She jolted. Her eyes inflated. Lightning charges exploded within her, one after another, throwing her body into convulsions and her breath into irregular huffing, until she could not breathe at all. She slipped from consciousness.

Ж
Chapter Twelve

Heavy, Kamara felt heavy. She opened her eyes. Gray skies above her. Something covered her. She slanted her eyes down. A black blanket, no a cloak it was. She moved her eyes side to side: shrubs, moss. The ground was hard and she was cold.

She lifted her head, straining her neck so much that it fell back down. She rested a moment and tried again. This time she pushed her elbows back and propped her upper body on them. A mass of sticker branches fell to her lap. Resting there a moment more, she pushed her palms back on the ground and propped her body against them. She realized then the cloak wasn't on her, but around her, securely tied in place, serving as a heavy dress. And she was grateful, for she was naked underneath. Her head throbbed. Dizziness sent her flat to the ground. She lay there for several minutes and tried again to rise, but could not. After a short while, with determination set, she pried herself upward and sat with sickened stomach and a spinning in her head. She threw the sticker branches off her, and stared at the ground to gain balance.

When at last the dizziness passed, she looked forward. Her eyesight blurred, then cleared. Through an opening in the bushes, she saw the back of a thin woman in a frayed brown shift with snow-white hair swirled in a messy bun. She was tending a fire. The woman turned around with a big smile. She approached Kamara holding a tin cup of steaming liquid. The nearer she came, the more her dark eyes glimmered, and cheer danced on her wrinkled face.

She reached Kamara in the scant space encircled with bushes, and handed her the cup.

Kamara clutched the warm cup gratefully. "Who are you?" she

asked.

"Drink child. I shall return in a moment." The woman headed back toward the fire.

Kamara lifted the cup to her parched lips. Her arms ached, heavy as stone, making even this small task a challenge. She sipped the steaming tea of peppermint, spearmint, and catnip as well. Flavor burst in her mouth. She savored the pleasant sensation of hot liquid sliding down her throat, washing down inside her, soothing the hungry ache in her belly, and the horrible thirst in her body.

She had nearly finished the tea when the woman returned with a piece of burlap that supported a little pile of walnut pieces, blackberries, and one carrot with the roots hanging off it. She rested the cloth on Kamara's lap and sat down in front of her.

Kamara gazed affectionately at the kind woman. "I thank you for your care."

"You need a lot of it," she said with whimsy, "and you will require more nourishment than usual for a time. Eleven days have lapsed since last you ate or drank."

Kamara's almost dropped the cup. "Eleven days! That explains my laden condition. That I am alive does not seem possible."

"Indeed," replied the woman. "Had you not fed off the energy you absorbed before your collapse, and if you were not part angel, you would not have survived. Even so, 'twas not easy hiding you from the many passing by." She pointed to the sticker branches, "Camouflage, you see?"

Kamara cocked her head. "How do you know so much of me?"

The old woman replied, "I am the Wise One, devoted messenger of the sisterhood."

Kamara's face jutted forward in frozen shock. "*You*—are the Wise One?" Her dehydration forbade tears, but the unseen tears of joy were there. "You *are* real. After all these years, I can barely believe you are here before me. I am too weak to bow at your feet. However—" she bowed her head, "I am humble."

"And yet, you believed I betrayed you."

Kamara hung her head in despair. "I no longer know what to believe."

"Feed your starved body child, and then I shall impart the untold story of your life."

Kamara's heart quickened. She shook her head in disbelief. Could it be the time had come at last to know all Teeah would not tell? After all the years of prying and begging for answers, was this the moment of truth? She popped one berry in her mouth, and then another, taking in the food perhaps too quickly, until every morsel resided in her stomach.

The Wise Woman clapped her palms to her knees in an act of triumph. "Now that you have fed your body. I shall feed your mind, but you must listen with open ears."

"I shall," promised Kamara, making sure burlap and cup were well to the side of her. She hugged her knees, and stared intently at the Wise One.

The Wise One spoke. "There are four secrets waiting to be revealed. Once they are, you shall not only understand your destiny, but you shall know how to fulfill it.

"The first secret is this: the Cold One is all that isn't. He is the hungry void that laps existence into a black hole. His goal is to nullify humanity. His method is to obliterate the Light Priestesses by usurping their spirits, and to pit the general population against each other until they become so destructive, no one survives. Their spirits then are easily sucked into The Nothing.

"You, Kamara, were born into a time of great wickedness, amongst thousands of people pillaging the heart with reckless abandon—rioting life with an absolute loss of moral constraint. These people were labeled evil and of the dark.

"The clergy feared the obliteration of humankind, so they proclaimed all people bad, and convinced many that in order to save their souls, they must abide spiritual laws. Those that turned to the clergy, many of whom were nobles, became lawful and extremely moral. So moral in fact that they persecuted everyone who did not

exercise their particular strict code of conduct. The clergy advocated punishment for the dissenters and claimed the right to dominate them, in the name of the Lord and in the name of the Law.
These clerical persecutors were labeled good and of 'the light.'

"But these clerics were not of 'the light,' even though they believed they were, for true light bearers judge not, and love uncondi-
tionally. 'Twas all the Cold One's trickery. These religious figures
did, and still do, exhibit much of the same violence executed in the
wayward world.

"The Cold One bred darkness, overwhelming 'the light.' Priestesses over-exerted themselves to teach true love and light while
they could. Most of the Priestesses grew weary and fell prey to the
Cold One. Others, who left their temples were deemed witches and
burned at the stake, even though they had never harmed another.
They were blamed for any and all mishaps anyway, because they
were so different.

"The Cold One was heavy upon them, but because Light Priestesses are not born with a destructive side, they did not fight back.
Instead, they loved him. They journeyed into his empty chasm to
find his spirit. But he has no spirit. And once they were in his
realm, he kept them. They learned all too late that to survive the
Cold One, they must become the whole breath of life, not only exhaling to give, but inhaling to take.

"The Cold One was simply meant to be the turning point of inhaling and exhaling, of night and day, a moment's pause in the way
of things. But he has gone astray, for we have gone astray. The Light
Priestesses exhaled and exhaled until they could give no more. And
the people inhaled and inhaled until now they are ready to burst.

"And the Cold One grows more powerful, because no one can
see that the downfall of humankind has nothing to do with what
law or lawlessness one lives by, but rather in the way that people
judge each other. Differences are not acceptable. Mystery is feared.
What we fear is to be conquered and forgotten. It is as if human-

kind is a magnificent tapestry that is unraveling itself, instead of seeing the greater picture.

"The Cold One laughs, for if this continues, he can win. And the humans lose, because they have no vicissitude to become more than they are and less than they've been. The takers must give, the givers must take; the warriors must love, and the lovers must war."

Kamara said, "That's why you gave me the sword!"

"Yes, for that reason . . . and another, which brings me to the second secret: You are the champion that the Priestesses created. They chose to mate your mother, the most powerful Priestess, with a mighty, yet honorable lord, so that you'd be born with a balance of the truest light and the most powerful dark.

"But there were complications and it became necessary for the Priestesses to ban your dark side, and once they did, they could not get it back. You, must get it back. We've waited long for you to come of an age when you could commence that process. We've sheltered you from the Cold One as long as possible, hiding you, manipulating you to stay on Lania Land. Without your dark side, you were a thousand times more vulnerable to the Cold One than any Light Priestess had ever been, for you were virtually void of male energy. You did not carry your father's legacy as did other Priestesses, even though their fathers were peace-loving men.

"But your time as a pure expression of love at Lania Castle has been well spent. You've created a true sanctuary of enlightenment, spreading hope into the vast and dark brutality of these times. You shine Lania Castle like the sun, balancing all who have come to you. The seeds of true love now grow in many. The Cold One abhors this.

"If love is restored in the world, then the breath of life shall stabilize and thereby halt the Cold One's out of control consumption of humankind. So he seeks you. He seeks you boldly and wildly. And you now shine so brightly that you cannot hide from him anymore, except behind a war shield. And you did—for a while. You allowed the destructive element to protect you."

"Kayenté?" Kamara asked.

"Yes," replied the Wise One, "you allowed him to protect you several times, did you not? And that essence that is him was in the red spirit sword that you absorbed."

Kamara cracked a faint smile. "No wonder I fell unconscious."

"No wonder indeed," the Wise One said with a sparkle in her eye.

Kamara's smile faded, thinking of Kayenté in bloodlust mode. Then she stared hard at the Wise One who seemed to know her so well. "How do you know of these many things that have happened to me?"

"I follow you child. I have, since you were born. I am your emissary, bequeathed with the responsibility of guiding you to fulfill the destiny for which you were created."

"What must I do now?" Kamara asked, her face earnest with appeal.

"You tell me, child. You are our champion. What must you do next?" The Wise One touched Kamara's forehead. "Let go of the teachings. Search your heart. What action feels right for you?"

Kamara shut her eyes. She soared into her own soul. Several silent minutes passed. Then she jolted, snapping open her eyes. "It cannot be!"

"What child?" asked the Wise One. "What cannot be, that already is?"

"I feel I must retrieve and return Kayenté's sword somehow, even though I—I ordered it destroyed. I must accept and wield my own sword. I must humble myself and ask Kayenté to teach me. There is nothing of greater importance."

The Wise One pat Kamara on the head and smiled. "You've done well, and fear not, Kayenté's sword has been spared."

"Spared! But I told Camille—"

"She did not undermine you. Great love was required for her to act in ways that you'd clearly misunderstand."

Kamara nodded. "That is true." She paused and then sighed deeply. "What then of the third secret?"

"You're not ready for the third secret, nor the fourth."

"But I don't know how to defeat the Cold One!"

"You've begun the process. You made him disappear!"

"But I don't know how I accomplished that feat."

The Wise One stroked her wizened fingers against Kamara's cheek. "When you pushed your hands against him, you reversed your flow, rejecting instead of connecting. He was not expecting that from you. No Light Priestess had ever done that before. And you can thank the Warlord for that act of rebellion, for it was from him—you learned it. The other Priestesses failed to—"

"Where are the other Priestesses? Teeah says they roam, but where do they roam, why do they roam? Why do they never come to me?"

Teeah held her hands. "Their spirits are gone, and they've lost hope."

"They live, but without their spirits?"

"Many have lost their bodies. Yet many have retained them—without spirit. Empty and alone they are, powerless and fragile, fading with each passing day—into The Nothing."

"And you, Wise One, does the Cold One seek your spirit?"

"The Cold One has my spirit."

Kamara's jaw dropped, horrified by the Wise One's confession. "But I thought the taken, lost hope? You have hope!"

"I have you. You are my hope. You *are* hope, and without you, there is none. Heed my words, Kamara Lania—the chosen one: Humankind is flowing into emptiness. The Cold One is emptiness. It is a non-place of stagnation, petrified time, so to speak. If the human spirits are gone from the earth, so shall follow the spirit of animal, plant, and all others; for all forms of life are connected. Without the fire of spirit, then water, air, and matter diminish. The earth shall dissolve.

Kamara gripped the Wise One's hands, even as they held hers. "Dissolve?"

"Yes. The earth was created to allow souls to move into physical experience, to learn about light and dark, to alchemize the polarities and experience change, like the caterpillar into butterfly, like the child who moves from the womb to the outside world.

"This earth is our vehicle for that transition. If we regress, rather than progress, if we devolve rather than evolve—then the earth shall fade away. We are devolving and that flow must be reversed. Only then can people begin to accept each others differences and discover ways to work together, and thereby insure the survival of humankind."

Kamara asked, "Evolvement then, requires all of us to bridge each other—even with the Cold One."

"Yes," affirmed the Wise One again. "But you cannot bridge the Cold One with your usual method. You must find a way, more different than anything you could presently imagine, that way which is the fourth and final secret. If you find that way, you shall free all the spirits taken by the Cold One, including me—including your mother."

Kamara squeezed the Wise One's hands tighter. "She's alive then!"

"Less than alive. But her heart beats."

"Where is she?"

"She's nowhere. She has no home, not even in herself. She can speak the wisdoms, but no longer can she live them. She cannot create anything anywhere, anymore, nor can she die and move on."

Kamara's face deepened with sorrow.

The Wise One allowed her this moment of anguish, for truth often rips and tears. But truth's fruits cannot be born without the labor.

Finally, Kamara's voice broke with pain, "Ah—the Cold One spoke of impregnating my mother, and Kayenté's mother as well. Is this true?"

Kamara's face held terror. She stopped her breath, awaiting the answer.

The Wise One replied, "The Cold One did indeed impregnate the Duchess Jela Ketola for he knew of Duke Ketola's power and he sought to control and manipulate that family, planting dissension and hate amongst them."

Kamara's voice quivered, "The rapist then, that bred Kayenté torment, he was the Cold One?"

"Yes."

Kamara's face tightened. "And what of me, Wise One? Is the Cold One the powerful lord with whom my mother was mated?"

"Would it matter? Would that knowledge change your course of action? Will you fight harder or more weakly if he's your sire? "

"Is he?" she cried out.

"You'll know that answer, in time."

Kamara flung her hands over her eyes and moaned. Her fingers slid down her face. "It's horror enough to think the Cold One might be my father, but I'm in love with Kayenté, and he may be my brother."

"It does not matter," the Wise One said.

"It does not matter! It does not matter that I would love my brother as a woman does a man?"

"No."

"No?" wailed Kamara.

"You must trust the mysteries, child, and judge not—anything. We care only that the Warlord has placed the seed of fight in you, and that your desire for him has made you less vulnerable to the Cold One's seduction. That is why the Cold One tries a more forceful approach with you than he did your mother."

"Tell me where she is! Tell me who she is! I *must* know. I want her with me—desperately!"

"No child," the Wise One said. "If you were to know who she was and be with her, connecting your childhood longing with her maternal love, the Cold One would feel it and he would work through her to seduce you into his oblivion. When you can free her by bridging the Cold One, she'll come home to you for all time."

Fantasy bloomed a smile on Kamara's face. "That's my dream." Her eyes beamed hope . . . for a moment. Then reality emerged and stole her smile. She lowered her gaze to the ground. "But I doubt my abilities."

The Wise One held out her hand. "You shall succeed, child. You must! Go now. You have several hours journey to Lania Castle."

She looked up quietly. "It will take me more than several hours I fear."

"By foot. However, your mare is still here. I have hid her, and tended her well."

Kamara's eyes lit. "Thank you. I am glad. What would make me gladder still is to keep your company."

"No." The Wise One reached over to Kamara's wine colored slippers and put them on her feet. Then she helped Kamara stand, wrapping the tattered cloak tighter around her. "I must move about and behold unfolding events. I am a messenger."

A cold blast of wind shot past them.

"Hurry child. The Cold One has sensed your awakening. Ride your mare swiftly back to Lania Castle and retrieve the Warlord's sword. There is much power in it—much."

Kamara cried, "I cannot leave you alone with the Cold One. He's merciless!"

"I know. But he can no longer harm me, and you are still far too imbalanced to ward him off for long."

The Wise One grabbed Kamara's hand and hurried her with strategic precision to a wall of lush ferns and ivy smothered saplings. Her mare turned her head to acknowledge her, and if a mare could smile, it would have. Kamara saw the riding regalia neatly hung in a tree. She saddled Twilight quickly, while the Wise One bridled her. Kamara created passage through the foliage wall, and the Wise One guided her mare through to the clearing.

Kamara mounted, straining against the weakness in her arms. The act made her head throb painfully, but her concern was for the Wise One. She reached her fingers toward her for a final goodbye. "Be careful!"

The Wise One did not reach back. Instead, she thumped the mare's rump. "Make haste child!"

The mare jolted. Kamara glanced over her shoulder saying her own silent goodbye. She faced forward, and galloped away.

By late afternoon, Kamara arrived at the Hot Springs. She had been delayed by her desperate thirst, and stopped often to drink by the winding creek that often paralleled her journey. She dismounted with a wince. Her chafed inner thighs had rubbed hard against the saddle. She said a silent prayer for the Wise One while she stripped Twilight of riding regalia.

She stroked her fingers over the horse's sweaty alabaster fur. "Thank you for carrying me home."

Twilight walked to the edge of the Hot Spring and slurped. Water appealed to Kamara too. She needed something to relieve her physical discomfort. She shed her cloak, and slid into the warm pool. She ducked under and shot through the water like a fish released into a lake. She reveled in the liquid heat that soothed her aching muscles, bruised bones, and throbbing head.

She popped her head to the surface, and inhaled deeply. The air cooled her face. At that moment, she knew pleasure. True pleasure. Not the kind you can have whenever you wished. No, this was the kind you experienced after being deprived. The deprivation made it delicious.

"Kamara!"

She turned to the commanding male voice behind her. Michael stood on the bank: tall, strong, and beautiful in a green tunic, black pants and boots. His sandy colored hair and beard were almost blond in the sunlight. He looked bright and well defined. Suddenly, all she'd experienced with Kayenté seemed a dream. Michael was real now. The Hot Springs were real. All else seemed a nightmare.

She stood up in the water exposing bare breasts, her modesty gone. "You look well, Michael. Very well."

Michael drank in her bareness. His heartbeat quickened. Beads of water glistened on her skin. He couldn't speak for a moment. He was surprised by her uncharacteristic semi-provocative behavior that aroused him as much as it worried him. He glanced at her mare grazing on grass shoots, and noticed the tattered cloak on the ground.

Seeing no other clothing, jealous suspicion reddened his face. "Where are your garments? What has happened? Kayenté sent men here searching for you!"

Her eyes lit with curious hope. "He did?"

Maybe Kayenté did care for her. But why hadn't *he* come. But of course . . . she knew. The Lord of Darkness serves himself, not love.

Michael said, "Camille had a hard time convincing them that you hadn't returned. Where have you been?"

Her face went blank, not ready to resurrect the terror of her escapade.

"Kamara! Speak to me!"

She spoke in a fugue of denial as if delivering a speech on wild-flowers. "Well, I tried to return home when I discovered Kayenté was Panther, when his men informed him that his realm had been invaded and he apprehended me and I hated him and I hated you and then I fainted at the sight of his murdered squire and then I became preoccupied with the seven peasants who wanted us dead and even more preoccupied when the seven peasants themselves were dead—by Kayenté's hand of course and . . . by my—" her voice broke,"—sword. And then—"

"And then?"

Her monotone voice hinted hysteria. "Then we journeyed to his father's castle where I was greatly disturbed by his bitter mother, his flirtatious brother, and a pig." She began to ramble, emotion rising in her tone. "I was allowed to heal the son of a vengeful servant, but not the prisoner in the dungeon whose pain was locked in me, like I was locked in my room—driven to hell, drunk on wine, jumped down a wall, battle all around—" She threw her hands over her cheeks. Her voice rose with wild intensity, "—taken from Kayenté's horse, swords, blood, warriors everywhere—tree, nightgown, ran away, the Cold One—" Her body shook violently.

"The Cold One?" Michael plunged into the water and enfolded her in his arms. "I'm sorry!" He rocked her gently. "You've been through much. I was only thinking of myself, behaving like a jealous husband. You're alive! That's all that matters!"

His kindness suctioned forth the deep fathoms of her grief.

He pressed her face into his shoulder.

She moaned.

He cradled one hand on back of her head.

She cried.

He kissed her ear.

She wailed.

He was anxious for her to stop lamenting, so he could inquire about the Cold One. But since he'd unleashed her emotional flood, he owed her a cavity of reception. He kept patting her back, hoping she'd stop, but that hope was not soon realized. His arms grew tired before she quieted. But at long last, she did.

He stepped back to view her damp face. "The Cold One found you?"

She nodded, shame in her eyes.

"Did he . . . violate you?"

She swallowed hard. "Almost . . . but then he disappeared."

"How much is almost? And what do you mean disappeared?"

She glared at him angrily, not only because he wanted to know details too painful for her to admit, but a kind of judgment seem to hinge upon her answer.

"Would you hate me if he went too far?"

"I would hate *him* if he went too far."

"Well, he didn't."

"Talk to me. Kamara. Tell me everything."

"The Wise One told me—"

Michael interrupted,"—you met the Wise One?"

"Yes. I was unconscious after the Cold One's attack. Eleven days, she tended me. She said that because I resisted, he disappeared, though not for long. She said he would eventually trick me into submission unless I learned Kayenté's way."

"Kayenté's way?"

"You know, the Way of the Sword."

"Oh," he said, unsure of his feelings but certain of his needs—her bareness intensifying them.

He enveloped her in his arms, wanting to feel more of her.

Comforted by his embrace, she felt him once again as her very best friend. "Oh Michael, I no longer resist my fate. You sprung me from the bow of my home, and like an arrow I'm sailing to the mark, and I don't know what shall happen, but it's too late now to arrest it."

"I'm—sorry for what I've set into motion. I believe I was wrong. I understand if you despise me."

She drew back from him. "I did despise you, Michael, but I can see the greater picture now. I've come to believe you were right, that I should accept the sword without forfeiting my light. I think it possible to somehow have both. *You* have both. Even though you don't touch the mundane sword, you use its power in other ways. You used it to protect me. So yes, you're instincts were right."

"But I was wrong to seek Kayenté. I should have championed you myself, as first I had wanted."

"No, Kayenté is the one. I know this. No measure of reasoning can alter that knowing. I am destined to touch the power he holds—the power that dances in his sword. When I do that, everything shall come to balance."

"His power? You desire his power? You surprise me, Kamara, I thought you were above all that."

"You misunderstand, Michael. The ultimate defeat of the Cold One involves me somehow reversing the flow of not only my power—but Kayenté's. The Wise One told me that the lovers must war and the warriors must love. Don't you see? I doubt that Kayenté can defeat the Cold One with a sword any more than I can with love. The middle ground . . . . Yes. The middle ground is where the Cold One shall meet his demise."

Michael shook his head sadly. "Then the Cold One won't meet his demise. You don't know Kayenté. Let me apprise you: Kayenté is a powerful lord, governing more territory than even the King. He administers justice, settles quarrels, coins his own money, collects tolls from roads and bridges on his own land, levies taxes, demands military service from his vassals, and he protects any and all in his realm, not only from outside forces, but from the criminal element within.

"He is supposed to owe loyalty to his uncle, King Aldos, but Kayenté is more wealthy and more powerful than he, so he does as he pleases because he knows Aldos depends upon his support. But I know Kayenté. He is waiting for the right moment to gracefully slide into the King's position. But first, he must secure control of the Rudels who, according to Sir Robert, may well be planning to overthrow Kantine.

"Meanwhile the Gates to the North have had their eye on Kantine for some time. King William of Gateland, Kayenté's cousin, has been squawking about his partial entitlement to our province."

Michael's voice heightened with bitter cynicism, "Kayenté is *completely* preoccupied with these matters. These matters are his life! In his pursuit to be King, he has killed thousands, Kamara, thousands. He has spent countless years devising strategy with a patience and genius that surpasses any lord of our time. He conquered the Provinces of Riseland and Jord for King Aldos, doubling the size of Kantine. He slew those who would not acquiesce and cut out their hearts to leave his mark. He gained the loyalty of every Sakajian lord in Kantine, Kamara, over sixty-eight warlords, who will do his bidding before or instead of the King's!

"He's not going to give all that up to slay the Cold One, who is to him no more than a magician whose only goal is to torment you! He won't do it Kamara, I tell you, he won't. You are wrong about him. You'd have a far better chance if you utilize me."

Michael saw that far away look in her eye. She didn't care about the truth. She didn't care. She was in love with Kayenté, plain and simple, and not all the reason in the world could free her from that fate.

Suddenly her body tightened. Urgency filled her face. "I must go to him! I must. Kayenté has influenced my spirit, saving me from the Cold One thus far, and if I'm not again with him, the Cold One shall return."

"Kamara, I implore you, do not leave. In spite of what you say, I don't believe Kayenté protected you well. He doesn't understand you. I know you better than I know anyone. I can champion you. Stay with me. I love you."

"Oh Michael," she kissed his shoulder, "life would indeed be delightfully easy with you, strong warrior that you are, dedicated to peace. You are in balance. I am not. Kayenté is not. And that is why I must return to him. I can take what he has to give, because I need it. Kayenté needs what I have to give, so he shall take it."

He sighed, staring at her in silence, shaking his head.

"I'm sorry, Michael, but it's just the way it is."

"If you must go," he took her hand to his lips and kissed it, "marry me first."

She gazed earnestly into his hopeful eyes. "I cannot take any action now save to return to Kayenté."

He repressed his sorrow, but not his love. "Then, I'll take you there, for the Cold One may again come upon you, and there are robbers and ravagers in the forests."

"No Michael. I need you here to aid Camille. You are the strongest male figure, and I realize now the importance of male energy. I have the 'mists' to protect me. Great Mother will lead me to my destiny. She smiled faintly, "but you could give me directions to his castle."

"Kamara . . ." Michael said hesitantly.

"If you don't tell me, I'll yet locate it with my senses, albeit more slowly."

"Very well," he sighed, "go south. Follow the river past Kanis. There is an old trail there that will take you beyond the nunnery. In two days time, if you move fast, you'll come upon his castle."

"Thank you, Michael."

He sighed, "Return to me, Kamara. I will wait and remain devoted to you. When you are done with Kayenté, and he is done with you, you will see that I am your true love."

"Perhaps you are Michael. I don't know. I admit that I actually know very little. I am the student now in your old world, just as you once were the student in mine. But no longer are you flailing in a sea of what you do not understand. You've faced your demons, but not I."

Michael dropped on his knee. Water bobbed around his chest. He took her hand to his lips and kissed her soft flesh. He looked up at her, devotion blazing in his eyes. "I'm here for you, dear lady, I am." He rose, and gave her a short sweet kiss on her lips.

She uttered lovingly, "No stronger or gentler a man could I ask for."

She thought to herself that Michael would not throw her over for riches or for the lust of another, as would Kayenté. Even though, in many ways, she craved Kayenté for her mate, she knew his cruel side would be far too great to bear. Once she learned that which she did not know—yes, then she would return to Michael.

She glanced around the springs. "I'm sure by now Teeah and Camille have sensed my return and my need. They are likely to arrive soon." She touched his shoulder. "You'd best leave. I shall return dear Michael, some way, somehow. I do love you, though I know not what course that love shall take."

She urged him away despite the look of longing in his eyes. He waded out of the water, turned back to her and waved. "Fare-thee-well, Angel."

"Fare-thee-well, Michael."

He walked beyond the cedar trees disappearing from view.

Moments later, Teeah arrived. Her long crimson velvet gown brushed against the wildflowers as she walked. She stopped at the edge of the spring, smiling knowingly at Kamara. Draped over her forearm, were garments of beauty: an elegant gown of velvet white, a pale pink under-tunic, the Red Cape that Kamara had earlier rejected, and a white blanket. In her hands, she held a white cloth sack, and red slippers. She set down everything but the blanket by a clump of purple heather.

She stretched open the blanket toward Kamara. "Do you still believe me of the devil?"

Kamara waded out of the water sheepishly. When she reached the blanket, Teeah wrapped it around her.

"I'm sorry," Kamara said. "I hurt you greatly by making such an accusation."

Teeah pulled the blanket down over Kamara, wiping her body dry. "I would have expected no less from an advocate of true love." She slipped the pale pink under-tunic over Kamara's head, pulling it over her body with motherly care, and then followed suit with the white velvet gown.

Kamara ran her fingers down her thigh over the velvet. "Why such fancy clothing?"

"You want to look nice for the Warlord, don't you?"

"Tee—ah." Kamara face reddened.

"Kam—ara." Teeah echoed Kamara's tone, and they both giggled.

Kamara slid her feet into the red slippers and sat down, knees bunched before her. Teeah sat beside her. Kamara leaned her head, child-like, on Teeah's shoulder. "You gave me everything, and still I doubted you." She lifted her head and looked at Teeah hopefully, "Can you forgive me?"

Teeah nodded with tear-glossed eyes.

Kamara dropped her head once more on her guardian's shoulder.

Teeah slipped her arm fondly around Kamara's back. "I love you as my own daughter. So great is my bond that I see everything that happens to you even when you are miles away. I would allow no force to harbor me that would destroy you. I am far too clever for that."

"My mother wasn't clever or strong. The Cold One seduced her and she left me behind."

"She left you behind, Kamara, *because* she was clever and *because* she was strong."

"She abandoned me!"

"She abandoned you to protect you from the Cold One."

"But I'm her child. I would rather have gone through everything with her, than anything without her."

"You aren't a mother, so you don't understand a true mother's heart, so filled with love that she'd do anything and everything to spare her offspring pain."

Camille walked up behind them, wearing a soft red gown like Teeah's. She carried a long white bundle in her hands. "I've brought you Kayenté's sword."

Kamara rose, facing Camille.

Camille implored softly, "Pardon me. I did not have the Warlord's sword melted."

Kamara touched her shoulder. "All is well between us Camille. I know much of 'the light,' but little of 'the dark.' Why, you know more of the dark side than I. In that, I must respect your decision to have preserved the sword."

Camille smiled. "I am glad."

"Lay down the weapon," Kamara said.

Camille knelt and laid the sword on the grass. Kamara knelt by her and unwrapped the cloth, exposing the large shining blade etched with ancient symbols that read, "Warrior. Strength. Protection. Gateway. Wholeness."

Kamara was surprised. Why, these were very noble runes. She had expected something more like "Blood. Kill. Conquer. Rule. King."

The gold hand guard was sculpted into two panthers back to back, their heads facing outward, hissing. The panther's backs touched as if they were a team guarding the home front. She thought it most interesting that the designated Ketola coat of arms was the reverse: two panthers leaping toward one another, like in attack, not unlike the manner in which the Ketola's behaved, or in fact, not unlike the way the people of Kantine treated each other.

Was Kayenté, perhaps without realizing it, trying to reverse that malicious behavior? Was his urge to rule Kantine actually motivated by an unconscious yearning to unite the factions? Perhaps he had the stuff of which saints were made, but because of the Cold One, he'd just lost his way, or lost his heart. If he did have a predisposition to reverse the inverted flow of humankind, then all she need do was restore his heart. That would be no easy feat, according to Michael. But perhaps that was a secret the Wise One did not tell.

She gazed upon the sword and murmured, "I must find my darkness." She thought of all the bodies Kayenté's sword must have slashed and how she had to develop the willingness to integrate such brutality into her being. The sword seemed to emanate him, and she could not help feeling his presence.

She reached for the sword, slowly and exactly, her hand quaking. She grasped the black bone handle and lifted the blade to the sun. "I believe in you Kayenté. I shall fight for your heart, and for the Priestesses, and for humankind. I shall fight. I shall use the sword—" her voice cracked with pain, "in the name of love." She touched her forehead to the blade. "For still—I believe in love. I believe in love with all my soul."

Teeah draped the Red Cape over Kamara's shoulders and then knelt next to her, arms touching. "And I too."

Camille moved in closer, sandwiching Kamara. "And I."

The three women, like faith, hope, and charity, bowed before the sword as disciples to an omnipotent being.

Kamara vowed, "Upon this day, we accept the sword to champion our love."

She turned the sword downward and pushed the blade into the soft ground. The three women sang their songs of light for several hours. Then they dined on fruit, nuts, and bread, talked, shared, laughed, and cried. When the sun began to dip in the sky, Kamara saddled her mare and bade Teeah and Camille farewell. She embarked on her journey with new strength in her heart, her way lit by the radiance of her Priestess spirit.

She traveled two meditative days, enveloped in her crimson cape, accepting the blood of new life—accepting all that she had denied.

Ж
Chapter Thirteen

Kayenté's Castle

Kayenté's long hair flew as he ripped a black and gold tapestry off the wall. He paced the Great Hall with caged agitation, the wildcat he was, black hide tunic and pants lending truth to the view.

His once cool demeanor had blown into a rare frenzy. He barked orders, and mistreated servants. A wide circle of pounding silence kept all at bay. His usual ability to fashion anger into action that yielded greater success, had failed him. He felt helpless now, ensnared in his dark heart.

Where was Kamara? Where! He had sent three men to retrieve her, among them Sir Robert who had worshipped her, since the day he'd tried to rape her. He had unbelievably become the most chivalrous of knights. Surely she would be less resistant to one whom she had bonded.

He wanted something to punch, maybe himself. He'd had the choice to retrieve her when once he'd found his warhorse. So what if he had learned Rudelians were making way to his castle once more. It would have taken but minutes to recover her, minutes that probably would have cost nothing.

Instead, he had been swept into war's drama, rationalizing that Kamara was better off returning to her home, safely, by virtue of her mystical powers. The Cold One, if anything, seemed a ghost, and Kamara was more versed in the ways of magic than he. He was a swordsman. He fought men, not phantoms. He'd decided that the

Wise One's utterances were nothing more than fairy tales. *Light must come to dark, and the dark must come to light.* No. He'd dismissed the theory. Let "the light" stay with Kamara in Lania Castle. That is what he rationalized—then.

But now . . . he wasn't rational. He stopped at the large bay window overlooking the courtyard, and gazed at the lonely clearing, absent Kamara. Where were they? His realm had been five days secured, and thirteen days they'd been gone. They could have traveled to and from Lania Castle five times over by now. Were her powers so great that she could hide from skilled warriors trained to track their prey? Or had they found her at her castle and been pacified? Or were his men dead? Was she dead? Was she lost? Had she been burned at the stake as a witch? Did Taran find her? Did the Rudels find her? Did the Cold One find her? He grabbed his head in anguish. He sighed through gritted teeth. Time to gather his senses. No woman was worth this.

He walked over to his favorite tapestries, and glared upon the hand woven stories of he and his men overcoming enemy castles. So, he left Kamara. So, he chose war. So what? This was him! He craved enemy blood and the taste of victory! If he had retrieved her, she would have been in his way. The Rudels simultaneous and consistent attacks on the most powerful warlords in all of Kantine, indicated massive armies, and immediate danger of losing Kantine and his power. No single woman was more important than expediency in preserving all he'd earned!

He started pacing again, teeth, fists, eyes a' glare—honing in on the gray marble pedestal that supported an obsidian statue of lovers in a primeval embrace. Embracing Kamara in the long throes of battle would have required him to stash her in the nunnery for safekeeping, costing precious time that could have decided victory or defeat! Minutes *did* make a difference.

He stomped toward the statue. As he neared, his face grew hot. When he arrived, the heat flew to his hands. No woman would drive him off course! He swiped the lovers off their pedestal and sent them crashing to the floor, breaking off their heads. Already, Kamara had begun to change his guile into guilt, and his lust into love. Soon she'd have him pruning roses, sewing clothes, and weeping in front of his men! His men, not Duke Ketola's. And what wasn't the Dukes? Even Kamara was likely his. And she, like Taran, could lay claim to true nobility. He, however, being the son of a rapist, could not.

He kicked the broken heads across the room. Kamara was just another heir who made him feel nudged aside from the heritage he wished were his. His mother was not a noble by blood, so what did that make him? Why should he not nudge Kamara aside? Why could he not? Why?

He went over to the heads and picked them up carefully, staring. He took them back to the pedestal and set them softly on the marble. "I'll fix you later."

He wandered back to the window, looking to a hawk soaring away. He felt compelled to ride out after Kamara and collect her himself, but with the frequency of Rudelian armies creeping into his realm, he dared not. Kamara had told him that he would have many opportunities to champion heart to the forfeit of conquering. Well, his choice had been clear. He'd tried to warn her though, that she'd credited him with a far more "noble heart" than he had deserved.

He drew her sword from the sheath at his side. The blade caught a glimmer of sun, sparkling in his eye. He held the sword in front of him—Kamara's power, untaken. So fresh, so pretty. Why would he *not* desire to seize her as he seized all else! Yet, why would he desire to seize what agitated him? He didn't want to want her, and he fought the need to need her. And he cursed that he cared for her now, and why, oh why did he not care for her then?

He slid the sword back in its sheath, and pushed his chest out with a deep sigh of prowess. He had wealth. He had power. He could protect his lands, his castle, his riches. His chest caved. But not his heart. No—not his heart, bludgeoned with a thousand swords named Kamara, his heart—laid waste to her shining face, throwing him on the edge of his childhood nightmare when he could not save his mother. He *could* have saved Kamara.

He sighed. He would save her yet. She would return to him. She must. He cracked a crooked smile. And when she does, he will calm the pacing wildcat and become the regal ruler of the land, in control and in possession of *all* he desires. He will force her to bow at his feet, where safe she'll be, and safely he will reign, free from her influence. His smile faded slowly, as his turned to the window once more, gazing out forlornly.

The sunlight glimmered upon the forest's wild beauty. The thick, fragrant pine trees were stocked with frolicking squirrels and a menagerie of colorful chattering birds. Lush green ferns carpeted the earthen floor.

Kamara drank in the gaiety, taking a holiday from her fears, even though she was ever moving closer to the dark nest that bred them. She heard a soft rustling in the bushes to her right. Peeking through the foliage, she spotted a doe birthing a fawn. Oh, elation!

She dismounted quietly, keen to view the little latecomer, this mid summer babe that missed the procession of spring. She slipped the hood off her head and approached the scene reverently, her step light on soft pine needles. When she was very close, she knelt and watched the miracle unfold. The little fawn's head popped out, tiny little nose, breaking free from the sac.

The body would soon follow. Oh, the darling little thing! Birthing was sacred, and beginnings a joy! She smiled sweetly. How fortunate she was to witness this precious event.

A silver flash streaked before her, cracking beauty. Blood splattered the air, spraying her face. The doe was cut in half. Kamara jolted when another slice of silver crashed down, cutting the fawn's head clean off. She numbed, staring at the scene that could not be real. Could not! She clutched her heart, beating heavily into her palm. The pain was too enormous to bear! Broken mother, broken child. A blood drop slid down her forehead. She wiped it before it reached her lashes and stared at the smudge on her fingers. The blood of new life.

Her body had numbed and nothing felt real. Cruel laughter floated down to her ears from the other side of the massacre. There, a bloody sword hung in front of bare muscled legs. She raised her eyes. The Cold One stood before her, loincloth bare. He'd come too soon! She wasn't prepared!

She rose and edged backward, slowly with protesting eyes and lungs of lead.

He stepped over the slaughtered animals, matching her step for step as she moved toward her mare. The Cold One's eyes grew mesmerizing, drawing her attention into him like a whirlpool sucking down a leaf.

His deep rich tone rolled over her in waves. "I am not evil. I've merely demonstrated how unable you are to accept the brutality of this world. Your suffering is great. Come into my emptiness. Let your terror fall away. Rest your weary soul in my void—forever."

She felt tired, sleepy, tempted to do as he said, surprised that she actually considered it. But then remembering what the Wise One had told her about the Cold One's seduction of her mother, she forced herself to stay alert and to continue moving toward her horse. "Now you're becoming the . . . the . . . seductive vampire. I'll not fall for your trick."

"This is no trick. I'm the answer to all your troubles. You are far too weak to master the power in this Ketola sword. But your meager gesture is indeed a noble attempt to rectify your shortcomings—something your mother never did and still she pays."

She forced the weighty sword back behind her shoulder preparing to swing. "I shall free my mother. You shall not have me. Kayenté shall have his sword. And you shall be bridged . . . yet!"

The Cold One slashed his sword across Kayenté's, flinging the blade from her hands. It fell to the earth with a thud, kicking up dust around the steel, spooking her horse into a run. She mournfully watched her mare flee from her—again.

He chided, "What a fine little storm you have learned to conjure, but never could you champion yourself against me."

His large ferocious laughter made her feel small. He quieted abruptly and dropped his sword. He grabbed her waist lifting her high and landing her stomach roughly on his shoulder. He tromped across a small clearing and tossed her into a pile of thorns, taking the breath from her.

She propped herself up on one elbow gasping for air.

He squatted in front of her, sardonic in gesture and tone. "Lie down. Be comfortable." He slapped her face, driving her flat on her back.

The world was spinning. Her cheek felt on fire. She tasted a blood pool in her mouth. She wanted to spit it on him, but she swallowed it instead. She must outwit him. It was the only way.

He stood over her, feet straddling her hips. "You clearly prefer the barbarian. You will submit. You'll not resist me."

"Why?" She hissed, scooting back and sitting up, "because you fear I'll make you disappear?"

He leaned over and slapped her face again, knocking her flat on the large hard thorny stems that pricked into her back.

She pushed past the pain and the urge to faint, forcing herself to sit up once more.

He wiped his finger over the blood seeping from the corner of her mouth. "You surprised me then." He put the red fingertip between his lips, and sucked off the fluid. "But now I know you are not as the others." He grinned, showing chunky square abnormally white teeth. "But of course, I always knew that."

"What do you mean?" She touched her stinging cheek, and looked past the bubbles in her vision.

"You're not aware of the prophecy?"

"What prophecy?"

"The prophecy decrees that you will be my most prized inheritance, richer in light than all the others, more satisfying to consume then ten Priestesses."

She shook her head stiffly. "There is no such prophecy. You lie, I am certain."

"What you believe . . . doesn't matter. Remove your clothes or I will cut them from you as I have before."

Wits and surprise, she thought silently, *wits and surprise.* "Very well." She removed her cape and she shed her slippers, thinking about the red spirit sword that she had absorbed, the one that had knocked her out for eleven days. Surely, that experience had given her something!

"Now your gown," he commanded.

She called upon the power of the red sword and put herself under its protection. Her hands flew inadvertently to a pile of thorns. She smashed the stickers into his face, leapt up, and dashed to Kayenté's sword. The Cold One's feet thudded closely behind her. She swooped down and grabbed the sword with both hands, twirling on her heels, rising, slashing the blade inches from his chest. Her intention was not to kill, no—never that, but her attack might make him disappear.

He became very still and spoke with utter calm. "Slay me then, in cold blood, the way I slay. Drive the sword into my heart."

The surprise was hers to bear, unless she could kill him, in which case the surprise would be his once again. And it had to be. She *must* kill him. She had no choice. Her arms hung like icicles. They didn't move. She tried to make them move, but they would not. She could not kill! Suddenly, the sword became too heavy to support. She couldn't hold it anymore. It weighed her down, sinking her to her knees, the tip of the blade touching dirt. She squeezed her eyes shut, unable to face her failure.

The sword was ripped from her hands. She heard it thud on the dirt, clinking on a rock. She hoped the blade wasn't scratched. Kayenté wouldn't like that. She felt very small, very unreal. Even the Cold One felt unreal. Everything felt unreal, except . . . Kayenté. He was real. Only he, beautiful, stormy, able to protect himself—he. She felt herself lifted and slung over the Cold One, the Mean One, the Vacuous One's shoulder, gliding through space, hurled away, falling down backwards, back stabbed with giant thorns, breath gone. Can't breathe.

He laughed. "I'm co . . . m . . . ing."

"No!" she gasped, almost inaudible. Her eyes opened. She pushed herself against gravity and sat up clumsily, on her calves, in a Priestess pose. "No."

He waved a knife in front of her eyes.

"No," she said affirmatively.

He slid the knife down the front of her dress, and thrust it up almost to her chin, ripping the fabric from the inside. He proceeded with quick thrusting movements all over her gown and under-tunic, until the fabric fell from her shoulders to the ground, leaving her bare. His brute aggression sank her resolve. Kayenté would not see her in the pretty dress. Kayenté would not see her. She snatched a hunk of material and covered her front, trembling and ashamed. Tears washed tiny paths over her dirt and blood smeared face. She closed her eyes—defeated at last.

She sank down into the hollow of herself, far away from the outside world, disassociating from her body. From that inner depth, she heard muted commotion in that distant world where her body resided. She remained deep and dared not look. Dared not see the gruesome preparation the Cold One brewed for her demise."

Hands touched her. She jumped.

"Lady Kamara?"

This was not the voice of the Cold One! She snapped her eyes open.

Sir Robert was squatted in front of her. "Does this qualify as penance, my lady?"

"Oh, yes!" She flung one arm tightly around his neck, clutching the cloth over her bareness with the other. "Yes, indeed!" She released him. "The sacred light is powerful, is it not?"

"It is at that, my lady," he said, "Am I not proof?"

"Thank you, Sir Robert! Thank you!"

"Thank Lord Kayenté. He sent us to retrieve you."

"I thought he'd forgotten me."

Sir Robert smirked. "Hardly, my lady, hardly."

She heard other voices. She glanced over and saw two knights looking her way with manly stares. The large stocky blonde-haired man approached her with her Red Cape. She blushed as he put it around her.

She asked, with her face still blushed, "Where is he—the Cold One?"

"Disappeared," answered the blonde-haired knight.

"He has a way of doing that," she muttered.

Sir Robert shed the gray tunic that cloaked his chain mail. "Here my lady, wear this. You may feel more comfortable."

"Thank you," she said embarrassed. She turned her back to the men, and maneuvered the garment onto her body, while still underneath her cape.

The dark-haired knight said, "We had all but given up on finding you."

"We must hurry," said the blonde-haired knight. "Our lord is anxious for your return."

She put on her red slippers and stood, a bit wobbly on her feet. She pulled the cape tightly around her to cover the bareness of her knees and calves. Sir Robert steadied her as she walked over to Kayenté's fallen sword. She knelt and wrapped the blade reverently in the dirtied white cloth. She noticed the Cold One's sword had disappeared along with him.

Sir Robert motioned his hand toward his horse. "You can ride with me."

She asked, "Have you a place to keep Kayenté's sword?"

"Oh yes." Sir Robert grinned, "He'll be glad to see it."

"I should like to surprise him," she said, "so please, don't tell him that I have it."

Sir Robert's eyes softened. "Anything for you, lady."

He took the bundled sword and tied it on the side of his war-horse. Then he lifted her onto the saddle, letting her legs stay together. He mounted behind her, and loped onward, between the other two warriors. Leaning against his chest felt safe and warm, but not all enveloping, like Kayenté's.

By sunset, they reached the castle. Kamara was disturbed by its looming black greatness, five conical rooftops in the clouds, more massive than the Duke's domain. There was a heaviness to it—a malevolence, a foreboding air of doom that held its own kind of greatness.

She had never dreamed Kayenté's castle to be so expansive, or his power so enormous, even though she'd heard it told. *Into the mouth of the Panther,* she thought, *into the belly of the underworld.* On the other side of the mote, she saw layers of black stone barricades and watchtowers and strange huge wooden war machines that she'd never even knew existed. It all felt dreamlike. She felt dreamlike. What thrill, what adventure, what magical horror awaited?

They rode across the drawbridge. The men shouted cheers of arrival and victory. Trumpets sounded. She felt strange riding onto the grounds with the glory of fighting men—the conquerors! How foreign the taste of victory was to her.

As they rode through the defenses, she felt humbled and ashamed that she'd denounced the prowess and might that man had to offer. She had always altogether shunned male energy, never recognizing its merit. It was male energy that had saved her from the Cold One—twice. And it was male energy that she *must* integrate into her own feminine presence.

They rode into the front courtyard, and stopped. Sir Robert slid off the horse and helped her dismount. She tightened her hood and cape around her, embarrassed by her state of dress.

Sir Robert smiled fondly. He handed her the bundled sword, which she drew quickly under her cape.

He said, "Wait here. I'll return shortly."

"Sir Robert?" she asked urgently, "do you think he'll receive me kindly—or with fury?"

"Kindly lady, even though he's furious."

She frowned, confused by his answer.

He shook his head with affectionate eyes. "No need for fear."

He ordered the two knights to remain with her until he returned. He walked thirty yards to the black stone steps and ascended to the castle entrance. House guards opened the doors. When he entered, Kayenté was charging toward him.

"We found her, my lord," Robert announced proudly.

Kayenté reached him. "Where is she! What took so long!"

"She's in the front courtyard. She was difficult to find, and thus our late arrival. We scoured the path to her castle. We were met by two women who told us she was not there. We insisted a search that proved fruitless. We weren't convinced that she wasn't there, however we doubted you would have approved torture methods on her people to exact the truth, so we left, conceding defeat. But on our return, we came upon her. And we came upon her in time."

Kayenté's face tightened. "In time?"

"When we found her, she'd already been to her castle and was in fact en route back to you. But she'd been stopped by a man as savage as any I've ever seen. We heard a commotion and saw her fleeing from him. As we neared, we saw her run to a sword. When she picked it up, the savage bade her kill him. She froze. He flung the sword from her hands, slung her over his shoulder, walked for some distance and threw her to the ground. We closed in as he ripped off her clothing. We attacked, but he fled, and seemingly disappeared. We searched for a while, intending to take him prisoner so that you could avenge her . . . your own way. But he was gone."

"Who was this man!"

"She called him, the Cold One."

"So he *is* of flesh and blood," murmured Kayenté to himself.

Sir Robert continued, "I wanted to warn you also, that she'd been roughed up by him before we arrived, and her face, well . . . I lent her my tunic, so her manner of dress is, well . . . She doesn't seem hurt badly, though blood is present, and well . . . she's not in the best condition. She's terribly shaken, and fears above all that you are angry with her."

Kayenté's face flicked rage for her attacker, then softened by guilt as her docile face came to mind. He had failed to protect her. Failed! His head hurt, and his heart ached. And for a moment, he could not speak.

"Lord?" Sir Robert asked.

Kayenté closed his eyes and sighed heavily, shoving rage and guilt back into the pit of his stomach so that he could function. He opened his eyes, composed. "I understand. I will reward you well for all for your good work, and Robert—" He tapped Sir Robert's shoulder. His voice softened, "Thank you."

Sir Robert nodded respectfully.

Kayenté said, "Bring her to me. Then you and your men may bathe and dine. I have already commanded the servants to see to your every comfort should you return with her."

"Thank you, my lord." Sir Robert bowed lightly. He turned and made haste through the open doors.

Kayenté followed him to the doors, and watched Robert walk to the right across the courtyard to her. She was here—sandwiched between two warriors. She was here—wearing the Red Cape, which she had once thrown out her castle window. She . . . was . . . here.

The setting sun splashed behind her like the dragon's breath, hissing and spitting her upon the threshold of his own interminable barriers, ignobly erected so long ago. She was his nemesis and his need, coming to seduce his heart into final oblivion. If she was the weaker turning to him, then why was it he who felt humbled? He stepped back, waiting for her to come through the door.

Sir Robert led Kamara to the castle entrance. "Don't be frightened. He'll be glad to see you."

"Are you certain?" her voice quivered.

"I am."

They approached the opened doors. She slowed, breathing deeply, clutching the sword behind her.

"Come," urged Sir Robert. He led her up the steps into the entryway, then exited, closing the doors behind him.

She saw but a flash of Kayenté's hard-lined features and wild black hair, before she fell to his feet kneeling, face to the ground.

Kayenté was astounded. She had fallen to his feet—willingly! And he found himself lonely towering above her. He knelt in front of her and drew up her chin with two fingers. He gazed upon her shadowed face well buried in the hood of her cape.

She said softly, "Teach me?"

Her plea was like a balmy breeze that wrapped him in a warm embrace. "Teach you what?"

"The way—" her voice broke, engulfed in a moment of pain. She lowered her head and finished her sentence in a gasp, "—of the sword."

He gripped her shoulders gently and raised her to a standing position. Her trembling filled his hands. "Do not fear me," he said.

Her head remained lowered. He slid off her crimson hood to better see the graceful face that had beauteously haunted him. Black and purple blood stained swells covered the right side, almost swallowing one eye. Her matted hair lay long and messy over her tunic, laced with twigs and dirt.

His eyelid twitched, seized by imaginings of revenge on the Cold One. Then he saw her again, and tenderness took him once more. He brushed his finger along her unharmed cheek, as if to affirm that she was really before him. But instead of soft skin, he felt grit—the remnants of her struggle, the dirt of degradation, the proof of foul play that would not be there . . . if only he had been.

His tone was deadly calm. "The Cold One *will* die for this." He opened her cape a few inches, and saw her bare legged in Robert's tunic. "He *will* die," he said, closing the cape.

She looked up at him demurely. "I want you to teach me how to bring him down."

"You cannot bring him down, little Kamara," he smiled, "not you."

"I can, if you assist me . . . if we do it together."

"My plan was to shield you, Kamara, not to put a sword in your hand."

"If I put one in yours, would you put one in mine?"

He looked at her with question, hoping she meant what he thought she meant.

She withdrew the cloth bundle from her back through the opening in her cape. "Here." She handed it to him.

He took the long bundle carefully, and unlaced the tether that bound the cloth. Heart pounding, he unwrapped his gift. His companion had returned. At last. At last! He gripped the hilt with one hand, sighed voraciously, and began wielding the sword in a killing dance.

"You are happy?" Kamara said meekly.

"Yes," he said, finishing the dance with a thrust of the sword. "All will be well now." He held the sword up, feasting his eyes upon the dusty steel a moment more, staring, adoring, blade and man, two as one. He raised it to his lips and kissed the steel, staring beyond the blade to Kamara. "So, you did not melt it?" he teased.

"Oh," she said shyly, "you know about that."

He removed Kamara's sword from the sheath on his hip, and put his own in its place. He stepped up to Kamara with renewed vigor. She'd remained meek and motionless before him, still humble—still afraid. Was she earnest in her request to be taught the ways of war? He would soon find out.

He held her sword out to her, hilt first. "You want to learn? Then take your sword."

She pushed her face closer to it, curiously. "There are panthers etched on it, like your fathers coat of arms."

"We will discuss that later," said Kayenté. "First, you must accept it."

She stared at him. "I need help with that."

"Accept it Kamara, or admit that you can't."

"I'm afraid."

"Stare that fear down Kamara, or lose yourself to it."

She sucked in a long deep breath, and exhaled quickly. She reached her quivering hand toward the hilt—slowly. Her fingers wrapped around the grip, and she took it from Kayenté, anguished, and sickened. The sword, though much lighter than Kayenté's, drew her hand down. She brought her forearm up beneath the blade and raised it once more to behold what she had *taken*.

She perused the detail of the blade, this blade, her blade, beholding it truly for the first time. This blade with panthers, she must accept. She must claim the sword and all it represented: her willingness to fight, her willingness to—kill, the fact that she *had* too, even though she didn't want to.

Though it was grace that bade her claim the sword, it was disgrace that bowed her head, filling her eye sockets with liquid pain. She would not cry. She would hold the tears in. But one slipped away and fell upon the steel that Kayenté had already blooded so many times. Though his own sword had been blooded more, she had found his easier to embrace.

She peered up at him with watered eyes. "Why can I accept your sword with more ease than my own?"

He stared deeply into her. "Because your sword is your own power to destroy, and that Kamara is your greatest nightmare."

She nodded sadly. "You are right. And if I cannot—" she flung her head toward her shoulder in shame, "then—"

He cupped her chin with hard fingers and aligned her face gently to his. "Then what?"

She said tearfully, "Then not only I, but the Light Sisters shall vanish. Yet, to protect them, I must be cruel. I must cause injury. And I must stop the Cold One. Oh Kayenté, I don't think I can!"

He edged her forearm down, bringing her sword to her side. With one hand behind her head, he drew her cheek against his chest, and with his other hand around her back, he secured her chest against his. There he held her—like his life, in sweet silence.

Her free arm slipped around his back, clutching his tunic. Tears came, escalating to heart wrenching sobs. His little Kamara, always crying, ever crying. Would she never stop? He allowed her tears for an eternal while. Better she cry upon his shoulder, then he for her absence, ever again.

When her crying subsided, her words came. "What is wrong with me that I don't want to harm the one who threatens the very extinction of my beloved sisters?"

"You just love a little too much," he whispered "and I—not enough."

"But you do. Oh Kayenté, can't you feel the nobility in your heart as you hold me—as you comfort me? I still believe you shall one day choose heart above all else."

"Last time you spoke to me, you seemed to have been swayed from that belief, having seen me *as I am*."

"I was shocked to see how you *can be* Kayenté. But I do not believe that is who you are. It is not too late for you."

He withdrew from her and said insincerely, "We'll see." He kissed her lightly on her forehead. "Come." He wrapped his arm around her back, walking her forward. "I want you to tell me about all that has transpired since we were parted. But first you shall have your wounds tended, bathe, and be given proper clothes. Then we'll dine. I'll teach you what I can," he said, "but the Cold One—" he clenched his jaw, "—is mine!"

"And mine." She gripped her sword more firmly.

"If I am your teacher," he scolded, "then don't argue with my decision."

"This isn't your decision to make."

"You've made it my decision by turning to me."

"I turned your way that you might teach me, not make my decisions."

"Sh," he said. "Your woman talk dizzies me."

But she did not "sh," and they argued all the way up the stairs.

Ж
Chapter Fourteen

Kayenté had delivered Kamara to a candlelit bedchamber, decorated with paintings of hawk-filled skies, and ornately carved cherry wood furniture: armoire, vanity, and a small square table with two chairs. The extravagant bed was adorned with royal blue satin bedding and a curtained canopy to match. In the far corner, near the bay window, was a small octagonal wooden tub.

He had placed her in the care of a woman servant named Allysa, who with cautious resentment and envious stares, helped Kamara bathe, wash and comb her hair, tend her wounds, and lastly dress her in the white under-tunic, carnation pink silk gown, and silky pink slippers that Kayenté had gifted her. The long sleeves hugged her arms, and the scoop neck was not too low. The top part of the dress had a single fine layer of netted lace, interspersed with tiny pink silk rosebuds. Though the bodice curved in and the material proved slinky to her form, with the under-tunic, she felt comfortable enough.

However, she was not comfortable being tended, especially by one who seemed to despise her. She tried to dismiss Allysa several times, but she wouldn't go. Kamara wondered what she had done to deserve the woman's envious eye, when the woman herself had been blessed with so much: a fiery personality, a physical appeal sure to please men, the protection of the mightiest warlord in all of Kantine, and most of all—the sanction to live the life of a normal woman. Was that not a great lot?

Would she rather be the Cold One's prey, forced to learn a man's way, burdened with saving the world, and have a black and blue face puffed like a grape?

Or perhaps Allysa's bitterness stemmed from her relationship with Kayenté. Perhaps she was his mistress or some such thing. Perhaps she feared another would outshine her. Kamara sensed a grain of truth in that thought, but could not pursue it then, for Kayenté had arrived.

He ordered Allysa to serve them dinner in the bedchamber. They sat in a corner at the small table in ornately carved wood chairs. Allysa served them hot plums, whole cooked carrots to dip in a side dish of lemon sauce, fresh heavy grained bread with honey, apple juice, and malignant stares.

Kamara, however, felt shielded by Kayenté's tender gaze upon her. So penetrating and sincere it was that her terror-filled day began to melt. She'd not known him to possess such gentility. Was his behavior a product of guilt, compassion, or ulterior motive? She did not know. She did not care. She simply needed his kindness.

After a dessert of cinnamon crumb cake, he dismissed Allysa for the evening and bade Kamara tell him of her adventure. She adhered to his request, deleting the many details that she considered too embarrassing to reveal. She further withheld her newfound knowledge that the Cold One was not only Kayenté's childhood tormentor, but also The Nothing that could dissolve the world. The first might set him off dangerously. The second, he'd declare myth.

When at last she finished speaking, Kayenté leaned back in his chair, observing her as she sipped down the last of her apple juice. He stated bluntly, "Now tell me what you haven't said."

She wiped her hands and dabbed her mouth with her wetted napkin, dropped the cloth on the table, rose and walked toward the bed. "I've suffered much this day. I need rest."

He rose and faced her, eyes narrowed in contemplation.

She turned her face down when he approached. She would tell him no more.

He stopped in front of her, his presence warm, too sensually warm to be met further without trepidation. Her heart sputtered. She bade it still.

"Kamara?"

She tried to look up at his face, but her eyes stopped on his throat. And oh, what a fine throat it was! Mounds and gullies resonated in his deep and self-assured voice. "Kamara?" Long, black hair tumbled free and wild down the sides of his neck over his chest. "Kamara?" His tone so soft. Soft little v-shaped hollow at the base of his throat. She wanted to kiss it lightly, sweetly, ever so tenderly.

His hands settled on her shoulders. "Did the Cold One . . . invade you?"

Forget his throat! Oh, forget his ill speaking throat! Kamara shrank back, head hanging. "Please leave, I am weary."

"Tell me, Kamara."

She stepped backward, until the back of her thighs touched the bed's edge. "Leave me, please."

He probed tenderly, "Was it worse than what the Rudel and Sir Robert had done to you?"

She flashed on the horrible feeling of the Cold One atop her during the first assault. She shook her head with closed eyes, blushing hotly—lying . . . because truth bit hard.

"Did he *touch* you?'

She glanced up shyly. "Why must you know?"

He seethed, "Because I must assess how slowly I will kill him."

"Kayenté!" She snapped her head to her shoulder.

He slid his hand beneath her compressed cheek, and guided her head to face him. "Tell me, Kamara, what did he do to you?"

"I told you, your men came before he could—"

"That was the second time. What of the first?"

She pushed the palms of her hands against his chest to distance him, but his feet remained rooted on the wood floor.

"Oh Kayenté, he was so very deliberately and extremely cruel, the details of which I cannot bear, so help me forget! Please Kayenté, help me forget!"

He seized her arms and drew her mouth to his, slippery warmth, in a kiss of kisses with the sincerity of a heroic heart. His chest tightened. Caring hurt. He could not feel its joy. He stepped back, breaking the kiss.

"Kayenté?" She said innocently, "I did not mind that kiss. It was a kiss not meant to go anywhere but into itself. It wasn't like the others."

"You are mistaken," he said.

She felt what was in the kiss slip away, and she needed it still. "Oh, hold me Kayenté! Make me feel safe."

A chivalrous look came to his eyes. That—he could not help. He wrapped his arms around her gently.

She returned the embrace, her cheek against his chest. His warmth flooded around her body—and that relaxed her. His musky breath whirred over the top of her head—and that excited her.

He whispered, "Twice I wasn't there for you when the Cold One came," he said. "There will not be a third."

"You were there for me . . . in a way, you very much were there. The first time, I had some measure of fight in me, born only from the rigorous day you'd forced me to endure. From what I gather, that bit of darkness warded him away, although I don't quite yet understand why. The second time, your men, sent by you, found me before harm came."

"But harm did come, Kamara."

She was deeply soothed by the vibration of his low rumbling voice in her ear.

"If you could only see your face. I would kill him now for striking you as he did."

"But, he didn't take my spirit, or—you know."

"But how close did he come?"

"Sh," she said, "please let's not talk of it. Just hold me, for in your embrace I am so greatly comforted. I wish we could remain this way forever."

He parted her from him slightly, searching for honesty in her face. "Do you?" he asked, surprised by her proclamation.

She nodded. "I used to live in starry wonder, safe in the mists, steeped in spiritual love, yet—unfulfilled. Then, I was thrust into darkness. Wild creatures stalked, pounced, and pawed at me. Michael, like the hawk, swooped down to grasp me in his talons that he may sweep me to his mountain in the sky. Taran, like the wolf, lurked in the shadow, licking his chops, hungry to dine upon my flesh. Your father, like a stubborn badger, tried to drag me into his underground home with eyes of fatherly want. And this I don't understand. He isn't my father."

Kayenté stared at her blankly, laboring to hide his knowledge on the subject.

She continued, "And then there is your mother—" She cleared her throat, "hmm, your mother . . ." She tilted her head to the side, deepening the look in her eyes. "Your mother is like a viper, holding me in a secret, leaving me alone in the dark passageways of all that can't be told. She aims her poisonous tongue at me. Hate rules her eyes. She pains me nearly as much as the Cold One, who is as the bear with brutal claw and heavy swipe. And then there's you—"

Kayenté listened intently as she peered far into his being.

"You are like the sleek black panther stalking your prey to feed your kingdom: stretching and purring when gently pet, hissing and killing when harshly hit—seeking contact, yet maintaining a fierce independence. You seduce me into your mystery, deep blue eyes calling me to you with affection. Then suddenly, I am trapped in your world like a mouse in your paws and forced to play your violent games. But I have been safe with you, for though your sharp claws scratch hard, you do not scratch me."

She touched his cheekbone. He cupped his hand over hers as she slid her fingers on a journey down the valley of his cheek, chin, throat, and heart. Leaving her fingers there, she said, "And yet, you who have the power to protect me—can harm me most. You—are the most dangerous of all." Her voice grew taut with emotion, "You have more of me than anyone has ever had, parts of me that no other has ever known. If you turn on me—"

Kayenté's face tightened for a moment, despising that recurring accusation. Then he relaxed, knowing it false.

"—if you do, my fate shall be worse than anything the Cold One could bestow upon me. Why is it Kayenté, that with the many closing in around me, I've come to you?"

He squeezed her hand on his heart. "You're in love with me," he said soundly, "and you have been, since the moment I first touched you."

She sighed with a flushed face. "I *am* in love with you." She absorbed the charismatic wildness flaming from his body. Her golden orbs got teary, wetting her lashes. "And I cannot seem to fall out of love with you, no matter how dreadful your behavior."

He pulled her close, pressing himself hard against her. He would teach her about her body.

"Oh Kayenté!" she shrieked, "I mustn't feel this."

"Free your resistance, Kamara. Let go!"

She pushed her hands against his hips trying to separate their bodies, "I can't let go—this way," she cried, "never *this* way."

"But you want to—don't you?"

"Yes—but I cannot!"

He groaned lustfully. "Let me awaken the animal in you, nun-angel." He pushed her backward until they both fell upon the bed, caging her body with his limbs in a billow of satin. "No," she pushed her arms against his, "there's no animal in me to awaken!"

He answered like a flame, rising to a blaze, on its way to out of control. "Oh yes, there is an animal in you. She's a panther, like me, but she's under oppressive dark waters, toiling to burst to the surface into light open air that she may leap to solid ground and run lawlessly under the sun. Free her, Kamara! Free her now!" His body fell harder on hers and his mouth found her neck.

"No! I don't wish to be freed!" She clutched his shoulders, pushing against him while he perused her neck with forceful lips.

Strange strong feelings tantalized her body to receive the male seed, void of the required ritual to sanction such union. She would not betray her Priestess sisters. Worse, his manner was that of a man only, and she could not betray herself. The hero had gone, and only the hero may kiss her—only he. And only a kiss at that. "Cat! Find another for your play!"

"I don't want—another," he moaned with pleasure, "I want you."

He pushed her resistant hands down to the bed and poured his lightening energy into her mouth with a carnal kiss.

Her eyes stretched open frantically, shrieking into the suction of their lips.

He felt her tremble beneath him, a crying sad little thing. He would not force her. He'd rather die. He rolled on his back, their shoulders touching. He spoke in a breathless, yet matter-of-fact manner. "You must unleash that animal if you intend to fight. Making love would help you achieve that."

"Making love," she gasped twice, repressing her sobs, "or appeasing lust?"

He rolled on his side towards her, lowering his face to her ear. He answered with hot breath. "What's the difference?"

"How should I know?" she mewled irritably.

"You have a body Kamara," he rested his palm on her hip, "don't you want to explore its talents?" He rolled lightly on top of her.

"No!" Her palms pushed against his shoulders. "I know my spirit, my heart, and my mind and that's enough. I need not know my body."

"You can't fight without knowing your body." He kissed her neck, careful to avoid her bruises.

"I've asked you to teach me how to fight, nothing more."

"I want to teach you everything."

"You would teach me, I fear, then cast me aside."

He sighed and stroked her cheek lightly, the cheek that had not been injured. He nibbled on her ear and whispered, "I'd not cast you aside."

"Yes," she said accusingly, "yes you would, because you won't love me!"

"Love is inconsequential," he muttered nipping at her chin.

"Not to me!" she said. "If ever I tarry from the teachings of the Sisterhood, and offer myself to a man, I shall be his one and only, and it shall be forever. I'll not be the mistress of a man who is to marry!"

He stopped suddenly and gave her a blank look.

"Oh," he said, "so that's it. You oppose my upcoming marriage. You surprise me. I thought Light Priestesses not to have such— human goals. Sex is for . . . what is it—rituals and conception?"

"I know," she said, "I surprise myself. I'm not as other Light Priestesses who are at peace with such matters. I don't think I could do the ritual. And if I gave myself to you—that way, I'd give you my whole world and I would expect nothing less from you in return. And of course," she rolled her eyes, "that's impossible."

Kayenté sat up on the bed. "Such unions are rare between men and women."

"This I know," she sat up next to him, "but if I'm to take a man, then no less a dream have I."

He scoffed. "Such dreams—remain dreams. A dreamer cannot survive in this world as can a realist."

"I know your priorities, Kayenté. I even accept them. I'm here to integrate your way with my own, not to force my way onto you as I had when you were in my domain. I would like to help you find your heart, but that can't happen unless you want to find it—and you don't. And you can't help me find my darkness unless I want to find it—and I do. Therefore, I am grateful for your help, but I'll not be taken cheaply if there is a breath of life in me to fight such an oc-currence. This, I have learned from you."

He rose to his feet. "You have learned well. And I think you are right. You have committed to the sword—not me, and you do not bid me commit to 'the light'—only you."

The words, *commit to the light*, reminded Kamara of Kayenté's time with her at Lania Castle, and how he avoided committing to 'the light.' She suddenly viewed it all with new eyes, seeing things the way they *really* were, and she found herself laughing.

"My statement amuses you," he inquired, puzzled by her sudden merriment.

"It's just that I know you now. And when I think of who you truly are," she giggled, "compared to who you pretended to be at Lania Castle—a man needing a woman's help," she laughed a little, "well, it's quite amusing."

Kayenté squinted one eye, half playfully, giving her latitude—some.

She started laughing hard and could barely catch her breath to speak, and had to do so quickly before laughter took her again. "You no doubt had clenched your teeth until they had almost broken off, pretending to need a woman." Her laughter rose, "—and you probably flowed rivers of silent curses . . . playing the role of a—*common* warrior," she could barely get the words out through her laughter, "seeking . . . peace! You! Peace!"

He was somewhat relieved by her levity, though a little uneasy that she was laughing at him.

She chortled deeply, comedy tearing her eyes. "Lor . . . ka . . . james. Lord Kayenté James, Lorkajames!"

"Yes," he said. "Believe me, I wasn't too pleased with that one."

Her hysterical laughter continued, "Oh what you must have felt . . . when we confiscated your sword, and you could no longer wield it or spout your orders." She inhaled a jovial gasp. "You must have bit your tongue more than once at our ways forced upon you!"

He'd never heard her laugh before, and found himself entertained by her amusement, even if it was at his expense. He'd endure this innocent ridicule as atonement for deceiving her then.

"Yes," he said, "it was indeed a most difficult undertaking."

She continued her cachinnation as she slid her back down against the side of the bed to a sitting position on the floor, clutching her convulsing stomach. "Oh . . . what you must have thought when I . . . found my way into your childhood!"

He sat down next to her, enjoying her joy, and said dryly, "I wanted to kill you."

"And what you must have felt—" she wiped the tears of laughter from her eyes, "when I ordered your sword destroyed!"

"Melted," he corrected, the humor of it fading, "you ordered it melted."

'No wonder—,"she laughed, "—you wanted my sword. You must have gone after it at with great vigor!"

The glow of humor left his eyes. She'd crossed into forbidden territory. Matters involving swords were never funny.

His expression made her laugh more . . . until the purring cat's eyes took the look of the hunt.

"Your patronizing offends—" his eyelids lowered, "and offense commands penalty."

She half-quelled her laughter. "Oh come now, when at Lania Castle, did you not patronize me unceasingly?"

Her words made her remember that side of the story, and her tone turned more serious. "At least I'm not here under pretense."

"If you were," his eyes glazed, "and I found out, I'd not forgive you as you have me. And the consequence would be significant."

Her face became child-like. "Please, do not lace your words with threat. I couldn't endure you changing from friend to enemy. We are friends at last, aren't we?"

He peered into her, seeking her motives. Then with hesitant surrender, he nodded.

She said, "I shall always tell you the honest truth, even though you may deem it distasteful. I do not want to fear that you might strike me down for disagreeing with you. Remember Kayenté, I'll never betray your heart. Don't be deceived by appearances. Just as your past actions toward me seemed traitor-like, you had my best interest at heart, or so I believe. Did you not?"

He nodded again, shifting uncomfortably. His emotions were like water: slippery, and hard to hold once he let them flow. "Sleep now. You will have your first lesson in the fundamentals of warfare in the morning." He kissed her on the forehead, and left, closing the door behind him.

She stared at the closed door, canceling an irrational urge to race after him. And with that, she snuffed the candle flame. She'd seen and felt enough for one day. She shed her dress, donned the white nightgown that was folded neatly at the foot of her bed, and crawled under the covers. No sooner did she close her eyes, when it seemed morning had come, and her eyes opened once more. This day, she would learn to fight.

Ж
Chapter Fifteen

Kamara awoke to rapping on her door and the sound of Allysa's voice. "May I enter?"

Kamara sat up in bed. "Yes," she answered kindly, suddenly feeling nervous about her forthcoming lesson in warfare.

Allysa entered. She appeared neat and efficient in her ankle-length sleeveless dark blue tunic, layered over a long-sleeved white collared under-tunic that billowed slightly around her arms. Her fair face was cute and sassy like a squirrel, with her light reddish hair pinned in a bun. She carried a gunnysack in one hand and a breakfast tray in the other.

She swung the door shut with her foot, and set the tray of bread and fruit upon the table. Then she turned to Kamara and held up the gunnysack. "Lord Kayenté wishes you to don these garments for your warrior training. He has also sent a brush and soap and other toiletries. Later, he will stock your armoire with gowns."

"I don't require much clothing," she said.

"He will require you to wear them," answered Allysa, matter-of-factly. She tossed the sack on the foot of the bed, her eyes still harboring that same sad mixture of fear and hostility.

Kamara asked, "Why do you look upon me this way?"

Allysa bowed her head and blushed.

Kamara threw back the covers and dropped her feet over the side of the bed. "Please. I wish us to be friends. Come sit by me," she pat her hand on the bed, "and speak your heart."

Allysa looked at her hesitantly. "I fear punishment."

"What you say to me shall be kept confidential, and I certainly have no desire to punish you. I don't even believe in this servant-lord thing anyway. We are all equally valuable and should be treated the same."

Allysa sat on the end of the bed.

"Come closer," Kamara said, "right next to me."

Allysa's eyes sparked fear.

"Come on," assured Kamara, "I shan't hurt you."

"Forgive me," Allysa said, "but some say you are a witch—even though you look like an angel."

"I am neither—or both," Kamara said. "But mostly, I'm a person who wants to be your friend."

Allysa edged closer to Kamara until she was by her side, casting a timid look of admiration upon the witch-angel. "You have such brightness about you, and my Lord Kayenté, he notices." She lowered her head, staring at her lap.

"Why do you feel shame?" Kamara touched Allysa's shoulder.

Allysa answered tearfully, with flushed face. "I have lain with Lord Kayenté many times since I came to his castle over a year ago. I have hoped that one day—"

Kamara tightened, bitten by jealousy. Even so, she bravely finished Allysa's sentence. "—that one day you would wed him?"

"Oh no," Allysa shook her head, "that hope is far too high. I merely wish he'd fall in love with me. Not lust—but love. I wish to bear his children, but nothing grows inside me. Even so, to have his love, that would mean everything."

"I understand Allysa, truly I do."

"Do you love him too?" Allysa asked, seemingly dreading the answer.

Kamara answered, "If I did, nothing would come of it, for I shan't lay with a man who does not love me. Besides, if I were to lay with a man, it would be with my dearest friend, Michael." Kamara's eyes lit. "Perhaps you made his acquaintance when he came here several weeks ago?"

Allysa's face froze. She stammered, "Mi . . . Michael. Michael Randenscene?"

Kamara smiled. "You know him then?"

Allysa wanted to reply, *in more way s than one*, remembering her sexual interlude with him. But instead, she nodded her head up and down frantically, eyes wide, mouth tight. Suddenly she blurted, "uh—then—Michael loves you?"

Kamara nodded.

Allysa said with disgust, "I despise men."

Kamara said, "You despise men because Michael loves me?"

"Uh, no," Allysa fidgeted, searching for a lie. "I despise Kayenté for not loving me," which actually was a truth.

Kamara said, "Kayenté is blocked in matters of love, Allysa. He's far from his heart. His whole world is . . . well—" She swept her hands from her waist downward.

Allysa smiled through her tears and laughed lightly. "That's true."

"So you see, don't take his detached demeanor toward you, personally. His way is his way and I doubt he could treat you, me, or any woman with the decency we deserve. And as for me, rest assured, though I trust him with my life, I do not trust him with my love. And you are far too worthy a woman to spend your life as Kayenté's pleasure object."

"But I'm afraid to tell him, no."

"Tell him no, anyway. Tell him you feel shamed. He'll understand that."

"He'll punish me."

"If Kayenté is unkind to you, then I shall take you to my castle. There, you may live without fear."

"Truly?" Allysa asked with surprise, "you'd take me in?"

"Certainly," Kamara said, "and you'd be free, so long as your ways were not violent—and I doubt they are."

Kamara wrapped her arm around Allysa's back, the motherly way Teeah had done to her.

Allysa turned toward her, and Kamara hugged her fully, and tightly, so tight. "Oh dear lady," Allysa cried, "you are kind!"

They parted with tender ease.

"Tell me Allysa, how do you feel about his plans to wed lady Winnefred?"

"Oh, that does not concern me," she answered. "Noblemen seldom marry for love . . . and they commonly take mistresses."

Kamara was baffled about the rules, not understanding how a man could marry one person, have sexual relations with another, and love neither. She was on the verge of probing Allysa for this answer when a firm knock pounded on the door, followed by Kayenté's voice, "Are you prepared Kamara?"

They both jolted and faced each other wide-eyed. Then they both gaped at the door.

Allysa sprang to her feet and whispered frantically, "Oh, he shall be furious that I've detained you." She scurried to last night's dishes and picked up the tray.

"Calm down, Allysa, he's not God."

Allysa replied, "Oh yes, lady—he is. You'll see—he is!"

She opened the door, curtsied shyly to Kayenté, tray in hand, and scurried away.

Kayenté peeked in and saw Kamara sitting on the edge of the bed in her nightgown.

"Allysa has detained you, I see. I'll have a word with her."

"No, Kayenté. I detained her."

Kayenté scrutinized her for a moment. "Still mending broken hearts, Kamara?"

"Still breaking them, Kayenté?"

"Yes. I am good at breaking things, remember? Isn't that why you came to me?"

"You shan't break my heart, Kayenté."

"What of you will I break then, nun-angel?"

"My hesitation to kill," she replied with a pointedly fixed gaze.

"Break that, I will," he said. "We commence in fifteen minutes. You'll not yet need your sword. Allysa will lead you to the green stone deck on the third floor. There, we will have privacy. There, you will learn to fight. And there, I will expect you each morning at the hour of six."

She nodded apprehensively.

Kayenté started to leave, but then added, "And when Allysa comes, don't detain each other incessantly for hours as women do."

"Oh," she retorted, "and men do no such thing on the battlefield?"

He smiled wryly, a playful spark glinting in his eyes. Then he left, and sauntered down the corridor, wondering how she'd appear in his page's clothes, clothes from a boy of twelve, clothes fit for fighting. She wanted to learn, and learn she would.

He waited for her almost fifteen minutes on the deck, surveying his land. Five years he had used his sword to attain what he had. And another five years he had maintained his power. He was fast regaining the honor lost to him in his childhood, was he not? He was near thirty years of age, and soon he would be King.

Kamara appeared with Allysa. Allysa curtseyed and left. He surveyed Kamara in the dark gray form fitting pants, and slim fitting tunic with v-neckline. He was glad he thought to dress her in boy's attire rather than a man's. She was more pleasing to view this way, even with her half-beaten face. Her loose fawn-colored hair hid much of her body, and it seemed purposeful.

He approached her, and said stoically, "In the future, tie back your hair."

She nodded passively.

"Do the boots fit?" he asked.

"Well enough." She wiggled her stocking toes in the black, calf-high boots, feeling empty space.

"Good," he said, reaching her.

"However, I wish to have something to wear under this tunic. I could not manage the long under-tunic with these breeches.

"I will see to it," he said.

"Thank you." She peered at him shyly.

He dipped his head back slightly, eyes glinting. "I have a gift for you." He reached down to his boot and slipped out a knife in a black sheath with dangling ties. The black bone handle in the shape of a panther's head, had a tiny red jewel embedded in the eye. "It is the one you confiscated from me."

"How did you—"

He offered it to her. "You will keep it on you or near you at all times."

She stared at the weapon with uncertainty.

"Accept it, Kamara."

She cocked her head with a sigh, looking at him, rather pleadingly. "Is not my sword enough?"

"You are more likely to succeed with this."

"Is this necessary?"

"If you will not take it to you . . . I will." He knelt and tied the knife around her ankle. "This weapon has long been with me, a favorite of mine."

She gazed down upon his black hair shining in the sun. Oh dear Mother Lord! Had she truly consented to let a fighting man guide her?

Her eyes rolled up with him as he rose. His height and stature suddenly felt larger than before.

He said, "Later, I will show you its talents."

She grabbed her stomach, hunching her head and shoulders with closed eyes, imagining how talented a knife could be.

"Have you changed your mind, Kamara?"

She shook her head, tears welling.

"This won't work if you let tears take you."

She opened her eyes softly with a quivering sigh. "I *must* go through with this, but . . . thrusting an actual blade into the Cold

One . . ." she shook her head lightly, "I cannot do it. I want to. But I cannot."

"It was your idea to take part in his demise. You needn't."

"The Cold One's demise will require us both. However, I prefer not to . . ." she swallowed, "stab anyone."

He laughed, almost angrily. "What did you expect to learn from *me?* How to use poison? The fine art of drowning? Twelve ways to throw someone of a cliff? If the Cold One is suddenly upon you, these methods are not practical. If you want *me* to teach you, then it is blood you will draw, and a knife is the best defense for one so small."

Her face turned pasty white. "But the thought of stabbing the Cold One sickens me."

She started to lean forward to keep from fainting, but he caught her cheeks in his palms. "When the Cold One is upon you, will you say, 'The thought of stabbing you sickens me?' "

Her eyes amplified panic. "But it does."

He met her horror struck gaze. "Do you wish to fight—or surrender?"

"Fight," she said weakly, fear sparking in her pupils.

"Trust me then to teach you. If I'm not hard on you, you'll not learn. And we've no time to pamper your fears. The Cold One has come upon you twice already. The goal today is to strike your rage and unleash your will to defend yourself. Later, you will learn the moves that can save your life."

She just stared at him, squinting, as if trying to screen the truth from entering her head.

Kayenté softened. "I won't hurt you—well, maybe just a little, enough to make you uncomfortable, enough to make you mad, enough to make you fight."

"Yes," she said with sad angel eyes, "You are correct. Don't let me hide. *Make* me learn. *Make* me fight."

"The first thing you must learn is to shield those kindhearted eyes. Don't give away what is behind them."

"You mean, make my eyes lie?"

"In a way—for now. One day you will feel the truth behind your eyes: a smoldering rage towards anyone who dares harm you, the refusal to allow such an occurrence, and the compulsion to conquer such an offender!"

Her eyes turned passive.

"Your eyes aren't lying," he said.

"How can I conjure a killing look, when I've no desire to kill?"

"You will," he said, "before this lesson is over—you will."

He snatched herhair, yanking her head back slightly, aligning her face to his. His eyes changed from warm to ruthless.

She closed her eyes tight.

"Open your eyes, Kamara."

She squeezed them shut tighter. "Huh ah."

"Open them, or I'll not teach you."

She cracked them open slightly.

He reached his free hand to the dagger sheathed on the opposite hip of his sword. He pulled out the long blade, and waved it in front of her face, landing the point on her throat.

"Kayenté, I didn't expect the lesson to be like this."

"This isn't Sunday School." His expression was hard and cruel.

She averted her gaze.

His taut words came through clenched teeth. "What do you feel now, Kamara? Love . . . mercy . . . forgiveness?"

"Stop!" she cried, trying to push his wrist away from her face.

"The Cold One won't stop." He pressed his armed fist against her breast.

She grabbed his wrist with both hands, trying to push his fist off the place it should not be.

He raised a quizzical brow. "Touch frightens you more than the blade." Maintaining his grip on her hair, he slipped his dagger back into the sheath, and grabbed her breast.

"How dare you! You've no right to touch me this way!"

"Neither did the Cold One. Fight back, Kamara."

"How!"

"Give your resistance power."

She started crying. "I don't know how to do that!"

He yanked her head back harder. "Feel the rage."

"I *don't* want to hurt you."

"Do it!"

"I can't bring myself to hurt you," she cried, enduring the hot pain on her scalp.

"Get out of my reality, Kamara, and into your own. Don't protect me. Protect yourself."

"I *can't* forget about you. I *can't* hurt you."

He released her with a thrust that nearly made her fall. He removed his belt and pulled his black tunic over his head.

She stepped back and gazed apprehensively at his clearly defined muscular physique, unsure of his motive.

He pointed to a large scar across three ribs, and a deep scar in his side, then to marks on his shoulders, arms and back, and then several faint facial scars. "These are sword and knife wounds." He pointed to his leg and wrist and the fingers on his right hand, "These have all have been broken," he said. "Can you injure me in this way, this day, Kamara?"

"No!" she gasped, imagining the pain he'd endured.

"Well then, you can't hurt me." He stepped closer to her.

She crouched near the ground turning her side defensively to him. "This is too harsh for me."

He loomed over her.

She looked up and gasped. "*Please,* isn't there a more gentle way you can teach me."

"If you require gentleness, you are not ready to learn."

She rose slowly and stood with shoulders back. "I *must* learn."

He stared right through her, and she knew if she resisted further, he'd cancel the lesson.

"Forgive me for being difficult. 'Tis hard to turn the tides." She shifted her eyes to the ground. "If you get into your shirt, I will comply."

"Why must I don my shirt?"

"Well, it's just that, you remind me of—him. You know—him. He doesn't seem to wear much clothing."

He smiled harshly. "I want to remind you of—him. I'll do as he did, until you make me stop."

"I know I just promised not to resist, but oh please," she said, in a low tormented voice, stepping backward, "I'm not ready for that. This is my very first lesson Kayenté. Have mercy!"

"This is my mercy, Kamara,"

She cocked her head innocently. "I shall try to remember that when you hurt me."

He suddenly wanted to kiss her, but commanded himself otherwise. "You *can* stop me from hurting you, Kamara." He stepped closer and thrust his hand against her chest.

She stumbled again, almost falling.

He walked into her, making her back up. "You are weak. I laugh at your weakness."

She thumped his chest with gentle force, and looked to him for approval.

"That's not rage." He shoved her to the ground, not too hard, and it hurt him to shove her at all, given her ordeal with the Cold One.

"I hit you," she said, her eyes soft with confusion.

He chuckled sarcastically, "That was no hit, little girl."

She peered up at him like a punished child.

He lifted the toe of his boot to her shoulder, pushing her down to her elbows. "Child."

She tried to edge away.

He pushed his boot against her harder, forcing her flat against the green stone deck.

She tried pushing his foot off her, but there it stayed.

"Hit me," he commanded.

"I can't," she whimpered.

"*That* is not rage." He removed his boot from her shoulder, yanked her up, and hurled her across the deck.

Her right shoulder and hip fell hard on the stone.

He neared her with a deadpan face, for now it was *his* eyes that hid what was behind them.

She drew back her head, and raised her open palm in front of her. "Stop, wait!"

On he came. On he must.

She struggled to her feet and ran along the stone crenellated wall that surrounded the deck. "Wait, wait, please wait a minute!"

He dashed across the deck and cut her off before she could round the corner towards the castle entry. He loomed in front of her.

She begged through panting breath, "No more! No more!"

"Good," he said. "Now show me you mean it!"

She tried to lunge past him.

He caught her in his arms and flung her across the deck. Though she landed on her side again, the force of the throw rolled her to her back. He needed her to strike her rage soon, for the guilt he felt in harming her was too disturbing.

Her hip shrieked pain, her shoulder too. "You're too rough Kayenté! I fear you enjoy this!"

He pulled her to her feet and stared into her gold eyes, tearing like rain. He drilled his words into her. "With the truly 'cold,' tears and pleading have no affect." He pushed her down again, staring at her below him into her helpless pleading eyes, still and deep, yet racing in some silent beat for a cure to his seeming cruelty.

For a moment, he was dazed. Her very expression had possessed his mother's face long ago when her rapist had come to call. His constant assault had taken her apart, and turned her fear into a hatred that haunted Kayenté to this day. His mother did not find her rage until well after she was broken—and then it seemed aimed at him. His reverie broke with a thump upon his chest. Kamara had risen and hit him with the heels of her hands—hard, hard for her anyway.

"Again," he said dryly, feeling like he deserved to be hit.

She pulled back her arm, elbow to ear, intending to slap his chest, but her hand was not forthcoming.

And he became more determined to teach her. No man must ever bring that look upon her face again. She must find her rage—now, this day. Now it must be, so that it would never be—too late!

"Women are for the taking," he said, "objects to be used at a man's whim. I'll take you as I please."

Rising in Kamara was the old hate that had birthed in her on that awful day when Sir Robert and Sir Bradley had molested her.

Kayenté came at her.

"Wait! I'll strike you hard."

"No enemy will wait for you to strike him." He snatched her arms.

She pushed her hands against his chest.

"You can't push me away, little girl!"

"I want to hit you. My hand just won't do it!"

He picked her up and slung her over his shoulder.

"Oh Kayenté! What are you going to do?"

"I'm taking you to my bed."

"Truly Kayenté? Truly?"

"Yes."

"No!"

"If you need to be taken and humiliated before you will fight," his voice hinted sarcasm, "then I'll make that sacrifice."

She suddenly thrashed upon his shoulders with a vigor he'd never seen in her. "Stop Kayenté," she screamed, "I swear to Mother Lord, I'll strike you truly hard. You'll be pleased!"

He put her down. "Remember your fate if you fail to defend yourself."

She closed her eyes, drew her arm back, elbow to ear, and landed a heavy slap over his heart.

"That was a hit?"

She feared he'd attack her again, so she shouted urgently, "I hit you with all my might, Kayenté, I swear!"

"This time," he said, "Make a fist." He mimicked the action he wanted her to take so she could see how it was done. "Draw your elbow back and thrust your fist straight forward and aim for my guts."

"Oh," she winced, "isn't there a way to hit that's more . . . lady-like?"

Kayenté let out a short laugh. "Kamara . . . you'll not likely be fighting ladies."

"That movement seems most awkward, I mean, mightn't I strike you in a fashion that is more . . . me?"

"You dally too much in your pretty little thoughts and ways. If you cannot strike your rage and unleash your will, you're nowhere near ever being able to learn the way of the sword. The Cold One will not be as merciful as I have been. Now I will show you what he will do, and you cannot stop me!"

"I'll punch you! I'll punch you!" she cried. Before she could think or feel, she closed her eyes, drew her arm back, and threw a punch to his gut.

She snapped her eyes open to view his response, while holding her arm, which hurt.

His face looked pained. "You did it. You hurt me." He glided down to his knees, hunching over.

She knelt and touched his back warmly. "I'm so sorry."

He lunged, sprawling her on the deck beneath him.

"Don't feel sorry for me because I still plan to take you."

"You tricked me!" Her fury mounted. "You used my compassion against me!"

"Exactly!" Kayenté's eyes squinted shrewdly. "Just as the Cold One did when he bade you drive the sword into him, but you did not. He knew you wouldn't. Your enemy will play upon your compassion to defeat you. And you must be merciless when your survival is at stake. In this case, I was hurt little, but you believed my lie. You trusted the enemy. Do not do so again."

He stood up, pulling her to her feet. "Punch me again," he commanded, "with your eyes open or I'll take you as I please, and I may take you anyway." His hand came at her.

She flung it away. Her eyes burst with power, producing definitive speech. "You shall *never* do that to me—again. No man shall *ever* . . . do that . . . to me—again!"

He whispered low, "Feed your resistance *more* power."

And suddenly, she did. All her pent up rage toward men and the Cold One exploded all she knew herself to be. She hammered her fists on his chest with a blind and deaf fury, angry at the world for having a cold dark side. And then, even as her body moved, she had no awareness of it. She saw only herself in a red world huddling over a moon ball of light as if it were an infant. This light would not be taken, even if the she had to kill every vandal on earth. Then the image faded, and so did she, flat on the green deck.

Kamara opened her eyes, viewing the gray rough texture of a ceiling. She turned her head and realized she was in a bedchamber, but not the one that Kayenté had assigned her. She lay on wine colored silk that covered a comfortable mattress. Quite nice, considering her body bellowed pain.

She was startled when Kayenté suddenly appeared standing by the bed.

She gasped, "What happened?" She glared at Kayenté suspiciously. "Why am I here? You didn't—"

"Kamara, I'd never rape you. I would never rape a woman. I could never commit that act. You, who have uncovered my past, should realize that."

"But you said—"

"I wanted to make you fight, and fight you did."

271

"Oh, Great Mother, what have I done!" She rolled to her side, hands over face.

He knelt down by the edge of the bed. "You did exactly what I wanted you to do."

She drew her hands down, crossing them over her heart. "I'd rather die, suffering all the pain of the world, than do what I did!"

"No Kamara, you did well."

"I'm evil now. I've snuffed my light." Her voice turned low and shamed. "I was—violent."

He nearly laughed, and then apologized, "I'm not laughing at you—well, I suppose, I am. It's just that if you'd snuffed your light, remorse would not be felt after a fit of rage. I feel exhilarated after such an event. If you're evil, than I *am* the devil himself."

"But I so completely reversed my flow—from healing to destruction. I've sinned. I've betrayed 'the light' and all that I am. I have changed. I have changed forever!"

"Kamara!" he shouted, to snap her out of her frenzy. Then his voice softened. "Have you forgotten why you came here? You came because you learned that not everyone can be pacified, and those who can't will destroy you. It's then that you must throw the punch, again and again until they cannot harm you anymore. Are you too weak to protect your loved ones, Kamara? Are you too weak to protect your precious self? If I thought so, I would not waste my time to teach you."

She drank in the earnest glow in his eyes. He really did believe in her! "Kayenté, please, hold me for a moment, friend to friend."

Tenderness crossed his face. "Move over."

She edged to the middle of the bed.

He climbed onto the comforter and lay next to her on his back.

She rolled on her side to face him. "You don't view me bad then?"

"Self-defense is not bad Kamara. You remain pure of heart," he said, pulling her head to his chest, "as I once was, before darkness took my soul."

Hearing his heartbeat, she draped her arm over his waist. "I love you, Kayenté," she blurted. "I mean love. I'm not just in love. I care for you deeply, apart from my own needs."

"Yes," he chuckled cynically, "but you love everyone, or do you mean, love like—"

"Love like—" a tear sank into his shirt, "with all my heart."

"I thought you weren't going to let me break your heart." His voice reverberated pleasantly in her ear.

"You can't," she lifted her head to see him, "for this love requires nothing of you, and I shine it deeply into the fathoms of your own lost soul, into that child cowering under a wood table, trembling with guilt and terror at the violence forced upon his mother. I hold that child in my love and render him the comfort that he's never had. I shan't sell him out for money or position. I wish him to recognize that love . . . is . . . real."

"Real for you, Kamara."

She stroked his cheek. "And what is real for you, Kayenté?"

"Control over those who could take me down—nothing more."

Her hand drifted off his waist to her side, her stomach sick, her heart sad. His love was so blocked, and his heart so cold! She stiffened. "Very well then. I'll request nothing more. As you said, I have come here to learn your way that I may integrate it with my own." She sat up, facing him. "Once that is accomplished, we shall part forever."

"So be it," he said, ire in his voice. He swung his feet off the bed and rose.

"That is what you want, isn't it?" she asked. "I mean, you don't want me in love's name, and I don't want you without it."

He stood there a long moment, staring at her like she was a thorn in his side. Then he turned away and strode to the door.

"Kayenté?"

He faced her. "What?" he snapped.

"Did you enjoy hurting me?"

He looked at her blankly, turned away, and left the room.

She knew she had pierced his heart. And she knew that he hurt. And she didn't care. Perhaps she was becoming a warrior—after all.

Ж
Chapter Sixteen

Fourteen days passed. Kamara's wounds healed, and in truth lent her the vigor to take her lessons seriously. Kayenté had spent each morning teaching her basic swordsmanship. Her defense moves had become charged with finesse, quick and keen for a beginner, but her offensive moves lacked conviction. Her lessons with the knife faired worse, with almost no conviction at all.

Her conviction was still rooted in her rituals of "the light." After each lesson, while Kayenté held court (a time Kamara hated because she could always feel the dread of the punished), she distracted herself by bathing (drawing her own bath), washing her clothes in the tub (before it was drained), and while the clothes dried by the open window, she'd dance and chant her songs of 'light.'

Each day Kayenté hurried to administer court so that he could go to her door and eavesdrop, finding secret comfort in her clear toned voice. By the fourteenth morning, he leaned his shoulders against the stone wall outside her door and nearly began humming along with her. Her sincerity pleased him greatly.

Displeasing him, however, was the counsel she had been giving Allysa. Allysa continually spoke of Kamara, "Lady says this, or lady says that . . ." Allysa had refused him sexual favors twice, and he believed Kamara was responsible, and no doubt feeling smug about her accomplishment.

Another of her accomplishments was her growing reputation as the castle's healer, deemed angel rather than witch. In just two weeks, she had physically healed twenty-three people, servants, and soldiers, regardless of their ailment. She was earning much respect, and respect equaled power. He feared that if she publicly opposed him, that some, perhaps too many, would take her side, causing unnecessary dissension in his realm.

He was grateful though that she had not yet asked to comfort his prisoners. And he wondered why? Surely, she felt their pain. He decided that after he held council with his warriors, he'd pay a visit to the prison. He wasn't concerned with the torture chamber for he'd purposely left it empty, disdainfully so—for her sake.

Did he love her? Did he? No, he just wanted to avoid the havoc that she so often stirred. He grumbled and left her door, deciding he must stop pampering her. No more meals in her room, no more missing tournaments, and no more exemption from courtly matters, beginning with the visit from his cousin, King William, that afternoon.

Kamara, knowing Kayenté was there, waited until he was well away. Then she emerged from her room in her rose-colored gown. She met Allysa at the end of the corridor. Allysa gave her the gunny sacks filled with all that she had requested.

"Thank you," Kamara said. "Go now."

"Really lady, I don't mind helping you."

"No Allysa, I don't want you in trouble, should Kayenté find out."

Allysa frowned as she watched Kamara hurry down the stairs to the prison, wanting very much to become more involved in her escapades.

Kamara misted the guard at the prison entrance. He unlocked the door and let her pass. She entered and proceeded with her daily ritual.

Kayenté adjourned his council meeting and made his way to the prison. He climbed down the stairs, intent on warning the prison guard about Kamara's possible intent to befriend captives. He and his men were leaving the day after tomorrow to join his father and sixty-five other Sakajian armies to overthrow Wincott Castle, and commence the overthrow of Rudelia. He didn't wish to return, finding his prisoners eating desert and sleeping on silk!

When he arrived at the prison, the door was ajar. The guard stood in a daze.

Kayenté's face tightened. "Damn that woman!"

He raced past the guard, through the door, down the dark stairway and stopped, shocked by what he saw. The walls and floor were sparkling clean. He walked past the small lemon fragranced cells, looking through the windows, viewing immaculate compartments adorned with flowers, and his prisoners eating crab apples and long green beans!

As he walked by, the prisoners made comments like, "You are humane, Lord Panther Ketola. You are not an evil, lord. We will remember this kindly treatment."

He then heard Kamara at the far end of the long reaching oblong room singing faintly to a prisoner. "Through the dark the moon shines strong, nightingale sings all night long," He went toward her, as touched by her caring, as he was riled by her insubordination. Prisoners were *supposed* to suffer. He could care less if they thought him humane.

As he walked toward her, her song continued, "Melodies that heal your soul, tones that make you feel so whole." He had almost reached her, and yet she did not break focus from the prisoner, or her song, "and though the outside light has died, you are always—" He reached her and looked down punitively. She looked up shyly, and finished her song to his face, "bright inside."

He sighed, his brow drawn in contemplation. Her chaste face made scolding difficult. How does one clip an angel's wings? Or silence a lark?

"Come," he said in a low calm voice. He took her hand and led her toward the exit.

"Good day," she said to each man as she passed him on her way out.

Once up the stairs, Kayenté eyed his guard in disgust, then he looked at Kamara,."Undo your spell on him."

She looked to the guard and said, "You are free of my influence."

The guard shook his head, as if awakening from a dream. His eyes shot wide open when he saw his lord standing there. "Lord Panther!"

"Never mind," Kayenté grumbled to him, and rolled his eyes toward Kamara. "What am I to do about you? You can't decide matters absent my approval. I should have you beat."

"My actions are only to bring comfort to the ailing, lord. I did not free the prisoners." She bowed at his feet in submission.

He was shocked to hear her call him 'lord,' *so* sincerely. She'd not done that before. "Rise," he said gruffly.

"May I continue with what I have begun?"

He nodded, surprising himself, figuring it would be easier to let her continue than to try and make her stop. "But under certain conditions: the first—I don't want you personally going into those cells to clean them. My servants will do the job. And my guards will be present."

"But I misted each prisoner before hand, and all went well."

"No," he said, "something might go wrong. You may come across one who can't be controlled."

"Oh, very well," she huffed, "what are the other conditions?"

"The second condition: You must seek my permission before doing what you please. I'm still in charge of your safety and the safety of all the people of my realm."

"I'll try," she said,

"Try?"

"Well, there are times I am certain you'll refuse my ideas and the ailing must be tended."

"Vow to me you'll ask first, or I'll halt your prison project."

Her face drooped. "Very well. I so vow."

"Let's go," he said.

She followed him down the musty dark corridor. He looked over his shoulder. "The third condition . . ."

"Third? Just how many conditions have you?"

"Many more," he said sardonically, "many, many more."

"What is the third?" she asked, her voice hinting dread.

"I want you to stop turning Allysa against me."

"Against you." She held back her smile.

He stopped and faced her. "You know of what I speak."

Her eyes widened innocently. "I've not turned her against you. I am only helping her to mend her horribly broken heart. She loves you so, and she suffers because you do not return that love."

"She had no such problems with me until you arrived."

"She did Kayenté. You just did not know it."

His eyes narrowed. "Stop advising Allysa. That is the third condition. And if you do not obey, I'll not only halt your healing activities, but I'll forbid her to associate with you."

"All right. Fine! I'll stop."

"The fourth condition is this: Since you have insisted on integrating my people into your ways, I insist that you integrate into ours. You will take your meals in the Great Hall with the others, and you will accompany me in my courtly duties, attend tournaments, and present yourself in the fashion of a noble woman in front of my guests, beginning today. My cousin, King William of Gateland, arrives this afternoon for a social visit."

Kamara squinted one eye. "Don't you mean a political visit, so that you and he can cordially banter about who is to be the next King of Kantine?"

"Very good. I see you are developing an understanding of politics."

"Under great duress, I assure you. It's difficult to remain unaware, while I'm residing in your castle and living in your mind."

"Living in my mind? You know me well, do you?"

"Yes, perhaps better than you know yourself."

"If truly you understand me, then it's to my dismay that you don't support my kingly pursuits. However, you will be present when I speak with King William. And you'll appear supportive or your healing privileges will be revoked."

Her mouth dropped open.

He smiled. "It's fair, is it not? I have let your light into my castle, now you must enter, what you would call—the dark of it."

She glared at him. "This is coercion."

He raised his brows. "Indeed." He resumed walking.

She shrugged her shoulders with a huff, and caught up to his side. "Why do you wish me to participate in your politics? I mean—I'm not your wife. I'm not even Sakajian."

"You are—an asset."

"I am?"

"You are of noble heart, mistress of your own castle, and—you look good on my arm."

They reached her room. He opened the door and nudged her inside.

She said, "I don't think—"

"—you should say anymore." He blocked the opening with his elbow leaning against the side rim of the door jam.

"You can't treat me like—"

"—I can treat you any way I wish."

"I'm not an object. You can't treat me like a prized sword."

"That is precisely how I will treat you. Is that so terrible?"

She sighed heavily.

"Giving up on me, Kamara?"

"Certainly not, Kayenté." She looked up at him most earnestly, "You are my only hope."

"Then you must obey me," he said blandly, masking the stirring of his heart. "Remain here until Allysa comes."

He closed the door and left.

Kamara sulked in her room, upset that Kayenté not only treated her like a child, but insisted that she participate in the tyrannical system she so despised.

After several hours, Allysa arrived, holding a bundle of elitist garb, saying that Kayenté wanted her to look regal. Kamara grumped the whole while Allysa draped, puffed, and tied her up in black and royal blue silks, satins, and brocades—hooking, slipping and pinning sapphire jewelry on every part of her body that was yet exposed, making her feel quite the prisoner of hypocrisy. Though her own clothes were never that of a poor woman, neither were they of royalty.

Her hair was swirled up into an artistic mass upon her head, held by sapphire combs. Her breasts were plumped upward in danger of full exhibition. Her waist was made to look almost nonexistent, and her skirt belled out so greatly that no one could stand near her without upsetting its artistic integrity.

Kamara's face turned red. "I'm not going out there like this! I'm simply not."

Allysa said, "Kayenté said you would say that, and he bade me inform you that the prisoners will be beanless tomorrow if you did not abide his wish."

Kamara clenched her teeth.

Allysa chimed, "Besides, lady, you look ravishing! Even you're bruises are gone."

"My appearance is irrelevant! I don't want to attend this meeting. I *abhor* politics."

"But lady . . . you are to meet William—King of Gateland!"

"I dislike the idea of kings or nobles, or any division of the social classes. I don't even like it when you call me, lady."

"I know you don't, but I can't help it. Come, Lord Panther awaits you."

Kamara's face was drawn in a pout, and she moaned when Allysa took her arm and led her out the door. She whined as they journeyed down the corridor, stairs, and through the Great Hall.

However, her complaints fell into silence when they exited the castle and crossed the front bailey, for she had apparently caught the attention of several hundred guards who suddenly had silent lips and loud lustful eyes. So loud they were, she couldn't hear her own thoughts.

Allysa led her onward, under gray skies to the far west side of the front bailey where they came upon a rose garden, divided by a greenstone walkway. Kamara couldn't view such splendor as a mere rose garden. No, it was more like a magical rose forest. She stopped and looked around her with awe, hundreds of green manicured bushes, taller than her, bursting with large brilliant red roses, damp with the aftermath of a summer rain.

At the end of the thirty-yard walkway where she stood, she saw in the distance Kayenté and King William sitting in a grassy clearing in finely carved, cherry wood chairs at an oblong, cherry wood table, garnished with gold platters and goblets. The men looked almost . . . beautiful as they talked to each other against the backdrop of shorter bushes teaming with salmon colored roses.

Allysa nudged her and bade her move forth alone. She flashed Allysa a glance of uncertainty. Then she proceeded down the walkway, her heart pounding in her ears. She brushed the puff of her silk adorned shoulder against the bushes, as if to draw their support. The humid air was clammy on her skin, disguising the cold sweat that she felt breaking out upon her. She didn't feel like herself playing this role, dressed in these garments. She was disoriented by being so objectified.

When she neared the end of the pathway, her field of vision opened to an entourage of guards, Sakajian and Gatish, not far from their lords, setting the tone of the meeting. Their faces too, stole admiring looks her way. She then realized sadly, that most men actually viewed women in that manner, blind to what was inside them.

Kayenté and King William rose from their chairs as she neared. Kayenté's black leather vest adorned a white silken shirt, tucked into black leather pants that accentuated every muscle on his body. Leather belt, sheath, and sword of course, were part of his everyday fashion. His calf-high black leather boots had a white full-bodied leaping panther insignia branded over the ankle. His hair was combed back off his face, with two small black leather bound plaits on each side, hanging over the length of his shining mane. She fantasized stroking her hands over the long strands that lay seductively over his chest.

"Lady Kamara of Lania Castle." Kayenté said, eyes sparkling as blue as the sky.

Kamara realized she had been staring, taken by his appearance. She scolded herself, for possessing the very shallowness she'd just accused of men.

Kayenté continued, "May I present my cousin, King William of Gateland."

She curtsied, eyeing King Williams' beauteous presentation as well. He was more stocky, and shorter than Kayenté. He wore a v-neck burgundy tunic lined with gold brocade, and pants to match, black leather boots, belt, and sword by his side. The plush deep burgundy complimented his blonde hair and beard. He was a handsome man, but he did not stir her as did Kayenté.

The men's reverent gazes so unnerved her that she barely heard them invite her to sit at the table. Further, she was quite behind cue when she realized they were sipping red wine from the shiny gold goblets, and eating strawberries and muffin cake from the ornate gold platters strategically placed before each of them—while she merely stared at the men in a fugue, leaving her own food and drink unattended.

She commanded her self to snap out of it, and took a succulent scarlet strawberry to her lips. She managed to eat it even while King William stared at her intently in-between bites of food, almost as if he recognized her.

She had just bitten down on the second strawberry when King William asked her in a low resounding voice, "So Kamara Lania,

Mistress of Lania Castle, what is your opinion of my cousin? Would he prove a good king?"

She slanted her eyes nervously to Kayenté, despising political games. King William awaited her answer that was not forthcoming. Instead, she swallowed the strawberry.

Kayenté said, "Lady Kamara, would you care for some long green beans?"

Then she looked at King William and nodded vehemently. "Yes indeed, Lord Kayenté would prove an excellent king."

King William smiled and replied with whimsy, "Oh, because he feeds you beans?"

She cleared her throat. "No, your grace, I believe he would prove a good king, because—" she cast Kayenté a sly glance and then said pointedly to King William, "—he is a man of noble heart."

"And you know this—how?" asked the King.

"He has taken time from his busy schedule to protect me from a most dangerous adversary, and there is nothing in it for him."

The King eyed her slowly, up and down. "Well, I don't know about that."

She ignored his rather insulting insinuation, and labored not to blush. "Truly your grace, he's even teaching me how to defend myself. In addition, he stretches his protective wing over the people in his realm, upholding oaths, debts of honor, and loyalty in friendship."

Kayenté was impressed with her answer, not expecting her to speak with such sincerity or such length.

King William stroked his beard thoughtfully. "You think well of him, then. My cousin and I have always had a wager on who would one day rule Kantine, him, or me. Who do you think should win—you who are of Gatish blood?"

Kamara's brows drew together suspiciously. "How is it, King William, that you know my heritage?"

Kayenté said, "Yes, pray tell, how do you know her heritage?"

King William answered, "Your mother—"

Kamara's face tightened, "My . . . my mother? You know of my mother?"

"Priestesses of the Mist—"

Her hand flew to her heart and she expelled a short forceful breath. "How do you know of the Priestesses?"

King William continued, ignoring her interruption, "—first emerged in Gateland over two hundred years ago. Does that not make you Gatish?"

Her breathing grew shallow. The whole world seemed to slow down. The past was summoning her into a trance, but the present wouldn't let her go. She pressed her palm against her queasy stomach. "The Priestesses emerged in Gateland, yes, but that does not mean we are of Gatish blood."

"Your mother was birthed from a Gatish princess."

The color on Kamara's face drained and she stared at King William blankly.

Kayenté's expression matched, though he worked hard to shake it off. Kamara *was* royalty, with or without the Duke as her sire.

"Surely you knew this," said the King, bewildered.

"No," Kamara said in a daze, "no one ever told me." She swallowed hard between each breath, feeling her mouth go dry. "Who was the Gatish Princess?"

King William said, "Your great grandmother, Katara Lania married my great grandfather, King William the Terrible. He forced her, of course. She abhorred the power of royalty, as it is known Priestesses do, that is why I'm quite surprised that you endorse Lord Kayenté."

Kamara's heart pounded. She feared King William would stop telling the story she'd longed all her life to hear, so she held focus. "My great grandmother, Katara Lania . . . why did she come to Kantine?"

King William replied, "When she became pregnant with your grandmother, she fled, not wishing her daughter raised under an evil dictators influence. She and the Priestesses had much magic, but not enough to ward off William the Terrible, his band of advisors, and his multitude of armies."

Suddenly, a *knowing* stopped Kamara's breath, a knowing so hideous and so shocking, her face froze.

"Lady Kamara?" King William leaned toward her, "Are you ill?"

"Kamara?" Kayenté placed an assuring hand on her back, until he realized he was overtly showing compassion, and withdrew it quickly.

Kamara shook her head, and sucked in a jagged breath. "Priestesses in a collective can be *most* powerful. The profusion of Mist can create unparalleled camouflage." She looked up at King William. "Not even your great grandfather could have been such a threat."

"You give your kind much credit."

"What I'm saying is that William the Terrible had help in his treachery, for no human, nor army of humans can subdue the Priestesses without counter magic at play."

King William answered, though he was more preoccupied by Kamara's heart-stopping reaction. "William the Terrible had a sorcerer, yes."

Kamara breathed heavily, benumbed by her discovery. The Sorcerer was the Cold One, she was certain. He was timeless the Wise One had said—inhuman. He apparently borrowed human bodies, operating through one, until it died, and then another until it expired, and so on. Kamara's face looked broken.

King William reached a hand to her. "Lady Kamara, you've gone pale."

"Perhaps you should rest," suggested Kayenté, beating King Williams's hand to cover hers, forcing his cousin to retract his bejeweled appendage.

Neither Kayenté nor King William would believe what she knew, so she dared not explain—not yet anyway.

"I will be all right," she replied to them, still needing more information.

She addressed King William, "What happened next? How did my great grandmother escape him?"

King William replied, "She gathered her Priestess Sisters and fled to Kantine to get far away from him. The Sisters used their mystical powers to escape, and it was said that they used their magic to have Sakajians build a temple for the Sisterhood here in Kantine. As we Gatish are not much welcomed here, we risked a war we were not prepared for by our persistent search for her. The men that were sent could never locate the temple. But then, as you have just revealed, Priestesses in a collective are powerful. Queen Katara built a castle not a temple, which was an unexpected camouflage, not to mention the mists with which your kind are so fond."

"What did William the Terrible do when he couldn't locate her?" Kamara asked.

"He took his life."

Kamara's eyes widened. "What? Are you saying that he loved her?"

King William nodded. "Light Priestesses are easy to love, but most men, not unlike my great grandfather, resist love's power, fearing it will weaken them, and cripple their warrior ways. So . . . King William the Terrible remained terrible, even though his heart shattered when Katara left him." King William paused and then glanced at Kayenté.

Kayenté knew that William was wondering if history was in the remake with him and Kamara. And Kayenté wondered too.

Kamara withdrew her hand from Kayenté's and rested it on her lap under the table. She sank into deep contemplation. She jumped, startled by King William's voice, "And now here you are, William the Terrible's great granddaughter. And here am I . . . William the Terrible's great grandson."

Her head fell despairingly, and her hands covered her face, trying to put the truth to bed. Yet, out the truth popped with a heavy sigh from Kamara's weighted chest. Her hands slid down to her nose and she peeked over her fingertips at King William. Alas, her hands fell to her lap. "So, I am the seed of a man who bears the brand, Terrible? No wonder my guardian hid the truth. Who was your great grandmother? Certainly, not my great grandmother!"

"Certainly, not. Preceding your great grandmother, my great grandfather had another wife, but she died. I am a descendent of that union. So actually, you and I are cousins, just as Kayenté and I are cousins."

Kamara glanced at Kayenté. "But I'm not a cousin to Kayenté—am I?"

"I think not," said the King, "although, I'm not sure."

Kayenté felt stiff, in this heyday of surprise relations that had been unfolding ever since he'd taken Kamara under his protection. He was King William's cousin, and King William was Kamara's cousin. Didn't that make him and Kamara some sort of cousins, if not brother and sister, if per chance that they were both sired by the Duke?

"So," King William said, "would it not befit you to return with me and reclaim your Gatish heritage and your place in royalty?"

Kayenté nearly drew his sword to King William's throat, when Kamara blurted, "Why? So that you can show Kayenté how easily you can take me from him, and consequently Kantine?"

Kayenté was dumbfounded. He never dreamed that she could have found her way out of the web his cousin was spinning around her, to the purpose of unnerving him. But she did, not only by responding shrewdly, but also on his behalf!

King William replied, "You are an intelligent woman. But despite your theory, you belong in Gateland with your family."

"No. I belong with Lord Kayenté,for I believe in him. I believe in his noble heart, and further more . . . I love him."

Kayenté was stunned, and rather pleased by her public admission of love.

King William laughed. "Maybe so, but your love will be lonely. My cousin cares nothing of love and that is why I would better rule Kantine than he."

Kamara said, "You know love, King William? I mean true unconditional love?"

"Yes, Kamara Lania. You would not need to flee from my royal court as once Katara Lania did."

"If you know love—then why do you torment Kayenté?"

"And you don't?" King William asked. "Don't tell me that you aren't forever probing his soul in an attempt to save it? You are tormenting Kayenté, Kamara Lania, I assure you. Hell, I've only known you for ten minutes and you're tormenting me!"

Kamara shook her head. "You don't understand love."

King William shook his head back at her. "You don't understand men."

"I admit that. Can you as bravely admit that you don't understand love?"

"No Kamara, for if you understood men, you'd not ask me to admit such a thing."

Kayenté listened to them banter, one clever comment after another. And though he was subtly entertained, he felt that Kamara was doing his regular bit for him, and he actually felt left out of the fight.

King William said, "Return with me to Gateland, Lady Kamara, where you will be safe from the violent unrest in Kantine. If I return as Kayenté's enemy, I'll consider you the same."

Kamara gasped when a sword flashed over the table touching King Williams's throat. Kayenté stood tall with deadly rage. "You dare threaten an innocent under my protection!"

King Williams's bodyguards sucked in around him. King William ordered them at bay. "Forgive my poor manners, cousin. I expected no less from you in consequence."

Kayenté allowed his sword to fall back to his side.

Kamara adored it whenever Kayenté assertively defended her, an adoration that accompanied shame, for it was not very 'priest-essy' of her to delight in such displays.

"Lady Kamara, so you choose to remain here?"

She nodded. "My devotion lies with Kayenté."

King William declared shrewdly, "You err in your judgment."

"It is you, cousin, in error." Kayenté had a 'leave my premises' look in his eyes. "Kantine will be mine. And then, Lady Kamara will be mine too."

"That will never happen," King William said with assurance.

With the same assurance, Kayenté said, "I will give you Gate-land—for now."

"Give me? You could not take it!"

"I could—but it has not been in my interest do so." Kayenté was thinking of his bride-to-be and her Gatish dowry of substantial Gatish land. He would attain that first, and widen the boundary later. "However Kantine is my progeny. Even though your mother, the sister of my father and King Aldos, is Sakajian, thereby giving you Sakajian heritage, you have not spilled your blood upon Kan-tine's soil, as have I. You have not sweat your soul into the people of this province, as have I. And as for Lady Kamara, you could not survive the manipulative magic of this woman's boundless heart, just as you grandfather could not, Katara's. I can. I have. So be on your way King of Gateland. Kantine and the woman are mine."

"We'll see," said King William rising. His bodyguards flocked close. "My power is immense, cousin. When King Aldos dies, I'll challenge you for the crown. Causalities will be extensive."

Kayenté's men swarmed around him as he walked over to King William, and faced him squarely. He declared with cold confidence, "On both sides."

Kamara watched the lords, face to red face, dog to dog, on the cutting edge, teeth showing, sporting packs of men behind them.

"The next time we meet," said King William, "it will be with a sword."

Kayenté smiled coolly. "straight through your heart."

The King's eyes flared. "I've given you fair warning." He turned away from Kayenté, and departed with his men, exiting with drama fit for a play. Kayenté signaled his warriors to escort them off the grounds.

Kamara hadn't budged from her chair. She was speechless, overwhelmed by the power play, news about her heritage, family infighting, and what Kayenté mentioned about her manipulative magic. How could he! Why she chose him over King William was beyond her. No, it wasn't. She loved Kayenté—she did.

Kayenté neared her. "That went well."

"Well? How can you claim mutual threats a well event?"

"He came to see if I had softened. He found that I had not. It went well."

Kamara sat there in a glower, for to her, nothing had gone well.

Kayenté reached to assist her up from her chair. "So," he said, "was your support for me—about beans?"

She took his hand and rose. "No Kayenté, it was about love— unlike your support for me," she added snidely.

He kept hold of her hand and walked, ignoring the last part of her statement. Instead, he said, "So, you are of royal blood. Does that bother you?"

"Does it bother you? Does it give my opinions more weight?"

"Only the ones about how you think I'd make a good King," he said smiling. And then he asked more seriously, "Do you?"

She nodded shyly. "That is . . . if there must be a King."

"Anarchy doesn't work Kamara."

"How do you know? Have you ever tried it?"

"No. But you have, and look where you wound up—in the arms of a tyrant."

"And look at you, protecting an anarchist."

He glanced sideways at her, amused by her cleverness. "Well, my little anarchist, no more special privileges, like meals in your room. You will dine in the Great Hall tonight."

She froze.

He stopped, and examined the look on her face.

She glared at him as if he were a traitor. She wanted to rebel outright, but she had learned that such tactics only made him more determined to make her abide his wishes. So, instead she beseeched him. "Please Kayenté, give me one more day. I'm not prepared to sit in the middle of all that violence."

"Having dinner is violent? . . . Oh," he said smiling, "violence means eating dead pigs with warriors."

She nodded her head profusely. "I did well with the King. I believe I've earned one more day of freedom."

His eyes sparkled. "Very well . . . one day more."

She said, "That's a full day, mind you, meaning not until tomorrow evening's meal."

He smiled. "You bargain well. It's too bad you've decided to be an anarchist, for you're very good at getting your own way."

Her eyes glossed with tears.

"My words upset you?"

"No, I'm saddened because you are intent on getting yours. You are playing dangerous political games with frightening and powerful opponents. Oh Kayenté, I would give anything if you'd disqualify yourself and come home with me."

His voice grew sad and serious, "I can't."

She bobbed her head lightly. "I know."

She walked forward, seeking exile in her bedchamber. He escorted her in silence, tormented by the same lonely knowing that they would one day—part.

Ж
Chapter Seventeen

Kamara hibernated in her room until the following day. Kayenté never came for her, not even for sword practice. Was he sad too? Or did he just forget? He just didn't care that she loved him. He just didn't care.

That afternoon, Allysa arrived, saying, "Lord Kayenté requests your company at the tournament."

"Tournament? I can't witness a tournament!"

"Oh!" said Allysa, "tournaments are thrilling entertainment. The knights compete to ascertain the most skilled. Each man fights for a lady's honor."

"Is Kayenté participating?"

"No, the lord need not, for his position proves his supreme skill."

"Still, I can't attend. Inform him I've taken ill."

"He told me you'd say that, and to inform you that he would revoke your prison privileges if you didn't come."

Kamara's melancholy mood turned hostile. Why had he placed such cruel conditions upon her? Why was he insistent on integrating her into a lifestyle that she found so offensive?

"Lady . . ." Allysa said loudly, trying to get her attention. "You mustn't wear your fighting clothes, for his honored seat mustn't be met with boyish attire. Kayenté has stocked your armoire with many gowns. Choose one that will honor him."

"Oh, very well," Kamara agreed reluctantly, because she had to relent on some issues if she expected him to do the same. No, that wasn't it. She longed to see him again, despite the cost. She missed him more than she dared admit. She wanted to bury her face in his hair, kiss his lips in mutual, unconditional love—an impossible dream, for he could never relinquish control. Without that, they were doomed to fail.

She changed into a plain, velvet burgundy gown with a neckline that showed mostly the shoulders, laced close to the body with sleeves buttoned tight to the arms, reaching to the middle of the hands. She wore a small gold belt around the hips. She wrapped her hair in a simple bun, held in place by glittering burgundy clips. This would have to do.

Allysa led her to the field where the tournaments were held. The atmosphere was indeed festive. Off to one side, colorful blankets were spread for the servants. For those higher in rank, rows of chairs were neatly aligned. Taller ornately carved chairs, perched on a canopy-covered platform were reserved for the lord and his guests.

Allysa led her past people taking their chairs. Kamara was silently detesting the blatant division of social positions when Kayenté approached from behind and came between her and Allysa, interlocking his arms, one around each with an air of arrogance.

Kamara angered at his smug way of walking with two women whom he knew loved him. And he hadn't even offered an apology or explanation for abandoning her sword lesson that morning. Well, she would show him that love did not mean she'd allow herself to be taken for granted!

She broke away from him. She had to catch her breath, pretending she did not admire his kingly attire: White shirt with a cross-laced front opening, from neck to hem. Full yoke with wide gathered sleeves. Narrow collar, button cuffs. Black leather belt over shirt. Sheathed sword at side. Long black breeches with tie string cuffs, ending just above his calf-high black boots with the white panther insignia at the ankles. His hair was tied back at the top. His eyes were so blue. Her face began to soften, but no it must not!

Confused by her action, Kayenté observed the proud expression upon her face.

Allysa broke away too, and Kayenté became irritated.

He gazed at each of them. "Do you ladies not feel honored to walk with the lord of this Castle?"

Kamara raised her brows. "Do you not feel honored to walk with two fair women?"

He glanced around. "Should I choose two others?"

"If you like," Kamara said, "but it shall be your loss."

Allysa reiterated, "Yes . . . your loss."

He promptly dragged Kamara away from the crowd and pushed her roughly against the castle wall, placing his hands flat against the stone on either side of her head.

"If you hadn't already incurred so many bruises, I'd beat you for your insolence!"

"Oh," her lips tightened, "then you *do* enjoy harming me."

"You'll not school my people to disrespect me."

"Disrespect? I am merely upholding my honor."

"And what grave action of dishonor did I dispose upon you by escorting you and Allysa to your seats?"

"It was the manner in which you took us."

"And what manner was that?"

"In the same manner with which you wear and wield your sword—which of course is how ever you wish."

"And why pray tell, should women be so different? They all sell themselves to a man for the right price."

She huffed, and pushed against his chest in a gesture of disgust, attempting to leave. "I have no price."

He pressed his hand hard over her heart and pushed her back against the wall. "Your price is love."

She glanced down at the hand that pinned her, and then she looked him in the eye. "I would not let you treat me like property in exchange for a commitment that you would call love, because it would not be love—for true love is free and it cannot be owned, nor treated lightly."

"Like your true love for me?" Kayenté said in jest.

"Yes, Kayenté. I don't have to own you to love you. I don't even have to like you to love you. And there's nothing you can do to break that love, because no matter what you do, I'll always see the child in you—suffering."

He gritted his teeth. "I could make you hate me, lady."

"Your labor to do so would merely prove that you have feelings for me, not to mention a worthless attempt to sabotage the blossoming of such a love."

"I don't love you."

"Yes, Kayenté, there's some small part of you that loves me. I've seen it in your eyes."

"You've seen pity."

"No. I've seen love. You can try to degrade me all you wish, even in the same manner that you have been degraded, but I'll not wilt, because love, still I believe, in the end . . . conquers all."

He released her and stepped backward. "You've returned to your fairy tale world, I see." He grabbed her arm, slinging her back toward the crowd where Allysa waited.

"The fairy tale is real," she said.

"If you challenge me in public again—woman, you'll regret it."

"Are you saying I can challenge you in private?"

"Damn you," he said, half-serious, half-teasing, "I'll have to take out your tongue."

"I'd still have my eyes, lord. And if you take out my eyes, still I would have my love, and that—you can never obliterate."

He growled lightly.

When they reached Allysa, he interlocked his arm with her as before, and then Kamara's. "If you choose to defy me, you will be whipped."

Kamara knew he wouldn't whip her, somehow, she just knew.

Allysa dipped her head back slightly, behind Kayenté, worry lining her face.

Kamara met Allysa's gaze behind Kayenté back, and winked. Allysa gave a faint smile, and together they ascended the steps of the wood platform and arrived at the chairs.

Kayenté and Kamara sat in the two tallest chairs, under a red canopy. Allysa sat beside Kamara on a smaller chair. The crowd gathered. The trumpets sounded and a man called, "Let the games commence! The victor will partner Lord Kayenté and his officers when we ride into battle tomorrow!" The orator continued talking, but Kamara did not hear.

She was staring at Kayenté. "Battle? Tomorrow? Is that why you didn't show up for my lesson this morning? You were preparing for tomorrow?"

He acknowledged her with a slight nod, offering no further explanation. He must distance himself from his little bird, if he was to have the lack of heart to leave her. He needed to steal himself against the tenderness she evoked in him, if it was battle he must do. Tenderness and warfare were not comrades.

He beheld her endeavor to repress her usual tears. They dripped from her eyes anyway.

"I was wrong Kayenté," she uttered lightly.

He tilted his head. "Wrong?"

"Yes." She answered softly, her words like velvet. "There is one way you can break my heart—" she paused and then said, "—if you die."

He whispered in her ear, "Kamara, I am a survivor." He looked to the field where all eyes were upon him. He signaled the first competitors to charge each other.

Hearing the thud of hooves, Kamara closed her eyes. The smell of dirt rose in the air. She heard a man jousted from his horse, and the crowd cheering.

Her hands flew over her ears. "This hurts me!" She started to leave, but Kayenté snatched her arm, pinning her to her seat. How could he be so cruel? Or maybe he needed to be cruel. Block and parry. Love was the enemy.

She stilled and labored escape by going deep within herself.

Kayenté gazed upon her closed eyes and tear dampened lashes, searching for the truth that lingered beneath her paradoxical show of love and hate for him. How could she hate all he stood for, yet insist it was he she loved?

Kamara's mind played scenes of Kayenté jousting, gouging, and being gouged—while jousting, war, beheadings, de-armings, de-leggings, Kayenté's corpse rotting in the sun. An unwilled whimper burst from her mouth. Fearing for his life, for his style, and his choices, she slid her eyes his way, and viewed him looking upon her. "Please Kayenté," she said gently, "you know this is too harsh for me, and the news of tomorrow, harsher still. I can't help that I am—as I am, nor the fact . . . that I love you deeply."

Kayenté's heart ached, and he didn't want it to, so he released her wordlessly and turned his attention to the tournament.

She rose and began to walk away.

Allysa whispered, "Lady, do you need me?"

Kamara shook her head, and descended the platform.

Allysa studied Kayenté's face. Behind the hardness, his expression was quite clear. He prized Kamara. She defied him without punishment. He adored her. No other woman had he aided without payment of some kind—only Kamara was exempt . . . only her.

Allysa's heart ached as her own dream of making Kayenté love her—died. And in an act of true nobility, she decided to direct her efforts towards bringing Kayenté and Kamara closer together. If anyone other than she was to have Kayenté's love, she preferred that woman be Kamara, who was the kindest lady she'd known in all her life.

Ж
Chapter Eighteen

Kamara slunk to her room, locked her door, and fell heavy upon the blue satin bed, staring at the ceiling. She let loose her hair, and spread her arms over the soft satin as if she were preparing to fly. She wished she could fly invisibly alongside Kayenté tomorrow. Tomorrow Kayenté would leave her. Tomorrow Kayenté would ride into war.

Hearing distant cheering from the tournament, she rested her hands over her heart and rolled onto her side. A little gnat landed on her bare ear. She whisked it away and pulled her hair over her face. Hiding felt good.

Kayenté was hiding too, hiding from her, hiding from love. That brief, raw, wild spilling of their hearts on the day she bridged him at Lania Castle, had never recurred. It seemed the more tenderly he felt toward her, the more detached he'd become. Oh, how he fought love! He was better at battling warriors than love, but he clearly excelled in both.

However, fighting the Cold One was another matter. The Cold One was after Kayenté too. Why had she not told him? But then, she knew that answer. She didn't want ugly truths to emerge. She didn't want him to know that his childhood tormenter was the Cold One. And that the Cold One was The Nothing. And that Kayenté might be her brother. Nevertheless, he had to know before he left— He had to know just how enmeshed he was with the Cold One, and that the Cold One might try to destroy him while out on the battlefield.

She crawled under the covers, drew them over her head, and curled in a tight ball. The long arms of sleep enfolded her. When

she woke, she didn't hear the cheering voices of bloodlust that had
lingered in her ears when she had fallen asleep. The tournament must be over.

Light still filled the room, so day was yet at hand. Even so, she planned to hide under her covers until Kayenté bade her goodbye. Then she would tell him of the Cold One. Another fear burrowed deep inside her. Had she bonded with him too closely to detach from his experiences? If he survived, would she?

She heard a knock at the door and Kayenté's monotone voice. "Kamara, are you well?"

She went to the door, but she did not open it. "No."

"Unlock the door."

"It pains me to see you."

"Open the door. I've instructions for you while I'm away."

"No."

"Kamara, if you truly love me, you'll let me in. And if you don't—well, I do have a key."

She opened the door, hesitantly, but blocked him from entering. She stared at his feet, so that she wouldn't have to look at his face. "Tell me quickly and be gone."

He took her forearm and led her from the doorway, down the corridor, too fast. She was all too aware of her legs bumping against the thick skirt, taking her from the shelter of her room. "Kayenté, where are you taking me? I want to stay in my room."

"You can't pretend the truth away."

"Well, I am pretty good at that."

"I am going to show you an escape route, on the rare chance you might need it."

"I don't want to do this! I don't want to think about it!"

"Also, if I'm detained or don't return, I've left instructions for Sir Robert to continue teaching you the way of the sword."

"I don't want Sir Robert to teach me."

"Nor did I want Camille to teach me," he jested, trying to get a rise from her.

She gave him a sidelong glance. "We both know you never wanted to learn."

He cleared his throat and said more seriously, "Just the same, I've lined up several replacements for you, should Sir Robert meet with misfortune. If I don't return within a year, then my family will claim the castle if another hasn't seized it. You're welcome to stay as long as you wish," and then he added with a touch of humor, "as long as you don't free my prisoners."

She glowered at him. Through the glower, her eyes watered. "Remember the gift I gave you. Wear it always."

Kamara pulled away from him, her back landing on the corridor wall, hands over ears. "Stop this talk! You *can't* leave me. You *can't* expect me to use that knife on anyone but the Cold One. Moreover, I do not run from danger. I do not escape. I mist. I pacify the attacker. That there may be hundreds of them, presents a problem, but it is not in my nature to flee.

"Those events are unlikely Kamara. I just want you prepared— in case."

"You *can't* go to war. You cannot tell me these things. I will *not* listen! I will *not* hear."

He approached her, and drew her hands down from her ears. "You must face these realities, these possibilities."

She shook her head adamantly. "No. No, I shan't, I shan't face them. I can't think of you charging into a mass of swords and spears and all those other pointy, chain objects you fight with, flying from your body, *at* your body. I can't think of you in battle with the Cold One lurking in the shadows, ready to slit your throat!"

Time missed a beat. Silence ate it.

"Kamara? Why would the Cold One . . . be after *my* throat?"

She spoke so lightly, he almost couldn't hear. "He knows *everything* about you Kayenté, and I do mean everything. He's after you as much as he is me." She tightened her lips to stop more words from tumbling forth.

"Why did you not tell me before?"

"I feared your reaction."

"Talk."

Her gold eyes peered up at him full of answers, however, her mouth remained motionless.

"Talk!"

She said, almost in a whisper, "He knows you, your mother—and mine."

Kayenté's eyes turned dark with suspicion. "How?"

She swallowed hard several times, then inhaled intensely, preparing to speak. When she exhaled, no words came.

Kayenté's jaws flinched wrath. "This is no time for weakness Kamara."

"The Cold One said that . . ." she lost her breath suddenly and gasped for air to finish the sentence out loud, "he had assaulted my mother . . . and your mother . . . and that you and I would fall, along with—the world."

Kayenté's eyes smoldered. "De—scribe . . . him."

"He is a large stocky man, at least six feet tall. He has a wide face and round chin, with abnormally white squarish teeth, a flat broad nose, haunting black eyes, and a cruel and roaring laugh. There is a seductive way about him, like he is a whirlpool sucking you in, and it is hard to resist."

Kayenté became deadly still. He lowered his chin, but his eyes stayed high in the sockets, making him appear evil. "He is Ajento. He is my mother's rapist. He is my father."

She reached her arm to touch him, to bring him sane again.

He jerked back. He did not want her touch.

"I think he is my father too," she said.

He narrowed his eyes with seething hate.

"Kayenté, you're scaring me!"

Kayenté's face softened, barely. "It's meant for him, Kamara, not you."

"Still . . . ."

The submission in her eyes aroused his sympathy. He stroked the side of her head briefly. "He is not your father."

"Maybe fate has brought us upon each other, Kayenté, because we are brother and sister."

"No," he said, jaw clenched at the thought. "We are not brother and sister."

"How do you know? What do you know? Why do you know?"

He thought of the Duke's confession, and the Wise One not affirming his assumption that the Cold One sired her. He decided not to tell her, yet. Too much was already at hand. Just another secret to toss into the graveyard, where it could haunt him from the shadows and drive him to secure his future, because he couldn't change the past.

"I know," he said. "Besides, you don't carry the evil legacy of that devil in your heart. I do. I thought him long gone, but he will never be gone, until I make him gone." His eyes twitched pain, more so than rage. "He sired my mother's child. He'll *not* sire yours. When I return, I *will* hunt him down, and I *will* destroy him."

"Oh dearest Kayenté, please remember, we must fight him together. A sword alone shall not end him, for he is supernatural. Magic, alone cannot kill him, for he possesses a human body."

"You are not going near him again, Kamara. I forbid it. But we will talk of this when I return."

She shook her head uneasy. "None of this feels right. We—you and I—must *not* be separated. Must you leave tomorrow?"

"Yes."

"But you're not safe out there. I say this Kayenté, because my love for you is great,."

"Love is free," remember Kamara. "You need not *have* me."

She stepped back, hurt by the mask he'd raised. "Even at this final hour, you distance yourself from love. You will leave then, with armored heart, and eyes glazed cold, perhaps forfeiting your life to escape love, and forfeiting the world to escape defeat."

"Kamara, this is reality. This is war. Your visions blind you from here, from now, from what must be done. Kantine must be saved from slavery. Guarding boundaries is your weakness, not mine. I leave tomorrow to save Kantine, to empower it. All Sakajian lords have sworn to meet and join forces to end the Rudels' aggression once and for all. When I return, I'll devise a plan to outwit and slay our demon. He took her hand gently. "I promise this with my life."

"What if you die before you can return?"

"I won't."

"What if I die before you can return?"

"You won't."

"I may. I won't use an escape route. I won't run. I will face what comes . . ." her face saddened, "and come what may."

"I will show you anyway, though I doubt you'll need it. You are safer here than anywhere. No sign of the Cold One yet, and when there has been, it's been in the woods when you were alone."

A little white mouse scurried along the edge of the corridor, small in a big castle. She became silent inside herself, small in a huge fear.

He led her by the hand down a spiral staircase, through two secret openings into a little room. A ladder reached to a hatch on the ceiling. Once up the ladder, they emerged outdoors into dismal gray. He took her across a yard, through a hidden opening in the curtain wall, over to the moat. With his boot, he cleared away the earth next to where they stood, showing her a covered tunnel. He bent over, and opened the lid. "This tunnel goes under the water and comes out the other side."

She smiled faintly. "You must have love for me, or you'd not show me this."

He replaced lid, and the dirt that covered it, ignoring her words. He rose and pointed north. There is a nunnery, twenty kilometers that way and there you will find sanctuary for at least forty days. Should the Cold One find you again, let him think you are still the pacifist at heart, and then, when he lets his guard down, kill him . . . anyway you can."

"Do you believe I can defeat him?"

"To succeed, you must let yourself be as cold as he. He'd never expect that."

"If there is a fairy tale Kayenté, your words and actions weave it. There's only one truth for me now. If you die, I'll belong to the Cold One."

He glanced down at her with an assuring eye. "I'll survive, if only to purge that devil from this earth. I will avenge my mother, your mother, and I will not allow the Cold One to give me further cause to avenge you. As for the battle, I'll be fighting with over sixty thousand men. My war experience borders fifteen years, Kamara. I return. I always return."

"A thing of miracles. What I witnessed that day at your father's castle showed me the death toll in war. It all seems so predictably fatal."

He smiled. "That's what I like about it. Achieving the undo-able."

She glared at him.

He took her hand. "Come, it is time for the evening meal, a feast for my highest ranking warriors." He began leading her back toward the stone wall.

"I'm not hungry."

"I hold you to your bargain."

"Well, I'm breaking it."

He looked at her, astonished. "You lied to me."

"*You* lied to *me*. You said you'd protect me and now you're running off to kill people, and maybe get killed yourself."

"You *will* dine with me."

"I can't sit at a table with dead animals."

"I've instructed the servants to put them off to the far side of the table."

"No, that shan't do!"

They entered the castle and climbed down the ladder.

"I refuse to eat at that table," she said again.

He grumbled, then snatched her abruptly, lifting her upward, landing her stomach on his shoulder, and walked.

"Kayenté, release me at once. It is cruel for you to carry me in this manner."

"It is cruel for you to refuse my dinner invitation."

"But, I don't will this."

"And what of my will?"

"Your will! Must every little thing revolve around your will? I'm always forced to do things your way."

He carried her through the second passageway. "Have you forgotten that I let you pamper my prisoners? Have you forgotten that I've not punished you for your many breeches of my command? Have you forgotten that it was you who fell to my feet begging for help? I think the least you can do is sup with me."

Her frustration was such that she wanted to yank the back of his long hair. "You turn everything around to make yourself look perfect, while I am made to look like a disruptive rebel!"

He carried her down the stairs. "To the contrary Kamara, I've been more than willing to claim my part in disheveling Kantine, that I may control it. I am of the devil. And on a more glacial note, I am of the Cold One."

"Stop Kayenté, put me down," she said seriously.

"No," he said, "the exercise does me well, readying me for tomorrow's battle."

"Kayenté," she said calmly, "please, I must tell you something."

He stopped at the bottom of the stairs at the entrance of the Great Hall, and landed her feet gently on the floor. His expression held question.

She gazed at him, child-like, full of emotion. Then she lunged forward, rising on her toes. She wrapped her arms around his neck, clinging hard. "You're not bad Kayenté. You're not!"

He wanted to return her earnest embrace. He wanted to absorb the sweet kiss she gave to his neck. He wanted to believe that he was not bad. But he was. So he gripped her arms and pushed her away.

"I am what I am, Kamara. And not even you can save me."

"Love can save you."

He threw his head back derisively. "No," he said. "Love can't *even* save you."

"But—"

"Come." He walked ahead of her into the Great Hall. She followed, feeling sorry for him.

He led her silently to the three enormously long trestle tables moved together in the shape of a square with one side missing. The feast was set: meat, fish, cabbage, turnips, and more. Kamara averted her eyes from the table. The meaty aroma made her ill. She clung to Kayenté's arm, still intimidated by the great many warriors that dwelled in this area of the castle. She felt their male eyes assessing her.

Kayenté sat at the center of the table, and seated her to his right. A few hundred knights took their chairs, and Kayenté signaled that the feasting could commence.

Kamara recoiled when hands jutted everywhere, snatching food and drink, stuffing mouths with hearts and livers and victuals she'd never before seen, sloshing wine over gluttonous faces, toasting over and over, "Death to the Rudels!"

She stared at the hungry mob, stupefied: her plate empty, her appetite ruined.

Kayenté glanced at her—twice, for her skin paled by the moment. "Sup, Kamara," he said, hoping to spark some life into her. "You can't be served in your room forever."

Allysa eyed Kamara's paled faced from the kitchen, surprised to see her attending the courtly feast. Kamara's head dipped down several times, and Allysa knew she struggled. Since one of her jobs was to assure Kayenté's culinary pleasure and hers, perhaps he would not mind if she intervened.

She approached the omnivorous mob bravely and stopped before Kayenté. "Lord, may I be permitted to serve Lady Kamara,"

He nodded with a sigh.

Kamara stumbled on her words, "Uh . . . better yet, may I dine with the servants?"

He stared intensely at her fragile face. He had been trying to harden her, though it was her softness that held the appeal, which was one reason he wanted her hard. However, she was frail in these matters. He could not dismiss that fact, nor did he wish her to faint again in her usual manner. He signaled his hand, meaning away with you.

She went with Allysa, holding her sickly stomach all the way to the kitchen where the servants ate. The huge charcoal colored kitchen was dotted with servants busy by the stone ovens, fiery spits, and hot cauldrons. Allysa bade Kamara sit at the mammoth butcher-block table, and then went to a corner of the kitchen where potatoes, and green cabbage were abundantly heaped.

Kamara did not sit. "I cannot dine while others labor."

"Nonsense," said Allysa. "No one here will think less of you if you do. It is the way of things."

"But—"

"Sit!"

Kamara sat reluctantly.

"Allysa returned with a steel platter of grapes, long green beans, cooked cabbage, red baked potatoes, and fresh hot bread with blueberry jam. She set it on the table in front of Kamara. "Please eat. You are going to melt away into nothing if you don't."

"I regret that you must baby me so."

Allysa sat next to her. "Dining in Kayenté's castle is rougher than at the Dukes. I think the Duchess demands refinement. Kayenté can take it or leave it."

Kamara noticed Allysa had no plate. "Aren't you hungry?"

"We can't eat until everyone out there is done. "

"Nonsense." Kamara pushed her plate toward Allysa.

Allysa pushed it back. "No, I will eat well when it's my turn. You eat now. I insist."

Kamara felt bad eating in front of Allysa, but her appetite had returned stronger than ever and she had not eaten well in days. She bit off a hunk of soft warm bread that practically melted in her mouth, almost as delicious as Teeah's.

Allysa made small talk while Kamara ate, not wanting her to stop, which was sure to happen with the bigger news she had to tell. When at last Kamara finished, Allysa touched her arm. "I'm glad you joined me. Now that you have finished your meal, I have news to share."

Kamara scowled, not sure she wanted to hear it. The meal already felt sour in her stomach.

Allysa spoke, "The warriors say King Aldos is ill and soon to die. He has bequeathed his throne to Kayenté. Even though the King's advisor, Drudel Battling, has made an oath with Kayenté to uphold the Kings choice, there is suspicion that he will instead challenge Kayenté for the throne. And further, William of Gateland, who also seeks rule of Kantine, will wage war on the Sakajians if they don't submit the throne to him. But the Sakajians will resist, for they want a Sakajian lord—not a Gate. Harold Wincott of Rudelia also seeks the throne.

"The battle the Sakajians fight tomorrow is enormous Kamara, aimed to cut down the Rudels before reinforcements arrive. But the battle after . . . ." Allysa shook her head. "If all these men and their armies should fight for the throne, the chaos will be enormous. What will you do Kamara if such a battle should ensue? Will you stand by Kayenté as a Sakajian, or return to Lania Castle and stay neutral?"

Kamara threw her head back, squeezed her eyes shut, and held her breath. She sighed, and looked at Allysa squarely. "I don't know what I shall do," she said, agitated. "I don't know the right or wrong of dark matters. I'm more concerned about *cold* matters."

"What do you mean?" Allysa scooted her chair closer.

"The prey and the predator shall dance, and I suppose there are lessons to be learned from each, by both. But what if something happened to make both prey and predator disappear. What if nothingness swallowed both sides, all sides of everything and everyone. Then what?"

"Why, that would be dreadful!"

"So you see, I'm more concerned about preserving humankind, than I am solving the squabbles amongst them."

Allysa's face creased with alarm. "The world could end?"

Kamara nodded, "I fear so."

Allysa scanned the kitchen as if searching the world for danger. "Ah!"

A woman stood in the shadow of the doorway. She appeared emaciated and weary. Long white unkempt hair flowed over her tattered brown shift.

Kamara followed Allysa's gaze.

"Wise One!" She sprung to her feet and bolted to the door. She grasped the old woman's hands, and pulled her inside the kitchen. "You are well! I'm elated to behold you. How did you get past the guards?"

"I'm clever," she said, "and because of my cleverness I bring you information. I've much to tell you, child. Where can we speak privately?"

Allysa jumped up. "I know a place!" She grabbed an oil lamp. "It's outside, but no one ever goes there. It's an old storage house. Come!" She raced past Kamara and the Wise One.

"Enthusiastic child," the Wise One said, trailing Allysa.

"Very." Kamara followed the Wise One. "She would do well in our way of life."

Allysa led them into the warm night across a stretch of ground to a shed. She opened the door, and from her oil lamp, she lit three white candles sitting on a crate. You can sit there on the straw mat. This has been my thinking place."

Kamara turned to Allysa and smiled. "Thank you."

"You're most welcome." Allysa left, closing the door.

The Wise One sat upon the mat. "Come child."

Kamara eagerly joined the Wise One. They sat facing each other, bright-hearted in a moment of potent silence.

Then Kamara asked, "What guidance have you for me?"

The Wise One placed her cold rough hands over Kamara's. "The time is upon you to now perform the male-female ritual with Lord Kayenté."

Kamara's face froze. "You mean," she gulped, "I must engage," she gulped again, "sexually with him?"

"You have known that we perform sacred rituals through the sex act? Teeah was to have instructed you."

"Yes," she blushed, "but I've never done it."

"The time has come. If you do it, you shall be fortified against the Cold One. If you do not, the Cold One shall succeed in making you submit to him—be it by seduction, a show of brutality, or intimidating you into surrendering the hope of defeating him. If you surrender—all is lost. You *must* not surrender, no matter what he does to you. And you will, unless you are stronger. You simply are not prepared for the next attack. You need Lord Kayenté's power by virtue of his seed, before the Cold One comes again to plant his own child inside your womb."

"Is this the third secret?"

"No, child, you still are not ready for the third secret. You're learning to wield the sword and to walk into the Cold One's world, a feat no Priestess of the Mist has ever accomplished. To walk in his world, you must know how to become as cold as he."

Kamara said, "That's what Kayenté told me!"

"Yes. Kayenté is the sole reason you've not yet been taken. And the sooner you learn his way, the safer you shall be."

"But I'm changing too much, I fear."

" 'The light' shall be there for you Kamara, when you need it. It shines in your heart. Fear not that you'll lose your beauty to the cold world you have begun to journey. You'll only lose it, if you stop. You must defeat the Cold One. You must! I've come to tell you, do not hesitate to use the sword upon him. I give you permission to champion the Priestesses with all the darkness you can summon."

"Can I do it, Wise One? Can I?"

"There's no time for doubt. You simply must succeed."

"I shall then," she cried adamantly, "somehow, I shall!"

"Then listen well."

A rap sounded on the door.

Allysa said hurriedly, "Lady Kamara, Lord Kayenté searches for you."

Kamara jumped up, and said to Allysa through the door. "I'll be out shortly."

Allysa said, "I'll be in the kitchen should you need me."

The Wise One blurted, "You'll not be safe when Kayenté departs. A traitor comes to the castle. You cannot stop these actions from happening, but you can alter them by how you react. I tell you," she said powerfully, "fight Kamara, fight like the demon in your nightmares! If you do not, Teeah and Lania Castle shall soon fall, and then there shall be no hope of salvaging this world. If you succeed, you'll bridge The Nothing with light and dark, and the world shall breathe and spirits shall transform as planned."

Kamara shot her very soul into the Wise One.

The Wise One inhaled deeply. "Yes, my dear, that feels good, but remember, do not do that with the Cold One. He shall keep you, unlike the bridged, who give you back. Remember, it's this very act of soul merging in which each Priestess was lulled into the Cold One's prison."

Panic clawed Kamara. Doubt bantered with her resolve to save the world. "Fare-the-well," she said quickly, so that her tears would not spill. "I'll have Allysa bring you food and a new cloak. Please wait for her. I love you." She raced out the door.

The Wise One called out, "Love is real, Kamara. Don't let anyone trick you into believing it is not!"

"I shall remember!" Kamara cried. She fled into the kitchen. "Allysa can you provide a cloak and food for her, please."

"Lady, what of you?"

"I *need* to be alone."

She raced into the Great Hall, slowing to a walk, trying to appear normal. She dare not loose her tears until she reached her room. The terror of all that was, weighed heavy in her chest, and each step felt like forever.

Kayenté glimpsed her moving up the stairs and followed.

Kamara arrived at her bedchamber. She raced inside and closed the door, leaning hard upon it, hands pressed against the wood, as if to seal it from opening. The waiting was over. The time was at hand to face everything. No. Not yet! But she must. Oh, she *must*. She ran to her bed and threw herself on the soft covers, sobbing her ruptured torment.

Kayenté pressed his ear to the door, hearing her muffled sobs. Had she been assaulted? Had she some dark revelation? Had she seen the Cold One? He flung the door open and rushed to her side. She was face down on the bed wailing into a pillow, as he'd never heard her wail before. And that was no easy feat, for he'd already heard her whimper, cry, weep, and sob, every which way, in all ranges and intensity's imaginable—for the woman was ever in tears. He was unable to handle any more of her fervent emotions when his own were so unstable. Her tears always undid him, and this day before battle, he could not be undone.

He ripped the pillow from her, and yanked her off the bed to her feet, shaking her shoulders. "Enough!"

She drew her trembling hands into prayer formation, touching her fingertips to her lips and rambled dramatically with closed eyes. Tears washed her cheeks, dripping into the corners of her mouth. "You leave . . . shield gone . . . traitor comes . . . Cold One, must defeat . . . world ends . . . be as cold as the Cold One . . . ." She shook her head, tears streaming harder, and she repeated in a gasping whisper, "Cold as the Cold One." Then she blurted, "I can't. I cannot do it."

"Kamara," he said assuringly, rubbing her arms.

She looked at him pointedly, face red with pain. "When you go tomorrow . . . the time shall come . . . for all—or nothing."

He drew her into his arms, mustering empathy after all. "There is no reason to your talk. I'll leave men to protect you. And the Cold One cannot end the world."

She pulled back from him slightly to see his face. "Oh yes, Kayenté, he can, and I must merge with you before you go."

"Merge?"

"I mean—merge," she said, "in every way, but you must meet me with your heart and soul, as our bodies join."

He cocked his head slightly, narrowing his eyes with interest.

"I tell you, if you do not help me . . . all shall be lost."

"I'll help you Kamara." He brushed his fingertips down her throat, toward her breast, edging his fingers along the square neckline of her burgundy gown.

She placed her hand over his roaming fingers, stopping them before they reached their destination. "It must be done right, or it shan't work, and the Cold One shall win."

He withdrew his hand. "You speak madness. Sexual relations with me will not help you defeat the Cold One, though I'd like to tell you it could."

She pushed him away, hurt by what she deemed his rejection of her proposal. "Then go!" she commanded pointing her finger toward the door. "I've no time for doubts or judgments. There's a far greater battle here to be fought than you realize. Don't you understand? If a child of 'the light' and a child of 'the dark' can find each other and bridge completely—the Cold One cannot take either of us. But if he should take even one, the other shall fall."

"You are a peculiar creature," he said, more interested in her solution than her problem, "and deluded to some extent, I'm sure." He circled his arms around her body. "I don't know if I believe half of what you say, but for this one night, and this night only, I'll grant your request with its conditions."

She sighed with relief, and returned his embrace. "This is a ritual Kayenté, and I've never done it before, so I ask for patience and good will. We must be outside, under the moon in the mid of night. Is there a place we can go, perhaps near water?"

"Yes," he brushed a strand of hair from her face, "but I've yet to prepare for tomorrow's battle, so I'll come for you later."

She bowed her head slightly. "Very well."

As he turned to leave, she said, "Kayenté!"

He gazed softly upon her.

"This is crucial. Don't forget."

"Kamara," he said with a dash of bravado in his eyes, "this is not the sort of thing a man forgets." He gazed at her with masculine want. "I'll return. I will."

She nodded, staring urgently upon him as he stepped backward to the door. His male stare ignited her body, an ignition she resented, even though she invited the ensuing act.

Only the closing of the door broke their mutual gaze.

She sank to her knees. "Oh mother, I'm coming! I'll free you from the Cold One. I'll be your warrior . . . me, your daughter, who once lived in pure love." Her voice quivered, "I'll turn cold for you, and cruel, and dark—and . . ."

She outstretched her arms and hung her head back. Her long hair dangled over her ankles. From her throat came a drawn-out strenuous whisper that held all the strength of a scream. Her eyes, like full moons dripped liquid agony.

Who she was to be, murdered who she had been. Her heart of light plunged into darkness. She fell forward into a heap, her quintessence spiraling down, down, down.

Ж
Chapter Nineteen

At eleven o'clock Kayenté knocked firmly on Kamara's door. The door opened slowly revealing Kamara in her fighting clothes. She glanced at Kayenté's face—barely, then stared shyly at his boots, lifting her eyes no further than the knees of his leather pants.

"Are you preparing to fight?" he inquired, with whimsy in his eye.

"I'm preparing *for* a fight."

He lifted her chin with his finger. "This is good." The blue gray blanket draped over his shoulder, defined his eye color in brilliant shades of sky. His sleeveless black leather tunic exposed the hard contours of his arms. And the hand that slid to hers, adorned no rings, just the callused knuckles of warfare.

She took his hand. His warm strong grip engulfed that which was vulnerable in her. Her knees weakened with pleasure, but she did not want him to know. Being under the wing of one who could fight, and fight well, soothed her deeply, even though she ever wished fighting need not be a part of life.

He led her through a maze of dark passageways until they came outside into the warm breezy night. The full moon lit their way, capturing shapes with an eerie glow, giving view to the play at hand. When they reached the curtain wall, Kayenté pushed open a stone door camouflaged in the barricade, creating passage to the other side.

She gazed upon him with a woman's eye. Oh how sensual his moonlit form cocksure against the night, of an aura confirming the successful inheritance of primeval man's undaunted spirit. His hard chest protected his wounded heart against the forbidden love of woman. He had his space. None shall trespass.

His hard-lined face bespoke defiance. Would he allow her fingertips to dip softly into the hollow of his cheeks and rise along the slope of his cheekbone? Would he let love sink beneath his skin to the tender one within?

The passageway was open. His sharp eyes flashed through the dark at her. His mighty arm, signaled her to pass through the square opening. She climbed through, awaiting him to join her.

He emerged. Hair strands blew about his shoulders. He drew her against his chest. Her head tilted back, his forward, their lips nearly touching.

His musky breath made her feel wild. Oh, what phantom panther was this that sprang forth from the den of her own womb, not of lightning as before, but of the whole wild ocean! Perhaps she did have a primeval beast in her, ever lurking in the shadows of her soul. Perhaps Kayenté's beast was simply more—prominent and ever alive in his conscious presence. Could he ever be tamed by love?

He took her hand, and led her down the grassy hill to a lightly forested area that circled a small water hole, fed by a smooth flowing creek. "Will this do?"

She inhaled the pine-scented air to fill her head and calm her nerves. She exhaled, "Yes."

He spread the blanket near the water and motioned her to sit.

She sat with her legs curled to one side, staring at him, enveloped in the sound of her own breathing.

He sat next to her, elbow on one raised knee, hand hanging. "Apprise me of your ritual."

She clasped her hands in a prayerful pose. "This ritual is sacrosanct, used to strengthen both man and woman by exchanging power. During the height of the sexual act, I shall let you access the deepest secrets of female power, and you must send into me the power of man. After the ritual, it's said that man and woman shall experience a wider spectrum of abilities, and each shall be fortified by the other."

"Can two such energies blend without upset? If a man and woman are antithetical in nature, wouldn't the ritual serve to worsen matters?"

"Only, if the ritual is done incorrectly. We must bequeath our total power to the other. We must accept the other's gift completely. And we must do this, even though the other's gift makes us feel odd. Non-compliance from either of us, shall harm us both. The one who gives, but does not receive, shall feel robbed and fall into despair. The one who receives, but does not give, shall feel over-charged and driven to insanity."

"You fear I'll hold back, don't you?"

"I must tell you, Kayenté, I fear you'll view this act as another conquest, and that attitude shall destroy us. I'm not an object. I am a living being. I'm loyal and true and full of heart. I'm all that you were deprived. Treat me sacredly, as I shall you, and together, like bow and arrow, we'll hit the target—the Cold One. Then we'll accomplish our goal: to bond so deeply that we become one connected motion. As I go up, you go down. As I go in, you go out. If there's no power struggle between us, we'll force the Cold One back into his cavern where again he'll become only the pause between our breaths, a fleeting moment of nothing, a glimpse into the emptiness of inaction, only a short unit of stagnation in the range of a life."

"What happened that he is not so now?"

"We freed him with our intolerance of each other. He's separated light and dark so extremely that one falls without the other and the other falls without the one, until there is nothing anymore."

"You are admitting then, that you no longer rebuke what you call evil?"

"This is true. I can see now that the stars would be not stars without the night sky. Joy could not be felt without first knowing sorrow. Oh how divine the dance of light and dark! Mistakes teach us. Discomfort forces change. Pain drives us to freedom. Without light and dark, we cannot transition into greater worlds. Do you understand, Kayenté?"

"You believe that your life without storm was not fulfilled, and that mine was not fulfilled without love. What we lack makes us vulnerable to the Cold One, for he is emptiness. And if the emptiness grows, nothing survives."

"Yes! Yes! Oh Kayenté, can you believe what I tell you?"

"Well," his eyes hinted skepticism, "it sounds mythical, a mission to dethrone—nothing?"

"How it *sounds* is unimportant. How it *feels* is the key."

"We will exact the ritual then, whether I believe in the power or purpose of it, or not."

Kamara became silent.

"Kamara?"

"Very well," she said, hoping the ritual would still work. "Then let us link so that our connection cannot be broken, not even for a moment. I shall fill you with what you have been deprived: love, light, and the way of woman. And you must fill me with what I have been deprived: storm, the sword, and the way of man."

He barely nodded, as if only half absorbing the importance of her message. He reached to her leg and untied her knife sheath, laying it carefully on the ground. He pulled off her boots, one by one. Then her stockings. She stiffened. She didn't want her first time with him to be like this, loveless, and lacking shared belief. Suddenly, the ground felt so hard.

She watched him remove his boots, and lay his sheathed sword reverently on the blanket edge. Then he moved toward her. Her mouth felt dry, and drier still when he took her trembling hands and guided her up to her feet.

"Oh Kayenté!" she blurted, her eyes pleading for comfort. " 'Tis a hard thing to give myself to you in ritual only, and harder still to receive you within the confines of a method. It hurts!"

He enclosed her in his arms. "I will relieve your pain, Kamara."

"I'll require your help somewhat," she lowered her eyes bashfully. "I've been trained to an extent, but having never done it. I . . . don't know what to expect."

"Leave that to me," he said, enveloping her head in his hands. His mouth found hers, hawk to mouse, lifting her dark doubt into the pale sweetness of surrender.

Pleasant pangs shot down her body, hanging there like hungry dogs in the street. Warm lifeblood pulsed between them in a full moist kiss.

She felt her belt untied while his lips discovered the northerly world of her neck, tongue exploring to the southerly world of her shoulder. She sighed quietly, trying to conceal the fact. The kisses stopped, and his eyes met hers, shanghaiing her curiosity into his fanciful ship of love making secrets, promising exposure once the ship sailed into seas unknown. Was she under a spell? Had he bewitched her?

"Am I dreaming, Kayenté?"

"No Kamara, you are not."

He raised her shirt over her shoulders and head. Her hair flipped back behind her. The shirt fell haphazardly to the ground. She wore no undershirt, and he was pleased.

A warm breeze played over her abdomen. Her breasts felt receptive to nursing a babe. His perusal of her flesh tickled her skin.

His eyes found hers. "I savor this sight, that which I have dreamed to see, that which I might never see again."

"You do love me then?"

"I . . . appreciate you."

"That's love, is it not?"

"I don't know what it is." He touched her breastbone. "I don't care." He trailed his finger lightly around the circumference of each breast.

"It must be love," she whispered.

He took his breath to her ear, "Hush Kamara. Just . . . feel it."

He trailed his fingertips down to her navel as he knelt, and unwrapped her pants over her hips.

Kamara felt like a thousand swarming fish possessed her body.

Kayenté pressed his ear against the heat of her breasts. "Your heart thunders," he said.

"Is this always the way of it?" she gasped. "Am I the same as all the others?"

He looked up at her. "Stop thinking, Kamara, just feel." He kissed the inside mound of her breast, sliding his lips down her body to her womb, breathing hotly there while helping her lift each foot, one by one, out of the pant legs.

He rose like the glorious sun. A breeze blew his moonlit hair about his shoulders.

"Uhh," she whimpered. "You are so beautiful. I am overcome. I fear these feelings."

"Relax, Priestess. The ritual, remember?"

"The ritual," she swallowed hard, "yes, the ritual."

He moved like melting wax, discarding his clothing leaving only the naked wick of his hard-scarred body.

She stared at his face, too frightened to look anywhere else.

He stepped close to her, and clasped her hands, lifted them outward like wings unfolding. His hair dangled over her breasts with feather softness, a cave of sorts, protecting motherhood—fostering a pleasant sensation.

He took her hand and rubbed it down his bare hip over a scar.

Touching his skin there, that way, made her want to kiss his hip, his scar, but oh, she dare not. This act mustn't be personal. It was a ritual, nothing more. Yet, in that, it seemed so much would be lost. But even if the ritual was not at play, no, she dare not. Kayenté was not ready for her love, nor did he have the where-with-all to give it. And what lay ahead? Though moments away, she could not welcome the event. Love was important to her. It just was. Plus, Kayenté knew too much, mechanically speaking, and she didn't feel safe giving him control.

"I'm still afraid, Kayenté."

"Me too," he whispered sensuously in her ear.

"You are? How could you be afraid of . . . you know?"

"No . . . I'm afraid of what *you* know. Magic and all that."

"And I am afraid of what *you* know. Seduction and all that."

"Let us be brave then." He slipped his arm under her knees and lifted her into the cradle of his arms. The momentum flung part of her hair over his shoulder, down his back over his own mane—gold and black, shining. He carried her waist deep into the cool pool of dark water, dipping her in, all but her face.

He rocked her back and forth, watching the moon's reflection on the black water ripple from the movement of her body. He raised her body just enough to see her fleshy contours break the surface with moonlit sparkles on her skin.

"Oh Kamara."

"Oh what?"

"You are lovely."

"Me, or what you view to be me?"

"Both."

She wanted to downplay the physical part, but she couldn't. She wanted Kayenté to find her body lovely. Oh, shame upon shame. The ritual. She must focus on the ritual.

Her hair swirled around his forearms, tickling pleasurably. He paused, mesmerized by her angel tresses, weightless about her flower soft face, afloat in a world of sharks that cared not if that face was ripped to shreds. He cared. He did. Strange feeling. Suddenly, he was embraced with the knowing she *must* survive, and that he *was* destined to save her. The feeling he'd had long ago about his lure to Lania Castle—this was why. And here he was— saving her over and over again, since the first day he met her.

"Remember the first time I held you in water."

"At the Hot Springs?"

"Yes."

"I was shocked to learn it was you who had held me."

"You dared not believe it was me."

"That is because I'd promised Michael that if I should need the closeness of a man, that man would be him."

"You love Michael too, I know."

"Yes, in a way . . . different than you. I could be happy with Michael if I were to choose a male partner, but I'd feel unfinished."

"Unfinished—or unfulfilled?"

"What about you Kayenté, will you feel unfinished or unfulfilled marrying Winnefred?"

"We are talking of you."

"We always talk of me."

"Is that a crime?"

"It is a crime of the heart."

"Then it is no crime to me."

"You ever trick me into disclosure, that you may reveal less of yourself. You ever turn the tables, drawing out information, but exposing nothing of you."

"I would say it is you turning the tables, Kamara. You fear revealing what the woman in you desires of me."

"Why should I?" she said, "for you give but half a heart to the vows bequeathed upon this night."

"Half is more than I've ever given."

"And yet I fear, 'tis not enough. Put me down Kayenté! I'll reveal nothing more." She struggled to escape his arms, hands and legs flailing.

He released her.

She stood rigidly, the water line even with her breasts. She stepped back. "This sacred ritual was entrusted to me. Oh!" She flung her head to the side in shame. "How could I think to share it with a man whose heart is but half?"

"Kamara—" He wanted to speak, but he didn't know what to say.

She stepped back and shook her head. "You seemed the only hope." Her glare intensified, even in the dark. "I reached for you in desperation, but you'll scrap me as you do Allysa. If you can't seriously receive the impact of what has been revealed, then we're lost!

The world is lost! "Give me the whole heart," she flung her hand toward the castle, "or be gone!"

Water glistened on the golden glow of her shoulders and breasts. He did not want to be gone. He grabbed her abruptly, holding her body in a vice against him. She fell limp. Seems *she* was the one gone, lifeless, and filled with despair. He lifted her feet from the silted ground and walked her out of the water hole, guiding her inert body down gently to the blanket.

He stood over her, feet straddling her hips, dripping water on her smooth belly. He drank in the view of her shimmering dark wet body. Adrenaline surged. He'd waited long for this moment.

To Kamara, Kayenté seemed a mythical giant in the night sky, naked body glowing against the full moon behind his head. His black hair dangled from star sprinkles. A god—a god. Were his staunch legs rooted to molten earth? Were his hands lightning? Was his heart thunder? He appeared omnipotent—the Deity of Storm, and she prayed his intent was benevolent.

The giant came to the earth, licking water off her neck. Each lightning bolt lick made her want more. His body hovered slightly above her. The tempest awakens. No, the tempest must not! His licking traveled downward.

She writhed beneath him and gasped. "I am consumed! Wait Kayenté! I mustn't' be consumed. I can't exact the ritual with this rising inferno distracting me."

"You'd better find a way, Kamara, because this is what you asked for."

"I didn't know it would be this intense, Kayenté. I didn't expect this veracity of feeling. Is there some way to minimize it?"

He laughed. "You want to get right to it? You don't want me to make love to you?"

"I . . . I don't know what that means exactly—just that I can't focus on the ritual. I feel I might forget about it and get swept away in something."

"It would do you good, Kamara."

"This act isn't for me, it's—"

"—to save the world, I know. Well then . . . let's save it." He straddled her thighs and leaned forward.

"Kayenté, wait . . ."

"Wait for what, Kamara?"

"I never believed I would actually have to do this . . . I—"

His lips parted and met hers, dancing fire.

Her body produced heat, pouring from her mouth, blending with the blaze.

He captured her hands and pressed them over his heart. He lifted his head, impassioned words slipping from his mouth, "My heart beats with the blood I've taken from others. I've lived by the sword and I shall die by the sword. This that I have lived by, I now bequeath to you." His mouth found hers again, his probing tongue drilled warrior rushes into her. His lips washed down her neck, potent with the agreed upon oath.

She moaned ecstatically. "I can feel the male charge, Kayenté! I think it is working."

"There is *much* more. Let me all the way in Kamara," he said, as his mouth encountered her breast, exploring first one, then the other with baby bestial vigor.

"I am losing myself again! We must finish the ritual now!" She lifted her head to see him, but only the top of his head was in view. She arched her back and cried, "I need man's power, all of it! I need storm! I need it—now!"

"Take it, Kamara. Take it now." With his knees, he pushed her thighs apart, and entered her.

She shrieked, pain searing her, burning, pounding. Was he truly giving the gifts of man to her? Or was he serving himself as usual? "Stay pure with me! Stay pure with me!"

He whispered, "Stay pure with yourself, Kamara. Don't throw your doubts on me, for I have none." His movement inside her was such that time seemed lost in a sensation that became all that existed. When the sensation peaked, she moaned long and loud, crying out with a tear strained voice, "I open to you, Kayenté. I release unto you all that I am. All the powers of woman, I send into your being!"

Though sexually heightened, and ready to burst, Kayenté felt dreamy and disoriented, as if he and Kamara were laying upon the moon.

Remaining joined, he rolled her on top of him.

She panted with sated relief, having given of herself. Now her intent was to extract from him the ways of man. She gazed into his eyes, delving fathoms deep into his spirit. She brushed her hands over his hairline with the lightness of bubbles, and traced her fingers over the contours of his face, making his skin prickle. She massaged his chest with Priestess fingers, opening his long locked heart.

She began moving in ways that Priestesses were taught to excite a man. "Men. Men!" she called out louder. "The power of men!" Then she wailed, "Men! I call for the power of all men!" She flung her face skyward. "I call with all my heart and soul, through all space and time, for warriors great and powerful. Come through the Warlord Kayenté! Through him, come into me—now!"

Kayenté was overcome with a lust exceeding his experience. The moment of a thousand kills exploded in him. He whipped Kamara on her back, and thrust his manhood in her over and over—and over again.

Kamara felt torn betwixt and between the realms of agony and joy. The pleasant sensation of undulating ocean waves pleased. But what pleased was also accompanied by the painful blows of man's violent capacity, and the terror of receiving man's power. She screamed and screamed as silently as she could, and she did not stop screaming until Kayenté burst his seeds into her womb and collapsed in a heap upon her.

After a moment, he heard her labored breathing and slowly withdrew.

"As you withdraw," she said, her voice nearly gone, "you take the mystic woman . . . the sister of 'the light.' The Angel is within you Warlord. And the Warlord is in the Angel. We are bonded."

He rolled slowly on his back, panting, and pulled her on top of him. "Only you could give your chastity to all great warriors in the span of a single moment."

She stared at him in silence.

Warm night breezes blew against their sweat dampened skin. Tears hit his chest.

"You cry," he said softly.

"What do you feel, Kayenté?"

"Changed."

She nodded lightly. "Me too."

"Do you regret our act?"

"We did what was necessary."

"You felt no pleasure?"

"Pain, Kayenté, I felt much pain."

"Women suffer the first time."

" 'Tis an act I should not like to repeat."

"What about before I had my time with you—did you not enjoy that?"

She was silent.

"Kamara?"

"Yes, I liked it."

"And that, would you like to repeat that?"

"I shan't answer you."

He rolled on his side, easing her down onto her back. He stroked his fingers along her breast and stomach. "I respect you, Kamara."

"Do you?" she asked unbelieving. "As a mystic, I feel much changed within me. As a woman, I feel opened. As a person, I feel demeaned. I see that I cannot do as my sisters, who perform such rituals and walk away detached. Perhaps it was I who was not prepared for this undertaking."

She sat up and reached for her clothes. "Just as you detach from me, I must detach from you."

"What makes you think I detach from you?"

She rose, trying to disguise the pain from Kayenté's initial thrust, and slipped on her pants. "Kayenté," her voice fought tears, "you've chosen to spend your life with a woman you do not love. You bed whom you wish, and I'm sure that shall continue after your marriage."

"Those women shall never have anything to do with us."

She donned her shirt. "We must defeat the Cold One." She wrapped her belt around her and tied it. "And that's the extent of my relationship with you." She pulled on her stockings and boots, "When that's finished, you'll not see me again." She tied the knife around her calf and then bolted to run away, when she felt herself thrown back onto the blanket, landing on her back.

Kayenté lunged on top of her. His velvet voice was charged with threat, fanning around her face, gripping her like teeth, "You made an oath with me woman, and I to you. With no other have I made such a vow. I hold you to it, and I'll not let you treat me like I've bequeathed you with nothing."

"But have you bequeathed me with something, Kayenté? "

He rolled off her slowly and sat up with his back to her, propping elbows on bent knees. He said, "I've given you a kind of—"

"What?"

He murmured feebly, "—love."

"Love?" She scooted around in front of him, hope rising.

He turned until his side faced her.

"In what way?" She crawled in front of him once more pounding.

"Listen," he snapped, "I don't know in what way, but it's there. I don't know what to do with it, but it's doing something to me. So be glad. You're not a mistress for my pleasure as others have been."

"What am I?"

"I don't know," he retorted, "this is new for me. I haven't a clue how to regard you. Mistresses and wives are not for love—not for me anyway, so where should I place you?"

"In your heart, Kayenté—in your heart."

"I don't much like you there." He grabbed his pants. "I'd prefer you anywhere but there."

She watched him dress, so in love that her heart ached. He pulled on his boots and strapped his sword about his waist. He took her hand, led her off the blanket, reached down and slung the blue grey cover over his shoulder. He placed his hand lightly on her back, and guided her toward the castle wall.

Her steps were strained from hurting in a place ladies don't mention. He seemed to know, for he swept her off her feet and carried her like an infant, into the night, under the moon, back toward the castle.

Kamara looked upon his face in a backdrop of stars, while bobbing gently with the gate of his walk. He held her securely, yet preciously, like a thing that must never be dropped. This was a dear moment of her life. His gentle manner made her heart burst with human love. But she held the brightness within, afraid Kayenté could handle no more than he had already received.

He brought her to the door of his bedchamber, and lowered her feet to the floor. "Sleep with me," he said, "these last few hours before dawn. Who knows when I will behold you again. Out there under the moon, you gave yourself to all great warriors. Now Kamara, in my bed, give yourself to me. Only me. Let this time be for you and your pleasure."

She placed her palms firmly on his chest. "If we are to make love, you must commit to me with all your heart."

"I will try," he said, "in as much as I can love."

They sealed themselves in the room, and shed their clothes slowly, locked in a gaze of affection. They climbed under the covers and touched, locked in timeless devotion. They rode in an ocean of sexual storm, locked to each other 'til dawn.

Ж

Chapter Twenty

The first rays of morning light shone on Kamara's sleeping face. Kayenté kissed her goodbye. She awakened and threw her arms around his neck. "If you must go, come back, my love."

He noticed the mist rising from her breath, floating all around him. "You're going to make certain I do, aren't you?"

"I'll keep you misted. You'll find it of great benefit. You'll be easily overlooked, and feel charmed in all your endeavors."

"Don't pacify me, Kamara. It could mean my death."

"I shan't. I'll let your aggression shine through. You'll still be able to utilize your male power."

"And so must you, if it becomes necessary. Stay safe for me. Remember all I've told you."

"How long shall you be away?"

"Weeks maybe, hopefully. If all goes well, not months. I've instructed the servants to care for you and a small force of my men to protect you. Do not fret when Lady Winnefred arrives. Just remember, you are the one I love."

A sharp pain hurled through Kamara's heart, something like the opposite of Cupid's arrow. "You still plan to marry her?"

"We'll talk when I return. Meanwhile, her bark and bite might prove challenging to endure. Just steer clear of her."

"You made love to me, Kayenté. You said I was more than mistress or wife. If so, how can you shove me aside for another woman's possessions? Does love mean so little?"

"Kamara, do you wish me to ride into battle thinking of you pouting in my bed?"

She thought of him riding into battle. Tears formed, as they always seemed to, where Kayenté was concerned. She said nothing, but soared into the glimmer of tenderness shining in his eyes.

"That's better." He brushed his fingertips over her cheek.

She wanted to scream, '*Don't go!*' when he rose to leave, but she knew it would be futile.

He left, closing the door behind him.

She muttered, "Do not betray me Kayenté. I beg you, do not betray me."

She sprung from the bed, and dressed quickly in her fighting clothes, oblivious to the soreness of lovemaking. Her heart suffered more. She went to the window and flung open the wood shutters, gazing down at the bailey, waiting, waiting to see her Kayenté one more time. After a heart-pounding half hour, Kayenté appeared. His squire helped him don his armor, and then the red and black panther tunic he sported only when declaring, or responding to a declaration of war. It seemed to be the code of them all. Hundreds of men were suiting up and mounting their horses. Within the hour, they rode away.

A traitor comes, she thought, echoing the Wise One's words, *a traitor comes.* Could Lady Winnefred be that traitor? Even if she was innocent, how ever could she conduct herself decently with . . . well, actually—her competition? How could she feel mercy and love toward a woman she'd rather spit upon and blow away?

Oh, she was changing. Never before had she been consumed with such jealousy. Now she knew why Allysa had once scorned her so. Allysa! Kamara's eyes popped wide. Allysa would surely deem her a traitor, after all she'd preached about never giving Kayenté her body because she distrusted him with her love.

A rap on the door startled her. "Lady Kamara! Are you in there? I hold your breakfast!"

Allysa! Kamara went to the door hesitantly and opened it, half-shamed. "Come in Allysa. Set down the tray. We must speak."

Allysa set the tray on a cherry wood dining table. Kamara led her to the edge of the bed where they sat.

"I know," she said, "you slept with him, didn't you?"

Kamara nodded with a blush, then rambled defensively, "It began as a ritual that my kind performs to defeat great danger. A ritual to—I don't wish to frighten you or make you think I am an evil witch, but it's a ritual whereupon a man and a woman give their powers to each other. And then—"

"Lady! There's no need for defense. I already decided that I'd hope for love to come between you and Kayenté."

Kamara touched Allysa's hand. "Allysa, is this true?"

"Yes. When you touched me with your heart, I realized that it was love itself I needed—just love. You care for me. Commands never roll off your tongue. You treat me well, and you have invited me to live with you. I should like to live in your castle one day."

Kamara squeezed her hand. "And so you shall."

"So, do you now trust Kayenté with your love?"

"I believe so, although I could be wrong." She rose, walked a few steps, and turned back toward Allysa. "He still plans to marry Winnefred, and I am unable to cope with that."

Allysa stood. "I'll help you all I can, lady."

"Thank you Allysa. You have been a true and loyal friend in every measure. You remind me so of my dear friend, Camille. I should think you would adore her. You'll like Michael too, when you get better acquainted."

Allysa's face turned red.

"What Allysa?"

"Oh, nothing." Allysa fidgeted.

"You're embarrassed. What happened between you and Michael?"

Allysa bowed her head, while peering at Kamara. "You know."

Kamara was stunned by Allysa's implication. She exhaled hard several times trying to accept it, and then she swallowed down a pang of envious rage. "You and Michael? Why that two faced . . . he . . . I—"

"I know lady, but I didn't know you loved him. I detest him for betraying you. And as for me, I was only following Kayenté's orders."

Kamara snapped, "Kayenté's orders? Why would Kayenté order such a thing? Did Michael fancy you, and you him? Is that why Kayenté brought you together?"

"No. It was just the one night, and it had nothing to do with anyone fancying anybody. It was purely sexual. I think Kayenté pushed Michael into it, because Michael seemed rather nervous before, and regretful afterwards."

Kamara huffed. "Forget Michael. What about *you* Allysa? Kayenté made you have sex with another man!"

"He didn't make me, exactly. I always did what Kayenté asked. I wished to please him."

"Oh Allysa!" Kamara huffed again, and she couldn't seem to stop.

Allysa's face went soft. "You're ashamed of me."

"No, I'm not. I am enraged with Kayenté! He arranged for Michael to sleep with you for no motive other than male conquest. That swine! He . . . I . . . oh!" Kamara threw her hands over her temples, pressing hard. "I knew it was a mistake to become involved with men. I just knew it! I was fine until I let myself be enchanted by their dancing eyes and bold manners. Oh!"

"Lady!" Allysa said in surprise. "Remember Kayenté has changed, and so have I . . . and so have you. I've not ever seen you this volatile!"

Kamara made a fist over her heart, cupping it with her other hand. "I know. Look at me! I'm cursing and fuming and envious and . . . and this isn't like me! This isn't like me at all." She lowered her head. "I am changing too much, and this change I dislike."

Allysa eased Kamara's hands down. "I like it. You're more human, like the rest of us." She stepped back, releasing Kamara. "I'm sorry about Michael." She bowed her head. "Forgive me."

Kamara shrugged her shoulders. "Oh, I understand Allysa—about your part anyway. However, I don't in the slightest understand those men!"

Allysa raised her eyes. "Are we still as sisters then?"

Kamara set her fury aside to give Allysa the assurance she needed. She nodded with a smile. They hugged warmly for a long moment. When they parted, Kamara said, "In time I'll teach you the ways of 'the light.' But for now, I'm much more concerned about what shall transpire here during Kayenté's absence. Let's each choose a warning symbol we can send to the other's mind."

Allysa shook her head. "What?"

"If danger comes and we can't reach each other for what ever reason, then we must reach each other with our minds."

"Can that truly be done?"

"Oh, yes. You'll see Allysa. Your mind is sensitive. Close your eyes."

Allysa closed her eyes.

Kamara said, "Envision me in my fighting clothes, holding my sword."

"I see you, lady."

"If that image should pop in your mind, then know I am calling you. Keep watching and listening in your head, and you'll receive the details of my message."

"This is exciting," Allysa said, opening her eyes.

Kamara said, "Soon it will be a common place occurrence. Now you choose a symbol for me."

"Very well."

Kamara closed her eyes.

Allysa said, "See the image of a black heart."

Kamara snapped her eyes open. "Why did you choose a black heart?"

"I sense betrayal, my lady."

"So do I, Allysa, so do I! When is Winnefred to arrive?"

"In two weeks, but don't fret. You let me tend her. I'm getting quite good at handling Kayenté's interests."

"Thank you, Allysa. I don't think I can bear to chat with Kayenté's bride-to-be."

"If she's the traitor," Allysa asked, "shall we throw her in the prison?"

"I must first try bonding with her. If I'm unsuccessful, then and only then will I resort to unkindly action."

Allysa groaned, "I disagree with your plan, lady," she sighed, "but I believe in you."

"We must make her feel welcome. I'll make that effort when I can, perhaps a few days after her arrival. I'll need time to rally my heart."

"Very well," Allysa said, dejected, wanting to play pranks upon Kayenté's bride to be, like mice in her breakfast and glue in her hairbrush. "I'll leave you to your breakfast."

She went to the door, stopped, and faced Kamara. "Sometimes, it's good to be bad, lady."

Kamara absorbed Allysa's words that indeed carried truth. This she knew, for her heart sank upon hearing them. She didn't want to be good regarding Winnefred. It was more like she *had* to be good. "You are probably right, Allysa."

"Winnefred's a bitch," Allysa said, "she's going to make you feel awful."

"Leave me now, Allysa. I have absorbed your point."

Allysa still looked worried, even when she left and closed the door.

And when that door closed, when it did, something horrible opened in Kamara. The opening spawned a possessive fuming monster that overcame her. She went to the nightstand by the bed where she had laid her sheathed knife the night before. She took her hand to the handle, withdrew the blade, and slashed the air repeatedly. "Lady Winnefred, take this . . . and that . . . and this. I shall hack you to pieces, destroy you through and through!"

She froze, suddenly aware of her contemptible behavior. She collapsed to her knees, and hung her head in despair. "Oh Great Mother, be not appalled by my conduct. What can you expect from me, when oh so very suddenly you toss me into a pit of darkness and shout, resist! Fight! Survive! How can I do these things void of rage or fear, or hate? Do not condemn these feelings—or me. Please . . . forgive."

A wave of nausea rolled up her body. She pulled the chamber pot out from under the bed and wretched, but nothing came up. Nothing.

She shook her head. "There's no substance to me now that Kayenté's gone. The rage and fear that I heave are empty. Shall the sword crumble in my hand when finally I gather the courage to wield it? Shall my words charge the enemy, and at the last moment lick instead of bite? Oh warriors! If you be in me, I cannot feel you. Make your presence known. Oh please!"

She walked over to the window, stretching her hand outside in the direction she'd last seen her warlord. "Kayenté!" she cried, "Come back! Oh please—please come back!" She fell to her knees, threw her hands over her face, and wailed her grief.

Ж
Chapter Twenty-One

Kamara found great solace that day hibernating in Kayenté's room, hating him, loving him, clutching the pillow upon which he'd last rested his head. When she pressed her face in the puffy fabric, his fragrance would flood her with replays of their sweet lovemaking. Breathing him in brought such pleasure. It made him feel near, though he was far. She napped frequently, and often sprung to the window hoping to see his wild eyes and virile gate, hoping to see her beautiful storm, hoping to see him—Kayenté.

What at last she saw was what she least expected. Kayenté's servants rushed out to welcome a gold-lined carriage in a procession of red and gold satin decorated horses, and warriors wearing the shiniest metal armor with red plumes in their helms. Oh, what a show of glamour and glitz. When the carriage stopped, a woman emerged. Her tawny hair was swirled fancy upon her head, her billowy red gown even more dazzling, and her face exceeding the latter.

Kamara surmised the woman could be no other than Winnefred, two weeks early. Oh, how dare she! Kamara imagined that Kayenté had instructed his warriors and servants to give her the finest welcome whenever she should arrive, and that monster jealousy turned Kamara's face red hot, and then white. It was too odd that Winnefred arrived on the very day Kayenté departed. It almost seemed that she had waited to come at precisely the moment when Kayenté was well away from his domain.

Winnefred promenaded into the castle with all the elegance of a queen.

Kamara threw herself upon the bed, face down, realizing she could never compete with such a stately woman. No wonder Kay enté desired Winnefred for his wife. Oh, no wonder! She'd be a fitting mate for the sleek and powerful Panther Man.

Kamara closed her eyes and saw a black heart. Allysa was warning her of that—that woman's arrival. The vision also showed Allysa tending Winnefred. She thanked the Great Mother Lord for Allysa and then promptly moped in her insecurity for hours.

That evening, Allysa pounded on her door. "Lady Kamara, allow me to enter!"

Kamara hurriedly raced over to the thick wood barricade and flung it open.

Allysa burst into the room. "Winnefred's here! Did you get my message?"

Kamara nodded, clutching the sides of her black pants.

"She's asking to see the room where she and Kayenté will sleep! She's coming any moment. Hurry lady. Go to your own chamber so I can make the bed."

Kamara felt trounced upon by the ugly talons of the Winnefred demon. She left the bedchamber, dazed and sinking into the quicksands of defeat, nothing new really. The first time she'd heard Winnefred's name at Duke Ketola's castle, she began her descent. Since then, she'd felt haunted by the phantom lady who evoked from her less than dignified emotions. And now the phantom lady was here, a phantom no longer. Her physical form radiated a womanly grandeur that paled Kamara. The quicksand covered her head.

She pushed her stiff body down the dark corridor dotted with oil lamps. Each lamp she passed seemed to mock her with its steady burning flame, for indeed her own—was out.

Oh, what hell hath come upon her, exceeding past experience—sinking down, down, down, into a quagmire of nothing. Nothing? Nothing! Something was terribly wrong! This despair was what happened to the Light Priestesses once the Cold One had taken them. The Cold One had not taken her—had he? Kayenté was not in league with the Cold One—was he? Oh, what trickery was at play? Had all been lost even before she'd begun to fight?

Winnefred appeared at the end of the corridor with crimson lips, and scarlet nails, and a ruby necklace blaring beauty, dipping into the cleavage of her plumped up breasts. Her pink flesh and shiny red gown blazed like the candle flames on the black stone walls, as she strolled toward Kamara with a treacherous smile, one red spiked shoe in front of the other.

Kamara felt the sting of envy's wicked lash. Her heart sputtered in her sunken chest. She felt—missing, shipwrecked, and indeed—empty of spirit.

Winnefred stopped before her, licking her bottom lip as if preparing to sup.

Kamara couldn't stop staring at Winnefred, at her command of beauty.

"Who might you be?" Winnefred asked with spellbinding elocution.

"I'm Lord Kayenté's pupil."

"In what?" she asked with regal disgust.

Kamara's original intent to befriend Winnefred was overwhelmingly thwarted by a primitive instinct to smash her head. Was that not a spirited urge? Maybe her spirit, though low in vitality, was yet intact. And perhaps the ritual she'd exacted with Kayenté, was successful.

She charged Winnefred with sardonic wit. "He's teaching me to kill."

Winnefred turned up her nose. "What reason could you possibly have for such an endeavor?"

"I must learn to defend myself against the cold and heartless."

Winnefred curled her lip, exposing pointed teeth.

Kamara nearly choked when she saw them. Surely, she was no vampire, though she certainly was a vamp. Teeah had told her once such blood-sucking creatures truly existed. Kamara had found that hard to believe. Even now, it seemed far-fetched.

Winnefred asked, "When do you plan to vacate the premises?"

"Maybe tomorrow," taunted Kamara, "then again—maybe never."

Winnefred squinted, appraising Kamara. Then she raised a wicked brow and cracked a malevolent smile.

Kamara was amazingly unaffected, so she decided to conquer her antagonist, then and there. She jumped into Winnefred's spirit, but landed—in emptiness.

They both gasped in simultaneous revelation.

Winnefred words dripped with venom. "I'm surprised I found you so quickly. I thought you'd be cowering in some hall of light somewhere."

Kamara strove to rally herself from the shocking awareness that there was more than one the Cold One. She half smiled at Winnefred, feigning confidence. "Oh, you sought me?"

"An easy find," Winnefred gloated. "You blaze so brightly, my eyes are offended."

Kamara shrugged nonchalantly and continued her charade. "I'm not so light anymore, in fact—" she paused and enunciated her next words with impure mysticism, "—I've grown quite dark."

Winnefred tossed her head back and released a demented laugh.

Kamara cringed.

"Dark?" Winnefred's eyes flared, "Oh come now—dimming maybe, but dark? I think not."

Kamara fought against the feeling of defeat. She rehearsed the Wise One's warnings, *Never give up, and do not submit. Only through submission can the Cold One usurp your spirit.* She'd clung to her frail line of hope and spoke poignantly, "You plan to dazzle Kayenté—into quite an illusion."

"And you have not?" spat Winnefred haughtily.

"My purpose is love," Kamara said.

Winnefred's face contorted into a vulgar expression. "And you call yourself dark!"

"Love is dark, to you—witch of all witches. If I love Kayenté, you can't take his spirit."

"I do believe—foolish girl, that he must also *return* your love."

"Love me, he does."

"Love you, he won't—" her eyes glazed prankish horror "—for long." Winnefred tossed her head back laughing, languishing in her malignant machination. Then she lowered her head with a caustic smile, and gave Kamara a heavy lidded wicked stare. "He'll love—" her eyes flared, "me."

Kamara swallowed, forcing herself to stay composed. "No. Never. Not even by your magic spells shall he love you. True love can't be swayed."

"Oh, and you believe you have true love with my husband-to-be, my cruel Lord of Darkness who even now is slicing off limbs of poor, less able soldiers. He is causing men to gasp with bulging eyes and spurting blood. Red pools form, so shiny and deep, Kayenté can see himself smiling."

Kamara nearly screamed for Winnefred to stop, but then realized that the vamp's goal was to lure her into hysteria, so instead she stated, "Come now cold lady, surely you feel 'the light' in Kayenté. Surely you know that if he links his light with me—which he has, and I link my darkness with him—which I have, then together we can defeat you and other the Cold Ones like you."

Winnefred snickered. "You underestimate the powers of the truly cold and heartless . . . little fallen angel, melting like snow before me."

"So I've been told," Kamara said, "by those who underestimate me."

"You are no different than other Light Priestesses, drowning in your own syrupy goodness."

"No," Kamara said, "Not I. I've released the wildcat in me. Do not think I would not unleash her upon you."

Winnefred's face became animated with jesting arrogance. "You!—harboring a wildcat? Don't be ridiculous! You're but a little kitten purring at the slightest touch, mewling for a drop of milk, sparring with clawless paws, and barely audible hissing. You're no threat to me. You serve only to make the big cats laugh." Winnefred discharged her derisive cackling once more.

Kamara fought the urge to crumble. Instead, she replied coyly, "Then you shan't expect much from me?"

"Of course not!" huffed Winnefred rudely.

"Good." Kamara straightened her shoulders, and sauntered past Winnefred.

"I didn't dismiss you, little kitten!"

Kamara looked over her shoulder. "You think I care?"

She walked to her room. Once inside, she fell to her knees, crumbling at last. She rocked back and forth with clasped hands pressed against her mouth. Her true feelings gushed out in silent prayer. *Great Mother be merciful! Such treachery is upon me. I am a neophyte warrior fighting a seasoned best.*

Her hands floated down, overcome by the thought of her opponent and the battle before her. Winnefred was right. She was a kitten in a war with the big cats. And her big cat was Kayenté, and he was not here to protect her. And even if he was, Winnefred would cast a spell on him a thousand times more horrible than she herself had ever cast on anyone. Had Kayenté bonded with her sufficiently to ward off Winnefred's vampish charms?"

And she—had she received enough from Kayenté to survive these next days? In a fit of rebellion, she rose, head tall, chest out. No more of this! What would Kayenté do if in my position? Why, he wouldn't whimper all day, he'd make a plan. No, he'd make a dozen plans to cover every possible situation.

She went to her bed and flopped down on her back, clutching the blue satin comforter with both hands. Power flowed through her veins. "Kayenté's power is in me—somewhere. I can use his dark side and I damn well shall!"

"Kamara." Allysa's voice sounded on the other side of the door. Kamara feared it was Winnefred in disguise. She ran to the door and commanded, "Send the signal to my head."

"Kamara it's me! Let me in. I have your dinner."

"Send the signal, Allysa!"

There was silence and a black heart popped into Kamara's mind.

Kamara opened the door. Allysa's stood there bewildered, holding a tray of rolls, almonds, apricots, and cherries.

"Allysa!" Kamara pulled her into the room by her forearm. She took the tray from Allysa and placed it on the wood table. "I'm sorry that I distrusted you, but I had to be sure. I know who Winnefred is, and if ever there was a witch, it is she."

Allysa's face contorted in horror. "No, lady, no!"

"Remember what I told you in the kitchen last night about Nothingness ending the world?"

Allysa nodded, fear brewing in her eyes.

"The Nothing can inhabit bodies. I call these soulless creatures, Cold Ones.' Winnefred . . . is a Cold One."

Allysa froze.

Kamara continued, "She intends to steal Kayenté's spirit, and I'm sure she means to use him and his castle as a trap to take many more spirits."

Allysa blurted, "We must get word to Kayenté!"

Kamara shivered. "No. He'll not believe me. He'll think me merely jealous and then before I can prove him wrong, Winnefred will have enchanted him into her lies. I must deal with her *before* Kayenté returns. I must!"

Allysa's voice turned cold, "Then let us do away with her."

Kamara stepped back. "What . . . do you mean?"

"You know, your knife—right through her heart."

"Oh!" Kamara gasped. "I can't," Kamara swallowed, "do away with her."

Allysa scowled. "You said, if you couldn't bond with her, you'd fight her."

"I know, but cold blooded murder? No. No. No. Even if I could, Kayenté would exact vengeance upon me, I'm sure!"

"Then you don't truly believe he loves you."

"He loves me, yes, but enough? I don't know."

Allysa's eyes sharpened. "Well, she treated me like a dog all day." A devious smile spread across her face. "I for one would delight in killing the witch. Poison perhaps?"

"No Allysa. That must be a last resort. There must be other solutions. And maybe I am viewing her unjustly. I don't truly know the extent of her powers. Maybe she lacks her spirit because it was taken from her. Maybe she's not a Cold One after-all."

Allysa said. "You close your eyes to the truth, lady."

Kamara bowed her head. "I know."

"Then what shall we do?"

Kamara shook her head lightly, walked over to the window, looked out, then paced the room mumbling. "I hope she can't conjure a Black Wind. Without a spirit, I can't conquer her with the mists, but I could pacify the house guards so that they wouldn't harm me."

Allysa eyes grew wide. "You're scaring me, lady! What are you talking about? Why would the house guards harm you?"

"She can bewitch them, I am sure. And even more certain I am, that she's doing it this moment. So, I must mist the whole castle."

Allysa furrowed her brows. "Mist . . .?"

Kamara approached her, and held her hands. She stared into the face of her friend who didn't know much more about the world that what she could concretely see. "I'm a Priestess, Allysa, of the Sacred Order of the Mist. The Mists are the creative life force that bind us all together, bringing the deepest mystical truths to the forefront. Those I mist, respond in one of three ways: they bond with me, they are immobilized, or they flee. But the mists have no affect on the Cold Ones, for they have no soul."

"So, there is more to you than your ability to heal?"

Kamara nodded.

"What else can you do with the mist?"

"Its true purpose . . . my true purpose is to unite the world. However, the Cold Ones sabotage this endeavor at every turn."

"Well," Allysa swallowed, dumbfounded, "how may I help?"

Kamara sighed, glancing at the door, as if Winnefred were on the other side. She squeezed Allysa's hands. "Just be my friend without Winnefred's knowledge. She mustn't know you are aware of all this. Recall the initial attitude you had toward me. Place it around you like a curtain that hides your true thoughts and feelings, for she can read what your words and actions do not reveal. Don't let her engage your eyes. If you are in trouble or you come to my door, send me the signal. I must begin misting. Go now. Stay well."

They dropped hands. Allysa said," Very well then, as you wish." She nodded in a daze and left.

Kamara locked the door, eyeing the food. She had no appetite. She lay on her bed, and began chanting the mists to fill the castle. Minutes became hours and hours became days, and soon several weeks had passed. She had misted and misted and misted, with little sleep in-between, even while Allysa fed and bathed her, dressed and undressed her, and untied and tied the sheathed knife to the calf of her leg with diligence. After three weeks, the castle was noticeably thick with vapor.

Winnefred popped another grape in her mouth and leaned back in the leather chair in Kayenté's sitting room, careful not to mess the swirls and curls of her pinned up hairdo. She traced her ruby ringed finger along the bust line of her scarlet satin gown that addressed every curve of her body. Her eyes glazed cold. Her lip curled in disgust. "Little Kitten is trying to outsmart me. Her punishment can no longer wait for Kayenté's return." She lurched up from the chair, out the door, and snatched a house guard's arm. She fixed her gaze upon his with womanly charisma and lulled his spirit inside her. "You will obey me completely because you desire what I can grant. Come with me!"

The guard obeyed, and trailing her up the stairs to Kamara's room. Winnefred rapped upon the door. "Kamara," she said in Kayenté's voice. "I have returned!"

Kamara's concentration broke. She had longed to hear those words! Her thinking was clouded from lack of sleep. Desperate to see him, she raced to the door, and flung it open.

Winnefred stood there with a house guard.

"You tricked me!" she cried.

"Indeed." Winnefred snickered and touched the guard on his shoulder. "House guard. This woman is a traitor. Take her to the torture chamber."

Winnefred glared coldly into Kamara's horrified eyes.

Kamara felt pressure crushing her chest and throat. She could hardly breathe.

"Winnefred, stop!"

"Are you insane?" Winnefred replied.

The guard approached Kamara in a wild-eyed trance.

Kamara flung her hand in front of his face, mist oozing. "You love me. You and I are one." His vaporous face turned passive. She touched his spirit that was sitting in Winnefred. Suddenly, she could breathe easier.

Winnefred said, "Look at me,"

The guard looked passively at Winnefred.

Winnefred said, "She is evil. Take her away."

Wildness sparked in his pupils, and he looked at Kamara.

Kamara said, "I am light. We are one."

Passivity glazed his eyes.

Winnefred said, "Look at me."

He looked serenely at Winnefred.

Winnefred huffed. "This is ridiculous. Leave house guard. I shall punish her myself."

The house guard departed in a dazed stupor.

Winnefred shoved Kamara backward. By the time Kamara caught her balance, Winnefred had sealed them both in the room.

Kamara gulped. "Kayenté shall be furious if you harm me."

"I do as I please." Winnefred opened her mouth, sliding her bottom jaw back and forth ghoulishly.

"So I see." Kamara stepped back.

Winnefred glided into Kamara, forcing her to walk backwards until she bumped the stone wall by the window. She didn't know what to do. Should she take Kayenté's gift and bludgeon Winnefred? She could imagine Kayenté's reaction, *You killed my bride!* No, she must use wit and magic.

Winnefred said, "You'll stop misting this castle or I'll bite you."

Kamara gulped. "Bite me?"

Winnefred bared her teeth, exposing two of the longest pointed fangs Kamara had ever seen on a human being.

Kamara gasped, "You're not . . . you're not a . . . a—"

"Yes, I am a . . . a . . . ." Winnefred sneered. "Unfortunately I'm not after your blood. And I've promised your spirit to another. And he has promised Kayenté to me. So you understand why I won't let you interfere."

"Another?" Kamara asked, barely audible, unable to get her sights off of Winnefred's teeth. "The Cold One? Is he a vampire too?"

"Stupid child," lashed Winnefred. "What is a Cold One? What is a vampire? You've been cold too me, does that make you a Cold One. Kayenté seduces women, does that make him a vampire? You access the minds and hearts of so many, but not mine? Right? So you are no Priestess to me. What does that make you?"

Kamara endeavored to keep afloat in Winnefred's suck down imagery. She turned her nose up. "You're trying to drive me into illogic, and I'm not going. Cold One's have no spirit. Vampires suck blood. And Priestesses mist."

"And you will cease . . . or I'll bite you."

Kamara swallowed hard before she could stop it.

"A tad terrified, are you, little runty kitten, weak and defenseless before me."

Kamara *was* terrified. What would happen if she were bit?

Winnefred read her mind. "Maybe you'll become a vampire if I bite you . . ." or Winnefred's eyes grew big, "maybe you'll turn into a bug-eyed pig that Kayenté's men will eat for supper!" She threw her head back and cackled.

Kamara's stomach turned. She kept swallowing over and over, trying to breathe, trying to act calm. She must retrieve her cunning to ascertain Winnefred's true power. That knowledge was imperative, not only for her own survival, but to defeat Winnefred. Was Winnefred as mighty as the Cold One? Was she a Cold One? Could she disappear? Could she conjure a Black Wind? Could her threats be actualized?"

Kamara summoned her courage, and stated coolly, "I'll bet the Cold One is far mightier than you."

"I am his number one servant." Winnefred curled her lip with pride.

"Number one? There are more of you?"

"Silence," barked Winnefred, "you challenge me too much . . . and for that—" She bared her spiked canines.

"Very well—" blurted Kamara, "you win. I'll mist no more."

Winnefred lowered her chin, and raised her brows punitively. "If this mist does not fade at once, I shall come for you." She pressed her fingers underneath Kamara's chin and jerked up so hard, Kamara almost bit her tongue. She wanted to speak, but Winnefred's glare commanded silence. Silent she was, but inside, curses flew like bats from hell.

Winnefred spun around and promenaded across the room, out the door, slamming it with enough earth shattering vehemence to wake the world.

Kamara sent Allysa the symbol of herself in fighting clothes with sword in hand, followed by a call, *Come quickly!*

She peeked her head into the corridor, waiting. When Allysa arrived minutes later, Kamara yanked her into the room and shut the door. "Allysa, I need your help. We've got to trap Winnefred, lock her up somewhere. She's a—a vampire. I think."

Allysa's eyes popped open. "A vampire!" She lowered one brow suspiciously. "Surely there is no such creature. I don't believe it."

"Nor did I. But she must be one. If you could only see her teeth."

"Her teeth?"

"Her canines are razor sharp!"

Allysa gulped. "Oh mercy." She shook her head as if trying to dispel the truth. "A vampire. A vampire? She's a vampire. A vampire?"

"Yes, I am almost certain."

"I just can't believe it. I think I preferred her as a Cold One."

"I think she's both."

"Both!"

"Even more reason that she does not discover you are on my side."

"I don't think she does. When I'm with her, I shield my feelings by rousing the old hate I felt for you."

"Excellent. Now . . . is there a remote room in this castle?"

Allysa thought for a moment. "Yes. Several. Well, many."

"We need to lure and trap Winnefred into one."

"Well, Kayenté's treasure room would appeal to her. It would serve as an excellent trap."

"Perfect. Can we access that room?"

"Kayenté hides the key, lady. Where, I don't know."

"If I could find the key, would you be willing to tell Winnefred that Kayenté left a gift for her there? Once she is inside, you can slam the door and lock it."

"Yes." Allysa's face lit, excited to at last be more involved in Kamara's rebellious escapades. "But then what? Do you plan to let her starve?"

"If she's a vampire, then she'd not need food, would she? Or, maybe she needs blood? I'm most certainly not going to supply her with blood. Maybe vampire myths differ from the truth."

Allysa propped her hands on her hips. "I say, let her starve!"

Kamara jerked her head back slightly. "Oh Allysa, please don't speak that way. Perhaps we should place food, water and a chamber pot in there with her."

"Lady, I should think you'd want her dead before Lord Kayenté returns because he will just release her and then she'll balk about her unfair treatment. Then the two of them will have you exiled, or maybe executed!"

"I must trust that Kayenté won't turn on me. If I can get to him before Winnefred, I have a chance. But if she reaches him first, than mortal danger may befall both you and I."

"But how shall you come by the key?"

"Like this." Kamara closed her eyes and sought the key with her mind. "It's in a satin cloth, red satin. The satin is in a cubical compartment made of stone, under a wood plank . . . in his room under the bed, under a rug . . . in the floor. It is in a bedchamber of his, not his usual—another he sometimes goes to—with a lot of black color."

"Lady! How did you—"

"There's a key to that compartment behind his clothes chest against the wall."

"—know! That room is right across from his wine colored bed-chamber. He goes there when he wishes not to be disturbed."

"Yes," said Kamara, "I can feel that. It makes sense that he wouldn't want servants where he hides the key to his treasures."

"Well," said Allysa, "he keeps that door locked too, but unbeknownst to him, I know where he keeps that key. There are things one learns when concubine to the lord."

Kamara looked to the floor, not savoring such thoughts.

"Forgive me," said Allysa softly.

Kamara nodded and sighed. "All is well, Allysa, go now, and retrieve the key to the black bedchamber."

Allysa smiled, and then scampered out to the corridor. Kamara followed discreetly. By, the time she caught up with Allysa, she had already snuck into Kayenté's wine colored bedchamber, and retrieved the key to the black bedchamber.

They went to the door of the black bedchamber, used the key, and entered cautiously, for Winnefred was keen on surprises.

Allysa closed the door, while Kamara sprinted to the large black leather chest. She strained her muscles struggling to push it to the side, but it didn't budge.

Allysa went to her, and together they inched it away from the wall. Kamara found the stone compartment, opened it, and grabbed the iron key. They pulled the rug out from under the bed. Kamara slid under and discovered a loose wood plank. She lifted it and felt the stone cubicle, then the keyhole. She inserted the key and opened the lid. Reaching her hand into the small compartment, she found the satin pouch and apprehended the key to the treasure room. She hurriedly replaced the compartment lid and scooted out from under the bed.

Kamara held the treasure room key up to Allysa, quite proud of herself.

Allysa smiled. "I'm impressed!"

Together they put the room back in order.

Kamara said, "I'll keep the key to the black bedchamber, and the key to the compartment that hold the treasure room key."

Allysa handed her the black bedchamber key.

Kamara slipped the compartment key in her boot. "This way we can replace the compartment key later without having to push that burdensome trunk aside any more than necessary.

Kamara handed Allysa the key to the treasure chamber. "Are you sure you want to help me? She'll suspect you've turned on her."

Allysa took the key. "I know my lady, but she's bound to find out sooner or later, if she hasn't already."

"Very well then, show me the room. Then you can commence our ruse."

They left the black bedchamber. Kamara locked the door, and slipped that key in her boot with the other one.

Then Kamara and Allysa crept through passageways until they came upon the chamber. Allysa fit the key in the lock and opened the door. The room was stocked piled with fine paintings and detailed sculptures, gold and silver ornamented weapons, bags of coins, boulders of gold, and trays and trays of exotic jewelry . . . even crowns.

"Oh Allysa," Kamara glanced over the treasures, "Kayenté would have to be a freebooter to possess such riches!"

"He is, lady. I mean . . . well, he's taken possession of foreign castles and robbed them of their wealth. What would you call that?"

Kamara scowled. "No. I don't want to believe it."

"Lady, he never claimed to be noble."

"There is nobility in him, there is." Kamara bobbed her head lightly and said with certainty, "His heart will come through in the end and he'll change his power mongering ways."

Allysa scowled, tucking her chin in doubtfully. "Lady Kamara, you evade truth—again."

"He'll change."

"Uh-huh," Allysa's said cynically. "Shall we proceed?"

"He *will* change Allysa."

"Like I said, uh-huh."

Kamara glared at her, red faced. "You are such a cynic."

"Someone has to be."

"Perhaps," Kamara said, "Just as there must be someone to keep faith."

Allysa pointed playfully to Kamara. "Let it be you."

"Enough of this," said Kamara, "Let's get on with it."

"Yes. Let's do the deed."

"Must you speak that way?"

"Oh, pardon me, let's make Winnefred comfortable in her new quarters."

"Need you jest me?"

"Forgive me lady, but I worry about the way you paint things pretty. Sometimes the truth is ugly. Sometimes solutions are too."

"I know what I am doing, Allysa. Trust me."

Allysa threw her hand forward dramatically. "Lead the way."

"You don't think I can lead the way when it comes to war, do you?"

"No, but I will trust you. Forgive me. My cynicism has nothing to do with disrespect."

They stared at each other a moment, washing away the hardness that had developed between them. Their eyes soon turned soft. They hugged abruptly, then left the chamber, locking the door. As they walked a short way up the corridor, Kamara discovered a small storage room, unlocked and empty.

"Allysa, I'll hide in here."

"Yes. Good. It is near the treasure room."

"Remember, place a curtain around your true thoughts and feelings."

"I'll remember."

"Come and tell me when it's done. Oh! Remember to leave provisions in the room before you place Winnefred there."

"Yes, my lady," Allysa said, thinking Kamara foolishly naive.

Kamara backed into the tiny room, not much larger than she, and eased the door shut. Soft spider webs bent against her body until they broke, sticking on her shoulder and head. She brushed off the residue the best she could, so that the spiders wouldn't slide down the remnants of their broken homes and bite her in retaliation. She sent love to the spiders wherever they may be, and she wished she could deal with Winnefred that easily.

She waited. This was her first diabolical act, and her heart pounded from the drama. She cleared her mind in case Allysa needed to signal her. She waited, listening for Allysa's footsteps marking her return with the provisions. But a long time passed and still Allysa had not come. Was something wrong?

"What?" Winnefred said, as Allysa helped her don her blue-black satin gown. "A gift, for me?"

"Yes, my lady. I'm most sorry, I am late to tell you, but I carelessly misplaced the key. At last I've found it." She bowed before Winnefred.

"Give me the key!" Winnefred commanded outstretching her hand.

Allysa clutched the key tighter. "Oh lady, Lord Kayenté asked me to tend the key. I'm to show you to the room and let you select your gift."

Winnefred snorted, "You obviously are too addle-brained to care for the key yourself, so hand it to me!"

"But . . . but—."

Winnefred rapped her on the side of the head and swept the key from her clutches.

Allysa held her aching head. "I must follow my lord's orders. Return the key!"

Winnefred said, "Rise child, and take me to this room at once!"

Allysa sighed, hating the very guts and bowels of Winnefred the witch, the vamp, the devil herself. Circling that hate with an illusion of allegiance was growing more and more difficult.

On the way to the room, Allysa sent Kamara the black heart with words that followed, *she took the key.*

Kamara received Allysa's message and wrung her hands. Cold sweat dripped down her face, stinging her eyes. She reiterated Kayenté's words in her head, *Protect your body with a furious love to maintain your own life, be it by the tongue of deception, the might of muscle, or the swiftness of your blade.* Well, she might have to use all three. She prayed, *I summon thee warriors within. I summon thee.*

She heard two sets of footsteps pass her. All right Kayenté, she thought, I shall follow your advice. Her body rushed war, the way it had when Kayenté first made love with her. After another minute passed, she emerged from the room and crept down the corridor.

Allysa stood at the opened doorway of the treasure room.

Allysa noticed Kamara, and gave a faint apprehensive smile.

Kamara tiptoed over and offered Allysa an assuring eye, artfully masking her own true terror. She peered into the chamber viewing Winnefred's profile examining a jeweled crown.

Kamara said, "Kayenté bequeaths you with a gift and not me?"

"Yes?" Winnefred turned to face Kamara with an evil grin.

"Well, I'm entitled to something." Kamara approached Winnefred, noticing the key in her right hand.

"Back child." Winnefred bared her teeth and pushed her free hand against Kamara's chest.

Kamara feigned fear, not that she wasn't actually afraid, but the fear she was feigning wasn't the fear she felt, and somehow that made a difference. She took a step back and bowed submissively.

"That's more to my liking," Winnefred said.

Kamara asked, "You care for treasures? I thought Cold Ones sought only the incorporeal."

"Don't be ridiculous. A queen needs a crown."

"A queen?" Kamara asked, "Are you planning to be Queen?"

Winnefred tilted her head back and scoffed, "Kayenté has that plan for me. He needs a shrewd rich woman who can manipulate the masses favorably his way. I am the woman behind the man and Kayenté knows it." Her bottom jaw circled malevolently under the top, exposing her fangs. Her ocher eyes ejected the poison of mal-intent. "Without me, he'll not rule Kantine." She grinned confidently.

"Oh," sighed Kamara with distasteful realization, "so that is why he wants you." Her respect for Kayenté began to fade when she awoke suddenly to Winnefred's scheme to maneuver her out of love with him! Winnefred's claim was ludicrous because Kayenté would never credit a woman with the ability to conquer Kantine *for* him. He'd want that credit for himself!

She rallied herself to the cause, taking heed to dodge Winnefred's clever manipulations. Back on course, she focused on getting the key. She recalled a fighting move Kayenté had once taught her. She shot one foot in back of Winnefred's while shoving her chest. Winnefred fell. The moment she hit the ground, Kamara grabbed the key from her. Winnefred seemed stunned. Kamara raced out the door, slammed it shut, and locked Winnefred inside.

Winnefred said, "Servant girl, unlock this door at once!"

Kamara replied, "I've put her under my spell, and she'll now do *my* bidding!"

"Servant girl! Servant girl!" shouted Winnefred, "I can reward you greatly!"

Kamara pulled Allysa away from the door. When they were well down the corridor, Kamara sighed with relief.

Allysa smiled. "We did it!"

Kamara returned the smile. Then a revelation stopped her steps. "I never heard you pass with food and water."

Allysa faced her tentatively. "I know. I thought it not best, even though I had to disobey you. Your kindness was going to get you murdered, lady. Please understand, you must be as cold as she would be. You must be as cold as the Cold Ones."

"You are the third person to tell me that, and each time I hear it, I loathe it more! There simply must be another way to handle such matters. We *cannot*, in good conscience, let her starve."

Allysa grabbed her arm. "We can. We must."

Kamara swept Allysa's hand off her. "Oh, let me think on this."

"You can brush me away. You can brush my opinion away. But you can't brush reality away, lady. You cannot."

"I must remain true to myself, Allysa."

"True to who you have been, or true to who you are trying to become?"

"I retaliated, and that proves my gain."

"It isn't enough, lady, not nearly enough! You can't just point the sword and parry. You must drive it into your target."

"I don't want to kill her. Hush . . . please!"

"You're the one who'll be hushed."

"Allysa!"

"Lady, please listen to reason."

" 'The light' is not a thing of reason, but wisdom."

"You are being unwise."

Kamara walked on. "I know the realm of wisdom. I know it well, and now it decrees that I return to my room and resume misting."

Allysa said, "She is locked away. She can't hurt us now."

"Maybe not. Maybe so. No telling what powers she may have even though she is imprisoned. A Black Wind once almost carried me away, and the Cold One was nowhere to be seen. The Cold One can appear and disappear in a moment's time. Can she?"

Allysa moved to her side. "Well, if you follow my initial advice, we may not have to find out just what power she possesses."

"No more, Allysa, your talk sickens me."

"No more is what you'll be, if you don't get well fast."

Kamara sped up her pace. "Why are you being so stubborn!"

"It is you being stubborn."

"You are talking . . . mur . . . mur . . . murder."

"I am talking self-defense."

"I have taken measures."

"And your proposal of sustaining her with food is like taking them back."

"No, it isn't."

"Ask yourself, what would Kayenté do?

"I am not Kayenté."

"I thought you did a ritual to absorb his powers?"

"I did, but I am still me."

"Well, you are him too, right?"

Kamara grabbed her temples. "You are making my head hurt!" She reached the bedchamber door, and quickly went inside, blocking Allysa from entering. "I love you, but leave me be for a time, please!" Her eyes softened. "Please?"

"I ask you the same question, in the same way, to what is making *my* head hurt, my heart hurt, my hope hurt. Please lady, let us do away with her, please? Please? Please?"

Kamara's eyes teared. "I love you Allysa, I do. But you must trust me. I *must* be alone now. I ask you to understand." She closed the door on Allysa's earnest face, along with the prospects of that very bad M word, and the chamber of wicked acts. She had enough evil for one day.

Ж
Chapter Twenty-Two

Four days passed. Kamara had misted almost continually, listening periodically at Winnefred's door, hearing her whimper that she'd die without food and water, and that she wasn't really a vampire.

Kamara continued to wear her black fighting outfit with Kayenté's lethal gift strapped on her calf, but she'd shed her shrewd attitude. She lay on her bed, contemplating Winnefred's fate. Even though she remembered Kayenté's words about her enemies playing upon her compassion, she still couldn't, in good conscience, leave Winnefred to die in such a cruel manner. Perhaps Winnefred wasn't so powerful. Apparently, she couldn't disappear or conjure a Black Wind.

She decided to aid Winnefred—a little. She rose from the bed to apprise Allysa. Just then, Allysa knocked lightly and entered the room, cheery eyed, with a red dress and black shirt draped over her arm. She said, "I brought you a gown of mine that I've been saving for a special time. Wear it please, for when Kayenté returns." Allysa held the dress up for Kamara to fully view.

Kamara surveyed the beautiful bright red gown, a form fitting delight. It reminded her of liquid fire: soft yet stunning, a scoop-neck and long open shoulder length sleeves that draped down like scarves. The black wool long sleeved shirt hanging over Allysa's arm, was for wear underneath the gown.

"It's breathtaking," Kamara said, "but I can't wear your prize dress."

"Please lady."

Kamara was surprised and a little ashamed that she was so intensely attracted to a material object. "Well, if that's truly your wish."

"It is." Allysa handed her the garments

Kamara smiled warmly. "Thank you." She took the clothes appreciatively and laid them carefully over a chair by the window. "You're being most kind, and I have terrible news for you."

"What?"

"I must bring Winnefred food and water."

Allysa's face turned to horror. "Oh no!"

"Oh yes."

"Then take some house guards with you."

"No, our spells seem to cross cancel, so nothing happens. It's pointless to involve them. Although, I wish Sir Robert were here."

Allysa tilted her head. "Sir Robert Durham? Is he the one who brought you to Kayenté?"

"Yes, he'd help us. He'd believe me. I know he would. But he's not here, so I must tend Winnefred with my own wits."

"Leave Winnefred to her fate, I beg you lady!"

"I cannot Allysa. I know I should, but I simply *cannot*."

"I want to show you an escape route that Kayenté revealed to me before he left. I want you to know, in case something goes wrong. Flee if you must, even if you leave me in danger."

"I won't leave you!"

"You may well have to, if Winnefred turns on you. As for me, there's no place I can hide that I can't be found. The Cold Ones are relentless, and Kayenté and I are their targets. If you leave us, you could be free."

Allysa frowned shaking her head.

"Come," Kamara said. She led Allysa out through the secret passageway to the outside of the castle, and onto the secret tunnel by the moat. "Kayenté said that twenty kilometers east there is a nunnery. You could remain there for a while, and then if you can, find a way to get to Lania Castle. Tell them I sent you. I shall mist you for protection, if I am able."

"You talk as if something *is* going to happen."

Kamara ignored her and started walking back. "Come. As you would say, 'let's do the deed.' "

Allysa followed. "I fear the deed will do you."

Kamara realized giving Winnefred food and water was dangerous. She didn't feel confident, and how could they succeed when she
lacked confidence? They walked back into the castle silently. Kamara
bade Allysa bring food and drink and meet her at the treasure chamber. Kamara went to the treasure chamber and waited. Allysa didn't
arrive for a full hour. When she did reappear, she had a gunnysack.
Kamara peeked inside and saw only an apple, a loaf of bread, and a
jug of water.

"That's not much," whispered Kamara.

"She deserves nothing more," Allysa whispered back.

"Is it poisoned?"

"No," Allysa lied, mind shielding the truth. She had indeed poisoned the food to save Kamara's life.

"Well," Kamara sighed gathering her courage, "let's do it. You
open the door. I'll toss the sack in the room. Then you slam the door
and lock it."

Allysa shook her head.

Kamara glared at her punitively.

"Oh, all right!" Allysa whispered. She unlocked the door, and
opened it, just enough to get the food in.

Kamara tossed the sack, her hand barely in the room. Her wrist
was grabbed and her body flew into the chamber, smashing against
shelves of jewels. A pile of green gem necklaces fell on her chest as
she landed on her back, flat on the hard wood floor. Her stomach
caved from the pressure of Winnefred's knee pinning her down. She
could scarcely breathe. Winnefred towered above her, ugly and
hissing, bearing vampire teeth. The gruesome mouth dove swiftly to
her throat.

Kamara shrieked, then moaned deeply, feeling her neck pierced
by two huge lances. Surely Winnefred's canines were not this big, nor
that fat. Cold sharp pains intensified as the fangs burrowed into her
throat and seemingly beyond. Warmth filled her veins. An almost
pleasant rush of blood shot through her body, up her neck. She real-

ized that Winnefred was feeding on her and she didn't care, for her worries and cares were fading . . . fading . . . fading. She lost consciousness.

Allysa drew her hand to her lips, stunned, unsure what to do. Should she run away as Kamara had bade her? She could seek help. Should she attempt to get Winnefred off Kamara, and also risk being bit? Who would help them *then*?"

She finally decided to try and kill Winnefred, fearing Winnefred was killing Kamara. She raced into the room, snatched a gold dagger and plunged it down towards Winnefred's back.

Winnefred spun around and grabbed her wrists.

Allysa shrieked and inwardly recoiled with terror. Blood dripped down the corners of Winnefred's mouth.

Winnefred stated calmly, "Thank you for stopping me. I didn't wish to kill her, and I would have."

Allysa gulped, struggling to uphold her courage.

Winnefred spoke with mock sincerity, "Calm down child, I'll not harm you if you serve me. Drop the dagger."

"What will happen to Lady Kamara?"

"She'll sleep for a time. She's lost much blood."

Allysa clung to the dagger. Her trembling hand was numb from Winnefred's iron grasp. "You *are* a vampire then?"

"Indeed."

"But I've seen you in the daylight and you didn't burn."

Winnefred curled her lip. "Don't be ridiculous. Do you believe all the stories you hear? Has it not occurred to you that there are as many levels to becoming a vampire, as there are clergies to the pope, or servants to the king?"

Allysa stood in shock, petrified by Winnefred's confession.

Winnefred scolded, "Drop the dagger dear, or shall I bite you too."

Allysa didn't trust Winnefred, for she'd already proved herself a liar. She surrounded herself with phony thoughts of allegiance. "Release my hand. Then I'll drop the dagger."

"Very well." Winnefred released her.

Allysa clenched the dagger harder and dashed out the door. She fled through the secret passageways, outside the castle, through the tunnel, under the moat, and on toward the nunnery. Her every instinct screamed that Winnefred wanted her dead.

She felt guilty for abandoning Kamara, but at least this way she could seek help. She ran hard and long, most surprised that Winnefred was not on her trail, but then again, she was probably *more* preoccupied with Kamara.

In the chamber of treasures, Winnefred looked down upon her victim and licked blood off her teeth.

Ж
Chapter Twenty-Three

When Kamara opened her eyes, she was in her bed in a stiff yellowed nightgown. Kayenté stood over her, his hair tied back in a ponytail. He was wearing reddish billowy shirt, uncharacteristic for him.

"Kayenté?" she murmured confused. "Is it truly you? You survived the battle? All is well?"

She recognized his voice, but not his disposition. "I survived the battle, yes, and the Rudels are in temporary retreat, but the war is far from over. So, all is not well. As to you . . . you forced my Winnefred to knock you out. You should have known better, considering how fragile you are. You've been unconscious for three days, and you misted the hell out of my castle. You invaded my treasure room and stole my keys. Winnefred discovered them in your boot. You caused Allysa to steal one of my daggers. Have you gone mad?"

His response disturbed her, shocked her, ever so contrary to what she'd expected, and horribly opposite of what she needed.

"Oh Kayenté, hold me!"

He bent over and held her limply.

She blurted, "Winnefred is soulless! She is a traitor in league with the Cold One, and she means you harm, and intends to bring your castle down. I've been trying to stop her!"

"Kamara," he said hesitantly, releasing his unenthusiastic embrace. "That's a ridiculous story."

"You *must* believe me. Winnefred wanted me in the torture chamber. Instead, she bit me. She's a vampire!"

"Don't be ridiculous. Winnefred informed me of your jealous attempts to take her life, so that I couldn't marry her."

"Kayenté, she lies. Would I take a life? Does that sound like me?"

"You are a confused child in a delirium. You could attempt anything in this state of mind."

"I'm no child, Kayenté. Have you forgotten all we shared?"

"Of what do you speak?"

"Our night together . . . our ritual . . . making love!"

"We have never made love Kamara. That's ridiculous."

"Stop saying that word! You sound like Winnefred. Oh Kayenté, she has cast a spell on you!"

"You're the witch Kamara, not my Winnefred. Now relax and I'll have some food brought to you. Winnefred has begged me not to punish you, for she pities you terribly."

"*She* pities *me*? Now that . . . that is ridiculous! Kayenté look at my neck. What do you see?"

"Two swollen red and purple puncture marks."

"Your beloved Winnefred *sucked* my blood."

Kayenté laughed. "Your imagination runs wild, silly girl. I don't know what misfortune befell you, but I am certain, it was not that."

"Oh Kayenté, you're in grave danger!"

"Calm down, Kamara. If you can't behave, I'll send you away."

Kamara raised the back of her hand to her forehead in despair, and closed her eyes with a defeated sigh. Her neck ached worse now than during the initial bite. Winnefred *was* a vampire, and Allysa could attest to that. Allysa! Her eyes snapped open. "Where's Allysa?"

"Gone, three days now. Winnefred told me that she feared you."

"Feared *me*? She fled from Winnefred I'm sure, especially after watching me get bit."

"Kamara, get your strength back. We'll talk later."

She grabbed his wrist. "There shall be no later if you do not believe me now!"

He jerked his arm from her grasp and walked out of the room.

Her bottom lip quivered. Things had turned so bad. Her head fell to the side in defeat. The red dress and the black woolen shirt Allysa had given her were draped over the chair by the window. She sat up slightly, weak and lightheaded, and pulled the garments desperately to her breast. She rubbed her cheek against the red fabric, needing Allysa to comfort her.

She felt utterly hopeless. Had the sexual ritual with Kayenté been performed in vain? She was exhausted from holding all the responsibility to save the castle. Her heart ached unbearably. She wept into the gown, "Allysa, Allysa, Allysa," wishing Allysa could hold her in the way Kayenté would not.

Her tears drained her strength, and she fell asleep. She awakened sometime later in the thick black night feeling panicked. She crept outside her door, still clutching Allysa's clothes. It made her feel as if Allysa were with her. She went to the outside of Kayenté's room and heard his voice—and Winnefred's, and the sounds of lovemaking.

Her throat tightened. Breath trickled in and out, cracking her heart with pain. She wanted to die. Her beloved had betrayed her. He had. Kayenté had been thoroughly snared in Winnefred's web and he'd soon be devoured. However could she save him! Oh . . . however could she?

Weighted with dejection's heavy chains, she went back to her room and locked the door. She trudged over to the unmade bed and flopped onto the blue satin covers, drowning in agony. It seemed she'd been descending a spiral into darkness, like the one she'd once climbed out of in the Black Wind. Then, she realized she was in the Black Wind after all. Winnefred was that Black Wind. Black as could be.

She had the awful sense that the only way out of this wind was through it, climbing *down* to the bottom and out, instead up and away. Yet, each rung brought more suffering than the one before, this time, the downward spiral, worse than the up. Could any human survive the journey? Besides, she doubted her ability to even descend the rung she was on. It seemed to own her.

What she claimed Kayenté could not do, he had done. He *had* broken her heart. And he didn't have to die to do it. Her misery surpassed tears. Her body numbed with depression. And there she stayed, for two days, with Allysa's dress at her breast, rejecting food and water. She cared about nothing—and no one, except Allysa, who (having loved Kayenté) was the only one who could possibly relate to her devastation, or understood the complexity of the situation, or bring her the human caring she so desperately needed.

Kayenté entered the room. Three servants followed with food and clothes.

He touched her shoulder. "You must eat and drink to survive."

She didn't respond. Her eyes were blank.

"I have ordered you a bath, some food, and a new dress. I want you to attend my wedding." Her expression remained unchanged.

Kayenté commanded the servants, "Tend her, and escort her to the wedding at noon."

Why? she thought, *why is he doing this?* Had he forgotten that he once loved her? Had he forgotten she loved him, or was he bestowing such cruelty upon her for his own pleasure? Was he so weak that he could not see Winnefred had enchanted him, the way she herself had enchanted his prison guard?

The servants began filling the wooden tub in her room with pails of water. She barely noticed anything happening, until she was in the tub and Allysa's dress was ripped from her and cast upon the floor. She cried silently, *Allysa . . . dear Allysa . . . you are the only one who knows my pain. You are the only one who is real to me.*

She felt herself being dressed in new clothes, and she felt her hair pinned up and food pushed into her mouth. She found Allysa's dress and held it desperately over her heart, and she would not release it, no matter how hard the servants tried to pry it away.

She felt herself walked to a big room somewhere in the castle. She was seated in a large chair, and guessed that was supposed to make her special. The wedding took place in a blur and life seemed but a dream. She felt her spirit fading, and she thought only of Allysa.

After the wedding, she was taken back to her room where she remained for two more days in a silent deep fugue, clenching Allysa's dress. The servants tended her, leaving her in a white night shift for she clearly did not intend to leave her bed again.

On the morning of the third day, she received an unexpected visitor in her bedchamber—Taran. He appeared handsome and virile in his long sleeved chain mail tunic, and brown sleeveless brigandine. His tan pants showcased his taut leg muscles, sword on one hip, and knife on the other. His dark hair was longer than she'd last remembered. His blue eyes smiled, and oh, how so very much he resembled Kayenté.

He knelt by her bedside. "I told you Kayenté would break your heart; I told you I would be here for you when he did. So, here I am."

She gazed at him. Faint hope glimmered in her eyes. She loved his soft presence. He stroked her cheek. That tender action rendered a wave of emotion within her.

Taran brushed his fingers through the strands of her tangled hair. "My brother tells me you are in great distress. I want to help you."

"You cannot help me." She closed her eyes and shook her head. "I have bonded with one who has fallen, so I too—fall."

"Let me take you away from him, and you'll soon feel better."

"No." She peered wearily at him. "I haven't the will nor strength to go anywhere."

He slipped Allysa's dress from her hands, and tossed it on the chair.

"I'm taking you anyway." He pulled her out of bed, into his arms.

"What are you up to Taran?" she asked with semi-suspicion.

"I'm rescuing you," he replied.

He carried her down the corridor and descended the stairway.

She felt too weak to fight him, and honestly she no longer cared where she resided. She was already in hell.

When they entered the Great Hall, Kayenté took notice and followed them. Taran made haste for the castle exit.

"Where are you taking her?" Kayenté called in a hollow voice.

Taran stopped and addressed his brother, who had reached his side. "For some fresh air," he answered with a smile.

Kamara stared at Kayenté's perplexed face. He seemed to struggle with himself. Sparkles of pain dashed across his otherwise lifeless eyes.

"Away with you," he said flatly.

Kamara snapped her head toward Taran's chest and flung her arms around his neck. "Oh take me away indeed Taran. He loves me no more!"

Taran gave a twisted smile, turned away from Kayenté, and carried her out of the castle. Kamara realized that her sword, knife, and Allysa's dress were not coming with her, but those objects did not matter now, for Taran filled her with the kindly attentions that she craved. Nothing else seemed important. He helped her on his gray steed, mounted behind her, and took her away.

Three and half days passed as a dream, for as long as Taran fed her gentle whispers of affection, she no longer cared of her whereabouts. But when they arrived at an enormous greystone fortress, she asked, "Where are we?"

"Wincott Castle," he replied.

"Wincott Castle?" she asked, mildly alarmed, "Why have you brought me *here*?"

"You will be safer here," he replied. "The Sakajians have taken this castle. I am in charge of guarding it. Here, I have more power to assure your every comfort."

She sighed. "Very well then."

Taran tended her daily until her spirits again shone bright. He had taken her for strolls in the plentiful gardens, horse rides in the aspen woods, and picnics by the fish-filled streams. She began to forget that there ever was a Cold One. Memories of her past began to fade as if she had never existed before Taran had swept her away.

Five weeks passed into late autumn. Taran had wooed her every day, bestowing gifts of garments and trinkets, and stroking her ego with confessions of love.

A leaf from an oak tree fluttered down between them as they picnicked on a burgundy blanket by a creek dotted with trees of oak and aspen. They sipped on fine wine from silver goblets, chewed on soft bread and moist white cheese. Kamara wore an elegant white wool gown, covered by a pale blue velveteen cape. Her long hair, pinned up at the sides, cascaded down her back.

"You look sweet," Taran said. A chilly breeze blew against the tendrils of hair that outlined his face. "You are far too sweet for my brother."

Her eyes narrowed suspiciously. Did Taran woo her to spite Kayenté, or were his affections genuine? Sadly, she admitted to herself that she fairly did not care, for his attentions, no matter what the motive, lightened her suffering.

He took her hand in his. "Marry me."

Stunned, she replied, "What? Why do you ask?"

"I love you." He squeezed her hand.

She fidgeted. "I mean not to seem distrustful, but you and your brother involve women in your lives for ulterior motive: be it a night of pleasure, a castle to attain, or simply to spurn each other. I can't trust you to marry me for love."

"Kamara—" he dropped her hand, rolled onto his back, and peered at the cloudy sky, "—you've changed me."

"I think not," she said cautiously.

He turned on his side and propped his head up with his elbow. "Then why do you stay with me?"

She lowered her head, shame forming on her face. "I suppose I need you."

"And I need you," he said, "is that not reason enough to wed?"

Taran suddenly sprung to his feet and snapped his head toward a smattering of oak trees in the direction of the castle. "A rider comes," he declared. He stepped in front of Kamara and withdrew his sword until a man on a horse emerged from the trees.

"My brother," Taran sighed, replacing his sword in the sheath on his hip.

Kamara's eyes lit. "Kayenté?"

"No. Marc."

"Marc?"

Marc reached them and dismounted.

Kamara rose and stood by Taran.

Marc was fully armored, wearing a yellow and black panther tunic, helm at his side. He said, "I went to the castle, but the guards informed me you were out here."

Marc glanced at Kamara with confusion in his eyes.

Taran asked, "What business have you, brother?"

Marc addressed Taran, "King Aldos's health is fast failing. He's expected to die within the month. Word is, Drudel intends to break his oath with Kayenté, and take the crown for himself. William of Gateland has sent word to King Aldos that he should be named heir, by virtue of his Sakajian blood and proof of his long-standing kingship. And that mercenary, Merculus, he's regrouping the Rudels and planning to take back this castle and all of Kantine, thereby making Harold Wincott, King of the Sakajians. I have brought another two hundred men here to fortify this castle. All hell is about to break loose. Father wants you to stand ready for battle. We are going to make Kayenté—King! We've sent him messages but he does not return them. Something is amiss."

Kamara blurted, "Kayenté is bewitched by Winnefred!"

Marc narrowed his eyes in pause. Then he said, "Is that what puts you in the hands of Taran, Lady Kamara?"

She half nodded, not wanting to insult Taran.

Taran said, "Kayenté *isn't* bewitched. He's in love with Winnefred. He's sure to respond to your messages soon. Meanwhile, I'll prepare our army here at once and await orders. Until then, Kamara and I plan to wed and have a honeymoon."

Kamara looked at Taran with stunned eyes. "You think Kayenté not under a spell?"

"Of course not," Taran replied.

She faced Marc, her golden eyes pleading for understanding.

Marc stared straight through her. "Return with me now, Lady Kamara."

Her face held indecision. Taran had been kind. How could she leave him?

Taran protested, "She'll remain here. We are to marry tonight."

"Tonight!" Kamara said.

"We've waited far too long," Taran said, "it's time you were free of the pain Kayenté inflicted."

Marc accused, "You seem unconcerned about this war brother."

"I'm not concerned, for as always, we'll defeat our enemies."

Marc said, "Kamara, if you choose to come with me, I leave now. You can have sanctuary at my father's castle, while I pay a visit to Kayenté to see if your claim is true."

"You—believe me?" she asked surprised.

"I know Winnefred's capabilities," Marc said, "and never did I trust her."

She took a step toward Marc. Taran caught her arm. "You would abandon me after all the comfort I've given you. I've earned your loyalty, have I not?"

She looked at Marc, her eyes searching for truth.

Marc said, "She has the right to act on her own behalf."

Taran squinted his eyes with threat. "Leave *now* Marc."

"Very well," Marc said dryly.

Kamara's heart lurched. Why had he acquiesced so easily?

"Are you coming, Kamara?" Marc asked.

She wanted to go, but she felt paralyzed, caught between her debt to Taran and the truth shining from Marc.

Marc sighed, "Fare-the-well, then." He turned and walked to his horse.

She panicked and tried to speak, but no words emerged.

Marc mounted and rode away.

Kamara instantly felt trapped in a pit of deceit, and her only hope of climbing into truth had just ridden away. A gray rain of despair washed over her.

Taran suggested, in his most affable manner, "Let us return to the castle, and plan for tonight."

Kamara felt like an immobilized fly hanging in the spider's web, soon to be devoured by the two-legged Taran. She remained motionless while he packed up their picnic. And once he lifted her onto his horse, she felt lethargic. And by the time they reached the castle, she had fallen far, far away from the last remnants of who she knew herself to be.

That evening, someone dressed her for the wedding. Her daze was so thick she could barely detect the identity of the faces that came and went before her, and she wondered if this was how Kayenté had felt under Winnefred's spell. Had Taran such powers? Had he such motives as Winnefred? Oh Marc—why had he not just taken her away! Couldn't he see the struggle in her eyes?

When Kayenté had married, she was lost in her pain. But tonight, she was far more gone. She felt a thousand miles away from her own body, yet forced somehow to peer long distance through her eyes. Her physical faculties were no longer her own, and the physical world was a dream. Her thoughts pounded so loudly in her head, she could hardly hear the priest. She didn't even remember saying, I do, before she vaguely heard the priest say, "I pronounce you married."

Then she was in a bedchamber. Taran's—she thought. She was naked on the bed. When did that happen? She heard Taran say, "I'll return in a moment." He snuffed the light and the dark was pitch. Seconds later, a heavy weight descended on her body, crushing the breath out of her—skin against skin, moist and ugly. A shaft invaded her womanhood.

"I can't breathe," she cried, pushing against his arms, "you're so heavy."

She felt a void in the man atop her, despite his heavy mass. *This could not be Taran, but why would Taran not be atop her?* She knew this smell, and this queer breathing in her ear. *The Cold One!*

She screamed.

The chamber door flew open. From the oil lamps in the corridor, soft light stretched across the room. The shadow of a man raced into the chamber. The Cold One sprung off her but she didn't hear his feet hit the floor.

The man who had raced into the room moved about frantically, until at last he came to her bed. "Kamara, are you well?"

His kind, honest tone snapped her back into herself. She was being rescued! Suddenly she felt so alive. The man gripped her arm and pulled her out of bed toward the doorway. On a whim, she grabbed the garment draped over a chair by the exit.

Once in the lit passageway, she looked to the man. "Marc!" she said, with a glow of affection in her eyes. "You came back for me!"

He released her arm. "I know a spell when I see it." He perused her naked body with man's eye, "and not only you, but this whole castle is under one."

Her face reddened. While Marc talked, she slipped hurriedly into the garment she had grabbed.

"Even the men I brought with me today already mill about with lifeless eyes. They can't defend this castle. I must warn my father."

Taran's green silk barely covered her thighs. She desperately wanted a cloak, but felt blessed enough that she had a shirt, and more blessed that she had Marc who actually believed her.

Marc grabbed her arm, and swept her down the long corridor.

As they fled, she said, "Oh Marc! I'm greatly relieved that you can see the truth!"

He said, "Ever since Taran met Winnefred, his behavior has turned more strange and distant, just as yours was turning, and I have no doubt—Kayenté's too."

"Marc," Kamara said huffing, "There is one worse than Winnefred, and he was upon me, when you entered. I call him the Cold One."

"Taran was not with you?"

"No! You have no idea the fate you have spared me. The Cold One almost defeated me, and he cares not who holds the crown, so long as he can hold us all—I mean everyone in the world!"

They rounded the corridor toward the stairs. Taran stood before them, blocking the way, sword drawn.

Marc stood protectively in front of Kamara. "Let us pass Taran, or prepare to die!"

"It's *you* who will die," Taran returned.

Before Kamara could protest, the brothers struck swords, and engaged in a furious fight. Kamara called upon the mist. Her breath and fingertips emitted vapors. She aimed mostly at Taran. Taran stopped fighting so suddenly, Marc almost slashed off his head.

Marc gaped at Taran, immobilized in the moist cloud. "What is this?"

Kamara raised her brows. "I misted him."

Marc looked at her strangely. "You what?"

"Marc, I am a holy Priestess with the power to pacify. Has no one informed you?"

He glared at her for a moment, and then his practical side took over. "Well damn! Keep misting, and get us the hell out here."

She glanced at Taran compassionately, understanding that he'd likely suffered Kayenté's current plight. She wanted to save him, but Marc's grip tightened on her arm, and he yanked her away. She called, "Taran come with us!"

Taran groaned, squinted his eyes, and pointed his finger at her. "When these vapors fade, I will come for you! You cannot hope to win—" his voice trailed off, ". . . no one can."

Marc pulled her swiftly onward. "He's too far gone."

They journeyed out of the castle into the moonlit night, passing dazed guards who seemed uninterested in them. Huge torches mounted on lion sculptures burned near the castle walls, casting an elemental incandescence over the frontcourt. They sprinted to Marc's horse. He helped her mount. Before he could do the same, a voice shouted, "Halt or I'll fling my knife into Kamara!"

Several feet from Marc, Taran stood, the features of his face lost in the darkness, his long black hair edged with light. Behind him was a battalion of the very guards that moments ago cared less if they passed.

Marc raised his sword. "You'll first have to fling it into me!"

Taran's sword met Marc's, and again they fought.

The flurry of guards flowed around them toward Kamara.

Marc yelled, "Ride Kamara! Go to my father!"

"I can't leave you!" she screamed throwing her mists at the entourage of guards closing in around her, but there were so many, she couldn't mist them all in time.

Marc's sword blocked a heavy blow from Taran's blade. He yelled again. "Run woman! Let my effort be worth something!"

She kicked her barefoot heals hard and the horse ran. Her hair whipped her back. The frigid night air bit into her ears. She heard pounding on the earth behind her, and the snorting and panting of horses at her back. She exhaled the mists full force. Soon she was in a cloud, hearing nothing but her own mount and her own hard breathing. She had escaped.

She slowed her horse, afraid it would trip and break a leg in the dark. She entered the thick forest, and sent the mists to Marc, hoping it would offer some protection, though it seemed no one was protected from the Cold One.

She thought of Taran and shuddered. He was a part of that awful team. The whole courtship had just been a scheme to trick her into submitting to the Cold One.

She hung her head wearily on the horse's neck, her bare legs turning numb from the chilly air. It began to rain. She let the horse move onward, hoping it would lead her to Franz Ketola's castle where it lived, and if indeed it did, would Franz believe her? Would he believe Marc was in Taran's traitorous hands? She prayed Marc was alive. She did not feel him dead.

The cold rain soaked her, but she was already too sad to resent the downpour. And she was already too resentful to fear the task before her. And she was already too frightened about the world ending to feel doubtful about her ability to save it. She felt strangely alive even as icy droplets chilled her to the bone. Clip clop, horse hooves squishing mud. Endless rain. Endless hours. Endless night. Head burning, limbs weak. "Dark days ahead," she murmured, "dark days."

Ж
Chapter Twenty-Four

Near Franz Ketola's Castle-Kanz Region

By morning, the rain had ceased, but the sky was still dismal gray. Kamara was exhausted and sickly. Her head burned with fever, and her arms hung limp over the horse's moist fur. But as she'd hoped, Marc's horse had taken her toward Franz Ketola's castle. She saw the brown stone fortress looming in the distance.

She was embarrassed by her state of dress, or undress as it were. The dark green shirt clung damply against her skin. Wet ropes of hair, darkened from the rain, hung haphazardly down her body, most wild and unsuitable for the court. But she had to enter the castle this way, or not at all.

"Lady Kamara! You are well!" A man whispered loudly.

She turned to the voice and saw a mounted knight hiding in the midst of thick pine trees. "Sir Bradley, is that you?"

"Indeed lady. Come hither, away from the castle's view."

Kamara hesitated.

"It's all right," he said, "I'm a Rudel, but I'm also your friend and I seek penance with you."

She trusted him and steered her horse his way.

When she reached him, he said, "I see you are safe, though dangerously dressed. Stay away from that castle! We're soon to attack."

Kamara gazed about the forest and saw a hundred shining eyes, and presumed there were more she did *not* see.

Her mouth dropped open.

Sir Bradley said, "Leave this danger."

"But—"

"The others don't care if you die. I do."

Her mind spun in circles, trying to make sense of her feelings. She had come to warn Franz about his son's treachery, and now she was amongst Franz's enemies as a non-enemy, apprised of their intent to attack Franz. How could she be on no side and yet be treated as if she were on both?

Then she heard a charge of voices, footsteps, and horses. Sir Bradley began to move with them. Looking back to her he shouted, "Ride north toward Panther Ketola's castle, but do not go there! You will come upon a nunnery. Remain as long as you can!"

Before she could respond, Sir Bradley was racing with his warrior mass into battle, toward Franz Ketola's men, who were flooding from the castle, war cries rending the air. They crashed into each other, weapons flying.

Kamara turned her head from the chaos. This could not be happening! What now? Sir Bradley warned her to keep distance from Kayenté's castle. Was he going to be attacked? With Kayenté's bizarre frame of mind, there was no telling what would happen. Winnefred would probably invite the Rudels in for tea! She must warn Kayenté. She *must*, spell or not.

She galloped fast and hard toward Kayenté's domain. Fever ached in her limbs. Hunger, thirst, and cold, ached her body the same, but Kayenté must not die! By nightfall, she neared his fortress, haggard and drained of energy, flopped sickly over Marc's weary warhorse. She prayed no Rudels lurked in the shadows, ready for attack.

Two hands ripped her off the horse. Her knees smacked the ground. She glimpsed the red and black tunic. She sighed with relief. The perpetrator was Sakajian, Kayenté's man.

"Hurry!" she said, "Take me to Kayenté. I've come to warn him of an attack!"

"Lame excuse," said the guard, yanking her to her feet, shoving her ahead of him. "We know you're a spy for the Rudels."

"I'm Lady Kamara of Lania Castle. I've been Lord Kayenté's guest before. I'm no spy!"

The guard shoved her. She lurched forward, her tender feet stepping on sharp rocks. "Please. There's no need for brutality. Where is Sir Robert? I wish to speak to him."

"He's gone. He abandoned Panther. If he were here, he'd be in the prison."

"Why?"

"Because he too is a spy."

"Oh what foul lies that vampire Winnefred has made you believe!"

He snatched her upper arm. Another guard appeared, snatching her other arm. They walked so fast, her feet barely touched the ground, grazing her toes over pinecones and clumps of grass. They dragged her like this, all the way to the castle door. She misted, hoping it would help her. But it did not.

The door opened. The guards shoved her to the floor. She fell on hands and knees, staring at black boots. She raised her eyes slowly. Maroon leather pants, tip of scabbard, ruby ring on the finger of a limp hand. Black belt around a maroon leather tunic, chest draped with long . . . dark . . . hair, bare muscled shoulders. Throat with a soft hollow v. Soft . . . hollow . . . v. *Stern* face. *Ruthless* eyes. Kayenté. But—not Kayenté.

"Why Kamara?" he said, "why is it that you're always in some man's shirt when you come to me?"

Winnefred's voice sounded. "Because she was your whore darling, before she left to side with the Rudels. Don't you remember?"

Kamara's face contorted in horror. "Kayenté! Taran took me away. You remember that, surely!"

He looked down upon her red sickly face that peered up at him, and searched her pleading eyes through the strands of her matted hair. He murmured as if trying to remember, "My . . ."

"Whore . . . Kayenté," interrupted Winnefred while preening the folds of her crimson gown of sparkle and bead. "Make her pay for her betrayal. Take her roughly, fornicate with her like a wild animal. Remember, she meant to destroy you."

Kamara was momentarily stunned. Winnefred always amazed her with the cold-blooded trash that rolled off her tongue. She was placing suggestions in Kayenté's mind. Kamara knew well how Winnefred's magic worked, for it was not unlike her own.

"Kayenté," she implored at his feet, too weak with illness to rise. "I'm a Priestess of the Mist. Love . . . Kayenté, remember love. Remember your noble heart!"

"I haven't a noble heart," he replied flatly, and then added in a diabolical whisper, "why—I have no heart at all."

"You *do* Kayenté," she said.

Her head burned. She required sleep, but she must rise from the floor. She must show her power! She gripped her hands around the ankles of his boots. She sent her spirit into him and climbed up his steely body, fighting exhaustion. "You have a noble heart. You have love for me, Kamara Lania of Lania Castle. You are committed to—me."

He remained stiff, making no effort to aid her. When she was finally up, she clutched his arms for support, and gazed into his vacant eyes. She pierced images of herself and Lania Castle into his mind. She commanded desperately, "Remember me, the one you love. Remember 'the light.' I call for the Angel I placed within you. Angel—awaken him!"

His body quaked for a moment, his eyes beginning to focus far into her. Just when she sensed he was about to connect, Winnefred barked. "She's your traitorous whore. Rape her."

Kayenté looked at Winnefred with questioning eyes.

Winnefred grazed her fingers over her three-string necklace of pearl and ruby. "Rape her darling. Look at her. What lies beneath the shirt, what soft pleasures are there for you to enjoy."

Kamara saw his eyes explode with sick lust. She searched about for some house guard to enchant, but there was none. Even the guards who had brought her, had left. The castle was emptier than she had ever known it to be.

Kayenté groaned with desire and seized Kamara.

"Kayenté!" she said, "Stop! I came to warn you. I believe the Rudels mean to attack your castle, soon!"

Winnefred brushed her fingers through a little curl on her forehead. "She lies, like always."

He whipped Kamara over his shoulder, his forearm pressed across the back of her bare-skinned thighs.

She cried, "Can't your see you're under a spell?"

He hauled her across the Great Hall.

Winnefred trailed close behind.

Kamara tried to mist, but her fear and hate and panic stalemated her effort. She arched her back trying to slide off his shoulder. "Winnefred is seducing you into shame. You *abhor* rape. Your mother was raped. You shall *never* forgive yourself for such an act. This you know! Oh stop!"

He proceeded with her up the stairs. Winnefred followed with her clippity-clip spiked heals, spewing lies, dousing Kamara's efforts. "Take her, lord, for she means to take you. She's your enemy. Let your hate rise like rank bile and spit it upon her, for this she deserves. She has earned your fiercest retribution. And when you are done, to the torture chamber she goes!"

Kamara cursed beneath her breath. "Her and her damn torture chamber. Damn her. Oh, damn her!"

Kayenté reached the top of the stairs and sprinted down the corridor toward his bedchamber.

Kamara concentrated. *Love. Love.* Little huffs of mist emerged from her breath, but his speed remained constant. He pushed open the door to his black bedchamber, the one that harbored his treasure room key. He tossed her upon his black silk bed. She landed on her back with a bounce, but quickly rolled to her hands and knees, scooting away from him off the bed, the mattress dividing them.

She crouched on the floor. Her fingers curled over the bed's edge framing her terrified face. Sickness crawled through her limbs, more from Kayenté's defection than the fever. She watched him unfastening his weapons with mercurial speed and drop them recklessly to the floor. She was appalled, for never had he treated his beloved sword with such disrespect. She forced herself to control her fear and exhaled mist. The vapor floated toward him, then hovered like a ghost inches from his skin. It would not touch him. His body seemed to repel it.

She looked to Winnefred who stood at the door, watching with a wicked smile, and words to match. "I've acquired power in your absence darling. I've mist proofed everyone here. You are helpless. SUBMIT."

"Never!" Kamara shrieked.

Kayenté yanked off his boots and chucked them one by one across the room. They smacked the wall and fell upon his leather clothes chest. He stripped his pants and flung them upon the boots. His intensity mounted. A current of deadly lightning he was, fated to crack the sky.

"Kayenté!" Kamara shrieked. "Winnefred is tricking you into a shame that shall torture you for eternity. Stop at once!"

Seeing the conviction in his body, she rose and dashed to the foot of the bed, hoping to reach the door, even though Winnefred was there. She would knock Winnefred flat.

Kayenté lunged in front of her, blocking her path. His wild and furious eyes steamed hate. His erect manhood flaunted itself boldly— wanton steed, god of rape. His muscles were taut with a vengeance that bore no mercy.

She stepped back. "Kayenté, I beg you refrain! I swear by all that is true, if you do not, we shall be ripped apart *forever.*"

He hailed her with icy words born from his spellbound tongue. "No greater a wish have I." He clenched his teeth. "I despise traitors, and a traitor you are. Traitors must be punished." He lifted the back of his hand and hurled a sharp blow upon her cheek, propelling her backwards against the wall. She landed in a heap on the wood floor.

Though dazed, she raised her head tearfully. "I implore you, Kayenté." She gasped, barely able to breathe, "Don't do this." She gasped again and wailed words with lung-weighted pain. *"Please don't do this. Please don't destroy our love!"*

He charged her, slamming her back to the floor, immobilizing her beneath him. He entered her with a violent thrust, as sword to foe, over and over, and ever over.

"No . . . o . . . o . . . !" she screamed, "No . . . o . . . o . . . !" again, and again, and—ever again, sobbing in between, feeling her insides hacked to pieces. "Too—much—pain!" She fell into tears, of the deepest silent kind. She was but a thing to him, a thing, a thing, a thing— an object into which he dispelled his hate.

Kayenté continued the rape, seething revenge.

From the bowels of her pain rose a hellish hate, something borrowed from him. But even so, it gave wings to her anger. And it was the anger that helped her override the torment of her crucifixion. She screamed her ruptured grief. "I hate you! I hate you! I hate you . . ." her words trailed into sobbing, "so much."

He climaxed, shrieking his death kill with exposed gritted teeth. He fell heavy upon her, panting.

She hissed in his ear with a labored whisper, her words barely audible for her lungs were compressed by his mass. "I *loathe* you more than I've *ever* loved. I like you *less* than cruelty itself. You *disgrace* life. You deserve *nothing*. You are *nothing*. If you lose your castle, your dream, your *life*, it serves you right. I pray you suffer the measure of what you have inflicted."

He withdrew from her, panting lightly. He rose, towering over her with a weighted emptiness that seemed to crush even him—or what was left of him.

She propped herself up on one elbow, trying to sit, but the pain was fierce. With a trembling hand, she edged the green shirt down over her thighs, and glanced at the door. Winnefred had gone. Where had she gone? Why had she gone? What was next?

Kayenté's chest puffed arrogance. Sweat dripped down his viciously tensed jowl. "I enjoyed that—immensely." He wiped the sweat off his brow, and erupted a twisted smile.

Her words seethed through clenched teeth. "I returned to save you Kayenté, not only from Winnefred, but to warn you about Taran and the Rudels!" Her voice dipped into a course whisper, "What you've done—can *never* be righted."

"I seek no penance from you—whore." He turned away from her, walked to his pants, and slipped them on.

Kamara lay there, damaged.

Kayenté had barely finished dressing when Winnefred burst in the room. "House guards, take her to the torture chamber. Use the paddles. Beat her into submission."

The guards shot across the room, and snatched Kamara's arms, yanking her up to a standing position. It hurt. She hurt. They swept her past Kayenté.

"Wait," he said.

The guards stopped. She glared at him, unexpectedly startled by the way his eyes studied her, as if he were trying to pull a shred of memory into his blank mind. She linked herself to the sparkles of struggle in his eyes. Only he could save her now.

His eyes warmed with anguished uncertainty. Such was the way she had stared at Marc when under Taran's spell.

Winnefred said, "Off with her this instant!"

The guards dragged her out the door. She struggled against them, twisting her head back toward Kayenté. If she couldn't save him, then *she* couldn't be saved. Her blood-curdling scream echoed through the halls, "Kayenté!"

Far from Kayenté, her voice could be heard in a banshee scream. "K A Y E N T É!"

She was taken into a dark damp foul smelling place, not the prison. No—*this* place was far worse. Mangled people were hooked up to strange contraptions, some hung from ceilings, some from walls and posts. She had not felt these people here before. Winnefred must have stocked the torture chamber—after.

A guard ripped open her shirt, and yanked it off her body so hard, she feared her arms might break. Her chin fell to her chest, unable to bear the cold, empty faces of her tormentors. No expression was worse than lust, or cruelty. Anything was better than nothing—The Nothing.

Her hands were grabbed. "Oh Mother Lord," she whispered inaudibly, "help me."

A thick heavy chain was wrapped around her wrists. 'I pray with all my love to any and all who can hear me—any and all who care!'

The chain had been doubled and suspended from the ceiling. When the loose end was pulled, it drew Kamara's arms up, lifting her feet off the ground. The metal dug into her wrist bones. Sharp tendrils of pain turned monstrous. The guard attached the loose end of the chain to a giant hook on the wall. Kamara dangled in the air, agony searing her shoulders. *Please, please, please*—save me! Oh purity! Oh wisdom! I shall merge dark and light! I will do *anything* to neutralize The Nothing . . . I *do not*—submit.

Thick clubs slapped her body from head to foot. The initial blows stung. Then deep shrill pain filled the sting, sinking into her bones, intensifying with each slap. Veins breaking, bones cracking, bleeding inside. Physical pain eclipsed emotional pain. Screaming, shouting pain. Consumed . . . by pain. Must stop . . . pain. Pain. PAIN! She could not endure it. She simply could not. "A . . . l . . . l . . . y . . . s . . . a . . .!" she screamed, seeing herself in her fighting clothes, holding her sword. Then darkness.

Ж
Chapter Twenty-Five

A day and half passed. Kayenté stood on the green deck surveying his lands, feeling drowned. Was he under a spell? He knew he'd known Kamara but he couldn't remember how. She seemed like a character in a dream he'd had long ago. Winnefred swore Kamara was bad. And his beloved Winnefred wouldn't lie. Yet, when he thought of Kamara, sadness swamped his heart. Why?"

Suddenly, he glimpsed the fleeting bodies of an armored knight, and a woman in yellow holding a gold dagger, running through the barren aspen trees. They raced across the bailey toward the fortress by means of his secret escape route. What treachery was this! He rushed inside the castle and down to the escape entrance, confronting them just before they entered his domain.

He drew his sword to Sir Robert's throat with lackluster eyes and asked flatly, "What brings you into my court without permission?"

Sir Robert said, "You speak to us as if we were strangers, lord. 'Tis I—Sir Robert!"

Allysa blurted, "And I—Allysa! I served you for over a year," and then she blushed, "in more ways than I care to mention. You don't remember?"

"Allysa?" Kayenté glared at them with a twisted face of confusion, sword pointed offensively. "Why do you bear that gold dagger, woman?"

"It's yours. I took it when Kamara—"

"—threatened to attack you. Allysa . . . I remember Winnefred telling me about you. You'll not need it now. Kamara's been dealt with." He reached out his free hand and snatched the dagger from her.

"No, you have it wrong." Allysa said, "I fled from Winnefred! She was going to *kill* me."

Kayenté lashed, "You are from my dream, and now you attempt to trick me! You want my castle to fall." He pointed his sword at Sir Robert's chin, blade glimmering in the sun.

Allysa said, "You know us not from your dream. *You* are in the dream, Lord Kayenté. The witch woman Winnefred has cast a spell on you and she's torturing Kamara. Save her!"

"Kamara?" he said, still trying to remember what *he* knew about her, which was less and less as time passed.

Allysa could no longer hold herself back and she didn't care if Kayenté killed her for insolence. She *had* to be bold—for Kamara's sake. "Kamara's in trouble! Do you not love her anymore? I have a vision of her in a torture chamber. Is this true?"

Kayenté's sword fell gradually to his side as he struggled to find his memories.

Allysa slapped him across the face. "Wake up! Don't you care?"

Kayenté's eyes flashed irritation.

Sir Robert stepped in front of Allysa and drove Kayenté against the wall. Kayenté barely reacted, the sword and dagger limp in his hands.

Sir Robert shouted, "What the hell is wrong with you! The whole Sakajian dynasty is on the verge of fall and you've done nothing! Winnefred is a witch and you worship her like an angel. Your brother whose virtues are questionable carted Kamara out of here, and you didn't care. And now, though she's supposed to be under your protection, she's in your torture chamber. We've not betrayed you. You've betrayed us!"

"He's hopeless." Allysa said. She dashed into the castle's secret entrance, winding her way about, heading toward the torture chamber.

Sir Robert caught up with her, racing ahead. When they reached the torture chamber, blank-eyed guards barred the entrance.

Sir Robert ordered, "Let us pass."

The guards answered concurrently, "No one passes, by orders of Queen Winnefred."

"Queen!" Allysa said.

Sir Robert pulled Allysa back and drew his sword upon a guard. "Unlock the door!"

The other guard swung his sword, lunging at Sir Robert. "No one passes."

Sir Robert blocked the sharp steel with his own when a hollow command sounded from behind them. "Let them pass."

Kayenté came up behind Allysa, his sword loose in one hand, the gold dagger in the other.

The fighting stopped in mid-motion.

One of the guards said, "But Queen Winnefred—"

Kayenté shouted, "I am lord of this castle. Unlock the door and let them pass!"

The guards became flustered. One of them unlocked the door and opened it.

Allysa raced down the dark stairway to the dank floor, searching frantically for Kamara along rows of near dead and rotting bodies in the dim light. She didn't care that her feet sloshed in pools of blood or stepped on body parts, nor was she delayed by the foul stench that made her want to vomit. Robert raced after her. Kayenté trailed Robert as if he were following a path of truth that he vaguely remembered—and somehow *needed* to remember.

Allysa screamed. Robert cursed. Kamara dangled in the air by chains. She was naked, camouflaged by hideous black and blue. Her head was flopped forward, face hidden in the cave of her long disheveled hair strewn over the front of her body.

Kayenté stared at her—hard. Concentrating. There was something about her that he couldn't remember. What? What! And then it came. The memory. His once blank face transformed to horror. He dropped the blades, breathing hard. He grabbed his head and roared. He swooped down suddenly, grabbing sword and dagger, looking about the torture chamber—crazed. He burst into a violent rampage, thrusting blades into all the living tortured that had been left to die, releasing them from their misery. Then he flung the sword and dagger across the room in a gesture of denouncement. He grabbed a club and bashed the torture machines, single handedly destroying the contents in the room.

Robert and Allysa were deadly silent, breathlessly still. Never had they seen such a display from their lord.

Kayenté approached them, his eyes bursting with frenzied anguish. "Robert, loosen the winch."

He gazed woefully upon Kamara as Sir Robert loosened the winch, lowering her to him. He touched her cautiously, fearing he'd find her dead. She was cold, but not stiff. He braced her carefully against him, her shoulders above his, feather light, her chest near his ear. Her heart beat faintly. Kayenté's relief exploded with a sigh. Yet, each beat might be her last.

Down fell her arms, hanging by her ears. Allysa detached the small hook that bound the chain to Kamara's wrists. Her freed arms dropped limp to her sides.

Kayenté eased her down, until her icy cheek was against his, her feet not touching the ground. He turned her limp body slowly side to side, in a dance of regret. "Kamara," his voice rasped. "I remember who you are. I remember! I feel your life pulsing weakly against my chest. Do not die." Liquid glossed his eyes. He whispered, "I give you all the life within me . . . all the life." A tear slid down his hard-lined face. "You trusted me, Angel, and I let you fall, just as I let my mother fall—just as you all said I would."

He turned his head slightly, kissed her cheek, and whispered in a broken voice, "Forgive me."

He eased his arm under the back of her frail and broken knees, bringing her to a horizontal position. Her matted and bloodied hair fell back over her shoulders, much of the tangled mane yet pinned under his arm.

"Sir Robert," he ordered, "Capture that bitch, Winnefred, and deliver her to me!"

Allysa threw her pale yellow cloak over Kamara's black and blue body. Kayenté carried her up the stairs, revering each contour of her face, though swollen and discolored. His little angel had been tortured by the devils. She was his heart. He knew that now, and all that mattered was that she lived. *She* was what he couldn't remember, *who* she was, and *how* she was, and the love they'd shared before Winnefred destroyed it.

Allysa followed, weeping quietly. As she passed servants, she bade them follow.

Kayenté carried her into his bedchamber and laid her upon the burgundy silk comforter. He ordered the servants to bring water for cleaning and drinking, broth, and a gown for sleeping. Then he gazed upon his beloved. She looked even worse in the light that streaked through the window, bruised almost beyond recognition. She had fallen into such darkness and it seemed that true light would never touch her again. Even though he'd brought her up from the torture chamber, he somehow still felt her there.

He slid his hand beneath the cloak and skimmed his fingers up her blackened arm, to her bare shoulder, to a nest of tangled hair, up her neck and over the bulbous blue black knots on her forehead and cheeks. He bent over her face and softly kissed a red welt on her brow. "I want Winnefred's blood for this, but it is my blood that should be spilled."

Allysa touched his arm. "No lord, not yours."

"Yes, mine," he said, stepping back from Kamara with clenched teeth.

"No, it was partly her fault. I was there, remember?"

"How could any fault of this be *hers*?"

"This wouldn't have happened, if she had left Winnefred locked in your treasure chamber where we'd trapped her. She had everything under control until that point."

"Don't tell me." Kayenté said. He gazed lovingly upon Kamara's face. "She couldn't allow Winnefred to suffer."

"She had to get food and water in there, just had to. That's when Winnefred attacked her, when I stole your dagger, and when I fled. Her folly is her insistence on saving even the most treacherous. And in so doing, she sacrifices herself. She had bade me leave food and water for that vampire before we captured her, but I didn't. Perhaps it's my fault. If I had done as she'd asked, she would probably have left her in there until you returned."

"Did you say . . . vampire?"

" 'Tis true lord, Winnefred bit Kamara and sucked her blood. I saw it happen!"

"Vampires are fiction, exacted by storytellers."

"Well, whether you believe it or not, watch out for her teeth. I never should have let her go back in that room. I shouldn't have."

Kayenté sighed. "Allysa, what you've done pales to my folly—or hers. I not only abandoned her . . . I—" Kayenté choked on his words, "raped her."

"Kayenté, no, I . . . I can't believe it!"

"Shame weighs me. I will never be free of it. Winnefred is a master of destruction. I never thought a woman could take me. She did, and for that she will die. But for what she did to Kamara, she will die in a manner far worse. Even that will not make my vengeance sweet, for I've lost too much. I've lost Kamara's trust and love and maybe her life. I've neglected my castle and the people who serve me. How long before I would have been overthrown?"

Kayenté remembered the words that the Wise One once told him. *Dark comes to light, and light comes to dark. The risen shall fall and the fallen shall rise. So it has been and so shall it always be.*

His eyes swept over Kamara. "Who will heal her? Who will heal the healer?"

"You," Allysa said, "but her body is less wounded than her heart, and her heart less wounded than her spirit. You shattered her faith."

Servants entered with a bowl of washing water, bandages, a cloth, drinking water, broth, and a blue silk nightgown. Kayenté washed the blood and grime off her, and eased her bluish arms gently into the soft gown, hoping that lack of circulation had not impaired them. He cared for her wounds, and then covered her with a heavy blanket. He tended her into the night, taking water to her lips, and droplets of broth to her tongue, ever trying to fathom what she must have suffered, and what he yet did not know. Why had she been flung to his feet in a man's shirt—again? Had the Cold One taken her at last? Was his seed now within her? Kayenté sighed. Had he failed her so completely?

Even Winnefred couldn't be located. Sir Robert's grand scale search had proved futile. Midway through the night, Kayenté became extremely agitated. He ordered Allysa to tend Kamara. Then he went to the top floor of his castle, into the chapel. He had never been religious and had only built the chapel out of respect for the King, who believed in God, but he felt the need to call for help to something beyond himself.

There—he slept. Asleep, he had a dream—a prophetic dream.

The Rudels marched toward the sea to fight the Gates. He rode swiftly ahead of them on a radiant white horse. When he reached the ocean, he saw Gatish ships in thick fog, coming to claim Kantine. He strategized to let the Gates and Rudels battle each other. Then, with Drudel Batlin's aid, he'd battle the winning side. When the Sakajians won, he would wage war on Drudel and claim the throne for himself.

He rode back fiercely toward his castle, but when he passed through Kanis, a cold chill raced through him. He stopped and heard thousands of Sakajian ghosts wailing in pain, and William of Gateland appeared holding a cross up to him. He said, "If you fight me, many Sakajians will die, for Drudel Batlin will battle with you before you can battle with me. Your armies will be thinned, and though you can defeat me, the cost shall be great. Drudel has murdered our uncle, the King of Kantine. Let me be his doom. Panther Ketola, my cousin—submit, for you know I am a fair ruler in Gateland and I'm of Sakajian blood. Let there be unity."

When Kayenté awoke, he shared his dream with the priest whom he barely knew and only kept around to perform weddings and funerals. The priest told him that God had shown him the way to lead his people. Kayenté knew not if God had shown him *the way,* but certain he was, that something of a wise nature—had.

He saw the beginnings of a plan to set things right. King William must rule Kantine. He felt humbled and broken, yet blessed with a small ray of hope that brightened as moments passed.

He spent most of the day with Kamara, praying she'd come to consciousness. He spent that afternoon explaining to his armies that they'd all been bewitched, and that the witch was Winnefred. And with Winnefred gone, it seemed everyone was returning to their normal state of being, except Kamara. If only he could redeem himself with her—if only . . . .

He even had his sword retrieved from the torture chamber, vowing to use it differently. And he gifted his gold dagger to Allysa as a token of peace. He took to sleeping in the church, for there, he felt the easing of his oh so heavy guilt. His dreams revealed more and more the full scope of the truth at hand, and he was beginning to believe that there was a kind of penance he could exact to regain all that had *ever* been lost to him.

In the five days that followed, the Rudels invaded his realm twice. He always had men posted in waves, layered many kilometers outward of his fortress, deflecting most attacks from spilling too near his domain. Though he and his men had forced the Rudels to retreat both times, if they had attacked one week earlier, when all were bewitched, Kayenté knew his fortress would now be under Rudelian control.

Kamara had roused, but not much more than to sip broth in some only half-awakened state, for she seemed unaware of her caretakers, not able to open her eyes or speak. But at least some nourishment was going into her. Kayenté even bathed her once in her near comatose state. She had moaned with pleasure when he placed her in the steaming water. Her strength seemed to be returning slowly. He hoped so.

He had held vigil by her bed whenever he could. He needed her to open her eyes and acknowledge him, so that he could make his peace.

That afternoon, he received word that Taran had arrived and had asked to speak with him. He arranged for Taran to meet him in the sitting room. He was anxious to interrogate his brother about Kamara's activities with him.

Kayenté arrived first and sat in his chair. Moments later, Taran entered, appearing weary: his chain mail armor—bloodstained, his face—filthy, his black hair stringy over his brown brigandine. His hands trembled and his eyes looked lost. He didn't sit. "I have come for my wife."

"Your wife?" Kayenté asked.

"Kamara."

"What are you saying?"

"We fell in love and we were married."

Kayenté labored to repress the look of shock that nearly burst through his shrewd demeanor. He choked down his emotions and called upon his cunning survival skills. "What makes you think she is here?"

"She still loves you."

Kayenté sighed. "I think not."

Taran smiled faintly. "Where is she?"

Kayenté rose with wildcat eyes and stalked toward Taran. "I ask you again brother, what makes you think she is here?"

Sweat dripped past Taran's eyes that held the vulnerable look of a man before he dies. "She had some notion of saving you from Winnefred."

Kayenté heard the words like lead weights falling on his heart. Had she risked so much to save him? "Why did she come alone, bare under a man's shirt?"

"My shirt."

Kayenté glared. "And why was she in it?"

"She was with me at Wincott Castle." Taran said, conjuring a lie, "We were attacked and she fled."

"All the way to my castle, to save me,when she herself lay so vulnerable?"

"Actually," answered Taran, truth springing in his eyes, "yes."

"No," Kayenté said.

"No?" repeated Taran confused.

"No, you can't have her."

"She's mine. I can do with her what I please."

"She's no one's, for she's gravely ill, and I intend to see her back to health."

"I can do that. I've done it before."

"Leave my castle at once," Kayenté said sternly.

Taran inhaled deeply, and when he released the breath, he seemed his old self. He glared aggressively into Kayenté's eyes. "You don't trust me, do you brother?"

Kayenté answered with equal boldness, "No."

"Well then, I challenge you to a duel for her."

Kayenté gritted his teeth, a primitive light flashed in his eyes. "My pleasure. Swords?"

Taran nodded. "Swords."

"Let the duel begin now, for I'm weary of your presence. We will fight in the front bailey."

"You will be embarrassed to lose in front of your men."

"I have overthrown kingdoms so that I could rule them. Overthrowing you for a woman will be the easiest of my feats."

"Yes," Taran smiled, "but you've not been yourself lately, or so I hear. You're not the man you once were, nor will you be . . . ever again."

"Enough talk! Let us proceed to the bailey. I am eager to bludgeon your heart."

Taran bowed and motioned for Kayenté to go out the door. "After you, dear brother."

Kayenté glared at Taran suspiciously, as he passed him going into the corridor.

Taran followed, his eyes beaming cruelty . . . of the most super-natural kind.

Ж
Chapter Twenty-Six

Fifteen minutes later, Kayenté was in chain mail. Both men stood in the courtyard under a clear, blue sky, fastening their helmets that sparkled in the sunlight. They had drawn a great audience that stood off to one side. A signal was given to begin, and a furious sword fight erupted between the brothers. Kayenté was astounded at the super-human force behind Taran's blows—enough it seemed to break both swords, unlike anything he'd *ever* experienced.

He'd always been a better swordsman than Taran, but this . . . . Was Taran possessed by the devil himself? Devil or not, Kayenté could not let Taran win this battle. He knew that he must redeem his honor through noble acts of the heart. He'd no longer fight for the pleasure of the kill, but for love, for love of Kamara. If he didn't, then away he would slip, into The Nothing—forever.

He held his defense, strike after strike, but couldn't gain the offense. Minutes seemed eternal, and many passed.

Kamara became fully conscious. Her body felt all cracked up. She wasn't sure she could move, or even open her eyes. But her eyes did open. She saw burgundy décor. Kayenté's bedchamber. She noticed her attire. A blue silk nightgown. How had this happened? Then she noticed Allysa staring out the window.

Her mouth formed words but no sound emerged. She tried again. Her voice rasped, barely audible. "Allysa?"

Allysa twirled around. "Lady, you've returned to us!"

"Allysa. It is you! You are—" Her voice rasped then faded. She tried again. "You are actually here." Her mouth felt dry, and swallowing was hard. "What happened to you?"

Allysa noticed her swallowing, moving her tongue about her mouth in search of liquid. She propped her up with pillows, and handed her a golden goblet of water from the bed stand.

Kamara drank slowly, with head heavy, aching hands trembling, and coordination not up to par.

Allysa knelt at her bedside and babbled excitedly, "I felt you call, my lady, I felt you call so compellingly. And as I made my way back to you, I came across Sir Robert. He too had fled from Kayenté. He too had felt your call. You once told me he could be trusted, so we journeyed back to the castle together and challenged Kayenté to snap out of the horrible spell he was under, but he didn't recognize us. We finally found you on our own. Kayenté followed. When he saw you, the spell broke, and the old Kayenté came bursting through. He destroyed the whole torture chamber! He had your restraints removed. When you fell into his arms, he cried. I've never seen him cry before."

Kamara's shook her head with narrowed eyes.

Allysa said, "Does that mean nothing to you?"

"Not any more—" The water had helped, and speaking came easier, "and never again." She handed Allysa the empty goblet. Allysa set it on the bed stand.

"He's sick about what he did. He's shamefully sorry he didn't believe you, that he turned on you, that he damaged you so. He carried you here with tears falling. He's been tending you with all his heart for five days."

"He betrayed me, Allysa. That can never be undone."

"Oh, I never should have left you!"

"If you hadn't, you'd have been in that torture chamber with me, and today we'd both be dead."

Allysa nodded sadly. "That's true. I knew Winnefred was going to bite me if I didn't flee. I was on my way to the nunnery to seek God's help when the Rudels caught me. I was taken prisoner and made to serve a Rudelian lord."

Kamara winced. "Oh Allysa!"

"Don't fret lady. He treated me not so bad, though he grew tired of my incessant babbling that I had to leave so that I could save my friend, Kamara. One day a knight heard me speak your name. Sir Bradley—was his title."

Kamara suddenly realized now why Sir Bradley had been so surprised to see her safe.

Allysa continued, "He somehow got me released. He bequeathed me a horse and he even gave me this yellow dress to wear. He apologized that he could not be of more help, but he couldn't risk being accused of treason. I raced away from the fortress, intending to retrieve Michael that he may save you, but it was then I felt your heart-wrenching plea. I had no time to think or fear. I knew only that I had to reach you with not a single moment to spare. When I passed the nunnery, blessed be the saints, that is when I came upon Sir Robert. Now all is well, I hope lady. Let all be well, please."

Kamara closed her eyes and expelled a deep breath of pain. Opening her eyes, she said, "No Allysa, all shan't ever be well again. I accept the truth now. At last, I accept the truth."

Allysa bowed her head sadly. "This isn't the truth I wanted you to accept."

Kamara gritted her teeth. "Where is that vampire?"

"She fled." Allysa stood up and returned to the window. Her attention was drawn to something outside in the court.

"Fled?" Kamara reiterated.

Allysa talked while staring out the window, her words chopped by her preoccupation with what she viewed. "She fled before Kayenté could kill her . . . . He will though . . . when he can find her. I wish you . . . would have . . . just let her rot in the treasure chamber, when we had . . . the chance. At any rate . . . he . . . had . . . the . . . priest . . . annul the marriage."

"Allysa what are you looking at out there?"

"Kayenté's fighting someone."

Kamara said bitterly, "Kayenté is *always* fighting someone."

Allysa swung around, falling to her knees by the bedside. "Lady, he's changed!"

"It's too late," lashed Kamara. "Even though he was bewitched, I shall *never* trust him again."

"But—"

"I can forgive him that he married Winnefred. I can even forgive him that he didn't stop her from hurting me. But—" her voice turned weak, "*he* hurt me—. *That,* I cannot forgive. His love for me was not strong enough after all."

"But it was. It was he who stopped the nightmare."

"No, Allysa, it was you who stopped the nightmare."

"Please lady, give him a chance. He's a broken man. Don't desert him now."

"Oh, what good is a broken man to a broken woman? Besides, how broken can he be if he's able to engage in swordplay?"

"It doesn't look like play to me, lady. In fact—it appears he may lose."

"Lose, like lose the fight, or lose—like lose his life?"

"I don't know the terms of the fight, but I'm concerned."

Kamara said, "Help me to the window. I'm too weak to stand on my own."

Allysa wrapped her arm around Kamara's waist and helped her hobble to the window. Kamara looked out upon the fighting men. Her eyes widened. "Taran! That's Taran's armor. Oh dear Mother Lord, I pray they're not fighting over me!"

"Why would Taran fight over you?"

"He's my—well I suppose, husband."

"What?"

"I'm not sure. Does marriage count if one party doesn't comply and there's no consummation?"

"I wouldn't think so, but one thing is for sure: if Taran's here to take you, then Kayenté's fighting to keep you!"

"Why?" she said sarcastically, "so he can torture me more?"

"Would you rather go with Taran?"

"Taran would give me to the Cold One."

"Taran is a traitor?"

"Yes."

Kamara cringed every time Taran swung his sword. She didn't want Kayenté to die, but win or lose, she was going home.

Kamara turned back toward the bed. Allysa helped her back onto the mattress. Feeling sick and dizzy, she fell to her side. "Ouch."

"Are you all right?"

"My ribs hurt, my shoulder, my leg, and . . . oh, all of me hurts."

"It is a miracle that you live."

"I am a Priestess. We can survive rigors more so than others." She moaned in pain, sighed hard, and then raised her head slightly. "Allysa, will you secure my fighting clothes, sword, and knife?"

"Why?"

"Because I don't intend to be won by Kayenté or Taran. I shall leave for Lania Castle at once, and you with me, if you like."

"Yes, I should like to come, but—"

"Allysa. Please hurry. I am unwell."

"You are in no condition to travel."

"I will use the mists to improve my condition."

"Very well, lady." Allysa's heart sank. "But Kayenté . . . he will be crushed to find you gone."

"Good."

Allysa sighed. Kamara would not be convinced, but Allysa knew Kayenté *must* see her before she departed, lest he descend into irreversible depression. She exited the room with false haste, intending to stall as she had never stalled before. Somehow, the safety of the whole world seemed at stake.

Kamara took her hands to her injured bones, sending in the healing mist. She could not make bruises disappear, but she could repair broken bones and stressed organs, though full recovery was never immediate. She felt many fractures, and did not stop misting until her body was soaked through and through. The pain subsided.

She did feel better, and more energized too. But she still felt ill, and extremely sore.

What was keeping Allysa? Kamara sent her a mind message, 'Hurry!' Then she gazed about the bedchamber, for this would be the last she would see of it: the rich burgundy silks and velvets, bedding and curtains, ornately carved cherry wood armoire and table, gold lined trunk by the bed, the window. The window.

The window seemed alive, more defined than all the objects in the room, an ocular marvel, a gateway between two worlds charged with energy, daring her to peer outside. Kayenté was out there, fighting to keep her, though he could not. Though in a way, he had. He would always have that pure part of her that would never again love another man as she had him. He had killed that dream. Still, she didn't want him to die.

Kayenté panted heavily, unlike Taran.

Taran said, "You can't win Kayenté. Why ever would you want her anyway?"

"I love her," Kayenté confessed, as he blocked a mercurial blow coming fast over his head.

"*You* . . . love?" Taran scoffed, swinging his blade toward Kayenté's right shoulder.

Kayenté blocked, huffing. "And *you* love her I suppose?"

Taran answered, "She's fun to bed."

Kayenté burst into a fury that hurled him into a sloppy offense. "Kamara was right." Kayenté, slashed at Taran relentlessly. "You *are* less noble than I."

"Of course," Taran said, as he blocked the steel coming down toward his shoulder, "I'm the son of a rapist."

Kayenté froze, sword pressing against Taran's. Had he heard Taran right?

Taran lowered his sword.

Kayenté followed suit, still wondering if he'd heard Taran right. Hell must have frozen over, because Ketola secrets were about to spill.

They slipped their swords into their sheaths and removed their helms.

Taran wiped the sweat from his brow, studying Kayenté's reaction.

Kayenté gave the crowd a hand signal to disburse. The knights walked away mumbling their disappointments that the fight had ended so abruptly.

Taran gibed, "You thought *you* were the son of a rapist, didn't you?"

Kayenté narrowed one eye. "How did you know?"

"Because it was my job to create your struggles, Kayenté. You were never to suspect that I was the bastard son, for then you'd usurp my power as the first born son to the Duke."

"*You* were the bastard son? All the time it was *you*? You knew what was happening?"

"I knew." Taran nodded with a strange shame. "Yes, I knew."

"Why did mother comply with your scheme?"

"Because my father, Hansa—"

Kayenté interrupted, "Hansa? I knew him as Ajento."

"We all know him differently," Taran said. "He plays many roles and that's how he keeps them straight. Anyway, he threatened mother with your death, if she didn't cooperate."

"All these years, she did not curse me?"

"All these years, she's been protecting you."

"Protecting me? *She* was protecting *me*?" Kayenté absorbed this meaning like a hero who freed him from hell. His heart stopped, and when it started, it ached for his mother. Her actions had been executed . . . for love, all these years . . . for love!

Kayenté asked in a broken voice, "Why did Ajento—Hansa, want you to sabotage me?"

"Because he wanted me, instead of you, to influence the affairs of the castle. I was to make you doubt yourself and feel the shame of not belonging. I was to harden your heart, and drive you away from Franz Ketola's realm. Of course, my father didn't expect you to recreate the empire that you were forsaken. You became the lord of a castle and more powerful than the King, even ahead of your scheduled time."

"Scheduled time?"

"There was a foretelling that when a Ketola of the Dukes blood (you) came to rule a castle, five years hence, Hansa would meet his doom."

"How? Why?"

"It was prophesied that you'd be of noble heart, a high grade fighter, a fair and influential ruler, and one day—King. You were the one mystically ordained to shield from him a Priestess capable of destroying his plans and his power."

"Kamara?"

"Yes."

"Then Ajento, I mean Hansa *is* the Cold One?"

Taran nodded.

"Why didn't he just kill Kamara when she was a baby?"

"His plan was to kidnap the Priestess baby and make her into one of his own kind, for death would not be adequate—she'd simply be reborn. He needed her spirit. And a spirit cannot be taken unless it's seduced into submission through false love, intimidation, or by promise of fulfillment."

"So, why *didn't* he kidnap her as a child and seduce her spirit then?"

"He did. Or so he thought. He didn't know there were two babies—twin girls. The Priestesses knew of the prophecy and sensed his plan. While the child was in the womb, they performed a spell that split the fetus into two children, a child of light and a child of dark. After the babies were born, the Priestesses made it possible for him to kidnap the child of dark, knowing he'd think it was the child of light.

"The Priestesses sheltered Kamara from the outside world, hoping to raise her before Hansa discovered the truth. And he was fooled for a long time, certain that he had the right child, for the prophecy held that the baby would be birthed by the Priestess Jensa Lania, for her blood was powerfully mixed with the late King William the Terrible. Jensa conceived only once.

"So where is the child he kidnapped?"

Taran said, "The more appropriate question is . . . *who* is the child he kidnapped?"

"Who—then?" Kayenté asked.

"Your bride."

Kayenté's eyes widened. "Winnefred? Winnifred—is the child he kidnapped? Winnefred—was born to a Light Priestess? Winnefred—is Kamara's *sister*?"

Taran nodded.

"Does Kamara know she has an evil twin?"

"No."

"They don't look all that much alike. Well, kind of..." Kayenté said.

"Good and evil will do that to you. It is all in how they use their features. Malevolent eyes. Innocent eyes. Would they, could they look the same? Lips that spew venom do not match lips that speak love. Arrogance and modesty make different faces. In addition, Winnefred wears her hair up, head up, make up—long healed slippers, and scores of jewelry. Kamara prefers the natural look, hair down, head down—flat shoes, and little or no adornment. They are twins, brother. They are."

"Damn," Kayenté said, "and I thought *my* secrets were bad." His face dropped. "If the Duke is my real father, then Kamara *is* my sister!"

"No, Kayenté. She's mine."

"Yours? What are you saying, that *Kamara's* father is the Cold One?"

"That's what I'm saying."

Kayenté shook his head slightly. "*Her* father is evil, and *mine* is good? That cannot be. She's so loving. So radiant."

"She carries her mother's legacy, Kayenté. Winnefred carries her father's."

"When did Hansa discover that Winnefred was not *the one*?"

"When Kamara emerged into womanhood and began secretly calling for what was missing in her life—her other half, her dark side, unknowing that her call was carried across the winds and into Hansa's awareness. It was then that he began invading her dreams intimidating her to submit. He thought his task would be simple for Light Priestesses had always been taken easily, because they never fought when intimidated—they merged. And she was no different. She sought to merge with him through her dreams, each night giving herself a little to him. Each night he kept what she gave. Her spirit began to fade.

"Then, you came along and started filling her head with notions of retaliation instead of bonding. You threw her into situations that forced her to see the merit in resistance. And as if that weren't enough, you fulfilled her secret longing for the dark side of life with your own dark side, naturally shielding her against the Cold One. In this, her unconscious cry for her own dark side—Winnefred, ceased. You very much had gotten in the way, just as the prophecy ordained you would.

"We almost had you though, enticing you with Winnefred and her dowry, a handsome contribution that would have brought you one step closer to King. Winnefred was to take your spirit and use your empty shell as a facade to control your castle, *before* you became entangled with Kamara.

"But we were too late. Your friend Michael fouled our timing when he asked you to go to her. Hansa tried then to take her in the

Black Wind before you could reach her, but we concluded that you found her in time for her spirit did not come back with the wind."

Kayenté asked, "How does he always know what's happening?"

"He has second sight, like the Priestesses. Even now, he can sense disruption in his plan. If I don't return with her, he'll punish me and simply find another way to get her. He'll stop at nothing. He means to have her."

"Well, so do I," Kayenté said.

"He knows that. But even if you think you have her—you'll not have her. The Duke has our mother, but even though she's with him—is she really with him? Look how bitter she has been. Hansa murdered all that was pleasant in her."

"And what of Kamara's mother?"

"Your father hoped to help her conceive a Light Priestess. To this day, he believes he was successful, but he was not, for Hansa had detained her one day too long, and though she met with Franz the following day, she did not conceive. Before she could return a few weeks later, the Cold One seduced her and took her spirit. She never returned to the Duke."

"Why was the Duke chosen to conceive a Priestess?"

"The Priestesses needed the offspring of a powerful man, who had powerful sons, so that the child and her brothers could one day champion them."

"Hansa is powerful," Kayenté declared, "more so than the Duke. Hansa should have let the Duke sire her. She may have been less threatening."

"Yes," returned Taran, "but he has enhanced command over his own seed. Besides, allowing the Duke to sire her would have increased her chance of knowing you, and that was a fate he's long tried to sabotage. Even though he failed in that, still he seeks to disarm Kamara by making her like Winnefred and me—like he makes all his blood children—vampires."

"Damn Taran, that can't be true. Kamara and Allysa claimed Winnefred was a vampire. I didn't believe them. Are you really a—I mean how does one become a vampire?"

"First, Hansa lulls you into submission, then he locks your spirit in hell, which by the way is not burning flames. It's cold, empty, and stagnate, like being trapped in a coffin. He sets our bodies free to feed off of the life force in others on the condition we do his bidding. If we do not, he makes us starve in The Empty. And when we have vamped for him long enough, we forget more and more who we are, and become more and more what he wishes us to be—his demon servants. In time, we grow teeth that can suck blood, but it's not the blood that sustains us, it's the devouring of spirits. I'm not in as advanced a stage as Winnefred. My biggest project all these years was to deflect you from your destiny. But recently he's been pushing me harder through the process, so that I can vamp the women in power, while Winnefred vamps the men."

"But Taran, you were to marry Winnefred."

"I was to make you believe that, so that when the wedding plans fell through, you'd snap her up as an act of vengeance towards me. Of course, that was all planned when he believed that Kamara was Winnefred. By then, he'd turned Winnefred so dark, she bordered 'The Empty.' He deemed your union innocuous, for dark and light must merge, and she was light no more."

"So," said Kayenté, "I was to be Winnefred's puppet for the Cold One's play to end the world?"

"Yes, with Winnefred and I controlling the castles of the realms, we can suck hundreds of thousands into the void. Hansa has lured whole religions and even nations into obliteration."

Kayenté's eyes narrowed. "Why do you tell me this, Taran?"

"I don't know. Maybe there's a small part of me left that remembers you as my baby brother, for whom I once cared. Maybe through you, I remember something of what I was—once . . . long ago. Maybe because I know if I don't tell you this, all *will* be lost. Hansa will trick you into The Nothing. He was using me to that end when I came here today. I was to drive you crazy with rage. I was going to win this fight and take Kamara. I could have won, for Hansa's powers have grown strong in me, especially when I don't resist him. Then I would have told Kamara lies to make her hate you more than she does now. You would have lost her. Losing her would have doomed you. Your spirit would have faded into the Cold One. On and on, we were planning to make everyone turn against everyone, weakening all sides for our taking."

Kayenté inadvertently stanced his legs in a firm parted position. "But I would not have let you take her, even if you had won. I would have ordered my men to seize you, kill you if necessary. Kamara isn't leaving me again."

"But then your men would not have respected you for dishonoring the duel. They would have been less likely to listen to you in the future. That would still have been the beginning of your end."

"Then don't fight me," Kayenté said, "fight Hansa. We can beat him if we fight together, side by side, as once we did."

"I can't," Taran said. "He has a command over me that I cannot break. If I don't bring Kamara back, he'll punish me."

"She's your sister, Taran. Would you subject her to your plight?"

Taran sighed heavily, his voice filling with anguish, "I have no choice."

"You do," protested Kayenté, "you do. I would suffer for her, just to feel love."

Taran shook his head with great despair, and then said quietly, "All right. All right."

Kayenté approached Taran, stopping inches in front of his face. "This is the first time in all my life that I don't hate you."

Taran stared intensely into Kayenté's eyes as if burrowing into his very soul. "Do you *love* me?"

Kayenté nodded and said softly, "I believe I do."

Taran lowered his head, uncomfortable with the warm feelings passing between them. Then, he looked up. "I didn't bed Kamara. She was deep in a spell, so deep, I don't even think she was hardly aware of the wedding. I used the wedding as a way to get her to submit to Hansa who took my place that night."

Kayenté jumped. "He didn't . . ."

"No. He didn't get her."

Kayenté breathed a sigh of relief.

"He almost did," added Taran, "but Marc rescued her."

"Marc? So he knows of your treachery?"

"Yes. And for that, we had to detain him. He was going to warn your father about me. Winnefred's working on Marc, as we speak."

"We will rescue him at once."

Taran said, "I fear that I cannot help. If I'm not to do their bidding, I mustn't be near them. I can't resist their command. Even now, when they feel my resistance, I will suffer. In fact, if you intend to keep me here, you may have to lock me away so that I do not respond to their summons. I can't help you much anyway for I'm not Hansa's doom—except that I've warned you. But even so, you have no idea how many leaders he controls, or the intricacies of his plans, and the strategies he has laid out for your every move. Kamara's the key. She's the daughter of two supernatural beings. She has the power to destroy him, but she doesn't know this. And while she can defend her spirit and conquer him, she's not equipped to defend her body or attack. It's for you to physically defend her and keep her alive until she finds the answers. Feed her your encouragement, and make love to her again." Taran shook his head. "Hansa faded a little when he felt that occur between the two of you."

Kayenté replied, "I'll do as you say, the first part anyway. Come now into the castle. Let us shed this armor and decide how to best break you free, and then Marc. And then I'll labor to redeem myself with Kamara. I don't know if that's any longer possible, but if it is, I'll make it happen."

They walked over the field toward the castle.

Taran sighed, "You always make things happen Kayenté, even when the odds are against you. That's why I've hated you. You always succeed, even when everyone dooms you to fail."

"If that is so, then you *must* work with me," Kayenté said playfully, "for then you are sure to triumph over Hansa."

"We'll see." Taran smiled faintly.

They walked side by side, past the stables and the armory, toward the great black doors of the castle entrance.

Ж
Chapter Twenty-Seven

Allysa returned with clothes, weapons, and a stone cup of broth. She rested the pile at the foot of the bed.

"What took you so long?"

"I brought you some vegetable broth." She gave the cup to her. "Drink it."

Kamara sipped the nourishing warm liquid swiftly, feeling quite hungry.

"And I was keeping my eye on Kayenté and Taran. They quit fighting. I guess they are both all right."

"Wonderful," Kamara said sarcastically, then drank down the last of the broth.

Allysa said, "Aren't you glad?"

"They are all right," Kamara said, "but they have both made it so that I'll never be all right."

"Kayenté is not all right, Kamara."

"I don't want to talk about him any more." Kamara sighed deeply, forcing down emotion.

"I'm sorry lady. I'll try not to mention him again."

Kamara set the cup on the table and pulled the blue nightgown up over her head, but the action exacerbated the soreness in her arms, so Allysa helped her.

When it was off, Kamara noticed the shade of her body. "Oh Great Mother, my skin is purple! I look monstrous."

"You should have seen yourself when we first found you. Now that was monstrous." Allysa helped Kamara into her black shirt. She smiled faintly. "You're looking pretty good now."

"Well," Kamara slipped on her pants, groaning from the sharp pains that smothered her legs, "at least I'm feeling less dizzy and stronger than when I first awoke. The broth helped. Thank you."

"Are you sure you want to leave *this* moment?" Allysa asked as she helped Kamara slip on her boots. "Wait for Kayenté. He is desperate to apologize." She tied the sheathed knife around Kamara's calf.

"If I give Kayenté a single minute, he'll take me for a month." Kamara rose, and almost fell, but steadied herself in time. "I'm leaving *now*." She grabbed her sword for protection. She would not be thwarted. She looked over her shoulder to Allysa. "Are you coming?"

"Of course, lady, of course," She helped Kamara walk to the door, "but you can't travel in your condition."

"I can and I will. I must return to Lania Castle . . . to Michael . . . to gentleness, once again. I've had enough lessons in swordplay. If the Cold One should find me, I'll stab him in the heart with pleasure. I'm tired. I shall be done with this drama. I care not if I'm bad or evil. Enough is enough. We'll steal some horses, and make way, even if I must employ my sword!"

"My lady!"

"It's all right Allysa, being too good is bad, remember?" They walked out of the room, and made their way slowly down the corridor. "You'll see, when we get to my castle, how lovely life can be. The light shall shine, and we shall smile."

Kayenté and Taran rounded the corner, coming toward them.

Kamara stopped cold, and gasped at the dark visage before her: the mighty evil brothers who had so carelessly toyed with her love, twins in ebony, dark hair hanging long over arrogant puffed chests, battle swords hugging thighs, vicious minded, black hearted, mean spirited—

"Kamara!" Kayenté called. His heart lurched with delight to see her up and able. And though she was hideously black and blue, he wanted nothing more than to hold her and tell her how beautiful she was. He quickened his pace, but when he reached her, she aimed her sword at his chest, a two fisted grip with conviction—deep, as deep as the sea.

She said, "Your presence begs the attention of my sword!"

He looked down at the sword tip so near his heart.

She shouted, "Keep your boundary!" She glanced at Taran, "both of you!"

"Where are you going?" Kayenté asked, almost passively.

"Home!" She gripped the sword tighter, given to a sudden rush of energy. "Allysa's joining me, and no one shall stop us!"

Kayenté said, "You're not safe away from me."

She almost cracked her teeth clenching them. "I'm not safe *with* you."

Her words bit him sharply, and it took him a moment to get past them. He stepped closer, the sword point pressing into his chest. He extended his hand slowly toward her. "Your salty words make haste unwise."

"If you dare touch me, I shall thrust my sword clean through you," she said with fiery eyes, "so help me, Mother Lord, I will. Taran has doubtless convinced you to cede me to the Cold One."

"No," Taran said, "I wish to help."

"I've heard that before," she hissed. "Allysa, stay close!"

Allysa shadowed her as they edged past Kayenté, then Taran.

Before she could think or comprehend it, Kayenté compressed her purple bruised wrist with his hand, feeling guilty that he must. Her sword fell instantly, and clamored on the stone floor. Her jaw hung in surprise, and then clenched, words seeping through teeth, "I *hate* you!"

His other hand neared her face affectionately.

"Remove your loathsome hand you duplicitous fiend!"

"Aye, they are loathsome no more, precious Kamara."

"Precious!" Rage fired her body, giving her strength she'd not dreamed to possess. She yanked against his grip, but he towed her back toward the bedchamber. "Release me, you ogre, you oaf!"

Allysa cried out, "He will not harm you, Kamara. Give him a chance!"

"He had his chance!" She tried to dig her moving heals into the floor, and jerked her hand repeatedly against his grip. "Release me this instant you robber—you rapist!"

Kayenté could barely breathe by the tone of her brutal words. Though well deserved before he could 'see,' were not deserved—now that he could. Attaining her surrender was imperative.

"Hatred consumes me, and it is all for *you*. Not Winnefred, nor the Cold One, YOU!"

The old fire in his eyes had gone out. Now there was love. Only love.

She shrieked, "I despise you with all that I am! I detest you, you bastard, you devil, you demon!"

Kayenté spoke loudly to Allysa and Taran. "Leave her to me. Take her sword."

Allysa nodded and picked up Kamara's sword. Taran shot Kayenté a look that said, 'Good luck.' They made their exit down the hall.

Kamara screeched, "Don't believe them, Allysa! Don't believe *anything* they say! They are liars, deceivers, the foulest creatures on earth!"

Kayenté dragged her into the bedchamber.

She swooped her hand to her calf, and swung the knife toward his oppressing hand.

He snatched her wrist and squeezed. She wouldn't release the knife. He squeezed tighter.

"No!" she cried, trying to yank away her arm.

He didn't want to hurt her already injured wrist, but he had to squeeze even tighter. The knife fell. He kicked it with the side of his boot, sliding it out the door.

"Le t . . . m e . . . g o!" she cried, holding her wrist. "Our bond is— *broken*, you monster!

He dragged her to the bed. "We are going to talk." He released her with a 'stay put' look in his eye, and backtracked to seal the door. He felt her small form and large presence swell behind him. He turned and blocked the exit.

She tried to squeeze through the thin gap between his side and the door jam, but his body remained steadfast.

She grabbed her hips in an affirmative stance. "Release . . . me."

He shook his head.

She huffed, "You heartless, worthless, throw away piece of garbage, not fit for flies to feed upon," and then she screamed, "re . . . lease me!"

"*Never, never* again," he said.

She grabbed his shirt, and tried pulling him away from the door.

He didn't budge. He remained silent, as her pulling changed to pushing, and her pushing into ramming. Her diminutive shoulder pounded against his chest over and over. He absorbed the hits, wavering never.

"You shan't stop me!" She dove to his ankle and yanked, attempting to topple him.

He shook his head lightly, wondering how she would overcome the Cold One, when she couldn't even get past him. Or perhaps she was trying to get past herself. And that, most of all, he would not let her do.

She grabbed the empty stone cup on the table and threw it at his face, but it hit his shoulder, and fell by his boot, breaking into several pieces. She punched his gut the way he'd taught her, cradling her arm after to ease the pain. She didn't punch him after that, but she kicked his legs and slapped his face. Her breath grew ragged, but she didn't stop. Despite her exertion, he remained statue-still. She moaned and panted while pulling, and pushing him every which way, punching and kicking him every which where— and he let her. He assimilated the pain that he felt he deserved, never flinching. He held back the retching her obscene blows evoked, never giving away how he suffered.

He knew she needed to fight, yes, he knew that feeling well. She needed to purge her anger upon him, if she was to be free from its torture. He understood, for that had always been *his* way.

When she had no more energy to expel upon him, she dropped to his feet in despair, panting hard, moaning and weeping intermittently, between declarations of "I hate you!" and "I hate you . . . so much!" And it was the words that hurt him most.

He looked down upon her, a heap on the floor. Though his body appeared erect like an unfeeling monument to brutality, inside, he grieved for her plight. Innocence torn was the most sorrowful happening on earth, save to be the tearer of it.

Her voice rasped in a breathless expulsion of words, potent eyes scorching hate. "I detest your strength. I wish I was a ferocious warrior. I wish I was, then I'd show you. I'd show you that you couldn't treat me this way. I'd beat you until you died!"

He knelt, warm-hearted, and stroked her cheek tenderly. She thrust his hand away.

He spoke in a tone, soft and wise. "You've changed. That change is good. I too have changed, and that too is good. When the spell upon me broke, so broke my heart. And when my heart broke, it was set free, and in this freedom I see what I did not see before. I see that love *is* everything. I *do* have a noble heart as you have always believed. I have finally chosen heart to the forfeit of conquering. We must join our forces against the Cold One and Winnefred. They have managed to turn us all against each other. When the Sakajians took Wincott Castle, we pushed the Rudels back, but they retaliate constantly. Soon the Gates will wage war against the Rudels and the Sakajians. Even the Sakajians may soon fight against each other. You, Michael, Taran, me, and so many others, have been inter fighting. And in everyone's preoccupation with each other, the Cold One has positioned himself to make the kill on the lot of us. But I can now see through all the chaos. The real war is between the Cold One and everyone else."

418

She looked up at him with horror-filled surprise, then covered her face with her hands, letting out a blood-curdling whimper.

"What?" Kayenté said, his voice etched with pain, "You already knew most of this."

Heavy sighs slipped through her fingers, giving way to pauses that reflected a struggle for words.

"What Kamara?"

Her hands dropped to fists over her heart. "You've learned all this *too late*! I'm too wounded to care anymore about the doom of the world. I'm too tired to try and save it. All I can do is run to 'the light' even if I die trying—even if I must kill to get there. I just have to get there, and then throw the sword away, back into The Nothing— forever!" Her face and hands met again. Voiceless breathy sobs made her chest bob in tiny rhythmic spasms.

Kayenté touched her shoulder lightly, lovingly. He felt her body tighten. "Kamara," he said, almost pleading, "you possess great powers, beyond what you know, powers to defeat the Cold One and Winnefred."

She lifted her tear streaked face, leaving her hands hanging in the air in prayer formation. "What are you saying?"

Kayenté's velvet words brushed against her. "I have a tale to tell you—the tale of your life. Listen."

Kamara peered at him with intense hesitation. She knew he was going to reveal the third secret. Did she want to know? Was she ready? Or should she close her ears and run as far away from the truth as she could, because if she listened, she might shatter.

She couldn't decide. Confusion paralyzed her. She couldn't move, or hardly breathe, suspended forever in this eternal moment.

Kayenté broke the stalemate. "I know who sired you."

Her eyes narrowed, seething hate and wonder. Then she turned dead inside.

He slipped his hands around hers as if they were flowers.

She did not pull way, so he guided her up to her feet. Gazing lovingly into her eyes, he led her to the edge of the bed, sitting her down

419

on the wine colored comforter. He molded her left knee onto the bed, turning her body toward the pillows. He sat in the same fashion, facing her, their bent knees on the mattress, nearly touching.

He told her everything that Taran had told him, almost word for word. Her face remained expressionless. When he finished, she was silent.

"Well?" asked Kayenté.

"Well?" she said lightly, as if not understanding the question.

"Did you hear? Do you understand what I have told you? Have you no response?"

"You want a response?" She shook her head, closing her eyes, and when they opened, she exploded with indignation. "Do I understand what you have told me? You are telling me that I'm fated to defeat the Cold One, and that I must be chained to you or he'll turn me into a vampire," her tone piqued, "—that Taran's my brother and Winnefred's my sister and the Cold One's my father! No. I deny what you tell me. I shan't accept it. I denounce this task. I return it to those who bequeathed it upon me. Keep the knife, my sword, and the many tears I have shed on these premises. Take your secrets and shove them back into the grave where they belong. There is only one salvation for me, and that is to get far away from you as fast as I can, and return home to my castle of love and light to regenerate Lania Lands with the sacred mists!"

Kayenté touched her arm. "You can't escape the sword by hiding in love, just as I could not escape love by wielding the sword. Just dwell here a few days and examine what I've said. If you still choose to return home, I'll take you there. And I will stay with you until the end has come for us all."

"Take me home now, Kayenté, for I shan't change my mind. I no longer care if we all end. I shall never trust you again. *Never*. We are doomed to end *because* you cannot be trusted. Besides, what fate can be worse than the betrayal already exacted?"

"Your fate taught you how to be bad, Kamara. And for you, it is good to be bad."

"So they all say!" She threw up her hands. "Happy!"

"Yes. And fate taught me how to be good. Grant me the chance to show you how good I can be."

She cast her eyes to her fidgeting hands, which conveyed to Kayenté that though her words seemed final, she was truly undecided.

"We can succeed Kamara. I *know* we can. I've begun developing a plan to unite the warriors and the Priestesses, to calm the raging battles between us all. Remember the Cold One can only win if the Dark Ones keep taking and squabbling amongst themselves, and if the Light Ones keep giving until they are no more. If we bring this to balance, the Cold One will disappear. I disdain the task ahead of me as well. But I know I can no longer avoid it. I must relinquish Sakajian rule to my cousin, King William."

Kamara's lashes flew up with her head, followed by a suspicious pose. "You deceive me, Kayenté, just to induce my concession. That is cruel beyond cruel. You manipulate me. You play a game!"

"If I still wanted to rule, why wouldn't I just get rid of you?" He touched her hand. "I speak the truth, Kamara."

"Don't do this to me! I am comfortable hating you. I don't want to love you again. I don't *ever* want to take another chance."

"I have relinquished my ambitions, as you have long wished I would. Would you forsake me now?"

She shook her head, and then looked at him almost tearfully. "You would sacrifice your life long goal to be King? Truly Kayente?"

Kayenté nodded heavily. "My goal has changed. My new and only goal—is to champion love."

"Love?" she lashed. "You let me be taken to the torture chamber Kayenté... and... you... you...." she drew both her knees into her arms, "raped me—brutally! I cannot forgive as once I could."

"Then the Cold One wins," he said, but inside, guilt brimmed.

She felt his guilt. She knew he was shamed greatly, but still she could not forgive. Anyway, the Cold One seemed insoluble. She said, "The Cold One cannot be defeated, despite all effort. We performed a powerful ritual and it did not work."

"But it did. 'The light' you placed within me activated when I saw you in the torture chamber. It broke the spell, and set you free, sparking Winnefred to take flight. And in truth—you *saved me*. And look at you, you've grown tough—for you anyway. Look how you held your sword to me, took the knife to me, took your fists to me! The old Kamara never would have acted as such."

"Oh," she pouted, "so now I'm evil like the rest of my family!"

Kayenté smiled and held back a laugh.

She snapped, "I suppose you find that amusing, now that you know your heritage is pure!"

"No," he said, still smiling, "it's just that even when you think yourself evil, you are yet sweetly inoffensive, like a newborn kitten with little claws, and a miniature mew."

"Kitten?" she scowled. "*Never* call me kitten. Winnefred called me kitten!"

"Oh, sweet as honey. Will that do?"

Her pouting lips almost turned to a smile, almost.

He said, lovingly, "See, you can still feel joy. It's not the end of the world—yet. Take these next days to heal and contemplate my words. I'll continue to work on my plan."

He swung himself to the ground on bended knee and engulfed her hands in his. With strong glistening eyes, he met her gaze with an intensity that overrode anything she'd ever seen in him. He said with whole-hearted conviction, "Remember lady, I am at last, completely and totally dedicated to help you reach your destiny."

She proclaimed, "I will never make love with you again."

"I do not require that, nor do I expect it."

He kissed her hand and rose. "Your weapons will be returned. I am going to speak to Taran and devise a strategy to rescue Marc."

She said, "We *must* help Marc, at the very least."

"And you too," he said earnestly, walking backward slowly toward the door, staring at her as if she were a sacred jewel, even though she had laden him with pain lingering injury. He reached the exit. "You—most of all." He whispered, "I love you." Then he left.

Ж
Chapter Twenty-Eight

In the two weeks that followed, Kayenté accomplished many tasks. He had sent Sir Robert with six men on a mission to rescue Marc. Sir Robert was beginning to understand the power of spells and he was the most able of his men to do the task. Since Wincott Castle had supposedly fallen under Sakajian rule, he should find it easy enough to enter. Shrewdness would have to guide him from there. But he had confidence that Sir Robert would succeed, for Robert had not failed him yet. Even so, Kayenté waited nervously each day for his return.

He had also spent much time with Taran, who had become increasingly agitated, behaving more and more like a wild animal. Even Kamara couldn't help him. Kayenté had to regretfully lock him in a prison cell, accommodated of course with every comfort.

Kayenté had further spent many hours devising a strategy to defeat the Cold One. This plan shocked, even him, and he worked harder on accepting it than he did devising it.

He also spent part of each day pampering Kamara with Allysa's help. He was consistently kinder to her than ever before, but still she held him at bay.

He walked down the long corridor in the dark morning, heading towards the green deck where Kamara often watched the sunrise. She continued to resist him. She loved him, this he could feel. Yet, she would not let that love flow. He could hardly blame her. Her black and blue marks had faded and she was able to move about without too much difficulty. He wanted to engage her in sword practice, just to get some fight back in her. But she would not, claiming she'd lost the will to learn.

She still wanted to flee, but his plan required her to stay and rise to her fullest capabilities. Time was running short. He must actualize his plan before more trouble came to pass, even though a new trouble had already arrived. Michael rode in late last night, thundering demands to see Kamara. He'd come to see if she was well. Kayenté stalled him to wait until morning. Well . . . it was morning.

Kayenté feared she would flee with Michael, instead of staying to fight with him. Would she face her demon, or hide? Would she run into her destiny, or her doom? If she stayed, he still had to heal the personal wounds between them before they could be strong together. Could he heal them in time? Time was everything now. She *had* to be ready, or all his efforts would be for not.

Kayenté reached the green deck. There she stood, looking out over the barren aspen trees. She too, seemed barren, robbed of all that was once precious to her.

She wore her fighting clothes every day, refusing to accept the many gowns of silk, velvet, and satin that he had brought to her room. It was as if she didn't want to appear feminine or seductive, or some such thing. Apparently, she didn't know she appeared feminine and seductive to him no matter what she wore. She had never refastened her knife to her leg though, nor would she touch her sword, just as she would not touch him.

He joined her, leaning his elbows on the edge of the stone crenellated wall. He drank in her profile. Fine wine could not compare. She seldom looked at him anymore, and when she did, he considered it a rare treat.

She said, "I miss the quiet peaceful days I once knew."

He said, "You will have them again—soon, after we deal with the Cold One."

She glanced at him, quickly, as briefly as she could manage, so that her heart would not thump too hard. Then she resumed her trance-like stare upon the barren trees. His fresh image touched her mind like silk. So handsome he was in his leather boots and tight leather pants, tempting her to press her body against him, if only—

once more. The black vest over his dark blue shirt highlighted his azure eyes that shone so bright with pain. Oh, but to smell his musky fragrance once more! Oh, but to hear his manly voice fill her ear . . . once more! His midnight hair, long down his back, tempted her fingers to glide down its length. But she would not let them. She wanted to pretend he did not betray her. But he had, and she would never touch him again. There would never be a—once more.

She forced herself to wash away his beautiful image. "Once the Cold One is before us, how would we fight him? I don't feel empowered to win. Do you—truly?"

"We'll defeat him. I always succeed—except in *one* area."

Their eyes met, conveying the sad tension of their shattered hearts that held them apart.

She whipped her head forward to focus on the trees, scolding herself for viewing him again. "I feel lost in violence, Kayenté, stranded and alone in a warring world that's trying to take me down."

"I too feel lost," he returned, staring at her profile, "lost in love, stranded and alone in a caring place that has already taken me down. But you are not alone, Kamara. All you need do is reach for me. I'll take your hand, and I'll not leave you again—in any way."

"I can't." She gulped back the tears she would not let fall. She gazed down at her hands and spoke almost apologetically, "My heart cannot open that way with you, ever again. The wound is too deep. And I couldn't bear the sight of you and Winnefred together even if it were to kill her."

"I'll not be with her, Kamara. I'll be with you, against her. And what of you anyway? It won't be easy for me to set eyes upon the Cold One who has stripped you bare and touched you where he should not, thrice!"

She tensed her jaw. "But I did not sleep with him, as you so willingly slept with Winnefred."

"I was under a spell. You must remember that as naive as you were to the true power of man, so was I, to the true power of woman. The Cold One and Winnefred have shaken us both, and it is as you

425

said: If we are divided, they conquer. If we stay together, then they cannot succeed."

"Oh, where is the Wise One? So much has happened since last she spoke with me. I pray she's alive. And Lania Castle, I hope it did not fall when I did."

"Your powers are still with you, are they not?"

"Yes."

"Then you haven't fallen. You've been detained, that's all."

"But I've lost the will to succeed. If I fight at all, it's only to get away from this violent world, and back to my castle of light. I want to feel safe again, if only for a moment."

"Has Michael been on your mind?"

She nodded. "He's been good to me from the start."

"And . . . Michael wouldn't have done to you what I did."

"He wouldn't have. His love is too great, and he has no heart for acquiring power."

"But he has a heart for acquiring you. And you, I think, have developed a heart for acquiring him."

She nodded lightly with a sad expression, averting her focus to her fingertips brushing lightly along the stone edge of the wall. "I wanted and needed to touch the storm in you. You gave me permission to move into your wildness. I got lost in there, and you forgot about me. So predators took me. You didn't even know when it happened. Michael wouldn't have abandoned me in such a place." She choked on her tears. "I can't trust you in that way, Kayenté. You chose personal gain over honoring me. You did not choose heart to the forfeit of conquering. I so thought you would."

"Chose . . ." he said, "past tense. I choose differently now. I now choose heart to the forfeit of conquering. I do. Does that not mean a great lot?"

"It's just too late for us, Kayenté. I love you still, but . . . it is too late."

Kayenté resorted to his master strategy to win her back and he hoped he was not making a mistake. Her mind was not on war or saving the earth, so he decided to let her go through, whatever it was she needed to go through, to get her back on target. If he truly was the man for her, then back to him she would come . . . eventually—hopefully *not* to late.

"Michael is here, Kamara. Go to him and find happiness."

"Michael is here?" She faced him squarely, her eyes wide with surprise.

"Yes, he arrived late last night to see if you were well." His voice took a hint of sarcasm. "You no doubt called him to you with your incessant thoughts about falling into his arms to feel safe . . ." he almost choked thinking of how he failed her, "if only for a moment." He sighed with resignation. "I came out here to tell you."

"Where is he?" she asked softly.

She felt agony searing Kayenté's heart. Suddenly, she flung herself at his feet and grabbed his legs. "Oh, don't be hurt, Kayenté. I truly don't blame you for the priorities you had. I just can't seem to forgive, even though I know you were under a spell. I am *too* damaged."

She felt his hands grasp her arms. He had knelt before her with such whole-hearted intensity, she braved looking at him. He peered into her eyes, fathoms deep. A rush of energy flooded her quintessence. He had sent his spirit into her.

Her jaw dropped, struck with amazement. "I would not have believed you could do that!"

"What does it mean to you?"

She studied his eyes seriously, and fell into his arms. "I don't know!" she said, "I don't know!"

He braced his knees and cradled her tightly.

"Kamara!" she heard a stern voice.

"Michael?" she said lightly, twisting her head to his voice.

Kayenté reluctantly broke the embrace, water glossing his eyes.

Kamara considered making peace with him, but Michael, oh Michael . . . he was here! She rose and turned to see him. His chivalrous stance in tan riding clothes struck her with excitement. He'd always been loyal. He'd always known what she needed. He was so light and beautiful and he'd come to take her home! Oh beloved Michael! She rushed into his arms.

Kayenté rose, stepped back, and leaned against the palisade, watching Kamara give Michael the affection he wanted for himself.

Kamara squeezed her eyes shut joyfully, until she realized Michael's body was stiff. She drew back slightly, and looked up at him, perplexed. "Aren't you pleased to see me? Is our castle not well? Has someone died? What's wrong?"

"I came to see if *you* were well. I can see you are all *too* well."

Her face contorted with confusion. "Michael . . . is this you, the same man who had committed his love to me? I've not been well, not well at all!"

Michael shoved her hard. She lost balance; her hip and elbow smacked the deck. Devastation filled her face. She but blinked and saw the back of a dark blue shirt, black vest, and long black hair. Kayenté was shielding her. She saw his elbow draw back and plunge forward.

Kayenté's fist slugged Michael's stomach. "I forbid you to treat her this way—*ever.*"

Kamara heard Michael moan, but she could not see what was happening because Kayenté was in the way.

She heard Kayenté's gentle command. "Kamara, hurry to your room."

Michael said, "Don't you mean she should hurry to *your* room?" He approached Kayenté, sending his fist toward his face. Kayenté dodged it, but his gut was met with Michael's other fist.

Kayenté doubled over, trying to breathe. He spoke with strain, "She makes her own choices."

Michael charged past Kayenté to Kamara. Her eyes grew big, as he reached down and grabbed her wrists. "I doubt that. Maybe I should be more like you and take what I want."

Kayenté straightened and turned around to see Michael yank Kamara to her feet.

Kamara began to call the mists, when from *Kayenté's* breath, the mists came. He pointed his fingertips at Michael, emitting more vapor.

Kamara was stunned.

So was Michael, "Damn," he said, startled. "Good God, I have *never* seen a man do that before."

Kayenté looked a bit surprised himself, but spoke clear and strong as if he'd been 'misting' all his life. "I don't want to fight you, Michael. You are my best friend. But I won't let you harm Kamara. She's been harmed enough—more than a human could be expected to endure."

The mists enveloped Michael. A calm washed over him. He released Kamara's hand. He said, "Seems the last time we had this conversation, it was I speaking those words."

Kamara could not relinquish her penetrating gaze from Kayenté's breath. He really *had* received the mystic powers of female. Was the ritual *that* successful? Oh, whatever had taken him so long to utilize the gift? Kayenté could bridge—but could she kill?

Michael turned to Kamara and stroked her arms lightly. "I cannot believe I was rough with you and that Kayenté was kind. It's just that I've waited ages for you. I couldn't bear to think of you snatched out from underneath me."

Kamara looked to Michael and embraced him. "I'll always care for you, Michael, but we are as the rivers of life that flow as they may. Perhaps into each other, away from each other, or maybe side by side. We need to wait and see. Go where you must. Do what you must. Do not live for me. Live for you."

Michael held her lovingly. "I'm sorry," he said, then whispered, "I've missed you."

She wept lightly in his arms for a minute, and then eased herself from him, turning to where Kayenté had stood. But he was gone.

Michael pulled her back into his arms and kissed her with a soft wildness. She pulled her head away.

"Do you feel nothing?" he asked.

"I feel something," she said, "but this romantic type love, I'm learning is quite dangerous for me."

"Kayenté has hurt you?"

"Yes, but I do not fault him."

"He has taken you to his bed?"

"The first time it was a necessary ritual of light, a life or death matter."

"The first time?" he reiterated, "and what of the second?"

"The second time was for love."

"And then?"

"Nothing but heartache, and I am resistant to return to that kind of love. It nearly killed me. If you need that kind of love with a woman, then take it to another, Camille, or my new sister, Allysa." Kamara cleared her throat and added shyly, "as you have before."

Michael froze for a moment and then said, "Oh, you know about that."

Kamara nodded, blushing.

Michael asked, "Are you angry."

"No, not anymore. You needed someone in a way that I couldn't fulfill. You had every right to do whatever it was you needed to do."

"And what of now? Would you not be pained to see me with another?"

"Yes, Michael. But it would pain me more to see you without."

"You do love me, then."

"Yes," she said, "with all my heart."

Michael sighed heavily. "If you are to be with a man, I think Kayenté is the one."

"Why?"

"I've known you for years and you never performed a sexual ritual with me, not even when the Cold One haunted your dreams. You've known Kayenté for mere months, and look at all you've experienced. And Kamara, you bridged him—the unbridgeable Panther Ketola! You taught him to use female powers that no man at Lania Castle has *ever* achieved."

Michael looked into her anguished eyes. "I release you. It's clear Kayenté won't hurt you again and he is paying for his sins. I will leave as soon as Kayenté reveals how he will need my help to defeat the Cold One."

"He asked you to help?"

"Yes, it's time that we all work together."

She nodded. "Yes, it is."

She paused a moment, finding it hard to release him. "Oh Michael, when you leave, don't take your brotherly love from me! I have taken such comfort in your love."

Michael placed his hands on her shoulders. "I could never take my love from you—" he smiled, eyes twinkling "—for you are the sister I never had."

"The sister you never had?" she asked, puzzled by his comment. And then remembering his ruse to leave Lania Castle for his sister, she half-smiled and said. "Oh, the sister you never had. You were clever." She poked his belly playfully.

He brushed his hand against her cheek. "The people of Lania Castle will be with you in spirit Kamara, lending you all you need to defeat the Cold One."

"How are the good people of Lania Castle?"

"Well enough."

"And Camille?"

"She is love sick."

"She has always loved you, Michael. Mightn't that love be returned?"

Michael shook his head. "Not since Sir Robert came to Lania Castle, searching for you when you fled from Kayenté."

"She fancies Sir Robert?"

Michael nodded.

"That's ironic," Kamara said, "for she was raped once . . . and now she's in love with a reformed rapist." She raised her brows. "Life does have synchronicity, even with all its strange kinds of love."

"I hope so. Teeah told me that my love would be returned. I thought she meant you. I guess not."

"What of Allysa? Could you love her?"

"Without you monopolizing my heart . . . aye, I think I could."

"Allysa desires to reside in Lania Castle. Perhaps you could take her back with you."

Michael smiled, "I'd like that." He jerked back his head. "You've not yet told me of the perils you've endured since I last saw you."

"Allysa can apprise you Michael. I honestly can't speak of what happened. I'm still horrified and most unstable inside."

"All right then, I'll not press you." He stroked Kamara's cheek with her finger. "Let us find Kayenté and hear his plan."

She nodded with a smile.

He looped his arm around hers and opened the wooden arched door that led into the castle. "He is likely in his sitting room. He spends a great deal of time there."

They walked down the hall and began descending the stairs, when they met Allysa. She looked sweet in her yellow dress that pleasingly contoured her feminine form.

"Greetings Allysa," Michael said.

Allysa blushed.

Kamara touched Allysa's shoulder. "All is well."

Allysa sighed and relaxed a bit, still unable to look Michael in the eye.

Kamara declared, "We seek Kayenté. Come with us. We have serious issues to discuss."

Michael said, "Kamara, you go find him. Allysa and I will join you in awhile."

She looked at them both lovingly, tears brimming in her eyes. "Allysa—you released me to Kayenté. Michael, so did you. And so, in this same way—I release you to each other."

They both gazed warmly into Kamara's eyes, acknowledging her meaning. Then they peered into each other's eyes, acknowledging what was not spoken between them.

As Kamara turned away to find Kayenté, she heard Allysa tell Michael, "I can't bear children."

And she heard Michael reply, "Then we can have a lifetime of lovemaking."

Kamara smiled. They were well suited.

She headed toward the sitting room, ready . . . at last, to face Kayenté. But most of all, she was ready to face herself.

Ж
Chapter Twenty-Nine

Kamara stopped short of the sitting room, standing in the corridor. She was unsure how to approach Kayenté, unsure of what she felt, or what she wanted, or what it was that she must do. Maybe she didn't need to know. Perhaps events would just occur. She entered the room, standing in the doorway, hesitant.

Kayenté gazed upon her from his big leather chair. He sat slouched, his hair splayed about him in a less than regal fashion. His feet touched the floor, legs apart, one bent, and one straight, looking a little vulnerable in a tough sort of way. A warrior taking pause. A knight obeying heart. His arms were positioned like the letter L, one crossing his ribcage, the other perpendicular to his face, with his finger pressed to his chin in contemplation.

Suddenly she felt safe with him, sensing the honey of the bee and not his stinger. He would never sting her again. She knew this. Somehow . . . she just knew. Now he could rightly protect her, and make true his claim.

His voice twinged with pain. "I see you've not deserted me."

She ambled his way, stopping in front of him. "No, I have not."

His eyes interrogated her. "Has your allegiance found a home?"

She stared down into his bright blue orbs for a long deep time, seeing the dark of him, the light of him—him. He was beautiful with his mask of pride ripped away. She reached to his hand. "Yes, it has."

He read the truth boldly expressed in her golden eyes, and captured her wrist. He pulled her close, driving her knees up on the edge of the chair, bringing her mouth to his ear. "Kamara!" he whispered passionately.

"Kayenté!" she returned in a broken whisper.

He propelled them both to the wood floor, landing her gently underneath him, withholding his true weight. His mouth came against her lips and lingered there for a moment. Their breath mingled, and they felt each other—as if they *were* each other. He lifted his head to observe her face. He groaned and whispering gruffly, "I want you, Kamara Lania."

She answered with ragged breath, "Then take me, Kayenté Ketola."

"I will," he said. "I will." His head moved down to her face, his lips touched hers, light then rough, osculating with savage beauty.

After several flaming minutes, he said urgently, "Shed these garments!"

"But Michael . . . Allysa," she said, half not caring.

"I am not concerned." He rose to his knees, pulled off her boots and flung them across the room. Then he slipped her pants down over her legs and flung them over the boots. He untied her belt and pulled her to a sitting position, drew her tunic over head and cast the garment aside, and then the shirt underneath. He shed his clothes hastily and pounced upon her once again, bowling her down to the floor, kissing her with lawless abandon. Her neck tasted sweet; her breast tasted better. His hands roamed her body zealously, pressing across her pelvis and inner thighs. Cascades of mist blasted through his fingertips, soaking into all that had been wounded because of him.

The vapors finished curing her bones, aching still from her torture chamber days. She'd never thought to mist during lovemaking, and found it enhanced everything, and opened her more. She misted him too. Soon, white vapors enveloped them both. Who were they? What were they?

Overcome with the rolling sensation of unbound identity, they paused a moment, staring at each other, her beneath him, him above. His eyes burned blue-white heat. Hers burned deep orange. Together they were a flame, fire, lightning, storm. Storm with a purpose. A purpose created and fueled by pure spirit. They fell together in a thunderclap, rolling across the floor as one, a brawl of whitewater gushing into a waterfall. He anchored them, edging his legs between hers, and scooped his hands under her back.

Making love to her, he whispered loudly, almost violently. "I worship your life, Kamara Lania, Storm Tamer in the Mist. By all things sacred, I shall defend your person, and champion your love through the annuls of time. The parting of our bodies can no longer separate us—not even death can separate us now."

She accepted the whole of him as he moved inside her. Her childhood fell away, along with all the mysteries that had held her ignorant, unraveling the purest feelings of pleasure that she had ever known, akin to Creation, Utopia, and all that. Kayenté, man and mist combined, given to her—sent her over an edge of no return. She was the waterfall, crashing down into the roar of gushing river below, emancipating, coming home, finding peace. Tears. Tears of joy.

His voice rolled through her like thunder. "As I move within you now, so give I . . . all that I am—of man, of heart, of mind, and of spirit. This allegiance I pledge unto you and unto any children born of us." His breath become labored, gasping in-between words, "and by my own blood . . . this . . . I . . . do . . . swear!" He moaned in ecstasy as his seed exploded within her.

They had both released their love, their past, their potential. Kayenté propped up his elbows, panting, cradling Kamara's head with his forearms. He gazed upon her tear-streaked face.

He said, "I gave you my whole world Kamara, more than you ever believed I could."

Another tear slid from her eye. Her voice was soft and honest. "We have one of those rare unions, haven't we?"

"We will see," he said, his breath steadying. "I have married you with my complete self. You've yet to make the same vows—another time . . . another place, after we defeat the Cold One."

"I love you, Kayenté Ketola," she gushed, "with all my heart. I never dreamed that the storm I craved would sweep me off my feet and land me on a cloud. And from here, I behold your whole presence. And you fulfill me—completely. All is forgiven."

His head fell upon her with relief. "Thank God. Thank God."

"Thank Great Mother she said, thank her too."

"Thank you, Great Mother," he whispered, and he seemed to mean it. He withdrew from her slowly and rolled her on top of him just to feel her body limp on his, the way it had been once when he pulled her from the Black Wind, seemingly so long ago.

"Do you remember the first time we were in this position?"

"Yes," she said.

He half-laughed. "You asked Michael how he survived in the chaos of the outer world."

"And you answered, 'sometimes you have to use a sword.' Well, you were right. I accept the sword completely now, as I do you—my Kat."

"Your Kat?"

"Yes, I think I shall call you Kat, short for Kayenté, yet of the black panther whose power you carry. You are my big Kat, my defender."

"I like the sound of that Kamara," he lowered one brow, 'but I can't call you kitten, huh?"

"No, indeed," she said, "anything, but that!" She kissed him on the cheek and rolled off his body, sitting. "Michael and Allysa shall arrive soon. I blush to think of them finding us in this state."

He sat up. "Yes, I can see you blushing now."

She looked to the floor shyly in need of moral rescue.

And so he rescued her. "Come then, let us dress."

They dressed quickly, their eyes sparking love at each other.

Within minutes, Allysa and Michael entered, holding hands and smiling, a bit blushed themselves. Kayenté bade them sit in the chairs. Once they were seated, Kayenté stood behind Kamara, and draped his arms around her, his cheek against the softness of her hair.

"The days of Sakajian rule are coming to an end," he said. "And William of Gateland will claim the crown. We must support him. I will convince my father and as many Sakajian households as possible to strengthen that support. But in spite of my efforts, many will still choose to fight him. That battle will occur in Kanis."

"Michael, seven days hence, I'll need you to lead the people of Kamara's house to Kanis and chant 'the light' upon the soldiers. Kamara, you and Teeah and I, and any other who can mist, must do so. When the fighting men are pacified, the Cold One will be drawn out. When he comes, Kamara," he stroked the side of her head, "you will know what to do."

"What if that solution eludes me?"

"It won't. I'm certain. I'll protect you from the Cold One physically, but you must do the rest."

He looked upon Michael, then Allysa. "Are you with me? I have come to *light* as you have always wished. Now, I ask you and the people of Lania Castle to come to the center of dark, in Kanis, on the day of the full moon of next week. I ask again, are you with me?"

"Yes," said Michael.

Allysa nodded, "Yes."

He felt Kamara quaking in his arms. "We will succeed," he said, "You'll see, we will."

Michael said, "Damn Kayenté, remember when I first came to you asking for your help and you said *I'd* changed. I had changed all right, but not half as much as you. You're not only taken in 'the light,' you're damn well lit! I can't believe what I'm seeing. You, Kayenté— the Warlord!"

Kayenté said, "What good is lordship if the world disappears? What is power anyway? I've been shackled to my throne, running the lives of hundreds, tethered with responsibility, and upholding image, and in constant fear of downfall. Power cannot be held, for always in time, the powerful fall to the Cold One.

"Perhaps we're to let power flow through us, to come and go, freeing us from position and pride. Oh, what power I feel when I wield my sword from the fires of my gut, or sail swiftly on my steed with the speed of wind. What could be more powerful than the sun, ever shining, never overthrown, like the unrelenting love I have learned to feel for you Michael, and you Allysa, and you Kamara. What could be more powerful than the bond of friendship, like bee to flower.

"I have found this power, more deep and true than owning lands, riches, and people's lives. I can experience this power, with or without my fortress, with or without my position. As long as the earth survives, this power cannot be confiscated. And that's why I'll make every sacrifice to preserve this world. The Cold One *must* be brought to balance."

"Indeed," said Michael as he stood. "Allysa and I will leave at once."

Allysa smiled warmly at Michael.

Kayenté said, "Mended her heart after all, huh, Kamara."

"No," she said, "it appears Michael has."

Michael said, "I think all of our hearts are mending."

They exchanged deep glances of wordless kinship and unity was strong between them.

Ж
Chapter Thirty

Within the hour, Kayenté and Kamara had assisted Allysa and Michael in preparing for their journey. They bid their goodbyes at the stable, misting their friends in the chill winter air as they rode away toward Lania Castle.

Kayenté captured Kamara's hand and led her across the brown grassy courtyard. His fast anxious pace put him several feet in front of her, but his firm grip did not let her go. His long black hair kicked up around the shoulder of his deep blue shirt and ebony vest. She sighed, wanting to make love with him all over again.

He'd brought her to the tall barren rose bushes where he could express his feelings privately, without his soldiers viewing him unmanly.

He stopped and faced her, cupping his hands on her hips. With an energetic burst, he lifted her high above him, and lowered her until her face—met his. And he held her there, until her lips—touched his. And he kissed her there—until her tongue probed his. She *was* his. She was him: the bright and beautiful reflection of his own wayward preciousness.

"My little warrior," he said with sentiment. He lowered her feet to the ground, and then lifted her in his arms, cradling her like a baby. He turned slow circles, beholding her face. He stopped and gazed at her silently for a moment. Then, he said, "You fought for my heart—" his voice broke with emotion as he nuzzled his face against her ear and whispered, "—and won."

He eased her feet to the ground, and held her very . . . very . . . tight, pressing her cheek against his chest with a firmness that bespoke his need for her.

She said, "You truly love me. I can feel it."

He released her gently and combed his fingers over the top of her head, down her temples. Her golden hair fell over his hands. Sunlit wisps glowed from rays that had broken through gray cloud. "I *do* love you," he said, "even *I*—can finally feel it."

He harnessed her head in his palms, his eyes blazing hungrily. His mouth grabbed hers, gratifying his appetite with the taste of her lips. Then he tilted his head back a few inches to view her. With the clench of impassioned teeth and weighted breath, he gazed his storm into her receptive amber eyes. Man to Woman. And he crystallized this pose—*this ancient coalition, this cataclysmic completion of the ever happening now. And he hurled it into eternity so that it could never be lost in The Nothing.*

"We are as one," he said, "and when the time comes that you must defend yourself, you will feel me in you, moving through you. I want you to practice this today—now, in the form of a sword lesson. Tomorrow we must leave for my father's castle and I want you prepared—for anything."

"Yes, Kayenté," she said, her eyes soft with cherish. "I shall do as you say."

They walked hand in hand into the courtyard. Kayenté had her sword brought out and they spent the following three hours engaged in rough swordplay. She fought offensively with a vigor that amazed Kayenté. She no longer hesitated to strike. Her focus had become single pointed, and though years are required to master the sword, she showed great promise. She even nicked Kayenté once. Such a feat was rare. Then again, she had *him* in her.

Shortly after the practice, while Kamara bathed and Kayenté reviewed his strategies in his sitting room, King Aldos's messenger arrived. Kayenté received the news privately. The King had died and Drudel Batlin intended to rule Kantine.

When the messenger left, Kayenté sat alone in a dreamy shock, not by the news, but by the queer way he was reacting. This was the day he'd long awaited, for his power was such that he could override Drudel, but now . . . though this day was yet great, it was great for a different reason, for he no longer sought to be King. He could say goodbye to the angry ignoble person he used to be. The time for true nobility had come. At last, the time had come.

Kayenté called a gathering of his men in the front bailey.

Kamara viewed her beloved from the Green Deck. He stood beside the priest on the Lord's Balcony of Public Address, not far from her. He addressed his troops with a thundering voice.

"King Aldos is dead!" Though he did not believe in God per se, but rather Life itself, he decided he must use the word, *God,* to convince his people. "God has spoken to me regarding this matter. The wisdom He has given, I now share with you. God showed me the King's death, and God showed me the destruction of Kantine." A low hum swept through the crowd. "God also showed me how to save it!" An upbeat cheer buzzed amongst the men.

Kayenté continued, "The Rudels still threaten us from the East. The mercenary hired by King Harold Wincott of Rudelia is Sakajian, a traitor to his people and he has caused great conflict in Kantine. And even though we hold the Rudels at bay, they continue to attack in greater and greater numbers, gaining recruits from all the known world. If the Rudels rule Kantine, they will subject Sakajians to horrific degradation.

"Drudel Batlin also plans to take the throne now that King Aldos has died, even though Aldos has announced *me*—as heir. Aldos became sick *after* this announcement. Does that event not evoke suspicion? If Drudel, who has not even a drop of royal blood, comes to rule, then we will be at the mercy of a murderous traitor who does not have Kantines' best interest at heart, only his own.

"My father, though he is the King's brother, is old, and carries not the power or initiative that he once did. He does not want the throne. My brother, Taran, is neither any longer predisposed to such a position.

"And I—" Kayenté nearly choked in an effort to proclaim his next words. His knees almost buckled. His stomach churned sickly, and he had to breathe deeply for a moment before he could speak.

"Even though I hold the greater share of power in Kantine, I too, am no longer predisposed to . . . be—King."

A hum of voices rose from the crowd mounting to a chant, "Hail King Kayenté! Hail King Kayenté!" Kayenté could barely quell the water rising in his eyes, or hear over the heartbeat pounding in his ears. The realization of his dream was before him, and he *had* to shatter it.

He raised his hand, signaling for silence. "No! All I say is so ordained in the house of God, by this I swear, and upon you I bequeath allegiance with my own blood. I could be King, yes, but only at the expense of far too many Sakajian lives, which would substantially diminish our bloodline—for what purpose? To name me ruler when King William would serve just as well?"

Protest rose from the crowd, but Kayenté bellowed over them. "King William of Gateland, my cousin, will come from the North to claim the Crown, by virtue of his Sakajian mother, King Aldos's sister, my aunt. King William believes Kantine would profit under his rule. So do I. He has Sakajian blood, and he would respect our nobility and our ways.

"We must support William of Gateland with whom we already have royal alliance. In addition, he has proven to be a fair and noble ruler in Gateland. We must relinquish to him if our future is to remain intact.

"I would not have you forsake your lives to a mock cause, when your honor may yet breathe without such sacrifice. I tell you this prophecy, warriors, of loyal and worthy status in gratitude for the homage you have each paid me.

"While we'll not kill our Sakajian brothers, save self-defense, we will stand in support of King William, and this message shall be so sent unto him. Any man not so wishing to participate in my proposition, I release to join Drudel, who is now gathering armies."

Kayenté became silent, looking over the crowd, listening for objections. There was a strong drone of voices for several minutes, until his third in command moved to the forefront and shouted, "You have led us well and always rewarded us justly. Yes, we are with you!" The crowd grew strong with cheers and affirmation.

"Then," Kayenté said, "in one week, we will meet at Kanis where a great battle will ensue. We'll form a defense that stretches into a large circle, shielding the lay people of this province from harm. You'll not strike or kill unless the circle is invaded with violence. Though I know this way is foreign to us, it is ordained by God that we make this circle of peace. In time, the fighting will stop. And the dawning of a new and better way of life will be at hand.

"I'll ride to Franz Ketola's castle at once and render support. You are dismissed."

Kayenté watched the crowd disburse. Oh, he knew some would slip away, traitors after all. No matter. He had turned the tides, so completely, so utterly, and set true nobility in stone. He trembled, feeling his former self, ways, and dreams . . . dispersing, now that he'd finalized his new agenda. What had happened to his survival instinct? All he cared about now was defeating the Cold One, and he'd die *without* a fight—if that's what it took.

That night Kayenté held Kamara in his arms under deep wine satin sheets, skin against skin. "I was hoping Sir Robert to have returned with Marc before our venture tomorrow. But we can wait no longer."

Kamara nuzzled against him, stroking his chest. "If we can defeat the Cold One, then Marc shall be freed." She propped herself up on her elbow, gazing into his shadowy face. "But can we defeat him? Do you truly think *I can do* what must be done?"

Kayenté pulled her bare chest against his. "Yes. Remember the prophecy?" He pressed her cheek over his heart. His voice purred in her ear. "Even as the Cold One has tried to alter it, it's ever coming to pass."

She blurted, "I love you Kat. And even if tonight be our last, I can tell you . . . you have fulfilled me."

He stared at the dark ceiling, tear buds in his eyes. With mind and heart, he enveloped her like a womb. No danger must befall her. He envisioned himself as the red orange flame that surrounded the precious blue flame within. And with that vision, the night slipped away.

In the morning Kayenté, Kamara and twelve armored knights mounted spirited horses and rode out into the cold winter air. The dapple-gray gelding beneath Kamara complemented her black pants, dark gray shirt, and black brigandine, which was less encumbering than chain mail. She bound her hair in a long braid with a black leather tie. From a distance, she might even appear a male. Kayenté gave her the special pair of calf-high black leather boots he had made for her. The right boot had a built in sheath for the knife he bade her always wear. The handle peaked out, for quick access. Armed with the knife, and sheathed sword on hip, and her very own horse to ride, she felt quite the storm—at last.

They cantered off the grounds, through dense woods toward Franz Ketola's castle. During their journey, Kamara slipped loving glances to Kayenté, so proud of how noble he'd become. He still looked kingly, but in a fairy tale way, chain mail shirt, under black belted tunic that draped in princely folds over the hips of his black leather pants. His boots fit securely in the stirrups, his posture confidant. He wore no helmet. His hair hung long and striking, layered with a thin leather bound plait of hair on either side of his head. She loved his hair that way, pulled off his face. He seemed less wild and safer to touch.

He'd catch her smiling at him from time to time, and his eyes glittered delight.

Six hours passed of an almost enjoyable ride, when they came into a yellow meadow of dry grasses so tall, the group was camouflaged. As they crossed, Kamara's skin prickled, and the prickle did not diminish. A sick sensation brewed in her stomach, and she felt uncomfortably hot. From the edge of the maple trees at their right, a cold wind emerged, streaking across the clearing, mowing down a path of yellow grass. It slapped the entourage with icy fingers that seemed to probe their bodies.

Kamara snapped her head toward Kayenté. "The Cold One is upon us!"

"At last," Kayenté said, "at last I am with you when he comes!"

Sakajians charged out of the hills, equaling the number of Kayenté's bodyguard.

Kayenté shouted to Kamara, "Hold fast your sword and do not hesitate. I will guard you."

The attackers arrived, bellowing colorful accusations, "Deceiver! You are no longer Sakajian, Panther Ketola! We'll have your head!"

A flurry of maces, daggers, and swords clamored in war's symphony, cutting through tall yellow grasses that blew against them in one solid direction. Horses neighed their hot curses over the enemy's seditious tones spitting in the air. Kamara's head dropped to her horse's neck, resting her temple on its warm fur. She was overwhelmed, not ready to parry with experienced warriors.

Her head burned with the shock and horror of death dancing all around her. She felt on fire. Sweat poured down her body. The cold wind blew harder, cooling her face, steadying her against the gruesome ache of battle.

She tried not to hear the guttural moans surrounding her. Sharp phantom pains sliced her wrist as she glimpsed the gruesome bloody slash of a warrior's half-severed hand. She squeezed her eyes shut, trying not to feel the victim's agony. But she was failing.

Pale and ill, she was comforted only by the icy gale blowing steadily upon her. Hot. She was so hot. Cool . . . cold . . . wind. Sweat dripping over her skin. Cool . . . cold . . . wind. She knew from whom the comfort came, but no longer could she resist the intense urge to fall into its source, away from the battle, away from the heat, if only for a moment.

She forced her head up and rode swiftly into the wind, out of the skirmish, to the shelter of bare maple trees and thick brush. And she felt better. The wind died down, and she wondered if perhaps the cold comfort was *not* the doing of the Cold One, but rather of the Great Mother Lord.

She dismounted to better camouflage herself in the maple trunks. She peaked through the trees down the path of flattened grasses, to flashing pictures of warring men, through wildly moving tall yellow blades. She feared for her Kat. She glimpsed him on his mount, front hooves high in the air. His sword flashed in the sun. The grasses camouflaged him a moment, then his bloodied sword smacked high in the air, flicking off a red liquid stream. She winced and threw her hands over her face. *This is self defense, and gruesome acts are sometimes necessary.*

But why was this happening? They'd been fairly well hidden in the tall grasses. How could news of Kayenté's plan have bred such a heinous lust for revenge in his own people? Did he not have the right to renounce his appointment to kingship? Did he not have the right to recant his violent ways? It was as if the Sakajians were telling him that if he did not kill and control, they would assassinate him. *Or* had the Cold One manipulated them into such hideous hate?

From the forest, a chill wind seemed to tap her on the shoulder. She spun around expecting to behold the Cold One. She saw only the maple forest, and a trail of wind that led into it, beckoning her to follow.

She touched the hilt of her sword. *The prophecy said I was the Cold One's doom.* The knowledge of Kayenté's plan disappeared from her mind. Her feet took her into the woods.

Kayenté thrust his dagger into the stomach of an attacker who dropped off his horse, moaning as he disappeared into the tall pale grass. He scanned the path of flattened grass into the distant maple woods in search of Kamara, aware that she had ridden away from the fighting. Before another attacker demanded his attention, he rode off in the direction she had fled.

He came to the woods and saw her dappled horse, but not her. He feared she'd fallen into the Cold One's cleverly executed trap, so that he could attack her for the fourth and perhaps final time.

He rode to her horse and dismounted with pounding heart. He gripped his sword with one hand, and his dagger with the other. He scanned the trees in search of her. He glimpsed her back, sword in hand, moving steadily, cautiously into dense brush.

"Kamara!" he shouted in a loud whisper. "The time is not yet! Do not face him now!"

She had disappeared in the foliage, and she did not answer.

He sprinted to her, hot in his armor.. He tightened his grip on the hilts of his blood soaked sword, and dagger.

He finally reached her in a small clearing. "No, Kamara."

"He's here," she whispered. "I can feel him."

Kayenté sensed predators, huddling, ready to ambush.

He shoved Kamara sideways as a horde of *Sakajian* warriors pounced on him. "Get his sword! His dagger! He has two boot knives! He has at *least* two!"

"Kat!" she screamed, as she watched her beloved fight fiercely against the mountain of men attempting to subdue him. Men flew off him, but many more jumped on, shouting, "You are a traitor! You would give rule to a Gate!"

She swung her sword back, intending to slash into the crowd that surrounded Kayenté, when she felt her blade whisked from her hand and heard it thump upon the earth. Her wrists were yanked to her back. An arm emerged from behind her, curling tightly around her chest.

A cold blade touched her throat. She felt paralyzed, uncertain of her situation. She wanted to help Kayenté, but she could not even help herself. She exhaled the ghostly mists of love, only to feel the knife pressing more firmly against her throat. She stopped misting. Tears streaked her dusty cheeks.

Her eyes slid sideways to view her beloved Kayenté struggling to repel the sea of bodies, grabbing, punching, and pushing against him. He never gave up. And that is what she loved most about him.

After monumental minutes, he was on his knees, entrapped by his attackers who edged him like a portrait frame. His weapons, hauberk, and most of his armor had been stripped from him, and the black shirt underneath was torn, exposing most of his skin. His wrists were bound behind his back. The leather cut into his skin, but his proud face, marked with sweat and dirt, showed no pain.

Two warriors leashed his neck to a horse. The thin strap pinned most of his hair against his neck, almost choking him. A few shorter tendrils, stained with other people's blood, had fallen across his damp cheeks, dripping pale red into his sweat. The horde of men stepped back from him with evil smiles, huffing, puffing, and smugly moaning their victory.

Kayenté, still on his knees, glared darkly in Kamara's direction, eyes burning, chest bobbing breathlessly. "Winnefred, what evil do you now evoke?"

Winnefred, thought Kamara, *is that evil asp upon me again?* She vowed to herself that, sister or not, this time, she'd have no compassion for Winnefred, who had well proven the empty measure of her mercy.

Winnefred laughed and answered haughtily, "I evoke the doom of Little Kitten."

Kamara felt the blade cut lightly into her. Warm liquid trickled down her neck.

Kayenté's rage rose from his belly to his mouth. He fought to repress the venomous words on the tip of his tongue.

The Cold One appeared out of thin air, standing inches in front of Kamara. He puffed his bare hairy chest brazenly toward her face. His tight brown pants bulged obscenely.

She kept her head level, but turned her gaze upward, blazing her scorn into his empty ancient eyes.

"Ouch," he said facetiously. He bent his knees, lowering his face to her level as if mocking her size. With hypnotic eyes, he hurled himself into her stare.

She slid her eyes sideways to escape the sight of his face. "No!"

Kayenté clenched his teeth, riveting pain along his jaw into his temples. His heartbeat pulsed visibly in his flushed neck from the white-hot fury coursing through him. He was finally with her when the Cold One came, and he could do nothing! Just like old times with his mother, when the Cold One came to call. A master at breaking spirits, indeed.

"You will say, yes," said the Cold One. Then he slid a laughing glance to Kayenté.

Kayenté wanted to spill every last drop of blood from each foe present. But because he could not, he wanted to spill profanities instead. Yet he knew the Cold One sought to drive him over the edge, just as always. So to the edge—he would not go. The only weapon he had left, besides his will, was his mouth, so wisely he must use it.

The Cold One ran his fingers along the collar of Kamara's brigandine, and said. "You have toughened yourself, but you remain tender to me. Your only salvation is to submit, and let yourself become a creature that can live in eternity."

"A vampire?" Kamara asked with rhetorical cynicism, still averting her eyes.

"That—or nothing," he said laughing.

Kayenté cringed when he saw her glance submissively at the Cold One, revealing her weakness. He silently prayed for her to force confidence. And suddenly she did.

Her facial expression became cagey, and her tone coy. She glared dead straight into his eyes. "I choose—neither."

He raised one brow. "You are of my blood. I should not have so much trouble with you."

"I know who you are," she said smoothly, "but I do not accept you as such, nor do I accept as my sister the evil one whose blade is at my throat. Kill me. I'll die knowing love, for that you have failed to destroy. And you'll never have my spirit."

"*Never* is of my world," replied, the Cold One smiling.

He walked over to Kayenté and asked sardonically, "Are you disappointed that I am not your true father?"

Kayenté drilled his killer look into the Cold One, unaffected by his hypnotic eyes. "That may be who you *aren't*, but I know who you *are*. You are Ajento, my gremlin. You are Hansa, demon father to Taran and Winnefred. You are vampire to Light Priestesses, and nightmare to noble women. And I do believe that you are also Merculus, bedeviler of the Rudels. For why else, would the Rudels so suddenly wage grand scale war upon the Sakajians and coincidentally so, when Kamara began experiencing her troubles with you? And you let me believe you were a Sakajian traitor so that I would be zealously preoccupied with bringing you down, leaving Kamara vulnerable. Aldos is dead. Now you wait for the Gates to move in, so that there will be a three way fight, weakening all sides for your taking. And since I did not comply, you turn my people against me. Yes. You are Merculus, but most of all, you are the Cold One—" his eyes flared, "—*doomed* to fall by the Priestess Kamara!"

The Cold One glared in silence. His image faded slightly, then grew strong again. He said, "You've befriended Taran—got him back, or so you think. So be it. Fair trade."

Kayenté wanted to ask him what he meant by *fair trade*. Did he mean Marc? But he would not give the Cold One the upper hand. Instead, he proclaimed coolly, "I've been saved by love. I am safe in love. Even if you kill me—you can no longer destroy me."

"But *she* can!" He pointed to Kamara. "She'll turn on you yet, one way—or another."

Kayenté knew that the Cold One was trying to cause doubt in him, so he glassed over the pain evoked from such a thought.

The Cold One continued, "I was successful in destroying your mother's relationship with your father, Taran's relationship with you, and your relationship with your mother, was I not? Your mother would have chosen poverty to escape me, but as it was, she knew you'd die if you fought for her. So, she sacrificed and let you believe the lie, that you were my son, and that she sold your honor for the prestige and fortune of remaining a Duchess."

Kayenté's heart ached, still aware that the Cold One was trying to weaken him, but his sadness weighed heavy. All those years his mother's love was *real*, and tragically, he had never felt it.

The Cold One, as if sensing Kayenté's sadness, threw his head back and laughed. Kayenté fought harder to cap the emotion welling within him.

The Cold One walked over to Kamara and brushed her cheek, "And her—" he said staring at Kayenté. "—she carries your child. Soon she'll submit to me. And I will abort the little Kat with a roughness in copulation such as your Little Kitten has never experienced. Soon after, I'll place my seed within her and her spirit within me."

Kayenté's body contracted. Kamara carried his child? She was pregnant? Perhaps the Cold One was attempting to trick them, but no, somehow he felt it true. His delight in hearing such news was swallowed by the rage he felt for the messenger. Never had he wanted to spill blood so badly as he did this moment. Yet, he knew that sudden movement would send the horse into a gallop, dragging him behind, choking him to death.

Kamara was dumbfounded. Could she be pregnant? She was torn between the joy of possibly carrying Kayenté's child, and the fear of losing it.

The Cold One commanded, "Release her Winnefred."

Winnefred released her with a shove.

Kamara instinctively touched her finger to the small wound under her chin that still dribbled blood.

Winnefred sauntered over to Kayenté. Her slinky burgundy gown picked up twigs and stickers at the hem. She seemed impervious to the cold—in every way. She rubbed her hand over Kayenté's head. "Nice Cat, nice big fluffy cat."

His venomous glare bit her. And she felt it. She hissed and bared teeth.

Kayenté jerked his head away from her hands, feeling a flash of horror to ever think he had lain with her—to ever think he was enraptured with her. He shuddered and returned his attention to Kamara.

The Cold One stepped closer to Kamara. She held her feet to the earth, not backing up as once she would have. The Cold One blew a cool, soft wind across her face, blowing back a tendril of hair that had fallen loose from her braid. Then he gripped her forearms and landed a biting kiss on her lips, breaking skin.

When he finished, she wiped the blood from her mouth and stated calmly, "I do not submit."

He said, "You'll not birth the Warlord's child. However, your sister may."

Kamara gasped.

The Cold One taunted, "Remember how he bedded Winnefred, over and over. Remember how he cared only for her when she was in his sight."

Kamara swallowed and inadvertently took a step back from him.

Kayenté, seeing her weaken, said, "Kamara, trust your heart."

She took a deep quivering breath and took an affirmative step forward, pushing her words into the Cold One. "You can't alter destiny!"

"I can alter everything," he said. "I've done so for thousands of years. I'll lead you all like sheep into my black hole, as I have animal species, primeval tribes, whole religions, and once powerful nations. Within the next hundred years, I will have collected enough spirits from all over the planet that the earth will decay under the abuse incurred from spiritless beings who do not nurture their surroundings. And then the earth will be no more. Before the night of the next full moon comes to pass, I will have succeeded to a point beyond the earth's saving."

His eyes locked coldly into her. "This is your last chance. Come willingly, serve me, and you'll feel no pain. But if you resist, hell will have you for eternity."

She closed her eyes and the gate to her soul. "I . . . do . . . not . . . submit."

He ordered, "Winnefred, when I take the Warlord away, weaken her into submission with your newly acquired power. She is your twin . . . make her lose love."

"I won't lose love," Kamara said, "no matter what you do."

Winnefred sneered. "Of course you will. Don't be ridiculous."

The Cold One said, "When you have her spirit, bring it to me at Wincott Castle, along with her spiritless body. When her spirit is mine,—" the Cold One turned to Kayenté and said casually, "—his will follow. And now, I've one more place to visit to make my plan complete. I'll give you a hint." He watched Kamara's eyes for a reaction. "It's *misty*."

Kamara struggled to submerge the sad panic rising to her face.

The Cold One squinted, as if saying *I have you now.* Then he signaled the men to lead Kayenté away. He commanded with twinkling eyes, "Take his stallion back with you. I'm in need of a new warhorse."

Kayenté growled to himself. His heart lurched when the horse he was bound to, started moving, forcing him up to his feet.

The Cold One laughed. "You look real noble there, lord."

Kayenté's ripped up shirt hung over his dusty leather pants, and his hair hung messy down his back. He did not look the noble, but he never felt more noble than now: strong in love, willing to die in its name.

The group moved onward spouting foul words to Kayenté, but he could not hear them over the loudness of his own thoughts. He walked sideways so that he could view his beloved. He locked his focus into Kamara with an intensity that bespoke his knowing of her within him, and a command that she would know him within her.

The Cold One vanished. Winnefred approached Kamara. Kayenté shouted, "Kamara! Remember the gift!"

She snapped her head towards him.

He saw the pain in her eyes. He caught the flicker in her pupils that cried out his name with all her heart. And before she was out of his sight, he saw her right palm stretched toward Winnefred's forehead, mist oozing out of her fingertips. Was she being stupid, desperate, or clever, he did not know. He hoped it was the latter.

And even when he could see her no more, his heart remained with her.

"Yes," Winnefred said, moving in a circle around Kamara, "*mist me, the downfall of every Priestess.*"

Kamara moved in unison with her—never breaking eye contact.

Winnefred said in a low hypnotic voice, "Give me your spirit. I shall keep it for Hansa."

Kamara replied, "I can bridge you Winnefred. I know I can. You are my twin sister."

"Then give yourself to me Kamara. I won't even call you Little Kitten anymore. We can be as one, as the one we were meant to be."

"Yes, but you come into 'the light.' "

"No, you come into 'the dark.' "

Kamara felt sucking at the top of her head, enduring, letting Winnefred believe she had the upper hand. "You are beyond the dark. You are a shadowless servant of The Nothing. Come back into the dark. Then I'll give myself to you."

Winnefred stopped moving. Her eyes flickered hope.

Kamara wanted to believe the flicker was genuine. Could she actually make peace with her dark side? Suddenly she wanted to. Very much.

"Winnefred, you can do it!" Kamara said.

"I can never escape The Nothing. I was born into it!"

"You can escape it with my help. I am your light."

"I want to, but punishment will be too great if I fail."

"It is now Winnefred . . . or never!"

Winnefred closed her eyes and breathed deeply. The expression on her face tightened. "I'm coming to you . . . it's happening!"

Kamara could feel her sister moving from The Nothing into the dark. But she feared it was a trick. Maybe Winnefred just wanted her to banish her caution. But what if Winnefred *was* trying to merge with her? After all, hadn't Taran made peace with Kayenté?

"I've arrived," Winnefred said, tears dripping down her cheeks. "I'm dark and lonely. Come find me."

Kamara touched Winnefred's shoulders and closed her eyes to concentrate on merging. "Oh sister!"

Winnefred asked in a confused tone, "After all I've done, do you really, really want me?"

Kamara replied sincerely, "Yes, Winnefred. I need you—my darkness."

Winnefred's voice broke, "And I need you—my light."

"Then take me," Kamara said, emotion rising on her breath.

"I shall," Winnefred said.

Kamara felt herself falling into Winnefred. Is this what the Wise One had meant when she'd told Kamara she must take back her darkness? No wait, wasn't her darkness taking her?

How did that happen?

Kamara snapped open her eyes. Winnefred's eyes were monstrously large. Fangs protruded from her gaping mouth. Saliva bubbled on her lips.

Kamara lunged back trying to pull her essence out of Winnefred, but Winnefred snatched her shoulders and thrust her fangs against Kamara's neck, puncturing skin.

Kamara's mind raced. *Not this again.* Kamara jerked the knife from her boot and jammed it callously beneath Winnefred's left shoulder blade.

Winnefred shrieked, and fell to her knees.

Kamara yanked out the knife, void of emotion.

Winnefred gasped.

Kamara stepped away from her fallen sister, whose eyes had widened like two full moons.

Winnefred whispered harshly, "Light Priestesses...never—kill." She fell on her face. Blood spurted from her back and sprayed across Kamara's shirt and cape.

Kamara stepped back and said coolly. "Winnefred dear sister, don't be ridiculous." She wiped both sides of the knife across her knee, leaving a smear of blood on her pants. "I'll not likely be fighting ladies, huh, Kayenté?"

She placed the knife back in the sheath inside her boot. *If you want to defeat the Cold One, you must become like him, or her, in this case.* And Kamara had.

Blood squirted in beats from Winnefred's back. Kamara felt nothing. She suddenly understood how Kayenté could kill so ruthlessly. He was with her—in her. She had used his darkness and his coldness to conquer Winnefred.

Her skin began to tingle, itch, then hurt. Her heart started palpitating hard and out of rhythm. She could barely breathe or contain the charge of power coursing through her body, pricking her like the tips of a million lightning bolts.

Just when she felt herself begin to faint, the pain decreased until it was gone, leaving her highly galvanized. Was this bloodlust that she now experienced? She walked beyond her slain sister, who lay in the puddle of crimson liquid that had drained from her body. She went to her sacred sword, resting on a pile of maple leaves.

She picked up the blade and replaced it in the sheath upon her hip. She sighed, feeling like she had accomplished something great. Didn't Kayenté say he felt great after a kill? But how could she feel so great, when clearly she had failed to merge with her other half? But Winnefred had not desired such union, and now she was dead. And Kamara wondered if her chance to claim her *own* dark side had been lost forever. Perhaps if she could use Kayenté's dark side, she didn't need her own.

She traced her steps back to her horse near the field where she had left the men fighting. She had hoped to enlist them, friend and foe, to help her rescue Kayenté, even if by magic. If the Cold One could take any body and bend it to his will, then why shouldn't she?

She mounted her horse, and rode to the field of smashed down grasses. Stilled soldiers were sprawled everywhere. *All* had fallen—every one. She bravely surveyed the bodies with an emotional distance that surprised her. None were alive, just as the Cold One had surely planned: *let them kill each other and fall into The Nothing.*

Should she try to rescue Kayenté, or go to Franz? What would Kayenté want her to do? She deliberated for a long moment and then she knew. *Let the Cold One think his plan was underway.* But did he sense Winnefred's demise? Did he? If she and Winnefred, though estranged, were actually one being, then maybe the Cold One would not accurately detect the event. Whether he did or not, Kayenté would want her to go to the Duke and insure the execution of their plan. Her heart broke to make him second and not first. Never had she put the whole above the individual, nor logic above love, and yet she knew—this time, she must.

ЖК
Chapter Thirty-One

Kamara galloped to Franz Ketola's castle, compelled by something she didn't understand, a knowing without knowing, and doing without doubt. Several hours passed as a moment. She came upon the castle, immersed in a tangled uproar of fighting men.

There were so many factions of people warring with each other, she had no idea who would consider her friend and who would not. So she *misted* herself, and using her powers of enchantment, she slipped into the castle.

She sprinted up the keep, seeking Duchess Jela. She knew not why. She screamed, "Duchess Jela! Duchess Jela!"

She raced so fast that she bumped into a man clothed in smoky gray—Munson! He glared at her darkly. Why must he hold a grudge? She had, after all, saved his son's life. But she had no time to ponder Munson. She *must* find Jela, so she dashed past him.

The Duchess peaked her head out of her chamber. "What do you want, child!"

Kamara ran towards her. "I must speak with you!"

She reached Jela and fell to her feet. "I beg you indulge me, but a few moments."

"Very well," said the Duchess tensely, opening the door wider.

Kamara rose and entered meekly.

The Duchess closed the door and turned toward Kamara. "What do you want! Why have you barged in on me?"

Kamara was stunned for a moment, not knowing the answer. She stared blankly at the Duchess, noticing her royal blue dress, puffed and patterned as the one Kayenté had forced her to wear for King William. She thought it sad that noble women had to dress so uncomfortably to feel beautiful. The Duchess was hiding behind her appearance. Somehow—she was. Kamara searched Jela's eyes for the answers she herself could not furnish.

"Well!" shouted the Duchess, "Why are you here!"

Kamara replied, "I'm not sure. I don't know why I came to you." She paused and then said, "Wait, yes I do. You are to tell me the fourth secret." Her face became perplexed. "But why have I come to *you* for this revelation?"

The Duchess sighed heavily and turned her back to Kamara. She glided slowly across the room, lavishly decorated with paintings of angels, shelves of gold statues, and jewels brimming from silver boxes. It seemed to Kamara that these objects had failed to soothe Jela's silent unyielding agony.

The Duchess turned and faced Kamara in a pose of resignation. "You have come to me . . . because I am—was . . . a Priestess of the Mist."

Kamara's mouth dropped open. For a moment, she was speechless. And when words had found her tongue, they were spoken with astonishment. "*You*—were a Priestess? Kayenté is the *son*—of a Priestess?" Kamara gasped softly, "Then that is why the mists rose from his breath!"

"Kayenté misted?" asked Jela with warm surprise, her sad face barely changing.

"Yes. He has emerged as a bearer of light, but I—I'm confused, for I thought Priestesses only bore daughters. How is it that you birthed three sons?"

"The tides shifted. Warriors of the mist were needed, and so it was—they came."

"So your three sons were born to defend the Sisterhood?"

"Yes. But the plan was ever so disrupted. King Aldos was to be the father of my children. But before I could seduce him, the Cold One came upon me for he'd discovered the plan. He knew that his demise, according to the prophecy, involved the son of a Priestess, who would be chosen heir to the King's throne. A noble man with a king's power and a king's heart. A heart that sought good for the whole and not just himself. And so, no, the Cold One did not want my sons associated with the royal court.

"So, he robbed my spirit and impregnated me with Taran. The Duke found me when the Cold One's son was but freshly planted in my womb. I was helpless and alone, detached from my Sisters of the Mist, unable to feel anything—but emptiness. He didn't know who I was, and yet he took me in. And I don't know how or why, but he fell in love with me. Perhaps it was destiny, the Duke, being the King's brother."

"Did the Duke ever learn that you had been a Priestess?"

"No. I let him think Taran was his, and that I had no roots worth keeping. I feared that if he knew the truth, he'd banish me, and the illegitimate son in my womb. And I hoped that if my child and the children to come were raised by the Duke, who was not only brother to the King, but a man of great power, then perhaps my sons could still bring the prophecy to pass."

Kamara shook her head. "But the Cold One did not leave you alone, did he?"

"No, he did not. After Taran, I bore two more sons. He intended to muddle any positive foundation that may have been built for the security of my sons' futures. And he did. He bred deceit, and my sons were sidetracked from their pathways. Taran never had a chance, for the Cold One seduced him early. He used Taran to derange Kayenté. And with those two so fiercely competing, Marc retreated into his own world, and became a quiet boy who expressed himself only on the battlefield. Marc was left with no aspiration at all, save performing a fight well done. He was no threat to the Cold One."

"Franz was to be your father, but of course, the Cold One again interfered, for you were to be the other half of his downfall. He sought to sire and control you as he did Taran. We outwitted him, though. I'm sure you now know of that, for it was the third secret, and you are asking for the fourth."

"What *is* the fourth secret?"

"No . . . no," Jela said. "The fourth secret shall not be uttered by my lips. Anyway, there is no longer any hope of defeating the Cold One. There isn't."

Kamara replied compassionately, "You feel that way because your spirit has been robbed."

Jela's eyes deepened with reverie. "If the Cold One hadn't interfered, Taran would have been sired by King Aldos. I'd still be at Lania Castle with three sons who carried their father's legacy as great warriors, and they would have protected those of us too far in 'the light.' " Jela paused and then said distressfully, "No, that is just a dream I have—it was never meant to be."

"What *was* meant to be, Duchess, what?"

"It doesn't matter anymore. It's just a matter of time, before we're all gone. I never liked the prophecy anyway." Her face deepened with pain. "No, I never did."

"Does it have something to do with why are you so bitter toward me?"

Jela sighed and began pacing the room, wringing her hands. Suddenly, she blurted, "How can I not feel bitter when I know that my son shall die by your hand!"

Kamara gasped. "I would *never* harm Kayenté. What are you saying?"

Jela's eyes brimmed with resentment. "The . . . fourth . . . secret."

"Duchess Jela. I know that your powers are gone. I know that your spirit is captured. However, I beg you share your wisdom. Kayenté and Marc are already in the hands of the Cold One. Taran has moved into 'the light' but the Cold One haunts him terribly. If you are to save your sons, you *must* tell me!"

"It's hopeless," said the Duchess, almost blandly, "even if you defeat the Cold One, I shall remain conquered, for I must lose my son."

Kamara felt engulfed in a race for time. "What are you talking about?"

Jela's taut face twitched.

"Tell me!"

Jela flashed her eyes upon Kamara's sword, and then rubbed the side of her finger hard over her forehead as if contemplating. "If I tell you—my son shall die."

"And if you don't—then on the night of the full moon, your son shall be lost for eternity anyway."

Jela glared at her with tear- glazed eyes. "Draw your sword from its sheath."

Kamara acquiesced reluctantly, staring intently at Jela.

"Kayenté was born to be sacrificed, and you were born to perform the ceremony."

Kamara felt dead for an instant, then shook her head profusely. "Jela, I know you loathe me, but please be not so cruel as to bestow such a lie upon me—not now!"

"The prophecy ordains that you must kill the one you love the most. And the sacrificed must love you enough to allow the kill."

"But Priestesses of the Mist—never kill!"

"But you have, haven't you? You would not have arrived at my door if you'd not taken back your dark side. Winnefred must have died by your hand for that to occur. You *have* killed. And you will—again."

Kamara dropped her sword. "No! No. I killed Winnefred. How could I have taken her back?"

"Death is not an end child! It's a passageway. You took her back—through death, just as you shall give Kayenté away—through death!"

"There's another way! There must be. I'd rather suffer for all time than to take Kayenté's life."

"It's the only way. Light and Dark must become so blended, that a great power is created to force the Cold One back into his place. *Light comes to dark and dark comes to light. The risen shall fall and the fallen shall rise. So has it been and so shall it always be.*"

Kamara was in a stupor, unable to move. Only faint hope moved her tongue. "But Kayenté and I have done that—haven't we?"

"Not enough child—not nearly enough."

Kamara glared at her fallen sword, her face red, her breathing strained. "So that is why I was given the sword."

Jela nodded. "Yes. That is why you were given the sword. At first, I was most honored that my son was the chosen one, but then as Kayenté grew, less and less could I promote his fate. More and more, I just wanted my son safe, not caring of Ajento's plan. Void of my spirit, I have not been able to support the Light Priestesses. I've not the strength to help them, or even Kayenté, anymore."

"Oh Jela," Kamara said compassionately.

Jela closed her eyes and sighed. "What shall you do?"

Kamara bent over slowly, picked up the sword. "What I must."

Jela snapped open her eyes and lunged headlong into Kamara, pinning her against the wall. "No! You'll not kill my son!"

She struggled to dislodge the sword from Kamara's hand. Kamara resisted. "Jela, you *must* let me go. We are not trying to save bodies—but spirits!"

"No! I won't let you kill my baby! I w—o—n—t!"

The door burst open nearly hitting Kamara. Munson shot into the room, grabbed Kamara's wrist, and yanked the sword from her hand. Kamara hadn't even the time to react before Munson slammed her to the floor, flat on her back. He held one hand around her neck, and the other around the hilt of her sword, pointing the tip over her heart. "Say the word, Duchess, and I'll drive this sword through her! She bewitched my son away from me, and now she seeks to take yours from you!"

Kamara tried to pry his hand away from her throat, his grip pinning her down, more than choking her. She looked to Jela, pleading for mercy with her eyes.

Jela looked down upon her with the face of a demon, sputtering the falsehoods of a woman gone mad. "She's evil, isn't she? She's the daughter of the Cold One. Yes. Yes. The Devil's daughter. The prophecy was a scheme of the Devil. Yes, he's played us all along. My son is not to die. She is!"

Kamara screamed, "J—e—l—a! N—o . . . !"

Munson's face was crimped in hideous hate, his lips and teeth were shiny wet from the bloodlust drooling in his mouth. Kamara was in such shock, she nearly forgot that she had the power to mist. Vapors seeped from her breath.

Munson shouted, "Duchess! Let me kill her now! She's using her witchcraft to protect herself!"

"Do it then!" screamed Jela.

"J—e—" Kamara choked, unable to utter another sound for the grip around her throat tightened. She stretched her hand to Jela, and drilled an imploring stare into her fanatical eyes.

Kamara felt the blade break the skin on her chest.

"Wait!" Jela cried suddenly.

"I'll not wait!" declared Munson.

Jela threw her body against Munson, upsetting his balance, but not his position.

He shoved Jela so hard, she fell on her backside at Kamara's feet.

Munson declared through clenched teeth. "I've waited long enough to bear vengeance upon this witch!" He glared hate into Kamara's face, tightening the grip on her throat and re-aiming the point of the sword over her heart.

Kamara forced her eyes open to view Munson's face, boldly confronting her situation, even though it seemed she would die. She thought to herself, *I'll not give up.*

Munson's eyes enlarged, and his crinkled red face unfolded. He moaned and fell to the side of her, a knife buried in his waist. Jela had stabbed him with Kayenté's *little gift*, sheathed on Kamara's calf.

Kamara scrambled to her knees and watched the fallen man with hawk's eyes. Jela's expression was identical. Munson lay still for a moment, panting, face beading with sweat. Kamara didn't know what to do. Neither did Jela. Should they kill him—or help him?

He took his hand to the knife handle and yanked hard, pulling the wet bloody blade into the air. Drops of red liquid splashed the floor. He pushed himself to his knees, staring at Jela, horror upon his face. He lunged on her, knife bearing down on her neck. Kamara came up behind him, grabbed his assaulting wrist, and squeezed, the way Kayenté had done to her to make her drop her weapons. Only, Munson didn't drop it.

Jela scooted sideways, away from the knifepoint. Blood oozed from Munson's side steadily, and he weakened. Kamara yanked his arm backward over his head with a death grip on his wrist, while Jela wrestled the knife from his hand. Then Kamara jumped on his back pushing him forward. He collapsed on his stomach. Kamara fell on his upper body, her head angled toward his head. Jela fell on his lower body from the other side, her head angled toward his feet. They weighed him down, hoping he would stay, fearing he would not.

Jela held the knife and stretched it toward Kamara. "Kill him."

Kamara wiggled her head, declining.

"Kill him Kamara, it is you duty."

"No, *you* kill him."

"You do it, for you are the one appointed to handle such matters!"

"But I've already killed today. It's your turn!"

"Kamara! You have become a warrior. Warriors duel for the *honor* to slay the enemy. They don't whine '*I have already killed today, you do it!*"

Their argument was broken when Munson, in a desperate act of survival, bolstered both women off him and rose feebly to his feet. Kamara scrambled to her sword lying on the floor by the door. She grabbed it and lurked behind him. Jela tightened her grip on the knife, rising to her feet, standing full fare in front of him.

Munson's voice rumbled rabidly, frothing acrimony. "I'll . . . *kill* you . . . both!"

The women's mouths dropped open with a whimper. Then, without thinking, they shot forth like arrows flying, bludgeoning his body from both sides, heart and spleen. With weapons protruding from his torso, gushing blood, he fell. They gazed upon him. He wasn't moving. He wasn't breathing. He wasn't—anymore.

"Go child," said Jela. "Take your sword and be done with your task, for my heart is so shriveled with grief, it barely beats." Jela's knees buckled. Kamara caught her and helped her into bed. The Duchess lay limply, eyes closed.

"Hold fast, dear lady," urged Kamara. "Your spirit shall be set free upon the defeat of the Cold One, which is soon at hand."

Jela spoke with closed eyes. "Leave child, and let me not gaze upon your face again."

"As you wish Duchess, but apprise me first about this current battle at your domain."

Jela muttered wearily, "The Rudels evoked the peasants to help them revolt against the Sakajians. The sheriff and his men came to uphold order, but the commoners number so many that all of my husband's men have also been forced to engage."

"So, there are no Rudels out there?"

The Duchess shook her head lightly.

"Duchess, I've a message from Kayenté for you to deliver to the Duke, if he, Great Mother willing, survives this battle."

"Tell me quickly, child," the Duchess said, drifting into slumber.

"Kayenté had a prophecy telling him that Sakajians must relinquish control to King William of Gateland, even though Kayenté has been appointed heir to the throne. Drudel is a murderer and a traitor. We mustn't support him. We must meet in Kanis on the full moon, not to fight, but to come together and find peace."

The Duchess mumbled, "My son does not wish to be King?"

"No, for he has found his heart and now bases his decisions on what is best for the people."

Jela murmured, "You *have* brought my son to Light. I shall tell the Duke, Kayenté's wishes. I—" The Duchess fell asleep.

Kamara brushed her fingers down Jela's cheek, envisioning her as a Priestess chanting 'the light' at Lania Castle. Then she walked over to the dead man, envisioning herself as a warrior on the battle-field, as she pulled out her knife, then her sword, both red with blood.

A wave of dizziness roared through her, but there was no more time for fainting. She must hold the sword now, for the three or-dained Warriors of the Mist—could not.

She replaced her sacred sword in its sheath, walked over to Jela, and lay the knife on her white marble bed stand. "You have earned the blade, dear Jela, the blade of truth that cuts so hard one can barely endure the pain, and yet once cut, beauty emerges. You whom I have hated for hating me . . . I now love. I know you don't love me. I know you do not. Maybe you would have though, if only you had embedded a knife into the Cold One, oh so many years ago, then per-haps—" She shook her head. "but no, it did not happen that way."

She slipped out of the room, away from the castle as smoothly as she had come. And now—she must rescue Kayenté.

Ж
Chapter Thirty-Two

Kamara moved not from logic, nor was she motivated by fear. Something else took her that afternoon. She galloped her horse through forest and field on through the night to the spellbound Wincott Castle, certain she'd find Kayenté there.

Once she arrived, she dismounted, hid her horse in the wood, and glided like a charmed bird into the castle, enchanting the enchanted.

She felt it though, the caged heartbeat of her loved ones pounding in her ears, louder when she moved one way, weaker if she moved another. She crept until the heartbeat exploded in her head. There they were. She was at the top of a stairway, peering down into a great black stone chamber . . . a familiar stone chamber, yes, the one where Taran had wed her!

Twelve people stood against the wall on the far side of the room, directly across from her. A fat red candle burned on a small protruding shelf above each person. No one appeared bound, yet they were statue still. If they weren't standing, she would have thought them dead. She couldn't make out the faces, so she crept lightly down the stairway into the chamber. Her steps echoed, so she dropped to her hands and knees, and crawled.

When she came upon the people, she rose and stared into their blank eyes, one by one. Sir Robert's men. One, two, three, four, five, six, Sir Robert. Marc. Allysa. Michael. Teeah? Oh Teeah! Camille! This *cannot* be. They were in a trance—all of them.

Where was Kayenté! She heard footsteps on the floor above her, moving along the path she had just taken. She went quickly to her hands and knees and crawled behind an ivory stone altar near Camille. She had to break the spell of the captive twelve before their spirits were irrevocably cast into The Nothing, if indeed they had not already been.

She heard pairs of footsteps descending the stairway. Her eyes stung from the sweat dripping down her forehead. The footsteps neared her, and stopped in front of the stone altar. Her breath barely trickled to and fro her lungs.

Kamara heard the Cold One speak, "Submit, and I'll release these people."

"Without their spirits," a voice replied.

Kayenté! The voice was Kayenté's. At least he was not under another spell. Perhaps after what he'd been through, spells were would no longer work on him.

Then she heard the Cold One say, "Submit or I will lay each one upon the altar and cut out their hearts. Then when your beloved returns with Winnefred, I'll torture her before your eyes. If you'll no longer sacrifice others for yourself, then at least you can sacrifice yourself for others. Love, do you call it?"

Then she heard Kayenté say, "As long as I do not leave Kamara by my will, you cannot win. Even though apart, we are together, if we neither one submit."

"Very well," said the Cold One, "then I'll begin with the woman on the end. Guards, place her on the altar."

Guards, thought Kamara . . . *the altar*. He was going to kill Camille! She had to do something, but what? Kill Kayenté in a sacrifice of love? No—not yet, maybe not ever. With Kayenté now before her, her resolve to fulfill the prophecy, faded.

She crouched down as far as she could, deadly still. Camille was laid face up upon the slab of stone. Kamara saw the dim glow of long yellow hair fall over the side of the altar. She wanted to touch it. She had to save Camille! She saw Kayenté's shadowy figure on the other side of the altar. He seemed chained. She summoned the powers of Light, suppressing the urge to mist, fearing it would give away her position. This was a most difficult undertaking, for she had never done one without the other.

"Wait," the Cold One said. "I sense Light in this room . . . and a Priestess at work! And since there's only one left . . . your beloved has escaped Winnefred. I believe she is here."

A voice echoed in Kamara's head, *Use Winnefred to shield you.*

What? asked Kamara, silently, but then without waiting for an answer she imagined Winnefred in front of her. Then she realized that Winnefred, upon her death, had indeed become a part of her. The Cold One had not suspected Winnefred's demise, because she was still here, in a way.

"No," the Cold One said, "it's Winnefred who has returned with The Light One's spirit. Make yourself known Winnefred."

Then Kamara knew that she could imitate Winnefred. Faithful in her realization, she stood in the shadow and concentrated on Winnefred's voice speaking through her own mouth. "Yes. It is I."

"You have brought The Light One's spirit?"

"Yes."

"Where is her body?"

"Upstairs, in the bedchamber where she once slept. You may see to her if you wish. I shall delight in nothing more than to execute on your behalf, the tortures of these prisoners."

"Give me her spirit now," commanded the Cold One. "I have waited long."

"Let me keep it for you until you have aborted her child, just to insure that all is done without mishap."

The Cold One nodded. "Yes. I'll go to her now."

He addressed Kayenté, "When I am done aborting the child, I'll come for her spirit. Once I have it, you will fall with her, into me—into nothing. Your love can no longer protect you."

Kamara suddenly realized that it would only take him a moment to disappear into the bedchamber to find it empty, and but a moment more to return, so she quickly created another lie.

"Hansa," she called in Winnefred's voice, "a troop of men arrived when I did. They are scattering. You may want to cloak them in your blanket of deception, before you take Little Kitten."

"I felt no stirring in the boundaries, except for you," he replied, his tone suspicious.

"That was not me you felt—but the new arrivals. They had once been enchanted by Little Kitten and I believe they have come for her."

"Very well," he said, "I'll return shortly."

He disappeared.

Kayenté clenched his teeth, preparing to confront Winnefred. His hatred for her had risen like a monument that he would thrust upon her grave.

She commanded, "Unchain the prisoner."

The guards did as they were bade. The chains dropped to the floor.

Kayenté wondered what cruel scheme she was about to actualize, not really caring, because he was planning to strangle her before she could say a word.

"Guards leave. I'll not need you."

The guards departed.

When they were gone, Kayenté watched the dark figure move out from behind the altar. Before she had a chance to get near him, he lunged at her. In one swift movement, he threw her to the floor, swinging his leg over her hips, grabbed her throat, and squeezed.

She tried pulling his hands away, but couldn't. She wanted to cry out, *It's me Kamara,* but she couldn't even squeak, much less breathe. What Munson had started, Kayenté would finish. Her mind flashed upon a terrible vision of the Cold One smiling when he discovered that Kayenté had killed her. Surely then Kayenté would submit his spirit, in utter shame for what he'd done. Her head deprived of air, throbbed—on fire, like burning ice. Would her head explode? This was it—her death. Velvet black devoured her. Visions of her childhood blinked through the black.

A thundering voice sounded by the stairs, behind Kayenté.

Kayenté turned his head to the sound and inadvertently loosened his grip, without letting her go.

The Cold One fumed, "I have been all over this castle! There are no arrivals! The Light One is neither in her room or anywhere else!"

Kamara uttered in a hoarse gasping whisper, "Kayenté, I am here. It's me—Kamara."

Kayenté's eyes opened wide. He pushed his face down to see her wheezing in the dark. He couldn't define her features or tell if he was being tricked, so he yanked her up quickly into the candlelight. Indeed, Kamara's face shone angelic and sweet.

He whispered in astonishment, "Damn Kamara, it *is* you! You are alive and well, and I almost killed you!"

"I'm glad," she gasped in a whisper, holding her throat, "you didn't . . . use . . . a knife."

The Cold One approached.

Kayenté nudged Kamara backward into the shadows.

She withdrew her sword and thrust the hilt into his hand. He received the blade firmly.

The Cold One said, "So, I've been tricked. Your Kamara is here, isn't she? I can feel her now." The Cold One drew his sword. "So, is this the moment you've been anticipating? The moment when you could challenge me at last? But why do you seek *my* obliteration? I am the one who has labored to protect you from the women who would have you destroyed. I have tortured them on your behalf. I never planned to send *you* into The Nothing. I was attempting to make you strong enough to be my protégé. When I leave this earth, there must be one to take my place. You—Kayenté Panther Ketola. You."

Kamara cried, "He is trying to trick you!"

Kayenté stepped forward. "You fabricate lies."

"No. I am what you have been seeking, but in the storm of your stubborn resistance you've not been able to see that. The woman you now protect has brought you nothing but turmoil. She is your nemesis, not I. She is your doom, not I. She is the one ordained—"

Kamara feared the Cold One would reveal the fourth secret. "Don't listen to him, Kayenté!"

Kayenté held his sword firmly in front of him. "I have waited long enough to spill your blood!"

The Cold One lunged at Kayenté, slashing his sword. Kayenté countered with Kamara's blade. The clang echoed loudly. They moved about the chamber, mostly in darkness, sometimes in the glimmer of the candlelight. Their blades collided with savage impact, sparking orange, at a vigorous tempo that seemed to exceed human endurance.

Kamara wondered how Kayenté could manage such precision in the blinding dark. She wanted to help—but how? She didn't want to do anything that would break his concentration. Even freeing the others from their spell could disrupt his focus, so she remained still and did nothing.

The fighting seemed everlasting. Were they so well matched? Surely, Kayenté would tire before the Cold One who was more supernatural. Even if Kayenté killed the Cold One, it would not help them for long, for The Nothing was more vast than a mere body.

She had to do something. Maybe she could break the spell on Sir Robert and his knights, and they could aid Kayenté. No. They had no weapons. She decided to find armed soldiers and enchant them to distract the Cold One. She crept over to the stairway, and summoned help with a silent chant.

Two guards came toward her. She blew the mists upon them, commanding in a loud whisper, "Behold your true master, Lord Kayenté. He is your heart and soul. If he dies—you die. Protect him . . . now. Hurry."

They flew down the stairs, and soon there was a greater commotion of footsteps and clanking swords. Kamara called Kayenté with her mind, not wanting to alert the Cold One.

In a moment, Kayenté was on the stairs, panting profusely. "We have to get out of here. We must be ready for the full moon."

"But the others!" cried Kamara.

"He'll not kill them if we aren't there to suffer by it. Besides, when we defeat the Cold One, all spells will break and all spirits will return."

Kamara shuddered, remembering all Jela had told her about how the Cold One must be defeated.

Kayenté grabbed her hand and guided her swiftly through the castle. They fled into the night toward the stables. The Cold One appeared before them, so near that they almost bumped into him before stopping. Kayenté edged Kamara back with his hand across her chest, standing protectively in front of her.

The Cold One's head fell back. He sucked in a large volume of air, more it seemed than lungs could harbor. He brought his head level to Kayenté's, and exhaled briskly, blowing Kayenté's hair over his shoulders, and Kamara's braid free from its tether. "Very well, you have convinced me. You two are inseparable. The full moon then." He grinned. "We will see if the inseparable—can be separated." He curved his arm behind his back, and produced Kayenté's sword. "Take it," he held the blade and pointed the hilt at Kayenté, "in case you change your mind and decide to kill her instead."

Kayenté took the sword. "Instead?"

Kamara held her breath, praying the Cold One would not reveal what Kayenté yet did not know. Praying that he would not reveal, what she already knew, and wished she didn't—but did.

As she thought that, the Cold One vanished.

Kayenté sheathed his sword and then returned Kamara's. She barely had it in her sheath when he took her arm gently and led her to the stable. He unhooked one of the many bridles mounted on the outside wall and began searching for his warhorse with his newly acquired power to mystically locate. He led Kamara into the corral to his horse, as if he knew its location all along.

He misted the horse, slipped on the bridle, then lifted Kamara onto its bare back. She very much liked the way he had calmed the animal. If only he could calm her. She almost fell off, hazy-minded from the raw truth pounding in her brain. Kayenté mounted behind her and secured her waist with his arm. "I had considered myself your savior Kamara. But indeed, you have been mine."

Kamara nearly burst into tears. She was not his savior. She was his doom, just as the Cold One had said. She stuffed down her mountain of sorrow, as they rode off into the icy night. Now was *not* the time for truth. No. Not now. She should have a few sweet days with him, just a few. Had they not earned that?

Several hours later, a warm fog rolled through the forest. Kamara's head rested pleasantly on Kayenté's shoulder. Her long hair cloaked his arm, and he loved it. He desired a pause in their wild adventure. Rest sounded good.

He stopped his warhorse, and slid off, taking Kamara with him, in a rainbow arc. When they hit ground, he enveloped her in his arms from behind—his beloved Kamara, so warm, so viable, so everything. He kissed the back of her head. "Let us rest," he said softly. He eased away and tied the horse to a thick branch. They found a sheltered spot, and arranged a nest of maple leaves, and snuggled love-bird close.

Kamara told him about her battle with Winnefred, and her meeting with his mother, and the death of Munson. She told him everything, except for his mother's true identity and of course—the final secret. And it was with this worry that she finally dozed in his arms.

He watched over her with cherish through the night, proud of her accomplishments, and in love with his little warrior-angel, no longer the nun-angel. She had forged a place in his world without relinquishing the beauty of her own—a feat he'd not dreamed possible. He didn't know that the tears and whimpers in her sleep weren't for the trauma past, but for the dreaded fate that awaited her beloved. He dozed lightly, on and off, at peace, despite the coming battle.

When the sun rose, he awoke and surveyed Kamara's sleeping face. Her throat was purple. He shuddered to think that he had almost killed her. He had been ready to snap her neck when the footsteps came. Ironic, he thought, that the Cold One had actually saved her. He placed his hands on her womb and thought of the baby she carried. His baby. He rested his head upon the infant's home.

Kamara awoke. Kayenté's head lay upon her womb, child-like and innocent. So pure was he, so pure he had become. And tainted was she, way over her head in deception, blood, and death. She ran her fingers through his smooth black hair, along the edge of his face. She must remember this, what he feels like—and treasure this, this sweet gesture of love. How would she keep his face from fading in her mind, or the beauty of his sword dance? How would she keep alive the scent of his musky breathe, the sound of his rich low voice in her ear, the sensation of nuzzling his hair with her face, or the feel of his manhood inside her? She choked down her pain, and said. "Your child shall always know of you."

He lifted his head to view her. "Why do you proclaim that? You speak as if we'll be parted. I'll not desert you again."

"I know," Kamara said, "nor I—you."

"What then, can answer to the sadness upon your face?"

"My heart is heavy when I contemplate solutions to the treachery at hand."

"Do you not trust the prophecy?"

"The prophecy ordains that the two of us shall bring the Cold One to balance. The prophecy says nothing of you and I living happily ever on."

He kissed the lone tear that rolled down her cheek. "We will." He rose, pulling her up to her feet. "Come, my dear lady. We'll move with winged heels and finish what we started. Then we'll create a new kind of kingdom, one hand bearing sacred mist, the other a mighty sword."

Her lips trembled. "I'm afraid, Kayenté. I'm terribly afraid."

He brushed his finger affectionately down her soft cheek. "You need not be. Nothing can stop us now."

He took her hand and led her to the horse. He seemed so confident. He'd never lost a battle. Never lost a fight. He always won in the end. Always. She wondered if he would feel so optimistic once he knew the fate that awaited him. Would he abide? However could she tell him? However could *she* abide? There must be another way. There must!

He helped her mount, and climbed on behind her. "I don't think Michael and Allysa made it to your castle before they were abducted, so let us go there and gather the people that they may return with us. Will they come?"

She was lost in the endings of all that would be, and barely heard him. Her thoughts had screamed above her voice, and she did not know if she'd answered him or not.

"Kamara, will they come?"

She pushed her voice through her lips. "I hope so. Long it has been since I have returned. I pray they still believe in me."

"Who could not believe in you," he whispered, and spurred the horse into a canter.

"You," she whispered so low he could not hear. Then she whispered even lower, "You should not believe in me."

By mid-afternoon they arrived at Lania Castle. The mists had faded completely. The people milled about like hungry cows in search of hay. But their eyes lit to see Kamara.

She called a meeting in the Great Hall and the people formed a vast circle. Kayenté stood next to her.

"All join hands," she said. "Close your eyes. Inhale the light of the universe. Let it fill your bodies, your hearts, your mind, and your spirit. Breathe the white pristine light into you . . . the light of hope, wisdom, mercy, and love. Now 'the light' is not only shining in you but all around you, expanding larger and larger to encompass the group. We are all as one large full moon. Feel the oneness."

The group, joined by hands and hearts, began to sway gently. "Yes," she said, "feel that beauty of togetherness. We are all each other. Now, from the center of the earth, let the orange flames rise into your lower body. These flames that temper the sword. These flames that burn away righteousness. These flames that are your desires, unfettered with your mind's analysis. Let that desire rise to your heart, and blend with the white light that fills your upper body."

Her tone deepened, flooding words rich with drama. "We are the flaming star. We shine bright in the blue-black sky. We shine bright in the vast mysteries, judging not how the web of life binds all existence harmoniously together in ways we cannot begin to fathom. One moment we blink, and behold ourselves in a sky of doom. Again, we blink and behold a miracle.

"Perception! Beware the rash conclusions born of a single point of view, drudging yourself into the hollows because such a rank sight did appear. When just overhead, the eagle flies majestically, bringing you welcome news. But you cannot hear or see, for you wallow in the pit of dark despair. The eagle flies by unnoticed, and your pain deepens because you will not see that the honeybee can bring forth sweetness. You only feel the sting.

"Trust life! Cast off the shroud that blinds you from the symbiotic whole! Awaken and accept all that you deny! Would you be told a story with parts deleted? To understand the story, you must receive all the words. So, do not jump to your misconceptions, that Teeah, Michael and Camille are doomed and therefore, you, as well. You don't have the whole story, no one does. It unfolds before us with each breath we take. So have patience . . . faith. Trust life! Trust life! Trust life!

"All of those who would trust and believe in the honey bees ability to bear forth sweetness and not just a sting, come with us to Kanis, and invite all peasants and townspeople to join our march to where the forces of dark and light will converge on the night of the full moon.

"We call for the breaking of all spells. Let all falsehoods be shattered, and oppression lifted. Let truths devour the fog of obscurity this day, that we may rise from our foul oppression, and lift our heads to see the eagle in her flight and receive her heavenly news!"

Kamara fell silent, so receiving her own words, for she did not conjure them. Language from the genesis of creation had floated from her lips, and she too, now lifted her head from despair to hope.

The people had also rallied.

Kayenté was impressed with her keen ability to inspire the group. He smiled faintly realizing what a great Queen she would have actually been, had his goals not changed. He had participated in the chants that rang from the heart and expelled the ache of the soul.

Kamara was delighted that Kayenté had so honestly performed her people's ritual. When they were done, they each cleansed themselves in the Hot Springs and prepared for their journey. By mid-afternoon, they marched and rode onward to Kanis.

Ж
Chapter Thirty-Three

After a few hours of riding, Kayenté and Kamara parted from the group and galloped to Franz Ketola's castle, arriving at dusk. This time there was no battle at the doorstep. Gloom hung thick in the air. The guards let them pass into the castle with all too little regard. The armies seemed thinned out. Many men must have died that last day Kamara had come.

They rode into the frontcourt toward the huge brownstone keep. The Duke emerged hastily from the arched double doors, and sprinted toward them. They dismounted. Franz embraced his son, rather startling Kayenté.

Releasing him, he inquired urgently, "Taran, Marc? Do you know where they are?"

"Taran is at my castle. He's safe. Marc is in the hands of Merculus. He's not so safe, but he will be father. Trust me to free him."

Franz sighed, "I have to trust you Kayenté. You are all I have left. Now that Aldos is dead, the Rudels have sent reinforcements, over eighty thousand men, I've heard told. They are marching this way even now. Drudel also has his men on the march, and has put out the call for us to join him to cut off the Rudels before they come any further. The Gates have been seen coming in from the North Sea. They have been marching for several days now. That should put all three armies in Kanis in less than two days. Your mother told me of your prophecy, and with all that has come to pass, I believe your prophecy is true."

Kayenté nodded. "Your men will comply then? They will come to Kanis not to fight, but only defend the defenseless?"

481

"Yes, but their hearts are heavy and their pride shattered. Some have left to join Drudel's army, the others well—look about."

Kayenté peered at his father, feeling for the first time that he really was looking at his father, and his heart filled with gladness. "All will be well, father. I am certain."

The Duke looked to Kamara. "You have changed since last I saw you. My son has treated you well?"

Kamara was tongue-tied, not sure how to answer that question. "Ask rather, do I love him, and he me?"

Franz glared at Kayenté. "Have you forgotten the words we spoke son?"

"No father. Your understanding of the situation was wrong."

"Wrong . . . what do you mean?"

Kamara beseeched them, "Yes, what *do* you mean?"

Kayenté and the Duke looked at each other. The Duke said, "We'll talk later, Kayenté?"

"No more secrets, father," Kayenté said, "it's time for truth."

A little voice in Kamara said, *no, no truth*, but a bigger one said, *yes*.

Franz nodded lightly and sighed. "Alas it is." He faced Kamara. "Kamara Lania, I had thought myself to be your father."

Kamara bowed her head. "I wish you were, but it is a dear untruth."

"Are you sure? How do you know?" asked the Duke.

Kayenté said, "We know unequivocally who—"

"—Kayenté!" Kamara blushed. She looked to the Duke. "If only you *had* been my father," her eyes turned inward as if contemplating that scenario, "but then of course, I'd be Kayenté's sister, not sanctioned to love him the way I do."

She looked adoringly at Kayenté.

He wrapped his arm warmly around her back.

The Duke said, "Well, all is well then. Come inside and spend the night. We march at first light."

Kayenté and Kamara agreed to stay. They entered the dim atmosphere in the Great Hall.

Kayenté's heart pounded. "How is mother?"

"She is gravely ill," said the Duke.

"I must see her at once." Kayenté hadn't loved his mother in years. Now that he did, he feared she'd fade from his grasp.

He headed toward the stairs, pulling Kamara along with him.

"No," Kamara said, "you must go alone."

"I want you with me."

"But I . . . I upset her."

"Not anymore you won't, not now, not when I can bring her love."

"More than ever, I would upset her now."

"Truth, remember? Face truth? Let it come to the surface now, burst through the fog."

He didn't wait for her to respond. He took her hand firmly and led her up the winding stairs. Franz followed. When they reached Jela's chamber, Kayenté knocked lightly, and then they all entered.

Jela was in bed, half-covered with a gold silk blanket, half-exposed in her white nightgown, propped up to a sitting position against tan silk-covered pillows. Two servants were trying to feed her hot broth.

The fireplace crackled with the blaze of hot flames, highlighting the shadowy bloodstains on the floor where Munson met his demise. Kamara wondered if Jela had told Franz the truth about how Munson died. Knowing Jela—probably not.

Franz dismissed the servants and lit more oil lamps. Kayenté released Kamara and raced to his mother. Her pale face was contorted with pain.

Kayenté asked, "Mother what illness befalls you?"

"You, my son—" she replied sickly.

She glanced at Kamara and whimpered. Then she addressed Franz. "I wish to be alone with Kayenté."

"No mother," Kayenté said. "This is a time for truth, the bearing of our souls."

"But—"

"I know mother—that the wretched lies you inflicted upon me were not born from your heart, but from Ajento."

Franz blurted, "Ajento? Who is Ajento?"

Kayenté said to his father, "He is also known as Merculus."

"This man has two identities?" asked the Duke.

Kayenté said to Jela, "Tell him mother."

Jela's head thrashed from side to side, and moaned.

Kayenté stroked her forehead lovingly. "It's all right, mother."

Jela's eyes filled with pain and apprehension. "I shall tell you both. I shall tell you both everything." Then she spoke softly—deliberately, the air of royalty still in her voice. "I was a Priestess of the Mist before you knew me."

Kayenté and the Duke exclaimed simultaneously in disbelief, "You?"

"Yes," said Jela, "difficult to believe, isn't it?"

Franz moved closer to her, his shoulder nearly touching Kayenté.

Jela continued, "A supernatural being, known to me as Ajento, known to Taran as Hansa, known to you as Merculus, and known to Kamara as the Cold One—took my spirit, raped me, and fathered Taran. After Kayenté and Marc were born, he returned to further torment me, and did so fifteen years hence."

Franz swooped over her. "Jela! Why didn't you tell me? All these years, I believed your coldness was because you didn't love me. If only I had known the truth, I could have prevented all this pain. I could have defended your honor!"

"Against Ajento? I feared he would have killed you with his supernatural powers."

"But—"

"Please. Let me tell this while I can."

Franz sat on the bed facing her.

She continued, "Kayenté knew of the repeated rapes. Ajento made me insinuate to poor little Kayenté that Taran was the son of the Duke, and that he was the son of a rapist. Ajento made me swear Kayenté to secrecy, to purposely torment and twist his innocence. Ajento enlisted Taran to do the same, convincing him he would be banished from the castle, if you were to find out he was not your son."

The Duke protested, "But I never would have—"

"Please Franz. I must go on. Ajento wanted Kayenté's heart so maimed and numbed that he would not ever forfeit his power to save a woman by virtue of love. But as you can see—" her voice became shaky, "—he has done so—anyway. I have suffered for years hearing Ajento's threats that he'd kill all whom I loved if I did not comply. But his efforts have been in vain and now my son . . . my beloved Kayenté, shall die for that woman, and then Ajento will be gone."

Kayenté sank to his knees, and took his mother's feeble hands in his. "What do you mean—die?"

Jela replied, "The wisdom that came to the Priestesses was that Ajento, or shall I say, the Cold One, would be defeated when a powerful Ketola warrior of the Duke's blood (that is you Kayenté) dies by the hand of the Light Priestess who loves him (and that is Kamara). If the warrior loves her back, he will allow the sacrifice. The givers shall take . . ." Kayenté mouthed the words for he knew she was going to recite what the Wise One had once told him, "and the takers shall give. Dark comes to light and light comes to dark. The risen shall fall and the fallen shall rise. So has it been and so shall it always be."

All three looked at Kamara whose back was against the wall, tears draining from her body. "I don't want to play this part. Truly I don't! Still I must believe there is another way!"

Kayenté went to her. He lowered his knees to the floor, placed his hands gently on her hips, and gazed up.

She looked down at him, her face puffed and red.

"It's all right," he said. "I told you once that I would die by the sword."

She tried to pull away from him, not wanting to accept his acquiescence. He pulled her down on her knees into his arms, and forced her face against his chest.

She fought against him. "No . . . Kayenté. No! No! No! I could *never* kill you. I would rather suffer eternally than to draw one drop of your blood. Oh please . . . please, do not let this be my fate!" Her voice filled the bedchamber with a scream, "N o o o o!" She gasped heavy sobs, unable to suppress her agony.

Kayenté held her steady in his embrace, though tears watered his eyes.

Franz pulled Jela into his arms and they too, wept.

Franz said, "I never knew how much you needed me . . . how much you loved me and our sons . . . how so very much your love was full underneath your bitter facade."

Jela said, "I tire of everyone thinking I'm bad. I was a Light Priestess. I was good and sweet and pure . . . once."

Franz held her tight. "You are again, my love. You are again."

The room was filled with heartbreak.

In time, Kamara calmed herself, but could not stop the whimpering that seeped from her ruptured hopes.

Jela said, "Come here, Kamara. I'll not look upon you with acrid eyes. I want you to know my heart. Come to me."

The Duke rose and stood aside. Kamara walked slowly to her, trembling. Kayenté was close behind. Jela lifted her hand. Kamara received her fingers and held them lightly.

Jela said, "Though pain is full in this house tonight, there is also love restored . . . and though you shall take my son's life, you gave him his heart . . . and for that I shall be forever indebted. For he shall die with a noble heart, and he'll not be a victim of the Cold One—anymore. I—it is true, I do love you."

Kamara threw herself into Jela's arms and wept.

Franz looked at Kayenté. "All these years, you thought me not your father. Is that why you left this house?"

Kayenté nodded. "I believed I was evil because I cared only for my own salvation and my own gain. I could not be free in this house of pain."

Franz sighed hard. "I'd like to be the one to take the sword to the Cold One's heart!"

Kayenté said, "That's not as easy as you might think. He is more skilled than any I have ever fought. Besides, the death of a body doesn't kill the essence flowing through it. If we want to alter him, we have to alter ourselves, which I would say we are all now doing."

When Kamara sat up, Kayenté extended his hand. "Kamara, let us sleep. We have a long journey tomorrow."

She took Kayenté's hand and rose. Then, she bid Franz and Jela goodnight.

Kayenté led her out of the room and down the corridor to his old bedchamber. Once inside, he shed his clothes and hers. They climbed under forest green satin sheets and laid their heads upon satin pillows.

He said, "My son will always know me—is this so?"

"Yes," she answered, holding back a veil of tears.

"Raise him in Lania Castle. Give him my name so that he will carry my power."

"That I shall do," she said, trying not to cry. "Why do you think I carry a son?"

"It seems the trend of late."

"I think you are right." Her voice broke to catch the sob that nearly escaped her.

"I'm not afraid to die, Kamara," he said softly. "It is easy for me to die for you and for our child, for love, and for honor. I have at last attained what I've longed for all of my life—a good and noble heart. I am at peace."

"Oh Kayenté," she rolled over on top of him, laying her head on his chest, "then why am I not!"

"You must cross through the gateway, as did I. When I beheld you in the torture chamber, I knew that I would never again forsake my love for anything—even life. You must cross through, the other way and not forsake your life for anything—even love. Don't you see," he said, "I have used the sword on so many, now it shall be used on me. You have taken the blows for so long, now you shall give them. Balance."

"I see," she sighed, "but I don't want to see."

"What about that speech you gave your people today. The honeybee can produce sweetness, not just a sting. Trust Life."

"Yes, it is so. Indeed it is so."

"Then make love with me. Make *love . . . with me.*"

And they united in a bittersweet embrace and gave to each other all their last goodbyes.

Ж
Chapter Thirty-Four

The next morning, everyone made haste, and rode out with the first rays of light that crept upon the land—even Jela, to the surprise of all. She rode along side Franz, proudly and lovingly, having found her peace with him.

They traveled all day and made camp by nightfall at Kayenté's castle. Taran was gone, and Kayenté feared the Cold One had repossessed him. Or perhaps Taran had never really submitted to 'the light.' Maybe he enchanted his way out of the prison and worked for the Cold One now, willingly or unwillingly, he did not know, and he had no time to find out.

That night they all slept outside, needing the strength of the stars that glittered above, assuring them that everything would come to balance.

Kayenté slept fitfully, not because he feared death, but because he feared that they might fail to defeat the Cold One. He coddled Kamara in his arms until the dark of morning, for she could not sleep at all.

They readied themselves for the day. Kamara wore the black wool shirt and red dress that Allysa had given her, and the red slippers that Teeah had given her, and the red cape that the Wise One had given her. The dress and slippers had both been given to please Kayenté, and this was the last opportunity she would have to do so. And the cape . . . she thought it a fitting day to wear it, since it represented the blood of new life.

Kayenté had told her that she was his flame from heaven and that he'd never seen her look so beautiful, and that to die looking upon such a sight would ease his pain. He had helped her fasten the sheathed sword around her dress. He'd said that it gave her a balanced look, blending lover and warrior. He said that he would remember her that way in the next world, always and forever.

Kayenté wore his short-sleeved black tunic lined with silver studs, black leather pants and boots—but he did not wear chain mail, no armor at all, and no weapons. Not even his sword. He gave his sword to his mother, for he would not need it anymore in this life. She was to lay it upon him in his grave, to be dug wherever he fell. And he felt a strange peace knowing soon his life of toil—would end.

Kamara rode on Kayenté's black warhorse, in Kayenté's arms. And Kayenté rode next to his father who enveloped Jela in his arms.

Other lords committed to Kayenté, having heard his word, emerged with their men from the forests, and melted into the fold of the newly created nation, moving toward Kanis, on this day, of the night, of the full moon.

Fifty thousand men journeyed under a strange glow of awakening as dawn broke over their heads. Fifty thousand men would not be fighting—today. They would not be killing nor be killed—today. Nor would they win the throne for Kayenté—today, as he once dreamed they would. *Today—was the manifestation of the apocalyptic meaning of life. Today was now and all eternity was in it.*

The passive armies soon enfolded the people from Kamara's castle. Many new faces had joined them along the way, among them, families of soldiers, peasants and clergy, numbering in the thousands.

Kamara reveled in the unity of the social classes, a dream she'd always sought to actualize. Yet, her heart was crushed with the weight of her responsibility, and the absence of her loved ones made her sadder. Her face lit, however, when she saw Sir Bradley in the crowd—a Rudel! He had chosen not to fight! And he seemed to have escaped the Cold One's kidnapping spree.

Fighting clamored in the distance as they approached Kanis. Cries, moans, and death screams sliced the air. They moved toward the battle, singing songs, never flinching, even when viewing the dense swarm of warriors slaying each other in the green rolling hills.

Kayenté and Franz commanded their armies to form a circle around the battle. Kamara ordered the lay people to form a circle around the passive soldiers.

The circles began wide and thin, but as the chant Kamara started continued, the circles tightened around the fighting men, growing thick with late comers.

The people's chorus spilled over the valleys and deep into the distant mountains; their low toned chant echoed in the brains of the fighting and passive alike. "I am you and you are me, we shall live in harmony. William is our noble king. Rest your weapons, and with us sing."

The surrounding crowd continued to grow, dotted with clergymen, who finally, finally felt 'the light,' not as they had deemed it to be, but as it truly was.

Kamara stood behind Kayenté misting her very life into the people. Jela stood behind Franz, looking forlornly at Kamara, knowing she had lost her power to mist.

When a fighting man would fall against the wall of warriors, he would be asked to join the circle. If the answer was no, then he was simply pushed back into the fight. The battle thinned as sunset neared. Then, the violence ended. All Sakajian and Rudelian warriors had either died, like Drudel himself, or become a part of the chanting crowd. King William and the Gates remained in the arena, victorious, but Kayenté knew that it was he and his men who had really won.

The chanting stopped. The silence was deafening, mounting, waiting for proclamation.

Kayenté shouted, "Hail King William!" Over and over, he said the words until the multitude of people joined him.

King William sat tall on his horse. He raised his hand high and the hailing simmered down. He pranced up to Kayenté, face dripping with sweat and dirt and blood. He said, "I received your message cousin Kayenté that you would honor me as King, an honor I dare say, I little expected to receive from you. And not like this, never like this."

"You were right," Kayenté said, "you are better suited than I to be King of Kantine."

King William declared loudly for all to hear, "By the support you have demonstrated, Lord Kayenté Ketola, and the leadership ability you have well proven, I hereby appoint you Governor of Kantine, to oversee all the lords and their realms and uphold the Holy doctrines of Gatish Law!" And then he added more softly to Kayenté, "not unlike Sakajian law, my cousin." He winked at Kayenté, for in truth, he had in a way, made Kayenté, King of Kantine, even though he had officially retained the title for himself.

Kayenté smiled and bowed eloquently before King William, for he knew his cousin had granted him the rule of Kantine—after all. And though Kayenté knew he'd not be alive to govern the province with the heart he'd found, he was fulfilled, because even though he'd released his dream, it had nonetheless come to pass. And not because he took what he wanted, but because he gave it up. He would die—a king of sorts, completely and nobly fulfilled.

King William nodded respectfully at Kayenté, making peace. He nodded at Kamara in the same fashion. She bowed before him.

King William looked down upon Kamara. "If you, a Priestess of the Mist, did not flee from Lord Kayenté, then he is indeed of the rarest noble kind."

Kamara and Kayenté glanced at each other with glossy eyes of shared love.

King William then commanded his men to gather prisoners and collect their wounded that they may move onward, away from the dead. Burials would be tended later. He kicked his heals into his horse and an opening broke in the crowd for the Gates to pass through. Late into the night, the crowds slowly disbursed, all but Jela, Franz, Kayenté, and Kamara and thousands of dead bodies dotting the countryside.

A gray whirling wind swept over the dead. They knew the Cold One was collecting spirits. After several minutes, the funnel shaped wind disappeared. Patiently they waited, knowing their time with the Cold One was soon to come.

They waited until the midnight moon was high above them. And then—a fierce icy wind blew against their bodies. The Cold One stormed over the hill towards them, loincloth bare. His tromping shook the earth. The Duke and the Duchess, Kamara and Kayenté, rose and drew close together.

Kamara said, "Each time I see him, he is more furious than the last."

Jela said, "That is because he has been drawn more and more into 'the dark,' for the Cold Ones are beyond ferocity. Now we must draw him into 'the light' with what we know must be done."

The Cold One approached, glaring demonically at Kamara.

Kayenté stepped forward next to Kamara.

The Cold One howled, "So the Dark and the Light unite and I am to shrink back into a mere pause? No. I still have the spirits of all the Priestesses—but one, and I still have all your beloved at Wincott Castle, and I still have an army under my command."

A voice sounded behind them from a smattering of baby oak trees, "No, you don't."

They all looked to the voice and saw under the bright moon, Taran. Behind him were Marc, Allysa, and Michael. Behind them were Teeah, Camille, Sir Robert and his men, and all the Sakajian soldiers that had manned Wincott Castle. They still appeared in a trance, yet apparently under Taran's command.

Taran said, "You are weakening, Cold One! Your spells are fading. Stolen spirits are coming home. Look at my mother. She is brighter is she not? Soon—"

The Cold One pointed his finger furiously at Taran. "You have betrayed me, son of my own blood, and I will send you into The Nothing—forever!"

"You'll not have the power to do so," Taran said.

The Cold One looked at Kamara, certainty glazing his eyes, relaxing his posture, and deepening his voice. "Yes, I will. When my daughter fails the final test, then I will restore the doom I have set into motion." He shouted at Kamara, "Daughter!"

Kamara swallowed so hard, she could barely inhale.

His empty gaze enveloped her. "You, who carry your mother's good heart, will never kill the one you love! And when you fail, I'll take you as I had planned."

Kamara *could not* let that happen. His reign of terror *must* end. She summoned her dark side to rise inside her. "Winnefred serves *me* now. Where I fail," Kamara's heart lurched, "—she will not!"

"On with it then!" ordered the Cold One, in the same tone of disgust once characteristic of Winnefred.

The group fell silent. Kayenté turned to face Kamara. She stared at him a moment, her beautiful Kayenté. She felt imaginary.

Kayenté said gently, "Do it, Kamara."

The harder she tried to draw her sword, the more her body constricted, visibly trembling. Her breathing became choppy, shallow, and almost not there. Gasping for air, tears filled her wideopen eyes, and gushed over her cheeks, down her neck, into the corners of her mouth. Her head felt on fire, burning away confusing illusions and dreams of escape, leaving only the horror of what was real.

Kayenté stared at her intently. "Do it."

She withdrew her sword from the scabbard. Her hands quaked so violently she almost lost hold of it. She tightened her grip.

"You *must* do it, Kamara," commanded Kayenté once more. His eyes teared with the intensity of oceans. "Save our baby's life."

She breathed harder. Her whimpers of agony mounted as she held the sword over her head, placing the point of the blade over Kayenté's heart.

Kayenté felt the sum agony of all the pain he'd ever inflicted upon others. His victims had died alone with no morsel of sympathy from him, and now he felt such sympathy for them as to break his very heart, even before it was bludgeoned. Kamara's whimpers were as theirs, and theirs as hers, and hers as his. He could no longer bear the cruelty of the coldness that once ruled his life. "Do—it!" he commanded.

"Ka—yen—té!" she wailed, pleading for rescue, "Oh, Ka—yen—té!"

"Your hesitation causes me to suffer! You are the warrior now! Do . . . it!"

She drew her hands back further behind her head to gain momentum for the blow, gripping the hilt of sword so tightly her fingers cramped. Her vision turned black. She willed herself not to faint. Her heart ripped with mercy for Kayenté, but there was no way around this dilemma. She must go through with it, or the world would perish. She found her conviction . . . at last, and her eyes stretched wider and wider. "I give myself to the realm, I do, beyond the sands of time!" She held her breath and propelled the sword toward Kayenté's heart.

A blast of apparitions exploded from the Cold One, streaking out in all directions. A thunderous groan and an ear-splitting shriek sounded from behind Kamara. She stopped mid-motion with the blade barely touching Kayenté's chest.

Jela had thrust Kayenté's sword into Franz.

Franz fell to the earth, first on his knees, then on his face. Jela screamed her grief so loud and so deep that the world stood still. And her sacrifice melted into the trees and the earth and the sky, and into the hearts of every living creature. She fell upon her husband. "Franz! Franz! Franz! I . . . love . . . you . . . . . . !" Then she took the knife that Kamara had given her and plunged it into her heart before anyone could waken from their shock.

The Cold One evaporated. Where he once stood, dazzling light sparkled so bright, it pained the eyes. The mass of sparkles shot upward out of sight. Moments later, the particles of light rained over the land, like fairy dust, charging everything with new life.

Kamara trembled, disbelieving what had happened. She stared at the fallen couple. Kayenté shot over to his parents and fell upon their bodies. He wailed, spilling the wells of liquid pain that had contained his life's sorrow. Taran and Marc sank down on either side of Kayenté and wept, freeing long imprisoned tears from their cold manly hearts.

Kamara's red eyes were fixed upon the scene, still shocked by what had transpired. She didn't have to kill Kayenté! Kayenté did not have to die! She stood still, numbed and panting profusely, her body yet trembling, sword still in hand.

And she stared deep and she stared . . . hard, at the backs of the three Ketola brothers lamenting with heart and soul, ending the fictional play called—real life. And hatching now, these three, the withered remnants of the once untainted spirit, made free to breathe again.

And from their breath rose the milky vapors of the cohesive life force that binds all creation together. *Dark comes to light. And light comes to dark. The risen shall fall and the fallen shall rise. So has it been and so shall it always be.* And as the vapors enveloped them, Kamara was beauteously touched to see her warriors in the mist.

They were her kind, of the Angel world. And—they were men! And—they were warriors! They no longer fought in the dark, for they had awakened—in en *light* enment and had at last tasted love.

Suddenly she felt a gigantic bitter relief for what had come to pass. Kayenté was alive! He and his brothers had united! She dropped her sword, and raced to Kayenté's back. Falling on her knees, she embraced him strongly, pressing her head between his shoulder blades.

And then she felt it, the brush of warm light, "Kayenté! Marc! Taran! Look!" She pointed to the sky. Two faint glowing figures flew away into the stars. "—your parents! They are together!"

Kayenté turned toward Kamara while rising, drawing her up with him. He held her in his arms so tight, her bones hurt.

Teeah approached, placing a warm hand on each one's back. "Kamara, Kayenté, release your sorrow, for indeed this is a great day."

They turned slightly toward her and listened.

"The prophecy ordained that the Light Priestess must take the life of the warrior she loves, and that warrior in the name of love, must let her. That fate was to be yours. And though you climbed the stairway to your destiny that the Cold One be defeated, Jela and Franz took your place. In that split second when you both sacrificed in the way that was opposite your nature, your willingness to do so and your act of faith was such, that it restored stolen spirits, and wilted the Cold One even before the blade pierced Kayenté's skin.

"This act restored Jela as a Light Priestess. She felt it then. She knew it then, that she and Franz could finish the ritual and she could save her son at last. You must honor them and carry forth a new generation of children, more balanced in light and dark, and in giving and receiving. We are all imperfect. If imperfection is badness, then we are all bad. Your children must learn that good and bad, joy and sorrow, hate and love, fear and faith, birthing and dying—are all a part of the magic dance of life on earth. When we categorize our thoughts and emotions into dark and light, when we label people, races, religions, and countries, as good and bad—then the Cold One comes for us all. We are all good and bad, dark and light. Let us finally accept that and let the blending begin!"

Teeah stood aside. "Look. Allysa and Michael have found each other. Camille and Robert . . . the same." She pointed to Marc and Taran, embracing. "Those two have made peace, and Franz and

Jela are together—at last. And you—" she gazed upon Kayenté and Kamara, "—our champions who were chosen to sacrifice, have gained everything. Let us bury the bodies of Franz and Jela here in this spot upon which they have made their mark for all humankind."

The next several hours were spent digging graves and enshrining the Duke and Duchess. When they finished, Kayenté addressed his brothers. "King William has appointed me governor of Kantine, and so Taran, I appoint you lord of father's house and lands."

Taran said, "Well, they should rightfully go to you."

"No, I'm going to live with Kamara. That is, if she'll let my sword live with me."

"Aye," she said, "as long as you bring your heart."

Marc said, "Who will oversee your castle and lands?"

"I would ask that of you, Marc."

"Me," he said, "lord of a castle?"

"Yes," Kayenté said, half-jesting, "it's time you had some responsibility."

Marc smiled, inspiration twinkling in his once unmotivated eyes.

Kayenté said, "We'll not rule as once we did, in heinous disregard for life, and a predilection for repelling—love. We three are Warriors of the Mist. Let us take the next few weeks and rearrange our lives. I've a wedding to plan with this young woman."

Kamara smiled brightly, "I thought marriage was for riches and power."

"Marriage is for love," he replied, "and love you, I do."

That night, under the stars in the wild heather, Kamara made love to Kayenté and bequeathed herself to him for all time. And the sunrise brought forth a newer, brighter day. Confusion was lifted, and the sky was clear when they journeyed to their respective castles.

In the weeks that followed, Kamara and Kayenté were married. One by one, the Priestesses of the Mist returned. Even her gentle alabaster mare came back, found in the frontcourt eating roses. They allowed an army of men to guard the castle, only for defense, never offense. Michael had regained his sword, Allysa her lover, and Sir Robert and Camille—their honor.

Kamara waited, hoping her true mother would return. Each time a Priestess came to the door, she would ask, "Are you my mother?" They each replied, "No." She was excited though, the day the Wise One rapped upon the door, for the Wise One knew the whereabouts of her mother.

"You have returned!" Kamara exclaimed, surprised at how much more attractive and youthful the old woman appeared now that her spirit had returned.

"I am glad for your return, Wise One, but still I wait for my mother. Is she yet alive?" Kamara held her breath, frightened to hear the answer.

The Wise One shook her head. "She is not dead. In fact, she's already here."

Kamara exhaled briskly. "Who? Where?"

The Wise One smiled and raised her brows.

Kamara tilted her head. "You're not—"

The Wise One nodded. "I am."

"But you are not a Priestess!"

"I am now, as once I was, before the Cold One came."

Kamara flew into her arms. "You never truly left me, did you?"

"No child, I never did."

In the following days, Kamara's stomach grew larger and Kayenté's love grew stronger. And milky vapors seeped from the ivory stone of Lania Castle, rolling over the woodlands, covering the *entire* province with the magical mists of love.

Nafysol's nixes: Jam

Printed in the United States
117026LV00004B/66/P

9 780979 566318